Barbara Ewing is a New Zealand-born actress and author who lives and works in London. She has a university degree in English and Maori, and won the Bancroft Gold Medal at the Royal Academy of Dramatic Art

THE MESMERIST

OR

THE MISSES PRESTON, OF BLOOMSBURY

Barbara Ewing

sphere

SPHERE

First published in Great Britain in 2007 by Sphere
Reprinted 2006

A CIP catalogue record for this book
is available from the British Library.

HARDBACK ISBN: 978-1-84744-065-5
C FORMAT ISBN: 978-1-84744-022-8

Typeset in Palatino by Hewer Text UK Ltd, Edinburgh
Printed and bound in Great Britain by Clays Ltd, St Ives plc

Sphere
An imprint of
Little, Brown Book Group
Brettenham House
Lancaster Place
London WC2E 7EN

A Member of the Hachette Livre Group of Companies

www.littlebrown.co.uk

To Chad and Kath

ACKNOWLEDGEMENTS

With special thanks to Dr Bob Large of The Auckland Regional Pain Service in New Zealand for fascinating discussions about hypnotism and pain; and to Simon O'Hara in London for instructive conversations about the history of coroners.

. . . I remember a Miss Preston in Bloomsbury . . . who died lately, practised mesmerism through the best part of her life; and I recollect that about twenty years ago numbers went to a magnetiser at Kennington . . .

Professor John Elliotson, *Human Physiology I*, 1835

ONE

1838

One

There was a clap of thunder.

It was not, however, real thunder; the stage manager was testing the iron sheet: if the iron split the sound was too tinny, lost its majesty.

Mrs Cordelia Preston, her cloak held tightly around her against the cold, leaned against a badly painted and somewhat misshapen castle wall, which was not majestic by any stretch of the imagination.

'That fat manager is a Beast from Hell,' she muttered angrily to Mrs Amaryllis Spoons, who sat on a square wooden tree stump. The empty, echoing theatre smelt of oil from all the lamps, and candle grease, and dust; and of last night's audience; and perhaps of actors. The footlights had been lowered by small wheels to the space beneath so that the wicks of the lamps could be trimmed; working candles lit the stage, gave dim, flickering light. The cold actors rubbed their hands together, breathed out faint mist. Mrs Cordelia Preston and Mrs Amaryllis Spoons, two of the three singing witches (the other was being played by the manager's mother-in-law), were required, from their meagre salaries, to provide their own costumes and hair and powder and paint; to eat; to pay rent; to travel. Yet the manager had called the actors in early to receive their salaries, and was now rocking back and forth on his heels at the edge of the gloomily lit stage, announcing that he had cut the salaries *again*.

'Audiences don't want Actors any more,' said the manager in a final, robust thrust, and Cordelia, with a flash of rage, considered how satisfying it would be to kick him into the auditorium. 'These days audiences want Spectacle! And what they mean by Spectacle ain't second-rate actors and that mangy old horse. I got a helephant arriving tomorrow – and next month I've got a Performing Boy.' And then he stopped rocking and abruptly disappeared into the gloom of the back of the theatre.

Second-rate actors? An elephant in Macbeth? The leading actor, Mr George Tryfont, stood centre stage in an agony of anger and recrimination, looking with disbelief at the money in his hand. The actress playing Lady Macbeth had already stormed off, weeping loudly. The other actors stood in little huddled groups mumbling complaints, pulling their cloaks about them; the dregs of winter, no sign of spring, and now, as Mr Tryfont leaned dramatically upon the boughs of Great Burnham Wood (which had not yet been removed after last evening's performance), he and the spiky wooden branches cast long and unlikely shapes across the stage. Amaryllis Spoons saw that Cordelia Preston, caught also in the candlelight against the painted castle wall, looked angry, and yet beautiful still: the unusual white lock at the front of her hair seemed to shimmer almost in the gloom and the shadows.

The property master plodded across the stage carrying large tin plates and goblets for the banquet scene; if he knew more than the actors about the future of this production and whether there was really an elephant, he wasn't saying. His footfalls echoed away into the wings.

Mr Tryfont's voice (he could not help this) boomed out across the empty auditorium, reached even the boxes and the gallery:

4

he knew exactly the timbre. 'An elephant in Shakespeare! Oh that I had chosen a profession with more honour! That manager is a disgrace, he pays more for horses to make an appearance than he does for Actors of my calibre.' The property master plodded back again, silent still, with the witches' cauldron balanced upon his back. 'I hear, by the way, on excellent authority, that tomorrow, as soon as the elephant arrives, all the *older* ladies . . .' Mr Tryfont cast a venomous glance across the stage, 'will be removed from employment. Audiences do not like old women.'

Mrs Cordelia Preston and Mrs Amaryllis Spoons caught each other's eye; the reference to 'older ladies' was meant for them (although they were both slightly younger than Mr Tryfont), and theirs not to reason why an elephant could take the place of the singing witches in a performance of *Macbeth* (but this was a number-three tour, so anything could happen). They had hardly the money to get home. But things like this had occurred a hundred times: they both kept money underneath floorboards in London for dire emergencies and they both did quick sums in their heads.

And then the actors were suddenly scattered by a loud shout of warning from below and the sound of more wheels: the wheels that were pulling apart the painted wooden trees of Great Burnham Wood and storing them out of sight in the wings on either side of the stage, until the climax of this evening's performance. The property master appeared between the moving trees. He carried a huge bowl of red liquid: the blood on their hands, the hands of the Macbeths, as they murdered nightly.

Their accommodation was some filthy cold rooms, part of a barn outside Guildford. Actors drank cheap whisky sulkily in corners before the evening's performance. Mrs Cordelia Preston toasted bread over the fire. Mrs Amaryllis Spoons ate two apples mournfully. They knew they should not have taken this tour,

5

they knew the vagaries of a number-three tour: the lowest salaries, performances at the worst theatres. But Mrs Preston and Mrs Spoons were over forty, commonly known as old (as Mr Tryfont had unkindly pointed out), and they needed the money.

'Yes, that fat manager is a Beast from Hell,' said Rillie Spoons.

That night the red curtains finally parted, late as usual, to the stamping and whistling of the impatient audience. The footlights were dimmed and the stage slowly darkened. The singing witches (the manager had insisted that the audience wanted singing) could just be seen on stage, ghostly, as smoke rose behind them. The manager's mother-in-law choked on the smoke and the stage manager rattled iron very loudly to make the sound of a storm (and to cover the sound of one of the witches coughing). Yet (whatever the appetite for old ladies) as the three harridans bent over the cauldron in the half-light, still the old silence fell as the familiar words caught at hearts:

> *When shall we three meet again*
> *In thunder, lightning, or in rain?*
> *When the hurly-burly's done*
> *When the battle's lost, and won . . .*

In this production Macbeth arrived on a horse: mangy it may have been, but the audience cheered. It was however the only cheer of the evening. Soon the horse was gone, but Mr Tryfont remained, interminably. Mr Tryfont's Macbeth favoured pauses, and tonight he seemed to be favouring them with more than usual diligence; disappointment and boredom began to waft up to the stage through the dust and the stink of the lamp-oil, and the smell of greasepaint and of the spectators: the audience wanted action, more smoke rising, more horses, drums, moving scenery. The production approached its climax and Mr Tryfont took a particularly enormous pause, stared upwards dramatically. *Life's but a walking shadow* came a loud whisper from the prompter's box underneath the stage, and Mr Tryfont looked furiously towards the prompter, who was only trying to be helpful.

> *Life's but a walking shadow; a poor player,*
> *That struts and frets his hour upon the stage,*
> *And then is heard—*

An apple core landed on the stage.

'*And then is heard no more,* thank goodness!' shouted someone from the pit.

'Get on with it!' shouted another. '*It is a tale told by an idiot,* you can say that again. *Signifying nothing,* like you, you old goat!'

'You old Ham!' shouted the first. 'You want to get on with it, you're too buggering ancient!'

Great Burnham Wood was whirring up to appear miraculously but Mr Tryfont, his momentous, poetic speech having been finished for him, suddenly exploded. He made a great leap from the stage ('Quite dangerous at his age!' whispered Cordelia from the back of the stage) and attacked his tormentors with his fists. The audience whistled in delight, other actors joined in, then more members of the public. It was thrilling. Mrs Cordelia Preston and Mrs Amaryllis Spoons looked at each other. *Out of work, freezing weather, no sign of spring.* They shrugged. Then Cordelia gestured at the property table and blew out the nearest candles. She and Rillie grabbed the large bowl of blood, and together they heaved the red remains out over the actors and the audience in the half-light; the glistening liquid dripped and splurged and splattered, bloodily. Then, still dressed in their witches' costumes – for the costumes were their own, had to be provided, and it was safer in the night to walk like a witch than a lady – they quietly, in the mêlée, collected up their belongings and disappeared.

* * *

And so they might have been seen: two rather weird shapes in the chill darkness, plodding onwards towards the London Road, stoic; two old friends, middle-aged actresses, out of work, cold February.

'If my poor dead mother could see me now!' said Cordelia. 'Oh how she would understand!'

'If my poor live mother could see me now,' said Rillie, 'she wouldn't understand anything at all,' and they half-laughed in the night; it was a half-joke, for Rillie's mother was demented.

> *When shall we three meet again*
> *In thunder, lightning, or in rain?*

They sang along the way, to keep their spirits up and the highwaymen away, and somewhere along the cold night road Cordelia thought she heard them: the tough, laughing spirits of her mother and her aunt, telling her, as they always told her, to keep going whatever happened, and to bear anything.

Two

Several nights later Miss Cordelia Preston (for although she was of course always advertised as Mrs Preston on theatrical posters, as was the custom for older actresses, she was not, in fact, married) sat in a basement in Little Russell Street, Bloomsbury, half dozing, tired still from the long, long walk home from Guildford. She was drinking port in a desultory manner.

She had not drawn the curtains: people would have had to get down on their hands and knees and crawl to see into the basement rooms. She saw and heard feet passing daily: boots and shoes and unshod dirty feet. The feet were thinning out at this hour but the neighbour's cat arched like a black question mark in the night on the iron basement steps, caught by the lamplight through the window. Cordelia's mother had died when she was ten; Cordelia had lived on in the basement rooms with her Aunt Hester. And when Aunt Hester had died, some of her last words to Cordelia were: *This is your home, girl, sit tight and make sure you pay the rent on time. And leave my stars when I'm gone, they'll watch over you.*

So Cordelia had left her aunt's shining stars on the ceiling (made from cheap jewellery and glass and paint) and paid the rent on time. And she had also left the mirrors that reflected the stars, and the tattered books on mesmerism and phrenology in the corner shelf, and the white marble head covered in numbers. She called the white marble head Alphonse because her mother was once in a play that had a character called Alphonse, who had no hair. Cordelia had learnt her numbers from Alphonse's head: 1, 2 and 3 were at the back; 14 was on the top; Alphonse was her friend and sometimes she draped him with red velvet flowers. A marble be-numbered head had been a strange thing for a little girl to play with, but strangeness never alarmed people in the theatre, who were used to a thousand strange-nesses: did they not live nightly with wax apples, and bowls of unreal blood, and skulls often, and live doves, and dead deer, and books with no pages in them, all sitting in the property corner?

So: her mother and her aunt might be dead, but along with Alphonse, and the stars and the mirrors and the red velvet flowers and all the other accoutrements her mother had stolen, those tough ghosts hovered always: Kitty and Hester.

Steps echoed down from the street to her door, a quick knock and Rillie Spoons appeared, come for a late drink: they kept odd hours of course, they were actresses.

'How's your feet, Cordie?'

'Same as yours!'

'Let's go to Mrs Fortune's,' said Rillie, 'just in case we can find out about anything that's going.'

'At least we're not acting with an *elephant*,' said Cordelia morosely.

'And it was almost worth it . . .' They both started to laugh, saw the red paint dripping, the shocked faces of the recipients. Cordelia knocked back port, handed the bottle across, then went to look for another glass, her laughter evaporating. 'And now of course we have to go down to the Lamb and enquire of Mr

10

Kenneth or Mr Turnour if they could kindly find us something just as bad! Oh Hell's Teeth, Rillie, I am so sick of it, I am so sick of packing my costumes and my paint and travelling in cold or rain or sun along terrible roads around the countryside, I've been doing it since I was born and *I'm sick of it!'*

'I've found something interesting in the newspaper,' said Rillie Spoons, ignoring Cordelia's mood. 'You know your Aunt Hester, and that mesmerism she used to do? Well, there's a show going on at the new University Hospital, look at this, I tore it out of the newspaper when the library man wasn't looking.' Rillie had a sweet voice still; she read from the torn paper holding it to the light of the lamp so that she could see, squinting up her eyes, dramatising her reading where appropriate. 'MESMERO-MANIA DIVIDES THE METROPOLIS! EXPERIMENTS IN MESMERISM AT UNIVERSITY COLLEGE HOSPITAL! PROFESSOR ELLIOTSON IS USING TWO CHARITY PATIENTS AT THE HOSPITAL, THE OKEY SISTERS FROM IRELAND – Irish you see, Cordie, they're different from us – TO SHOW THE EFFECTS, AND POSSIBLE MERITORIOUS USEFULNESS, OF MESMERISM IN HOSPITAL PATIENTS. Let's go and see this tomorrow, Cordie, it'll cheer us up and remind us of your dear old Aunt Hester,' (you had to be careful which bits of her haunted past you spoke of to Cordelia, you could not mention the word 'marriage' for instance; but Aunt Hester was always a safe bet), 'we'll go in the morning, after we've been down to Bow Street.' Cordelia's face was still bleak. 'Come on, Cordie, we're forty-five years old, we're not giving up after all these years!' and at last Cordelia smiled: her friend, or the port, or the mention of Aunt Hester lifted her mood. They began to laugh once more as they recounted again to each other the fight in the theatre and Mr Tryfont and the audience and the blood. And finally they sat back together in the basement in Bloomsbury with glasses in their hands and sang the latest number; they sang well and their voices echoed up from the lamplit window and drifted out into the night.

Max Welton's braes are bonnie
Where early falls the dew,
And 'twas there that Annie Laurie
Gave me her promise true.

Gave me her promise true
That ne'er forgot shall be,
And for Bonnie Annie Laurie
I'd lay me down and dee.

'I wonder who Max Welton was,' mused Cordelia Preston and Rillie Spoons simultaneously. And they laughed again, the port warming their throats and their hearts, as they put on their cloaks. Cordelia picked up the flat-iron she always carried for protection; Rillie always had a large stone in her inside cloak pocket. They set off on foot towards Drury Lane, to Mrs Fortune's rooms in Cock Pit-lane, up rickety wooden steps above a pawn-shop, where rumour and dreams kept most of the out-of-work actors from jumping into the River Thames. At Mrs Fortune's rooms actors would pass on information, or discuss their prospects, or boast, or weep, or drink. And eat – perhaps: Mrs Fortune regularly made a big pot of stew, added to it nightly: if actors became ill it was time to throw it out and start again.

And tonight as usual in Mrs Fortune's rooms all the riff-raff of the theatre were congregated: Mr Eustace Honour the comic; and Olive the ballet dancer; and James and Jollity the dancing dwarfs. And Cordelia and Rillie and Annie and Lizzie, out-of-work older actresses; and old Mr Jenks the retired prompter; and a bevy of the younger actresses: the Emmas and the Bettys and the Sarahs and the Primroses: including several who (although Mrs Fortune was against it) had brought in young gentlemen they had found in the street. Actors back from tours in Dublin or Manchester or Birmingham leant casually against one wall smoking cigars and talking loudly about their next

12

engagements; leaning with them often was Miss Susan Fortune, daughter of the establishment, who had found herself a very clever niche playing old ladies although she was only young. Annie and Lizzie and Cordelia and Rillie stared at her malevolently. Miss Susan Fortune had an extremely large bosom: managers found themselves employing her for old parts instead of the scrawny older actresses who were the right age.

The voices in Cock Pit-lane rose with the cigar smoke and the smell of Mrs Fortune's watered whisky and sausage stew as the actors and actresses spoke of their triumphs. The dancing dwarfs bought drinks for an actress who hadn't been working. Snippets of conversation could be picked up: Olive the ballet dancer complaining that she had had to do the hornpipe in her last engagement; Mr Eustace Honour the comic expostulating about having to appear with a gorilla; the laughter from the gentlemen from the street engaged the Emmas and the Primroses. Mrs Fortune counted her takings. And everywhere, all the time, underneath: the anxiety about finding work, about where the next money was coming from: the precariousness of their rackety lives. There was a harp in the corner from some long-ago triumph: Mr Honour tuned it up and began playing, voices were raised in song. Many of them had very good voices; the music from Mrs Fortune's establishment could often be heard with all the other cacophony of sounds down Drury Lane:

> While nostrums are held out to cure each disease
> And to parry with death or with pain as we please
> The protector of life and preserver of ease
> I have ever yet found in a bottle.
>
> And should love whose dominion is ever divine
> Drench my doating fond eyes in a deluge of brine
> Ev'ry tear that I drop at bright Venus's shrine
> Let me drown in the tears of the bottle.

13

Late that night, calling goodbye to Rillie at the corner of Long Acre, Cordelia walked home through the dim streets, on up Drury Lane and towards Bloomsbury. Port-warmed and the flat-iron in her pocket, passing the beggars, avoiding the ponds of piss, she sang softly still:

> *Ev'ry tear that I drop at bright Venus's shrine*
> *Let me drown in the tears of the bottle.*

Three

Cordelia's mother and Cordelia's aunt were both also known as Miss Preston.

The earlier Misses Preston had emerged, through determination and slog and grit and cheek and stoicism, from the fetid stinking rookeries of Seven Dials in the parish of St Giles' to the very respectable basement rooms in Bloomsbury. Long ago those two fair-haired Preston sisters, Kitty and Hester, finally ran away from home for good when their father smashed their mother's head in with a gin bottle and a chair. They were thirteen and thirteen and three-quarters respectively. They only knew one person to look for and they looked for him: Mr George Sim, who was their mother's brother and, by some miracle, employed as the lamp-man at the Drury Lane Theatre. Mr Sim had to snuff and trim and light the hundreds of candles and oil lamps used in the theatre; he had a tiny room off the lighting room where he slept, for each day he must be the last to leave and the first to arrive in the dark and famous theatre.

He was polishing the lamp glasses, holding them up to the window, when Hester and Kity came to find him. He saw their stricken, filthy faces and sighed. 'What is it now?' But the young girls could not speak properly. They did not cry, but their teeth chattered as if they were cold, only it was midsummer and the lighting room was hot and airless. He walked out on to the empty stage; they followed him, completely unaware of the gilt boxes where the people of fashion would sit, or of the decorated high ceiling, or of the red, heavy curtains; remained numb as he filled the oil lamps in the wings. 'It's got to be decent oil, mind,' he said, as if they had been questioning him. 'None of your train oil rot in Drury Lane, can't have the ladies and gentlemen getting the smell of oil in their hair and their finery, they wouldn't come now, would they, if we used bad oil?' He supposed his sister wanted money and had sent the girls. On a corner of the stage one of the musicians was playing his clarinet: high and crying, the notes drifted, like pain. 'How's Mary then?' The shivering girls looked at each other.

'We ain't going back.'

'Well you ain't staying here!'

'She's dead.'

Mr Sim sighed. Nothing surprised him. Many of his siblings were dead. He walked back to his little room; the girls followed him.

'Does your dad know?' Stinking good-for-nothing drunk. He was a sewer-man but he was usually too drunk to go down.

'Dad done it.'

Then he did look surprised and he gave a little whistle and their story became clear. He pulled out his ale, sat on a stool, supped, gave them a little. They were pretty, they were thirteen or so; he had troubles enough of his own without his nieces hanging around. But he knew their fate if he did not help them: pretty thirteen-year-old girls lasted only a few months on the streets before they got in the family way or the pox, or worse. It was a wonder they had lasted as long as they had; helped their mother take in washing, he'd heard. He thought for a moment, looked at them carefully, weighing them up. Then he directed them to a basin of water. 'Wash your faces hard,' he

16

instructed. 'Lucky for you they're doing a *tableau* this week,' and he disappeared.

And somehow he got Kitty and Hester into Drury Lane as Walking Ladies at *twelve shillings per week*, each (more money than they had ever seen in their lives; a working man with a family might earn no more), and it was their uncle, Mr Sim (who liked young boys, they knew), who found them the clothes each actress had to personally provide for the job: a gown and a hat and ribbons and shoes. In their new finery they laughed and danced round him in their gratitude: they were no more ladies than Mr Sim was a gentleman, but they were very pretty, which counted (especially Kitty, who was more than pretty: beautiful some said), and they watched and learned and turned their hands to anything they were asked to. They posed as soldiers' wives in *tableaux*, or nymphs; they sewed hats and gowns and mended swords for no money when there was no acting work; they hid money in their shoes; they improved their somewhat erratic reading skills, learning to memorise things; and they never complained. And *never* did they go back to St Giles', to the dark rookeries: the stinking gutters and the tramps and the herring-hawkers and the Irish and their father who had killed their mother. They shared a room in Blackmoor-lane off Drury Lane with five other Walking Ladies, next to where prostitutes roamed; they put the bed across the door all night as a locking mechanism. They never actually said thank you to Mr Sim but often they came in early and helped him with his lamps and his candles and his coloured glass, and just ignored the young boys they found sleeping in his room. He showed them how to wear jewels on their costumes and in their hair; how to move their heads slightly on stage so that the reflected lights would catch the jewels, and they would be noticed. The sisters listened and watched and learned and saw how actresses could *change their voices*, and changed their own. They would move and sound like real ladies if it killed them.

Kitty, as well as being so very attractive, had a pretty singing

17

voice, and after some time she was elevated to small parts; Hester learned with delight to walk on a trapeze because audiences were clamouring for more than classical theatre now and the second half of the programmes were musical or acrobatic. Sometimes they were not paid, sometimes even the famous Mrs Sarah Siddons was not paid, and often they were hungry. But they watched and learned and observed; saw how some of the young actresses would push others out of the main-light on stage; saw how so many of them paraded, smiling up at the red plush boxes: hoping for favour, for a lover, for a gentleman to notice them or (the bigger the part, the more likely this could be) set them up in a nice little room, and pay. They heard that Charles James Fox, the politician, had *married* Mrs Armitage and Mrs Armitage hadn't really been a proper actress at all, but something even worse.

Some time later Mr Sim disappeared; someone laughed and said he'd been thrown in the Thames with his nancy boys. The sisters went down to the Strand several times to see if they could find him; one morning when the tide was out they even walked downriver from Hungerford Market, walked far along the water's edge: past the barges and the sailboats and the rubbish and the stink and the calls of the watermen. It began to rain, the stinking Thames mud squelched in through their thin boots, they could feel it seeping between their toes, but on they went, along the shore, past St Paul's Cathedral, under London Bridge, just in case. They passed old newspapers and broken boxes and chairs with three legs and bones and pieces of rusting iron and the rolling bloated carcass of a cow and glass bottles and dead rats and old women searching for pieces of coal. They saw strange rivulets of bright metallic colours streaming down to the water from the factories on the other side of the river. But Mr Sim the lamp-man had completely disappeared: they never heard anything of Mr Sim ever again. Kitty got a whole song of her own and paraded, hoping for a favour, a lover. Men from the audience often wandered into the dressing-rooms after the

18

performances, there were attacks, and fights and tears; Hester once punched a minor lord and was fined *five shillings* by the stage manager.

And then Hester fell off the trapeze. Her face and head were badly smashed (she bled all over the stage) and she somehow damaged her knee so that she could never again walk properly; was of course summarily dismissed, and no Mr Sim to tide them over. The sisters were shattered: Kitty's salary was now seventeen shillings per week when she was working, but often she was not working and now she needed to support them both as well as buy her stage clothes and her face paint. In the shared room in Blackmoor-lane Hester was no longer welcome; the other Walking Ladies felt she brought bad luck, they saw her scarred face, they knew she was in pain. The sight of Hester reminded them of what could happen if for one moment they faltered, and when she left the room they gargled angrily with red-port and water. Frantically Kitty sang her short song nightly in the second half of the programme, smiled even more charmingly and laughed with the audience, pushed other actresses out of the main-light; her sweet voice rose to the gallery in panic. Once Hester and Kitty saw a dead woman in Bow Street and they heard people whisper: *She died of hunger.* At last Kitty acquired a gentleman of sorts; he was rather old and not very attractive and perhaps not altogether a gentleman (he seemed to be a great deal involved in horse-racing and the importing of wines), but he had money certainly and he admired Kitty's voice and her smile and (in particular) her animal spirits enough – the sisters laughed and cried and clung together in disbelief – to set her up in some discreet basement rooms in Bloomsbury.

'In *Bloomsbury*?'

'Yes, Hes, *yes*, near the church, near the square, near the lords and ladies—'

'—a room of our own? Just for us? and nobody—'

'—*two* rooms, Hes! Two rooms at the bottom of a house in Little Russell Street, just opposite St George's Church, in the

19

parish of Bloomsbury! We can watch all the ladies going into church in their best gowns and then we can copy them and wear them on stage! It used to be a kitchen, but they've made it rooms to let, there's still a little oven in the back room, a real oven like the gentry have in their houses, we can cook things and not buy!' There was never an oven in Seven Dials, only a fire outside that people shared and fought over.

'How will we know how to work it?'

'We can learn. I seen women cooking properly! We can buy a pot! And we've got our *own steps*!' Kitty and Hester had not imagined living in two rooms of their own even in their wildest flights of imagination. Mr du Pont (as he informed Kitty he was named) had managed – as far as the sisters were concerned – a miracle. He said the Italian landlord owed him a favour. And Mr du Pont was happy for Kitty to stay on the stage, for seeing her there and knowing she would be his (to do with as he wished) a little later in the evening did interesting, jiggling things to his dying libido. All he insisted was that Kitty return to Little Russell Street immediately after her turn. She sometimes watched other, more financially ordered, young people wistfully, but only for a moment: her gratitude for security overrode everything else. 'This is my sister, who will be my maid,' she said grandly to Mr du Pont, tickling him under his chin. He frowned at the scarred limping girl, but Kitty made sure he never saw Hester; the older sister kept to the smaller back room with the oven, nearer to the cesspit, when he was visiting and closed her ears to his exertions: she had after all grown up in the rookeries, and exertions were nothing to her. And Kitty considered that the things required of her, nightly, were a price worth paying and begged sweetly for money for a new gown, which she gave to Hester. The sisters laughed a lot about Mr du Pont as the church bells pealed from the big church across the road, thought of fifty ways for Kitty to please him, to keep him happy, to therefore keep themselves safe. Sometimes Mr du Pont brought a bottle of gooseberry wine. Kitty smiled gratefully. She and Hester *hated* gooseberry wine, would only drink red-port; instead they used the gooseberry wine to wash their feet and then emptied it in the cesspit, in his absence.

A theatre is a treasure trove if you know where to look. Kitty began to appear in Bloomsbury every night through the fog and the dark streets with small, hidden acquisitions. The basement rooms took on a strange, theatrical quality: a small mirror draped with a bunch of feathers; a goblet holding flowers made from red velvet that fell softly across a table in the candlelight; a curtain made from something left over from another *tableau*.

'Take care!' said Hester, half pleased, half anxious, remembering that one of the girls had been instantly dismissed for stealing a pair of white stockings. 'We'll end up in Newgate Prison if you're not careful!' but Kitty only laughed. Her greatest triumph was a backcloth of clouds that they managed to attach to part of the ceiling. The basement exploded with laughter when from under Kitty's cloak one night an odd, very large boot appeared. Hester adapted it and placed it beside the door to hold Mr du Pont's walking stick and umbrella.

Hester's scarred face was sometimes drawn down by the pain in her damaged leg but she never complained, was so immensely grateful that they had somewhere to live, somewhere to *be*; she visited the new circulating libraries and read the newspapers, slowly spelling out the hard words; she spent hours in the new museum in Montague House; from the pedlars and the hawkers she carefully bought food for their survival. Everywhere people noticed the scarred, but somehow pretty, limping girl with the quirky open face and the grey, enquiring eyes. But Hester was not entirely open: she secretly panicked about their future. *What if something happens to Kitty too, or Mr du Pont grows tired?* They had made themselves very presentable young ladies before the accident, and they talked nice now; they could even have found work in one of the new shops in Oxford Street or the Strand. But nobody would employ Hester, not now with her scarred face and her painful limp – unless she left Bloomsbury altogether

21

and crossed the river to the dye works or the glue factories. Kitty saw her sister's drawn look, sometimes heard her cry out with pain in the night; secretly panicked about their future too, sang louder, smiling at the audiences.

One night someone in the theatre spoke in awe about a Mesmerist at Kennington, just down past the coaching inn at the Elephant and Castle: how he put people into a trance and took away pain. The other actors laughed. But Kitty thought of Hester's face. 'It's probably all nonsense,' she said, 'but let's try, Hes,' and she performed new tricks in the front room in Blooms-bury and persuaded old Mr du Pont to give her half a guinea. They walked, Hester grimacing in pain sometimes, all the way to the Elephant and down the Kennington Road: the two of them slightly uneasy one early afternoon to finally find themselves knocking on a door of a house in Cleaver-street; to find them-selves then in a dark bare room hung with coloured stars and several mirrors, and a man with a foreign accent. Kitty carried a flat-iron beneath her cloak.

'We don't know what this mesmerism thing is, don't you do nothing funny,' said Kitty sharply, but the foreign man only smiled nervously and allowed her to sit in a corner. He bowed and played a little flute: some foreign, plangent sound. Then he placed Hester on a chair and sat beside her, asked her about her fall from the trapeze. His accented voice sounded as nervous as they, and the sisters both observed that his clothes were threadbare so his profession was obviously not financially rewarding, although he was charging them a whole five shillings. Then he stood above Hester and began passing his hands backwards and forwards, backwards and forwards, over her head and down her body, very near but never touching. Kitty watched carefully in case he did anything unsuitable – he was after all a foreigner – but she saw that his nervousness had now left him entirely, he seemed certain and calm. She saw her own sharp, strong, no-nonsense sister relax slightly, and then in about ten minutes she seemed to be asleep, but with her eyes open. She seemed to breathe *with* the foreigner, in and out. Kitty observed, half fascinated, half terrified: she blinked her own eyes, as if she too might have been caught up in some way in the odd atmosphere. The foreigner began passing his hands across Hester's leg, again never touching it although Kitty was ready with the flat-iron, just in case. Then when he passed his hands across his own leg, Hester passed her own hands over her own leg also. The minutes passed: ten, fifteen. Finally the Mesmerist moved his hands past Hester's face again and Kitty saw that her sister suddenly awoke – although she had never been asleep. And then, ordered by the foreigner, Hester stood. She swayed slightly at first. She looked at the man in amazement. She walked over to Kitty, limping as she always limped.

'It don't hurt the same!' said Hester.

They were much too sensible to believe in magic, but something had happened: Hester limped the same as usual but was in less pain than she had ever been since falling from the trapeze. She explained in amazement to Kitty as they walked all the way back to Bloomsbury again that she had felt a kind of hot feeling passing through her.

'It came from him somehow, a kind of warmth.'

'He never touched you,' said Kitty, 'I watched him like a hawk.'

'I know,' said Hester, puzzled.

'Well what happened?'

'I dunno.'

'Well – is it – is it something like – like rays of sunshine coming out of his eyes? What did it feel like?'

'I can't exactly say. I remember but don't remember, all at the same time. I *wanted* it to work. I remember wanting it to work so much.'

Kitty inveigled other half-guineas from Mr du Pont, Hester went again and again to the Mesmerist. Most times the pain became slightly less. ('Perhaps it was healing anyway,' she said to Kitty, bemused. 'Or perhaps I don't exactly *feel* the pain the same.') She stared at her leg sometimes, perplexed. Soon Hester could limp about the London streets at speed, pushing her way along the crowded, broken cobbled ways, past chimney sweeps and gentlemen, dodging horses and carriages and cattle on their way to Smithfield Market and the little boys with dancing white mice (always superstitiously giving a farthing to a beggar, as if to protect her and Kitty from a similar fate). Pedlars called of hot bread and cold milk, and shouting and laughter came from all the taverns. She read in the newspapers that Animal Magnetists (as they were sometimes called) were foreign quacks who trapped the unwary, especially young girls; she read other reports that said magnetic fluids could seem to pass for the good from one person to another, take away pain.

'But what is it exactly?' she said over and over again, to Kitty, to herself. 'What *happens*?' She found a meeting advertised: a German professor would give a lecture on Animal Magnetism in Frith Street in Soho.

Hester decided to attend the meeting, went down into a basement; found her own Mesmerist, Monsieur Roland, there among the rather eccentric audience of strange-looking gentlemen, and foreigners, and older ladies. The German professor spoke of Franz Anton Mesmer, and of Magnetic Energy and how it could be applied to bodily health. Hester listened, fascinated. A heckler stood up and shouted, someone else in the audience hit the heckler. Afterwards the German professor handed out cards but Hester approached Monsieur Roland in his shabby suit.

'Teach me,' she said. 'I'll pay somehow. I'll teach *you* things,' she added bravely (for it was brave to be so open when your face is scarred and you have a limp), and Hester with those intelligent grey eyes smiled at the foreign gentleman. The foreigner blushed to the roots of his hair, cleared his throat several times, and Hester, who knew she still had the remnants at least of her prettiness, smiled again. 'Teach me,' she said.

'Mademoiselle, the flute and the coloured stars are only to set up the atmosphere,' said her Mesmerist apologetically.

*   *   *

24

All these stories Cordelia had heard in bits and pieces over the years from her mother and her aunt, with their laughter and their tears and their rows and their reconciliations; had taken in with her mother's milk the smell of the carmine that actresses painted on their faces; had sat in a corner and watched her aunt passing her hands over visiting ladies. She drank in their lives. One of their favourite stories was about the famous politician who had married Mrs Armitage (who was worse than an actress), Charles James Fox, not because of his politics (they knew nothing of politics), but because once, before Hester's accident, he'd been at the theatre with gambling friends and had actually taken Hester and Kitty to dinner afterwards. 'Behaved like a gentleman,' they always said to Cordelia. 'We ate as much as we liked and he made us laugh, and we made him laugh, and he sent us home in a carriage after!'

Hester, known most discreetly only as Miss Preston of Blooms-bury, had turned out to have 'the gift'; that was what the ladies said who began to alight from their carriages in a circumspect manner at the door of the basement, and come quickly and quietly down the narrow iron stairs: *Miss Preston has the gift*. 'I only do what you do,' said Hester to Kitty, 'we transport people in our different ways,' and Cordelia remembered them polishing the cheap shining stars, and laughing. But even as a little girl she had understood clearly: these visiting women needed her aunt, and trusted her implicitly.

At first Hester could only make appointments in the middle of the day, so as not to alert Mr du Pont, who was after all paying the rent, but later, when Hester's fame grew and she became the main wage earner, Mr du Pont was no longer required and Kitty was banished into the back room with the oven. And Hester's business acumen meant that the sisters kept the rooms: she went to see the Italian landlord in person, found him at the Italian church rounding up small boys who sold doves in cages.

25

'I will pay you from now on,' said Hester grandly, with money in her hand. And so she did, every week without fail, even when the rent was raised. Other tenants in Little Russell Street carried their chairs and beds away in the middle of the night, or the bailiffs came; the Misses Preston, somehow, stayed. Through good times and bad they kept the rooms in Bloomsbury: it was home.

Mr du Pont had, of course, to be physically removed from their lives because they didn't need him any more; Kitty had had to tour the provinces as the only way to get rid of him and he had banged on the basement door for weeks.

'She's gone away for ever,' Hester told him at last. 'Goodbye.'

Kitty felt free for the first time, revelled in her new freedom, still young: literally yelled with delight and relief to be rid of someone she had found so physically repulsive: she was grateful for the security he had allowed them to have but she spat him out now, like a bad taste. She had done her duty and now she was free! But her title was quickly changed to Mrs Preston when she found she was pregnant. Furiously she drank gin and jumped off tables. Mrs Kitty Preston was a comedy actress and the unwanted birth of Cordelia was her greatest joke, for there was no Mr Preston of course, or Mr Anybody at all in the theatre in Bristol when Cordelia was born after a performance of *The Larcenist*, and no way of knowing whether Mr du Pont or any of the various passing actors was the father. One of the more erudite members of the company who had once played in *King Lear* decreed the baby should be Cordelia, decrying Kitty's rather more prosaic choice of Betty. The actors went on from Bristol, played in barns and theatres and slept in crowded stinking rooms in Hull, or Wolverhampton, or wherever they were required to be; the baby Cordelia, humped about, breathed in the smell of the paint they used on their faces and tallow from the candles and the oil from the lamps and heard the creaking of old theatres and the sound of the cardboard scenery being moved, as she lay underneath the props table or beside the costume baskets.

'Kitty, you don't have to do that any more,' Hester had harangued, 'not with a baby! I'll make enough money, you can be my assistant, you can play the flute in the back room.' But Kitty lived for the life she had known; after a short experiment at being the assistant of an Animal Magnetiser and playing the flute without seeing the audience, she wanted nothing more than to tread the treacherous boards once more, the little girl under her arm for want of somewhere else to put her, for Hester could hardly mesmerise, with a baby. So Cordelia appeared on stage: first as a baby when required, then as a little prince in a tower: and so she had learnt her mother's trade, and learnt to read as she memorised her parts.

Sometimes, if there was no acting work and money got a bit short, there were ladies visiting Hester in the front room, and gentlemen visiting Kitty in the back, and Cordelia was hurriedly sent out with a penny in her hand for the muffin-man; she would repair to Bloomsbury Square with her hot muffin, where she learnt to know every tree. Sometimes she had to walk out at night also so as not to be in the way, and then Kitty and Hester gave the eight-year-old girl special rules: always walk firmly, always carry the old flat-iron or a big stone in your pocket; have a basket or a letter in your hand as if you have some purpose. No dawdling by the trees at night. Scream your head off and shout FIRE if anyone touches you and hit them with the flat-iron. Cordelia made friends with the moon: she always felt so much happier if the moon was shining, the moon that she and her mother had travelled by on so many nights from town to town: 'my moon' she called it, looking upwards for it to come out from behind the clouds or the fog, walking around the park on her eight-year-old legs stoically chewing her muffin. There was nothing romantic about this fancy: the moon (if it could be seen at all) changed shape alarmingly (sometimes round,

27

sometimes crooked); it was unreliable, like most things in her life. But if, when she was alone, through the fog and the darkness the moon did appear, it *was* like a friend, for it lit her way. She was not educated enough yet to know that the moon was a symbol of romance, that people wrote poetry about it and spoke of love (had not yet heard of *Romeo and Juliet*). Stolidly – it gave her light in the darkness – she thought of her moon as a friendly presence lighting the square, nothing more. Sometimes she would sit in the branches of an oak tree beside the north gate of the square, even on cold nights she sat there for it was a change from walking around and around and her legs got tired; she would sit up there and look for the shining moon, the shape-changing, dark-banishing moon, and stare at it, dreaming in a silent voice, misty unformed dreams, till it was time to go home again.

Hester had occasionally allowed her young niece to be present, quiet and still in a dark corner, as she drew her hands down. Always, just before she started, Aunt Hester, who seemed a brisk, no-nonsense person in other aspects of her life, would say gently: *Let yourself rest in my care*. Her hands went not on the seated, anxious women (almost all the clients were women) but just a few inches from their heads and their bodies: over and over she passed her hands in front of them, beside them, in long, sweeping movements, never actually touching them. Sometimes the women were hysterical: Aunt Hester calmed them. Sometimes the women were in terrible, distressed physical pain: somehow Aunt Hester either took the pain away or helped them to bear it. The little girl in the corner would hear the breathing of her aunt and the patient, often it became a rhythm. And almost always, after some time, the women went into some sort of open-eyed, calm trance that – Cordelia was not exactly sure what was happening – seemed, she saw, to give them some rest.

And then another engagement would turn up, usually another third-rate theatrical tour, and off they would go, Kitty and

Cordelia. And Cordelia learnt to recognise that it would probably always be like this, and then to laugh, like her mother, at the unspeakable conditions under which they often worked: the cheating managers, the promised parts that didn't come, the cold, the dirt, the chanting of the crowds for lions and tigers even as the actors stood upon the stage in some worthy piece, the travelling to another town late at night as the moon shone down on them: all these things mother and daughter, shouting and swearing sometimes but stoic in the end, bore. Cordelia had a temper, flared up sometimes, uncontrolled. Kitty would hit her and Cordelia would subside, till next time.

And slowly but surely Cordelia learnt what Hester and Kitty had learnt from their profession, only she learnt it much earlier and achieved it much better: to talk, and to walk, exactly like a lady.

And then Kitty died of pneumonia somewhere near Birmingham, sleeping beside Cordelia in a cold room. The daughter and her aunt wept, but were much too tough to rant at the unfairness of life: it was part and parcel of the terrible apprenticeship.

The painted clouds had long since fallen to dust but the painted glass stars on the ceiling (stars that Kitty had acquired in her usual manner when Hester first started working) remained. Now, of course, mesmerism was talked of everywhere, newspapers were full of it: if doctors could not add a little mesmerism to their skills some people would not attend at all, for people, especially ladies, felt it more respectable and satisfying to be cured of an illness from the outside of the body, rather than anything more intrusive. Arguments raged over these matters in all the newspapers and journals; it was said that Mr Charles Dickens was putting mesmerism into his latest novel, *Oliver Twist*, and there were rumours that he himself had become a mesmerist.

But Miss Hester Preston, who had been a discreet pioneer, was dead and forgotten.

And now Cordelia was the only Miss Preston left.

Four

In an alley off Bow Street, seated in the Lamb public house, a corner of which, stinking of ale and pipe tobacco and humans, served as their 'office', Mr Kenneth and Mr Turnour ('Work Providers to the Stars') told Cordelia and Rillie that there was nothing immediate, but they would keep them in mind. The actresses heard the old familiar words, raised their eyebrows at each other in a resigned manner.

'Come on, we'll go and see the mesmerism experiment at the hospital I told you about,' said Rillie. 'Specially as we've got our ladies' hats on,' and they walked, glad to have something to do, somewhere to go, to the new University College Hospital where they understood with surprise that they may just have perceived Mr Charles Dickens disappearing inside. Along a corridor there was a lecture hall crowded with people and they heard excited rumbling chatter: learned, earnest gentlemen, doctors, and a few women in hats like Cordelia and Rillie, all squashed together on small seats, and certainly that *was* Mr Dickens, seated near the stage: *It is Mr Dickens*, they heard people whisper.

Professor Elliotson brought one of the young Irish sisters they had read about on to the stage in her hospital nightdress. She sat

31

demurely on a chair with her head bowed and her hands neatly clasped; they could not properly see her face. He spoke to the assembled people of the importance of the work he was doing: how mesmerism could help hospital patients, keeping them unaware yet not asleep during painful surgery. 'I believe that Mesmerism is a physical force acting on the body's machinery. I must impress upon all my learned friends here today that Mesmerism is not mumbo-jumbo, it is not spiritualism.' He looked about his audience: some friendly faces, some hostile. 'Ladies and Gentlemen, there have been too many battles between doctors and mesmerists: I am both: I am trying to bring Mesmerism and medi-cine *together*. I shall now demonstrate the propensities.' He sat on a chair opposite the girl in the nightdress. As he proceeded to pass his hands across her eyes, across her head, not touching them, passing near them over and over, Cordelia felt an odd, old tingle of memory – this was something she was so familiar with from her childhood, yet had never properly understood. In a very few minutes the young girl seemed to have fallen into a trance; the whole audience waited to see what Professor Elliotson would do next. Then, almost at once, something extraordinary happened: the girl stood up and began to sing, and to dance to her own music. To the assembled people watching this could not have been more shocking: the Professor had not indicated that she should do so: she had done it of her own accord, and what was more, she was singing a song that had only very recently become popular.

> Come listen all you gals and boys
> I'm going to sing a little song
> My name is Jim Crow.
> Weel about and turn about and do jis so,
> Eb'ry time I weel about I jump Jim Crow.

'That's from that show that's on at the Adelphi,' whispered Rillie in amazement. 'That actor from America makes himself a darkie. How would she know that?'

32

The audience (for they seemed like an audience) in the small crowded theatre (for it seemed as if they were at the theatre) was hushed and excited and disturbed all at once: great wafts of perspiration and old perfume seemed to fill the space as the girl in the nightdress went on singing and dancing. Cordelia watched with absolute concentration: she had seen mesmerism enough when she was young to understand what was happening, yet she could not be sure if she was witnessing a trance or a performance. She saw that Professor Elliotson looked surprised slightly, and yet proud. The girl's eyes were certainly blank:

> *Weel about and turn about and do jis so,*
> *Eb'ry time I weel about I jump Jim Crow.*

When the song finished several of the crowd began to clap, were hushed at once by others. An assistant came on stage and pressed something large and sharp like a nail or a big needle into the girl's flesh; the audience gasped, the girl did not move. The Professor began to speak to the crowd again, one hand on his hip. The girl put her hand on her hip also. When he began to walk about the stage, the girl in the nightdress did likewise. The Professor indicated that she should sit: she did so at once.

'I believe,' said the Professor, 'that this philosophy – for I truly believe it to be a kind of medical philosophy, not a spiritual miracle – can be used by the medical profession, most of all to relieve pain.' The assistant picked up a hammer and tapped the girl's shoulder sharply: not for a moment did she move or flinch. The assistant brought a small rope down hard across her back. The spectators stirred, uneasy. Not for a moment did the girl move or flinch. He took a handful of her hair and pulled. But her face was trance-like and impassive. 'If we can sedate, as it were, the patient before an operation,' continued the Professor, 'are we not moving forward? Who of us, who have observed such suffering in our hospitals, would not be glad to alleviate that? *and Cordelia saw her Aunt Hester calming the distressed women*

33

who came down the basement steps in Bloomsbury all those years ago – for surely the Medical Profession must be innovative, open to suggestion and change.' The Professor passed his hands at last across the face of the girl over and over: in a few moments she gave a kind of start, and then seemed to huddle in to herself, not at all a girl who could sing Jim Crow unaccompanied and dance in her nightdress to an audience of medical men.

'I think she is a very good actress!' whispered Rillie as they walked along corridors. They heard the murmurings behind and beside them.

'. . . and the patient should be passive, not active.' A dour gentleman passed them, frowning.

'. . . nothing but a kind of intellectual prostitution,' another gentleman was saying. 'Look at everyone, hanging on to her every word and movement, and being . . .' and his head seemed to wag in anger, *'excited* by it.'

But Cordelia's head, and her heart, were full of memory, half-pictures of the past. She felt odd, unsettled. 'Let's go home and have a drink,' she murmured. 'I got chops.'

There were the first signs of spring, straggling flowers round corners. They bought gingerbread from the gingerbread man, they half listened to a baritone street singer singing a penny song about a man murdering his wife in Camberwell, they bought some apples, they passed a man carrying a board that advertised India-rubber braces, they gave halfpennies to beggars in case one day it was them. The basement rooms were cold, yet stuffy. They lit the fires and opened the windows. Feet passed. They turned the chops over and over on the small open oven in the back room, the air filled with the smell of meat. Afterwards they ate gingerbread and drank port in the front room and spoke again of what they had seen.

'I think she was an *actress*,' said Rillie again. 'I know an actress when I see one! She was giving a performance.'

Cordelia was less sure. 'I have seen mesmerism when the patient had no need – or reason – to act,' she said slowly. 'It was – like that.'

'Singing popular songs! Did Aunt Hester's ladies sing?'

'No,' said Cordelia, 'not the singing. I never heard singing.'

Rillie wandered about the star-covered room, her glass in her hand. 'It sort of seems to me like what we do! Like I say, a performance!'

Cordelia still spoke slowly, oddly. 'My Aunt Hester believed implicitly in mesmerism – I'm absolutely sure of that, because it helped with the pain in her leg. But when I think back on it now – she was no doctor of any kind of course – when I think of all those women coming so quickly down the steps, so anxious to see her – from all different classes – you know, Rillie, I think she was more well known than I understood, there were real ladies sometimes, there were grand carriages, people quite out of the class of this area, and yet a shop girl with headaches used to walk after work from Bond Street I remember – all sorts of people. And I think what she did was – I can't quite explain, but . . .' Cordelia searched for words, 'tranquillise the mind. Make them calmer. Help them bear whatever pain it was – in their hearts or in their bodies. Some used to weep, she could almost always make them stop – they – they *believed* in her. But I knew it was odd. Even as a little girl I felt it was strange.'

Rillie picked up Alphonse, stroked the marble head. 'And was this part of it? Was it part of the treatment for the people she saw?' Cordelia held out her hand; when Rillie passed Alphonse over she too ran her hands over the head as she used to when she was a small child. 'What are the numbers?' said Rillie.

'This is phrenology – reading the head. The numbers are supposed to show where bits of your brain are.' Perhaps it was the port, but they both began to laugh. 'Or bits of your personality,' amended Cordelia. 'Look.' And she got up and picked up one of her aunt's books to check: 'Look, look! This is something different from mesmerism.' And she showed Rillie a picture of a head with numbers drawn on it, looking exactly like Alphonse. 'Look, see, here on the top of your head, like in this drawing, that's the spiritual region. And from the top of the head down to the forehead is the reason and the intellect.'

'I've only got a little forehead,' said Rillie and she looked into one of the mirrors to confirm this knowledge. 'I suppose that means I'm stupid!'

'No, no, look, see this number twenty-four at the front of this picture, that's marked OBSERVATION, now look!' She pressed Rillie's forehead, just above her nose. 'You are very observant, Rillie, you always notice things, and look! you've got a real bump there, look!'

Rillie said indignantly, 'That's where I fell down that track in the dark on the way home from Guildford!' And they were laughing again, and they picked up their cloaks and took their usual route to Cock Pit-lane and Mrs Fortune.

But seeing the Professor and the experiment had disturbed Cordelia somehow, disquieted her. Late that night, unsettled, home again from Mrs Fortune's she sat alone by the fire in the candlelight with the books and poured another glass of port: 'red-port' Kitty and Hester used to call it, from Portugal; (they liked red-port better than white-port when they could choose for they believed white-port to be poison.) Cordelia picked up the marble head again. She stared at the numbers, checking them in the book she had shown Rillie earlier. The numbers, as she remembered, were on the same place on either side of the head. She stood suddenly: *I suppose I must study my own head first of all*. Briefly she looked at her own head in one of Aunt Hester's mirrors and then quickly turned away. She did not always like what she saw in mirrors. She sat again by the fire and picked up one of the books.

No. 1: AMATIVENESS: love – impulse of affection between the sexes – the desire to marry. *There would be no such place on my skull*.

No. 2: PARENTAL LOVE: regard for offspring – fondness for

children generally, also for pets and animals. *I will not even feel my head for that*.

No. 6: RESISTANCE: energy – hastiness – destructiveness – severity – anger.

Anger. She dropped the book, picked up Alphonse, stared at the place wherein they said anger lay. As she drifted, half awake, half asleep by the springtime fire she thought that the space between her ears numbered 6 would be so immeasurable if she felt for it that it would be impossible to even touch, so great was her hidden, secret rage, and her terrible, life-consuming passion: *anger*.

For Cordelia had not always been known as Miss Preston.

Nor had Cordelia Preston always been the First Witch, picking up dregs of work in the Lamb public house from Mr Kenneth and Mr Turnour.

Cordelia's long apprenticeship, begun at her mother's side, had served her well. Some time after the new exciting young actor Edmund Kean suddenly took London by storm, Cordelia was, by some miracle of fate and luck and talent and good timing, employed to play in the prestigious company at Drury Lane where her mother and her aunt had once, long ago, been Walking Ladies. Edmund Kean represented the new style of acting; Edmund Kean did not declaim in the more old-fashioned style, Edmund Kean seized the audience by the throat. Cordelia, playing small parts at first with her friend Rillie Spoons, watched and learned. She saw Mr Kean play Hamlet. She saw a production of *Romeo and Juliet* and learned that the moon spoke of love. Cordelia was eighteen and pretty (more than pretty, beautiful: like her mother) and had been in the theatre all her life. She had long learned to walk and talk with elegance and grace, she had a particularly beautiful voice, and was well schooled by Kitty and Hester in how to catch the eye of the audience. She also knew how to make an audience laugh. She was ready for her chance.

Finally her chance came. But already, for everybody, working in the same company as Edmund Kean had turned into both a dream and a nightmare: he had become so soon, through his alcoholic excesses and his bullying, past his best, and would strike other actors if he felt so inclined. Cordelia was cast to act with him: in *Richard III* and then in *King Lear*, where she played the youngest daughter, her namesake: Cordelia. Like the others in the company Cordelia endured much for the intensity, still, of some of Kean's performances. And very occasionally something happened on stage to her, herself: Cordelia felt it, understood it: something between herself and Mr Kean affected the audience, some sort of magic concentration transported them into some other realm where they were one. Cordelia recognised it, but never spoke of it, understood only that it was a touch of momentary magic. But the arrogance and the drunkenness of the failing Mr Kean became unbearable even for someone as tough as Cordelia Preston, who was quite used to drunken actors breathing alcohol and madness all over her. So when she was offered the part of Nellie in *For Love of Nellie* during the summer season at the Haymarket she accepted this chance with great alacrity even though it meant saying goodbye to the extraordinary Mr Kean, and Shakespeare. It was a comedy and she knew how to make a success of it. The production was a sensation: *Nellie* was the talk of London that summer. And although she had become quite a favourite at Drury Lane, this time, at the Haymarket, admirers queued at Cordelia's dressing room door.

Rillie Spoons had learned not to ever, *ever* mention Lord Morgan Ellis, son and heir of the Duke of Llannefydd. But who could ever forget that young man, Ellis: handsome, charming, paying court to Cordelia at the height of her career. As her confidence in her success grew, Cordelia had never tried to exactly hide her rather eccentric antecedents, but developed a wry, humorous way of talking about her family and her past as if they belonged to a more distant branch of the family: the terrible conditions as she had toured the country with her mother, the hours in the dark back room while her aunt mesmerised ladies, all turned into fond, funny long-ago stories that left out pain and belonged to someone else, a distant outlandish relation. Cordelia herself was (it was said) of very respectable stock, her grandfather (so she said) having been an educated man, a lawyer. She was still, of course, an *actress*: there was no escaping that, and there was no way she could actually be a respectable woman, but she was also known among men of the world as a most entertaining woman who had had some very odd cousins. There were other admirers richer than Lord Morgan Ellis, there were others more powerful: Cordelia even dined several times with Lord Castlereagh, the foreign secretary, and made him laugh at the stories of the lamp-man in Drury Lane. When the Duke of Wellington came home in triumph from Waterloo the theatres presented many victorious *tableaux*: the Duke himself paid Cordelia, who had portrayed Britannia, special attention. But Ellis had her heart. And all her mother's and her aunt's real experiences came back to Cordelia then: how the actresses tried to find the main-light, to attract the attention of anybody who could rescue them from their lives.

'I will take you away,' said Ellis, 'from this whole life. I will take you to freedom! You and I and the sea and the stars!' He made it sound like the Garden of Eden.

He did not know that she lived with Aunt Hester in Little Russell Street; Cordelia was vague, and, after all, where a potential mistress lived was not a matter of concern to Lord Morgan Ellis. He would make suitable arrangements. But Cordelia's star was in the ascendant, she had money; quickly she moved herself to very cultured rooms in Mayfair, she had a maid. She was, in private, used to sitting with both her feet up beside the stove in Little Russell Street, drinking port with Aunt Hester; she now gritted her teeth and sat very straight and served tea in small cups to ladies and wore gloves and left calling cards. She had done such things so often on stage, or in public, that they came

39

easily to her: now she learnt to do them in private as well. She missed Aunt Hester dreadfully, hurried back to Bloomsbury to visit her.

'It won't be for long,' she promised. 'I know where my real home is but this is my chance; there are precedents; and he loves me.'

Aunt Hester was very wise in the ways of the world. 'He may set you up somewhere, pay. But never give up your career, for he will not be there always.'

'I am not going to be "set up". That is not what I want.'

'He will not marry you, Cordelia. He is the nobility. One day he will be the Duke of Llannefydd, it would be impossible for him to marry someone like you. You must not build up dreams that are impossible to fulfil.'

'He loves me.'

Her aunt tried again. 'Cordelia, you do not understand the difference between their world and ours; the barriers of class are unassailable for people like you and me. Appearing on his arm at respectable events is nothing, nothing at all: allowances are made for impressionable young lords. You cannot marry someone so far above you – I do not mean above you as a person, for there is nobody in the world above you in my eyes' – that fond, ironical look of hers – 'but I mean in society. It is impossible, Cordelia, and you are only storing up future trouble for yourself.'

'What about Mrs Armitage and Charles James Fox? You and my mother always told me she was something much worse than an actress.'

'That was entirely different. Mr Fox was a different kind of man who moved in a different kind of world, he was a politician more than he was a nobleman. What does Lord Ellis *do*, except be Lord Ellis? And Mr Fox lived with Mrs Armitage for many, many years before they were married. He loved her, he could not live without her.'

'Ellis says he cannot live without me!' Cordelia's eyes flashed, the temper she tried hard to suppress.

Aunt Hester was angry too. 'Perhaps he does say such things, but it is not the same situation at all. Be set up with Lord Ellis by all means, and take what you can from the time. But *marriage* is only a dream. Cordelia, we come from St Giles'!' She, more than anyone, who had supported Cordelia in every way she could, wanted the security for her niece that the earlier Misses Preston had not achieved, but was alarmed at her impossible and unrealistic hopes.

'He loves me!' repeated Cordelia again. 'Love changes everything!'

'No, it doesn't,' said Aunt Hester, her face expressionless. But she said no more.

Cordelia, from Mayfair, did appear on Ellis's arm at social functions. Heads turned to see her: she was recognised from the theatre and she was lovely to look at and had laughing eyes and the ways of a lady. She was seen at the home of the Dowager Duchess of Hawksfield where the chandeliers of Grosvenor Square glittered above the heads of the nobility when the fashion for things Egyptian swirled over London: that surely was some sort of acceptance by society; she wore the mysterious, untranslatable hieroglyphs in a beautiful medallion, given to her by Lord Morgan Ellis, around her neck. She was seen at Vauxhall Gardens, at Ranelagh.

It was of course assumed that she was Ellis's mistress.

But Cordelia was tough; much, much tougher than that. She did not want to be half rescued, like her mother and her aunt: in her deepest, most private heart she wanted to be married, and safe and secure. She was perfectly aware that she did not have the culture or breeding to be accepted properly by the nobility; she was perfectly aware that her mother was from the back of Tottenham Court Road even if Cordelia sounded like a lady and walked with grace. But she had had her own very special kind of education all the same: she had learnt to be entertaining and to please and her voice was low and musical. Once she did amaze, and shock, Lord Morgan Ellis – by throwing, without a second thought, a flat-iron at a man in the street who was hitting a woman. She was mortified at her instinctive reaction; the man was rendered unconscious and the woman shouted at her; Cordelia explained to Ellis that she sometimes carried the flat-iron in her cloak for safety.

'Safety where?'

'In the street.'

'You are *never* to walk in the street!' exclaimed Ellis, more shocked than ever.

'Of course,' murmured Cordelia, but she retained the flat-iron. He told her that exuberance and ebullience were unbecoming in young ladies; that real ladies were quieter, perhaps, than she. Cordelia did her best, tried to control her instinctive temper, and not throw things; did not suggest what she thought: that it was her ebullience and exuberance that had allowed her to survive and get to where she had arrived: that energy and strength and laughter. She held her peace, and was the image of a lady.

Night after night Ellis wooed her, often in the company of the fat and ageing Prince of Wales, who was still waiting to be King and whose alcoholic breath at least equalled that of Mr Kean (that fat old Prince who had once, also, married the woman of his dreams). Cordelia's stories entranced them. But Cordelia, drawing on every bit of courage and determination and worldly wisdom she had gained from her past, would not settle for anything less than marriage. She stopped seeing Lord Morgan Ellis, dined again with Lord Castlereagh.

And finally, unbelievably, Lord Morgan Ellis did marry Cordelia, on the promise that she would at once give up the theatre, and that her career and her past life would never, ever be mentioned. They were married in a small private ceremony in a small private chapel on the Gower peninsula in Wales: it was so private that none of his family came, except two smiling Welsh cousins, but Rillie and Aunt Hester made the long trip to Wales with Cordelia, to stand witness.

'You will meet my father when it is time,' said Ellis.

42

And Cordelia Preston left the stage, and her triumph, without a backward look, to become Lady Ellis.

Ellis's promise of 'freedom' meant, Cordelia learnt, living permanently on the Gower peninsula – Gwyr as she heard it called by the Welsh servants – a place far from anywhere (and days from London) where sheer, high cliffs fell down to the sea and the tide drifted outwards for miles and looked so safe and calm. 'I want you to forget about London and your old life,' he said, and Cordelia thought how wonderful it was, to leave the stink and the crowds and the noise and the fog of the city. They settled into a huge old stone mansion on the Gwyr coast, huge to Cordelia that is (perhaps once, long ago, a watch house or a gatehouse to the crumbling stone castle behind), for so her new husband decreed. The stone house was isolated, desolate, miles from the nearest small town. 'It is romantic,' said Ellis. 'We want to be alone.' He said they were to manage with only three servants: a maid, a manservant and a cook: '*Only* three!' said Cordelia, laughing at him. But she had not understood that Ellis would often be going back – to London – without her. 'Here is where you will be free,' said Ellis firmly, in the stone house where a high fence was built round and where grass grew wild and bright flowers shone, red poppies and yellow daisies and something unknown, blue and beautiful; and where yew trees and beech trees and a twisted oak tree bent away from the sea. 'I must, of course, still go about my business.' She watched until even the dust from the hooves of his horse had disappeared, along the rough coast path.

Cordelia had never been alone before in her life – ever. She had slept with her mother since she was born until her mother died; her beloved Aunt Hester was always there; on tour it was four or six to a room every time: now she was alone in grey stone silence. She went and talked to the servants but they hardly spoke any English, muttered among themselves in their own language: she at last understood that she was making them uneasy by crossing into their territory, they thought her voice

43

was that of a lady, did not understand that this was how actresses talked, for no one of course spoke of her as an actress now. She kept telling herself that this was what she had wanted above all things. *I am secure and safe.* Days crept by. There were old, mouldering books on dark shelves but she was not used to reading, except her parts; her sewing was costumes and hats, not embroidery. She was used to the sounds of people and carriages and pedlars' cries and the city, not the sound of the sea. She had seen the sea of course, on her travels with the companies around the country, but the sea at Brighton was not like this: not like the strange, moving water that almost disappeared at times in the day, and then came back like a snake across the sands and the green weed and the rocks until it lay suddenly almost beneath her, shushing and sighing, and there was no sign of rocks at all. And on Gywr there was a different kind of fog: a white, silent mist that came rolling in across the sea so that she could not see the huge old oak tree outside the window. She found to her amazement that she missed the noise and the shouting and the carriages and the laughter and the black fog and the *life* of London. At night she waited for her moon to come out: the new moon, the full moon, the waning moon: *my* moon: the same moon. But sometimes she lay in her lonely bed at night as the mist swirled and there was no moon; she would hear the sea: the drawing back, the silence like a sigh, and then the crashing sound again echoing into her broken dreams. But no moon.

For days and weeks she stared at that sea and the tides: it could look so safe: those miles of sand stretching out to the horizon, the infinite sand and the secret rocks and the shells and the seaweed; occasionally in the distance she would glimpse part of an old ship perhaps, long lost and ravaged. But then the tide would roll inexorably in again, covering everything, covering the rocks as though they did not, after all, exist. And often the wind blew wild and the sea tumbled and thundered into dark terrifying caves under the cliffs where nightmares lay. She felt

44

the sea's strength, and its hidden danger, and wondered if she would become mad.

Sometimes, in the middle of a dark (and moonless) night, she was sure lights flickered in the darkness, she was sure she heard cries and crashing in the darkness: one morning a new, lone hull with broken masts lay on its side beside the secret rocks as the tide went out, yet no sign of people, or goods, or life. And the hull of the unexplained, silent boat lay there, the sea covered it twice daily; the wood rotted; parts of it floated up to the shore on incoming tides. But when the tide went out, a long, twisted, torn piece of iron could be clearly seen: it pointed upwards to the sky like a finger of accusation, and no sailors. For the first time in her life her strength deserted her as she told herself over and over: *but this is what I wanted.*

At first Ellis came back often. Cordelia would run through the wild bright flowers and the grass to the gates when she heard at last the sound of horses, a carriage.

'My girl!' he would call, and he would alight and he would run too, and gather her up in his arms and the sound of the sea would recede in her head and she would come to herself again, chide herself for her weakness. Excited and young and in love and full of high spirits they would walk for miles and miles along the cliffs, and then walk home again, entwined in the cold, familiar moonlight. Sometimes there were wild storms, lightning across the sky and echoing thunder, but she was safe with Ellis. 'We will love each other for ever, Cordie!' cried Ellis in the night. 'For ever!' And she thought: *this is what I wanted.*

Later he came less. But now she had to learn something else: to be a mother. *I do not know what to do,* she would whisper to herself as her stomach swelled: it was the servants who did it anyway, the maid and the cook, as Cordelia screamed. She held the small bundle, terrified. Once she shook it, to make sure it was not dead. Later she would walk down the narrow winding paths cut into the cliffs to the sand, carrying that first child, Manon (after Ellis's mother, who had died long ago); beautiful

Manon who would stare and point at the shells and the rocks and the green seaweed that grew there, at the dark mystery of the caves underneath the cliffs. The next daughter was Gwen-lliam (after a Welsh grandmother), who had grey eyes, like her Great-Aunt Hester: the sight of Gwenlliam made Cordelia's heart leap in a way she hardly understood. She made necklets for the two little girls from tiny pink shells; they cried when darkness came and they must leave their paradise. Then Morgan was born, named after his father, *an heir at last, Ellis will be happy;* Ellis arriving on horseback lifted the tiny boy baby into the air and laughed with pride; later the boy wanted nothing but to be on the shore with his sisters, watching the sea coming and going. And some of their delight in the coast of Gwyr, like their father's delight, at last passed into Cordelia; she felt the wild lonely place enter into her breath and her bloodstream.

Slowly she taught herself to properly look after these small beings; the hardest thing was her flashes of temper: they were all so young, she was often so tired: once she hit Manon in impatience because she was crying on and on: the little girl stopped at once but Cordelia saw the other children stare, was ashamed, learnt to control herself over and over; at last did not hit them as Kitty had hit her.

The deserted shore was their life; Cordelia would see their blond heads far out on the sand as the tide snaked out, bent over rocks and shells, content for hours with their findings. All day their voices echoed upwards; she would hear them laughing and calling of their strange found treasures; wild sea birds flew over them, and there was the smell of salt and seaweed. Once Morgan wept inconsolably for hours: he had found a small fish, brought it so carefully home to show his mother, could not under-stand why the moving, flicking tail had become so still and the eye so glassy with blame. Cordelia comforted him and taught him to carefully leave the small fish in the pools of water caught in the secret rocks, explained that the water would come in again, and make the little fish safe.

And then there would come a storm, and heavy rain would pound the sea and the wind would blow the children back to the grey stone place that was their home as the ruins of the old castle shadowed behind them, and the fires would be lit, and sometimes Cordelia would sing:

> When that I was and a little tiny boy
> With a heigh ho, the wind and the rain
> A foolish thing was but a toy
> For the rain it raineth every day.

They built a treehouse in a big old twisted oak tree; she told them of the oak tree far away in Bloomsbury Square and her friend the moon. She spoke rather shyly when she told them how she thought the moon was hers, it seemed foolish now, and vain, but they liked that story too: *Mama's moon*, they called it, staring upwards.

They found wonderful hiding places in the old stone ruins of the ancient castle and told themselves stories of wild Welsh warriors: their father's heritage. Wild flowers grew taller, blue and red and gold; shells and seaweed dried in doorways. They found crabs. They found bronze buttons and wove stories of battles. They learnt to read and write (to Cordelia's best ability); left painstakingly written notes for one another high in the branches of the oak, their letter box. *Pick some flowers for the dinner table, Manon*, wrote Cordelia. *I love you, Mama*, wrote Gwenlliam. *I seed the big bird*, wrote Morgan, only four.

And they spoke of the mysterious shipwrecks on dark, moonless nights, the flashing lights that seemed to lure the boats inwards, the twisted iron of the hulls.

'Where did they come from?'

'What?'

'The boats.'

She could not answer their questions. 'Oh – let me see – America!'

47

'What is America?'

'Oh – another country, not this one.'

'Where is it?'

'Somewhere else.'

'But where?'

'Oh God's truth, just – America, for goodness' sake!' (for she did not know herself). Once she would have shouted for longer; now she breathed deeply. Then she said: 'America is a new country, far away, that sends us tobacco and – things. Beautiful things like' – she would search her mind – 'honey and carpets and strange fruit. It's where people sing all day long, this new place, America.'

'What does it mean that America is new?' Manon's beautiful little face.

'What?'

'What does it mean that it is *new*?' Gwenlliam's enquiring grey eyes.

And Morgan added in his very small child's voice, 'Did it just jump up out of the sea?'

She laughed. 'Yes – yes, it just jumped up out of the sea! And our sailors and explorers went there – and now they sing and have happy lives and honey!' New land sending carpets and strange fruit on ships, land emerging out of the sea for people to travel to and sing and have happy, honeyed lives: these things entranced them, became an ongoing story. Sometimes when the tide was right out they would plod out across the damp sand, and sometimes touch the rotting wood and the rusting iron that pointed upwards, and say, *America*. They whispered of invisible sailors.

If Cordelia had any regrets for her former life, no one ever knew. But sometimes by the tall, spitting open fire inside the grey stone walls as the rain came down outside she would, despite all Ellis's directives, recount to her children some of the real stories of her life: of her mother and her aunt and the theatre and Little Russell Street and Bloomsbury Square and London.

They were fascinated, she saw, at stories of Aunt Hester and her mesmerism and how it healed people like magic; they were entranced by stories of the theatre and Mr Kean and of their great-great-uncle, Mr Sim the lamp-man: asked questions about the lighting on the stage, whether there could be storms and sunshine. And she would sing them to sleep in the real storms:

For the rain it raineth every day.

Cordelia tried to keep in touch with her beloved aunt, and with her very old friend Rillie Spoons, but she was not a very accomplished letter-writer, although she tried, nor were her aunt or Rillie Spoons. Once Aunt Hester and Rillie made the long journey. They saw that Cordelia had strange foreign servants in this strange foreign land: they saw she still found it hard not to polish the floors herself. Rillie, privately, thought that Cordelia played the part of Lady Ellis, just as she had once played the part of Queen Anne, or Nellie. But the fair-haired children brought tears to Aunt Hester's worldly-wise old eyes, for she saw her own sister, Kitty, when Manon smiled. 'Look at me! Look at me dancing!' said Manon. And Aunt Hester at last saw the other grey eyes, for Cordelia and Rillie pointed out to her that Gwenlliam, the second daughter, looked like her great-aunt.

'It's true, I believe you look like me!' she said to Gwenlliam, and the grey-eyed, bright-eyed old lady and the grey-eyed, bright-eyed little girl laughed shyly at the strangeness of it and then Gwenlliam did an odd thing: stroked the old lady's ringless hands, looked at them carefully: perhaps because they were wrinkled, perhaps because she understood they held magic, kept anyway her young hand in the old one.

Rillie and Aunt Hester saw that the young boy, Morgan, was the most difficult, that he seemed consumed by some sort of rages or tantrums, much worse than Cordelia's rages had ever been; they saw that Cordelia calmed him by very gently stroking his head over and over, that this touch made him quiet and then

49

he would tell the visitors about his crabs and his shells, the storm in his head gone. They saw that he did not exactly look like Cordelia, yet he had her manner: somehow, something. He was *like* Cordelia. Then this very small boy, distress forgotten, insisted the visitors come down the cliff path to the sea, even the stiff and limping Great-Aunt Hester, so that they too could see the secret rocks that could be seen now (with the tide out) and the rotting hulls and the fingers of iron pointing upward.

'They comed from America,' he said.

Rillie and Aunt Hester saw that Cordelia had somehow taught herself to be a good mother, to half control her sharp, flaring way: 'Ye Gods!' she would cry in exasperation, and then they saw that she stopped herself, and laughed. They saw that her children loved her completely; they adored her: she was the centre of their lives. If they had secret anxieties, *was this a proper childhood for the nobility?* they kept such thoughts to themselves.

But the distances were so long, and the travel so difficult, that they wondered, as they said goodbye, if they would meet again.

When Ellis came he saw that his children were tall and wild and beautiful, and sometimes she saw puzzlement in his eyes that he would not explain.

'Morgan needs to go away to school,' he said.

'Let him learn here!' Her eyes flashed at him and he took her in his arms.

'No ebullience, my darling,' he said, holding her easily, so much stronger. 'Remember what I have taught you.'

'Don't take him away from me,' she said, but calmer. 'He has only just turned four. Let them all have tutors here! Manon and Gwenlliam and I will learn with Morgan.' Ellis looked at her oddly, but arranged tutors. And came less and less often. Finally, the last absence, he did not come for seven months.

It was Rillie Spoons, jobbing actress (like Cordelia's Aunt Hester before her educating herself in the circulating libraries), who saw the newspaper report: the Duke of Llannefydd's only son married, with fireworks, in a ceremony held at the Ranelagh Gardens mixing ancient Welsh and English families. 'It's Ellis!' Rillie exclaimed aloud in the library. 'It says it's Ellis!' People stared. She read again carefully, her heart beating. Ellis's new wife, the newspaper said, was a niece of a cousin of the King. She could not believe her eyes. 'Is Cordie *dead*?' She waited till her outburst was forgotten, quietly tore the article out of the newspaper when the library man was otherwise engaged. She ran to the basement rooms in Bloomsbury, showed old Aunt Hester. 'Is Cordie *dead*?'

'Cordie is not dead,' said Aunt Hester firmly, 'for I had a short letter from her only a month ago.' She read again, the breathing became faster. 'This' – she pointed at the newspaper – '*thing*, no matter all its pomp, is obviously a travesty. Ellis is already married.' She read again, shaking her head slightly: her mouth became smaller and smaller as she read over and over. 'He is a Beast of Hell!' said Aunt Hester finally, and they left immediately for Gwyr on the mail coach, jolted for days and nights; anger and foreboding gave the old lady strength.

Cordelia greeted them with love and delight and surprise. The children may have had tutors by now but they still ran about the castle ruins and the empty sands and the wild jagged cliffs by the sea; unruly but charming, they showed the visitors a huge dead crab. The boy, Morgan, seemed wilder than ever, told them excited, exaggerated stories of sea-monsters; pulled at their arms, wanting to show them more. Finally the children ran off. Aunt Hester sat down, her face drawn with tiredness, asked for port. And then showed Cordelia the newspaper cutting.

Rillie never forgot that day. It was spring. The old stone ruins shadowed behind them. High shafts of light streaked the small panes of the windows and there were wild flowers everywhere and the leaves of the huge, strange-shaped oak tree were green and they could see the children in the distance down on the sand and pain glittered like crystal in Cordelia's eyes and dogs barked somewhere and the childish voices drifted and echoed up and across the tall grass.

'Did you know anything of this?' demanded Aunt Hester.

They saw Cordelia's face, the disbelief, the doubt, and some crack in the façade. 'No,' she said in a low voice. 'I did not.'

'Surely the family know of you? They could not have let this happen!'

'Those two cousins you met at the wedding have been here once or twice. I have never met the Duke, Ellis said that they did not – get on well, he seemed not to – care for him. He said that he did not want his children . . .' her voice broke slightly, 'contaminated by their grandfather.'

'Does the Duke of Llannefydd live in Wales?'

'I – I do not know.'

'Where has Ellis been living, when he is not here?'

'I do not know.' Aunt Hester never, ever said *I told you so* – also, after all, had she not been present, and witness, at the wedding?

'But Cordelia, you who are so sensible – your mother's daughter – did nothing seem odd to you?'

'We – I – I have had little to do with the life I left . . . I suppose I did not question my new life. My children are – time-consuming, I had not thought . . .' Her voice trailed away.

'How often does he come here?'

She dropped her eyes quickly. 'When he can.'

Morgan ran inside, crying, shouting, his eyes wild. His mother stroked his head over and over and at last his eyes quietened and he became calm, listening to the visitors.

'How often, Cordelia?' Aunt Hester's voice was like a knife.

'He has not been here for some months,' she said painfully at last.

'Well, you are safe at least. He married you. We were there. We were witnesses. You are the legal wife.'

'Yes,' said Cordelia.

*   *   *

Aunt Hester and Rillie reluctantly returned to London, uneasy.

'It is some terrible mistake, there must be some explanation,' Cordelia had said to them. 'We love each other, I do assure you. And – he would never, never abandon his children, truly, I know that. I will write you a letter, I promise, when things are clearer.' The old lady limped to the carriage, biting her lips, the girl Gwenlliam, who looked like her, holding her hand, walking beside her. Finally Hester turned back to her niece. 'Remember there is always Little Russell Street,' she said fiercely. 'We could fit you all in somehow.' Cordelia looked at her in disbelief.

Only days after that visit, Ellis sent for her. She was to come to London at once, without the children; she was to go directly to an address off the Strand. *At last I will see our London house.* She had never been apart from the children: promised she would not be gone long, she would bring Papa back with her and he would never go away again. As the carriage rolled away she saw Morgan, crying and fighting, held by his younger sister; Gwenlliam's long fair hair blew across her face as she bent to him. Seven-year-old Manon stared stonily at the departing carriage: she had wanted to go to this place called London too, would not wave to her mother. Something, some instinct, made Cordelia rap on the carriage roof. She quickly jumped down, was almost blown off the narrow coast road as she stood there looking back, but she was too far away, already the children were shadows through the long, long grass; the broken stone of the ancient Welsh castle stood far above them as the wild wind blew.

On the long journey Cordelia went over her life, its too romantic, too unbelievable turn. The doubts she had pushed away over the years in the wilds of Wales reared up and her heart beat like a drum the nearer they got to her old home: London.

Waiting for her at the address off the Strand was not Ellis in their London house, but a solicitor in legal chambers. He had papers and a sum of money.

53

'Lord Morgan Ellis regrets, Miss Preston . . .'

She looked at him in surprise. 'Please do not address me as Miss Preston. I am Lady Ellis.'

'I am afraid you are not, Miss Preston. The – ah – marriage ceremony in the chapel all those years past was conducted by – a friend. It was a – jest.'

'A jest?'

'Ah – no – perhaps that is not the word. But it was not legal or binding.' He sniffed. 'You are not, and never have been, Lady Ellis.'

Something kept her upright. 'I would like to see my husband.'

'I am afraid that is impossible. And I must point out that Lord Morgan Ellis is not, nor ever has been, your husband. You are not to return to Wales, the estate has been closed up. And I am afraid that that is the end of the story.'

She again repeated his words in complete disbelief. 'The end of the story? *The end of the story?*' Suddenly she lunged out at the solicitor, taking him indeed by surprise for he had never been lunged at by any woman. She actually punched his head against the wall of the room off the Strand before he managed to escape her. '*What about my children?*'

'You bitch!' he screamed. 'You Actress Whore!'

'*What about my children?*'

'They are not your children, they belong, in law, to Lord Ellis. I have here two hundred guineas for your trouble,' and then observing the incredulity in her eyes the solicitor, before she could attack him again, was out of the room, dining out for some nights on the story of the harridan whore actress who thought she was a lady.

Cordelia returned to Wales that moment, that same day, hiring a private coach, not even going to Aunt Hester, travelling day and night, refusing to stop except to change the horses; she arrived back to find that a spring storm raged along the Gwyr coast, rain fell across their way and the wind was wild. As she approached the stone mansion and the castle ruins on the cliffs, as she saw through the driving rain that the tide was out as far as the eye could see, as she approached the gates, she knew: the children were gone, their home was closed and locked and no fair heads played among the seaweed and the rocks on the long sand. There were sparks of lightning as she stood there in the rain, and then the thunder echoed. Somehow she climbed over the iron gates by the stone walls, tearing her cloak; the house was closed and barred, of her children there was no sign, except for the house of branches they had built in the oak tree. *The oak tree.* She climbed quickly up to the small treehouse in the branches where they left their letters. The slanting heavy rain and the strong wind had already caught at, torn, a piece of white paper, it had spiralled away and up into the heavens: it had disappeared long before Cordelia had come home.

A great cry echoed through the rain into the long grass and the wild flowers and the castle ruins and the empty sands below as Cordelia ran like a demented soul in torment around and around the empty stone building. *Where are my children?* What would happen to Morgan with his anger and the storms inside his head? No one knew how long Cordelia Preston stayed outside the locked mansion in the storm, but the tide returned. The sea that had often seemed so benign smashed itself against the jagged cliffs below, drawing back and hurling itself, again and again.

Cordelia Preston might have hurled herself against the cliffs also, but she was the daughter of Kitty and the niece of Hester: she was, after all, Miss Preston. The Preston women did not, in the end, hurl themselves anywhere but at life.

Aunt Hester was kind of course and enclosed Cordelia to her in the basement in Little Russell Street, never once saying 'I told you so.' (*Cordelia, by the basement fire now, Alphonse with his space for **anger** on the floor beside her, stirred slightly, half sleeping, half dreaming of the past, yet her head pounding: outrage, passion, impotence, all the old, terrible rage.*)

She was so shocked at what had happened to her that a lock of her hair turned completely white, as if to make it clear At first she tried in every way she could think of to find the children: going back alone to Wales over and over again on the long, desolate journey, travelling through Gwyr, trying to find any information, any slight connection with Ellis or his family. Each time the old stone house and the ruined castle were more derelict; the treehouse had rotted away. Time after time she walked through the nearest towns, where unfriendly people spoke another language and only stared at her; once ladies in high hats danced. A blacksmith told her he had met the Duke of Llannefydd one time.

'An unpleasant man,' said the blacksmith jovially. 'You don't want to go looking for their sort. And he was short as a gnome!'

'But where do they *live*?' she implored.

'People like that have ten homes,' he said dismissively, 'all over our land. They own Wales, they hide away in the wilds when it suits them; they despise us, they *eat* us,' (she stepped away slightly from his venom), 'but their time is coming!' and he spat on the hot metal and there was a crackling, hissing sound. She understood Ellis had kept her very short of real information about his family – *perhaps they were fake cousins at the fake wedding* – only that the Duke his father was fierce and formidable and there was bad feeling between them: of that she was sure; she had seen the pain and the anger flash in his eyes. Cordelia did not care how fierce and formidable the Duke might be, would have been just as fierce and formidable if she could have found him, but Wales was so large and so far away from Little Russell Street, she did not have the money to stay for ever, searching and searching. Before she left she rather half-heartedly (the children were after all seven, six and five years old) put a message in the 'personal' column of the biggest Welsh newspaper, pondering long on the wording. *Mother is looking for Treehouse Children. Box*——

Back in London she had engaged her own lawyer, had soon

spent the rest of the money Ellis had paid her off with. The lawyer charged her a huge sum and told her kindly that she had no power at all: she was an unmarried woman: she had no right to the children: in fact whether she was married or unmarried they belonged in law to their father.

'But please will you *find* them?' she cried. 'Please, I beg of you, at least let me know that they are safe and well!' The lawyer said his investigations had ascertained that the children were apparently somewhere in Wales, unfindable.

'Investigations? What investigations?'

'Legal investigations.'

'Did you see them? Have you seen them?'

'No,' said the lawyer and he closed the papers on his desk, as if he was closing her life. Lord Castlereagh, whom she had once made laugh, the only man of influence who might possibly have remembered her and properly helped her, was dead. She was an ageing actress whom people had forgotten, her mother had been born in Seven Dials, she was impecunious, and power-less. Some instinct made her believe the lawyer, believe that her children were probably, still, somewhere in Wales, for how would Ellis have explained them to his wife and his father? Once a year, on Morgan's birthday, she put the same message in the same Welsh newspaper: *Mother is looking for Treehouse Children. Box*—— There was never any reply.

Soon after her fruitless searches and her final return to London she heard that the Duke of Llannefydd, Ellis's father, had moved into a grand house in Grosvenor Square. Grief made her mad enough to go to the square, enquire for the house, bang on the huge door and insist on seeing Ellis or the Duke. An elegant, rude footman barred her entrance: she actually hit him, and was extremely lucky that night not to get arrested. She stood for hours, for days, in shadows near the house, waiting for any sign of Ellis and his new wife, of her children. She haunted Mayfair day and night. But no small fair head ever appeared, nor even the man who had professed to be her husband; at last she understood that she could not stand, half hidden, near the house in Grosvenor Square for ever. Sometimes she would bang her head against the walls of the Bloomsbury basement: she felt as if she was banging her head against the world, felt rage and impotence choking her.

It was as if Ellis and their children had disappeared off the face of the earth and Cordelia was left with anger; and pain; and grief; and a disdain for the world.

And soon after her futile enquiries her old Aunt Hester died. In the very last hours, of pain, and falling away from the world, she spoke to Cordelia, just once, about Lord Morgan Ellis.

'It was your fault also, Cordelia.'

There was not time for Cordelia to pretend she did not know what the old lady was talking about. 'I loved him,' she said.

'Love is also understanding, dearest girl. You asked him to cross boundaries that were impossible for him.'

'He loved me.'

'Love . . .' Aunt Hester, who never spoke of such things, spoke with some difficulty, 'for people like us at least, Cordelia, love is only one of the answers of the world, for all the poets say.' She closed her eyes. *But she has not loved, like this*, thought Cordelia. Long silences now, in the fading basement rooms. The old lady slept and then woke. 'There are different kinds of love,' said Aunt Hester.

And because her heart hurt so terribly, to have lost her children and now to be losing this woman who had meant so much to her, Cordelia could easily say, 'Yes. I know.'

Later on, during that long night, Hester, after telling her niece to pay the rent regularly and keep her home safe, had smiled at Cordelia. 'I like to think, all the same – I am sure it is vanity – that there are children who look like Kitty and like me inhabiting the world still.'

*　　*　　*

Aunt Hester was dead and the two hundred guineas were gone. Miss Cordelia Preston, for that it seemed was her name, had nothing but Bloomsbury.

I will have to go back to the theatre, thought Cordelia in disbelief.

But she was no longer young. She had not understood that her best acting years were gone: no one remembered her now. Mr Kean was nowadays derided as a drunk. Lord Castlereagh had cut his throat, they said with a penknife. Some of the theatres were lit with *gas*, so a lamp-man no longer trimmed and cleaned lamps in the early morning; both Drury Lane and Covent Garden were doing pantomimes and burlesques and Shakespeare had become more unpopular. She had been so well known, but now the London theatre managers did not know her, or remembered her vaguely; there were other young actresses now. London Bridge had been rebuilt. Waists were back, and corsets, and petticoats. Sometimes she walked to the square: her old garden of dreams, Bloomsbury Square. Next to that oak tree a statue had been built: she was amazed to see that it was a statue of Hester and Kitty's old acquaintance: Charles James Fox, who had made them laugh and behaved like a gentleman and sent them home in a carriage and married for love. He sat leaning forward in Roman robes, as if to listen to Cordelia's terrible story.

Finally she went with her old friend Rillie Spoons to Bow Street, to ask work of Mr Kenneth or Mr Turnour, the actors' work-arrangers; to learn to be a jobbing actress again, grateful for any work, anywhere. She sang, and performed with children and acrobats. She appeared on ships that moved on a groove from one side of the stage to the other as a panorama of the sea unfolded from a roller in the opposite direction. She even appeared briefly as a mature Faerie Queen in some of the first lime-light: clear white light shining right down on a performer's face.

She laughed and sang and drank port, and had fights with

other actresses; sometimes Rillie Spoons thought: *there she is, the old Cordie.*

But Lord Morgan Ellis, her children, the lost years of her life: of these things, Rillie knew, Cordelia never, ever spoke.

When Cordelia woke, shivering in the darkness, her face was wet with tears. Alphonse, with the place for **anger** marked on his marble head, still lay on the floor beside her next to the port bottle. The fire had gone out. Hazily she got undressed, fell into bed.

Something: some strangeness in the basement night. Because the cold sheets took time to become warm, she drifted between dreams of her past and shivering wakefulness, and somewhere there, somewhere near, she felt her Aunt Hester. *Aunt Hester swept her hands in that remembered way, over and over, past Cordelia's face and her body: Cordelia felt, not the hands, but an infinite, life-giving warmth, taking away pain.*

Five

Rillie Spoons lived with her old mother in a room in Ridinghouse-lane, off Great Titchfield Street near Oxford Street. Mrs Spoons, who had been a small, kindly, busy woman long ago, very fond of company and loving nothing better than a good song, was now completely demented (but still very sweet-natured and musical), and now insisted on taking her clothes off at inappropriate moments. Rillie's rather jolly father (Cordelia remembered him) was dead; some children had died in infancy; one brother died in the navy, one had more or less disappeared long ago: dead, alive, who knew? The Spoons family had had two rooms now Rillie and her mother lived in one and let the other to an elderly, rather barmy-brained but oddly kind woman called Regina. When Rillie's work took her away from London, Regina, who was definitely strange but not nearly as demented as Mrs Spoons, would help. Somehow they all managed, more or less.

Regina had an overriding interest in murder. She knew the details of every important murderer in Britain; she was sure one was hanging about nearby in Great Titchfield Street. She consumed the penny broadsides and the *Dreadful Murder* pamphlets that gave all the gory details; when younger she had sometimes worked for, so she said, the patterers and the balladeers who would sing or recite news of the latest murder (or of a made-up one if nothing interesting was happening) which were on sale for a penny a yard. She knew many of the old murder ballads and sang them still to tunes they all knew.

> *O then he seized those lovely twins*
> *Whilst sleeping on the bed,*

she would sing, laying out her playing cards or making Mrs Spoons a cup of tea.

> *O then he seized those lovely twins*
> *Whilst sleeping on the bed,*
> *Now with your mother you shall die*
> *The wretch'd father said:*
> *He seized them by their little legs*
> *And dashed them to the floor*
> *And soon their tender lives were gone*
> *Alas! To be no more.*

Mrs Spoons, Rillie's mother, would tap her feet in time to the music and hum along, smiling her sweet smile. Rillie and Cordelia had often come home to the two old ladies, one often at least partially naked, asleep in their chairs; hands of cards were strewn about, and penny broadsides, and full chamberpots. Mrs Spoons however seemed not to be prone to pneumonia, nor malnutrition. Rillie somehow, working or not working, ran this interesting household cheerfully. Cordelia thought the saddest thing was that Mrs Spoons, who Rillie loved so much, no longer seemed to know who Rillie was.

'Never mind,' said Rillie briskly. 'She smiles.'

* * *

Cordelia, Aunt Hester still clear in her mind although it was morning, hurried now to Ridinghouse-lane, helped with emptying chamberpots in ditches in the lane outside, brought up coals, brought up water, and then begged Rillie to accompany her back to Bloomsbury. Rillie stoked up the fire and then fixed the fireguard to the fireplace in a manner she had perfected so that whatever else happened to the old ladies when they were alone they could not, if they fell asleep, burn to death. Regina was reading aloud to the room in general.

'He drowned his senses in wine and then returned home; undressing himself, the letter fell from his bosom, his wife picked it up, read it, and beat him about the head with a dishcloth.'

It was early afternoon before they got away, started walking into Bloomsbury.

'Regina should have been an actress,' said Cordelia drily.

'I'm lucky, my mum always loved people reading to her long before she went demented, so she is always enchanted, whatever the content! Regina says she learnt to read from the street ballad singers and the pattermen. I'm not sure she didn't actually write some of those street songs herself in the olden days.'

'Really?'

'She says she worked for them – she told me that a "poet" is still paid a shilling a song and she's very proprietorial about some of them!'

'Do you think it's true?'

'I don't know! But she's got some money, somehow. She keeps it under her mattress!' and the friends laughed and walked and gossiped on their way. They stopped pedlars near Little Russell Street, counted out their pennies and bought a *Morning Chronicle* ('There might be something about the Mesmerists,' said Cordelia mysteriously) and fresh bread and milk and eightpennyworth of tea and some sausages, which Cordelia said firmly they could have when they had finished.

'Finished what, Cordie?' said Rillie. 'I'm starving. And really we should be off to Bow Street again to see Mr Kenneth, I've got to find some more work.'

'And me, but tomorrow,' said Cordelia adamantly. 'I've had an idea.'

In the basement she sat Rillie in a chair, placed Alphonse and one of her aunt's books on the table. 'I'm going to read your head, like I explained yesterday,' she said to Rillie. She pushed at the white hair in front of her own head in some excitement. 'Your best qualities are loyalty and kindness. You are much nicer and kinder than me. Now, that's the number thirteen bump, right at the top of your head. If this book is right, I bet your number thirteen is bigger than mine.' And she read from the book:

No. 13: BENEVOLENCE: charity – sympathy – philanthropy, benevolence – mercy – fellow feeling.

Cordelia stood behind Rillie, her hands quite gently but firmly moving over her head, over and over.

'Oh,' said Rillie, surprised, 'that's nice,' and she leant back, relaxing slightly *and for a split second Cordelia, holding Rillie's head, caught at a memory of something and then, before she could grasp it, it was gone.* They heard the pieman down the street.

'Aunt Hester said the head was a map of the brain,' said Cordelia. 'So this Alphonse is actually a map, the numbers show you the parts. I've been reading the books. The brain is made up of many parts and some are bigger in one person than another and big bits show *propensity* for the numbered qualities. It shows people's *potential*.' She leaned over and studied the marble head carefully, at the same time feeling at the top and the back of Rillie's head. 'There,' she said triumphantly. 'There! Number thirteen. That's not where you fell down after Guildford; that is a part of your head that is very well developed, I can feel it quite

64

clearly. Your propensity for kindness. And look, look at me, feel my head, your kindness is definitely bigger and more rounded than mine!'

'Really?' Rillie sat up. She felt Cordelia's head gingerly, then she stood up so that she could see herself in one of Aunt Hester's mirrors. 'Really?' she said again. 'Where? Where's my Benevolence?'

Cordelia smoothed a part at the top of Rillie's head. 'There!' she said again. 'You are kind: your head says so even if I hadn't already known,' and Rillie half laughed but half stared at herself in the mirror and felt with her own hands where Cordelia's hands had been.

'Now,' said Cordelia, leading Rillie to another chair across the room, 'I want you to sit on this chair, here, and let me see if I can mesmerise you.'

'Get away!' said Rillie, laughing.

'Let me try!'

'But I don't want to be mesmerised!' Rillie got up, shook her skirts. Cordelia tried to push her down again.

'Rillie, I don't even know if I can do it! Let me try!'

'I'm not ill!'

'I know you're not ill! It's not to see if you are ill, it's to see if I can do it.'

'Well you won't be able to! I'll sing you a song if you like but I'm not going to be put upon!'

'Oh let me try! Sit down. Please, Rillie?'

Laughing still, Rillie sat down again and immediately sang, tapping her feet:

> *Weel about and turn about and do jis so,*
> *Eb'ry time I weel about I jump Jim Crow.*

'Amaryllis Spoons! Stop laughing and stop singing and look at my hands, and try to *want* to be mesmerised.'

'All right.'

65

'And trust me.'

'I trust you, Cordie.'

Cordelia took a deep breath, closed her eyes for a moment. 'Watching that – experiment they called it, didn't they? – yesterday has had such a strange effect on me, Rillie, and reminded me of the past. I'd forgotten.' She began to move her hands near to Rillie's face, sweeping them backwards and forwards, backwards and forwards, breathing in time to the movements. Rillie tried very hard not to laugh; she was very keen to break into 'Jim Crow' again but understood Cordelia was serious about something. The hands went backwards and forwards, over and over. Time passed. Rillie's stomach rumbled, they tried not to be distracted.

At last Rillie said, 'I'm sorry, Cordie, but my nose is really really itching.'

'Didn't you feel *anything*?'

'Nothing at all.'

'Nor did I,' said Cordelia gloomily. 'I just – wondered if I could.'

'I don't mean to be unkind, Cordie dear, but perhaps you just don't have the gift?'

'I am my aunt's niece,' said Cordelia rather portentously.

'Well – shall I try to mesmerise you? I saw what he was doing.'

'Go on then.'

They changed places. Rillie passed her hands over and over near Cordelia's face but nothing happened at all and Cordelia found she too was hard pressed not to laugh at Rillie's anxious determined little face and the concentration thereon.

'Oh Hell's Spite!' said Cordelia at last. 'Let's have some port.' They put the sausages on the small fire in the back room, burning meat smells drifted in their hair and their clothes but they were so used to such things they hardly noticed. They settled with their glasses of port and their bread and sausages, stretched their

66

arms, talked of going to Mr Kenneth in Bow Street. Cordelia did not speak more about her idea: she wondered if the odd dream she had had of Aunt Hester had befuddled her.

'Are you coming to Mrs Fortune's?' asked Rillie as dusk fell over London.

Cordelia stretched again. 'No. I don't feel like it.'

'We ought to at least go and see about some work first thing in the morning. You never know.'

'I'll meet you there.'

And so Rillie went off to see to her mother and then to go to Mrs Fortune's to see what new gossip was going around tonight, and Cordelia Preston lit the candle lamp and stayed in the basement in Little Russell Street reading the newspaper. Professor Elliotson's meeting was indeed reported: the journalist did not take sides regarding mesmerism but obviously felt some disapproval about the girl in the nightdress. Then with great interest Cordelia came upon a report of a riot on a stage in a northern town; she shook the paper out, to smooth it, she read again, more carefully. But it was not actors on a number-three tour: local doctors and travelling mesmerists had apparently engaged in fisticuffs over the merits of their respective professions: people (doctors fumed), especially women, were more and more preferring to be treated by 'Magnetic Quacks' (as the newspaper described them) because the mesmerists laid their hands near them, not upon them, when discussing their ailments. One lady's feelings were fully reported: '*No, no, not doctors with these new stethoscopes asking me to undo buttons. I like to see a mesmerist, he will advise me what is wrong without touching me.*'

Cordelia picked up Aunt Hester's books again, flicked through them: something caught her eye and she suddenly held one of the books very close to the lamp. She read carefully, not noticing evening feet pass by. Then she quickly picked up the newspaper again, looked carefully at the 'personal' column.

The tiny idea from her dream of Aunt Hester suddenly settled more strongly inside her head and all at once she could feel her heart beating very fast, as if she had been running.

Six

Next morning early spring sunshine sparkled on new leaves in Bloomsbury Square as if all was a new beginning. Cordelia walked round and round the square, as she used to when she was young: thinking hard. *I need to talk to Rillie. I must not be distracted or discouraged this time.* Later the neighbour's black cat ran inside as Cordelia opened the door to empty her chamberpot in the cesspool at the back of the building; he settled on the sofa where some rays of sunshine also reached, even in the basement. She heard him purring with satisfaction and she stroked him, teased his paws. He sat, lazy, relaxed. She lifted her hands from his head and passed them over him, near his eyes, down his body, and then again. He went on purring. She passed her hands over him again, could feel the warmth of his body. He stopped purring and stared unblinking, still. Because of the way the sunlight shone she could not see his eyes clearly but he seemed to be, as she passed her hands over him, in a trance.

She moved away slightly: the cat did not move, his head did not move. He stared ahead, as if he did not see her or hear her. She poured some milk into a saucer: he did not move. She called to him but the ears hardly flickered. *Have I mesmerised a cat?* Her aunt had brought her ladies out of their trance by moving her hands close to them again: gently she moved back to the sofa and again passed her hands over the cat's head. And then, as if he suddenly awoke, the cat jumped right past her and pounced upon his prey, a mouse in the corner.

'Oh Hell's Spite!' said Cordelia crossly.

Mr Kenneth amid the acrid blue smoke inside the Lamb, off Bow Street, shook his head. 'Not for old ladies my dears,' he said. 'Not this week. Well, we did have one old lady part yesterday actually, for York—'

'Oh, we should've come in yesterday!' said Rillie.

'—but the manager's took a *young* lady to do it for the run, well, managers, you know!'

'Miss Susan Fortune!' said Rillie and Cordelia in unison.

'We'll be missing the summer season,' said Rillie woefully. 'Maybe we should have stayed with *Macbeth*.'

'They were going to fire us from *Macbeth*, in case you have forgotten,' said Cordelia tartly. 'An elephant was to play the witches!'

'Yes, that's it,' said Mr Kenneth sagely, as if elephants played witches every day. 'I heard they acquired an elephant for that production. But come again next week,' he intoned, like a mantra.

'Come back again to Bloomsbury,' said Cordelia to Rillie. 'I've really, *really* got an idea.'

'I better see to Ma first.'

But in Ridinghouse-lane and Great Titchfield Street policemen walked importantly. Parts of the area were blocked off.

'Oh great God!' cried Rillie, not watching her language. 'I bet Ma's come out without her clothes!' She grabbed a policeman by the arm. 'What is it, what's happened?' She looked urgently up at her own windows, thought she could hear voices.

'Can't say, madam.'

'I must see to my old mother!'

The policeman relented slightly. 'There's been a murder, madam.'

'A murder? Not just round here?'

'In Great Titchfield Street, madam.'

Rillie and Cordelia looked at each other aghast. Just what Regina had been forecasting. Just around the corner.

'I *must* get up to my old mother,' Rillie repeated urgently; she pointed upwards. The policeman saw their extremely anxious faces.

'I'll let you in,' he said. And then confidentially, 'It was someone young,' to cheer them up.

In the two rooms the two old ladies were making enough noise for it to be absolutely certain that neither of them was the murder victim: Regina was now actually shouting out of the window: 'I told youse!' she yelled down. 'I told youse there was a murderer round here!' and she banged the door of her own room shut and wouldn't come out. Mrs Spoons was sitting on a small wooden chair keeping up, most unusually for her, an anxious, angry, unintelligible monologue and absolutely refusing any clothes at all, kicking at the chamberpots.

'I wanted the sheets!' said Mrs Spoons. 'It was a halfpenny, same as the table Bert said, and now there's a bag of cakes!'

'Who's Bert?' enquired Cordelia but Rillie only shrugged as they both rescued full chamberpots from Mrs Spoons' little angry kicking legs. The contents of the pots were emptied straight out the window at the back (which they only did in a crisis). They needed water: Cordelia went down and up. Regina was still yelling next door. Rillie was flushed and cross and relieved they hadn't been murder victims all at the same time, trying to make sense of her mother's discarded petticoats, and Mrs Spoons was now banging her bare feet on the floorboards, pulling at her own naked skin, still soliloquising loudly, she kicked some of the new water, it went all over the floor.

71

'How can it be done with the wood, tell me that?' cried Mrs Spoons.

Cordelia, trying to distract her, passed her hands over the space between them, the way she had passed them over the cat. After a few moments, her attention having been diverted, Mrs Spoons stopped talking, stopped kicking, followed Cordelia's hands, like a child watching a toy. Back and forth went Cordelia's hands: she concentrated on Mrs Spoons' child-like face.

Suddenly the room felt very quiet, punctuated only occasionally now by 'I warned you!' from Regina's room: Mrs Spoons became stiller and stiller. Rillie, who had been picking up dirty clothes, wiping up spilled water, trying to sweep up some of the dirt, stopped moving. Cordelia's breathing and Mrs Spoons' breathing finally came in unison, and Cordelia felt an odd warm feeling in her hands. And then Mrs Spoons quite suddenly fell sideways off the wooden chair.

'Oh God!' cried Rillie, throwing the dirty clothes into the air. 'Are you mad, Cordie, she's banged her head.' She ran forward to her mother.

'I'm sorry!' cried Cordelia; they tried to pick the frail naked body up, at last got her on to the bed that she and Rillie shared, covered her with a blanket.

Cordelia stared in horror, her heart was beating wildly. 'Is she all right? Is she asleep? Is she dead?'

Rillie looked at her mother carefully. 'She's alive. And she's not exactly asleep.'

'I'm sorry!' Cordelia cried again, her face white. 'I don't know what made me do that.' Mrs Spoons, her face quite still but very white also, and her eyes open, was breathing in and out very slowly. It was most peculiar.

'Do something,' said Rillie in a panicky voice, picking up again the filthy clothes that smelled, throwing them in a corner, coming back to her mother. 'Un-mesmerise her!'

'I don't know what made me do that,' Cordelia repeated.

'Well you undo it now, Cordie!' Rillie's face was even redder than before.

Cordelia took a deep breath, began passing her hands over Mrs Spoons' face and her poor defenceless little body. The old wrinkled hands were swollen and a purple colour. Three long minutes passed. Four. Nothing happened.

'Oh God!' cried Rillie, her face so red.

'Oh God!' cried Cordelia, and perspiration was running down her face. 'What have I done?' She tried again, exhausted now; saw Rillie's worried face; fiercely brought her Aunt Hester into her mind: her way: the passing of the hands, the rhythm, the breathing *let yourself rest in my care*; she made herself concentrate on Mrs Spoons absolutely. Finally after what seemed an eternity there was a little jerk and Mrs Spoons turned her head slightly, saw Rillie's face and smiled.

'You're a good girl, Rillie,' said Mrs Spoons.

'Hallelujah!' whispered Cordelia, wiping her sweating face with the back of her hands.

But Rillie wasn't listening, nor Mrs Spoons; Cordelia saw her friend holding her mother's hand very tightly in amazement. Her mother had *recognised* her. There were tears in Rillie's eyes, as she pulled the blanket lovingly about the little old body.

Cordelia, in a state of total shock, passed in a daze the policemen and the crowds and the white sheet and the muffin-man and the sellers of the penny broadsides who already cried 'MURDER', hot off the press. If the Misses Preston ever fainted, Cordelia would have fainted at what she had done. She went unthinkingly straight back to Bloomsbury Square. She sat on an iron bench, sat there as if she was in some kind of trance. She had done what Aunt Hester had done. She *had* felt a strange warmth in her hands: something untoward *had* happened. And for just a moment Mrs Spoons had recognised Rillie. Only at dusk did

Cordelia finally make her way back to Little Russell Street. Her face was pale, like the rising moon.

She did not dare to go back to Ridinghouse-lane. Early next morning she hurried to the circulating library, already waiting outside when the doors were opened. She borrowed some books about mesmerism and about phrenology. She sat in her basement rooms, reading, making notes. She lit more candles, bent over the books as the hours passed, spelling out words she did not know. She read about the cast that was made of the head of Mr Burke, in Edinburgh, the body-snatcher, after he was hanged. Phrenologists made a study: his bump of DESTRUCTIVENESS, it was reported, was very large. She wrote more things down. She had to talk to Rillie.

It was late when Rillie appeared in Bloomsbury.

'Is she all right?' said Cordelia at once at the doorway. Rillie nodded. 'I'm so sorry,' said Cordelia again. 'Rillie, I was too nervous to come again in case I set something off. I never got such a fright in my life.' The two friends stared at each other, still at the door. 'She knew you, didn't she?' and Rillie nodded again.

'You mesmerised her, didn't you?' said Rillie.

'Yes,' said Cordelia, 'I didn't mean to, but I think I did.' And for a moment both the women stood there, slightly ill at ease. 'Does she know you now?'

'No,' said Rillie.

And Rillie saw that Cordelia shook herself slightly and seemed to shiver. 'Come in, Rillie, come in, have a port for God's sake.' Cordelia bustled about.

'I went to Mr Kenneth this morning,' said Rillie.

'Nothing?'

'Nothing. And guess what.'

'What?'

'You know that murder yesterday.'

'Yes.' Cordelia filled their glasses.

'It was one of those young girls that turns up at Mrs Fortune's place!'

'One of the Emmas and Primroses?'

'One of them. Silly girls, that pick up men off the street. Mrs Fortune was always warning them.' And Cordelia thought of the risks her mother and her aunt had taken, so long ago; the men in the back room who would pay Kitty some money when Cordelia was sent out with a penny to Bloomsbury Square. She shivered again, as if something walked over her heart.

'I do think we need this drink!' she said. But she was only halfway through the first glass before she said, 'Rillie, listen to me. I think I've got an idea, really.'

'To get us work,' said Rillie rather glumly.

'*Yes!* Listen to me.'

First Cordelia took some papers on which she had written. She stood in front of Rillie, as if she were auditioning for a part. 'Listen, Rillie,' she said again, 'I've been wanting to tell you, but I had to do a bit more reading. I think I've had a really terrific idea to make us rich!' And she began to read.

'Unions of sexes are formed by chance, the laws
of nature are neglected, and the result is:
defective offspring, untimely death, and misery.'

'What? What are you talking about?' said Rillie.
'Shshsh!' said Cordelia.

'The rights of love and nature's law are violated,
and it is thought highly moral that man and woman
should live on together though the greatest antipathy
exist, because they have been joined together in
"holy matrimony" **whilst they were yet in ignorance
of each other's disposition** . . . it is not God who put
them together but their own ignorance . . . and a
religious ceremony does not alter nature's laws.

75

'Now, Rillie, I read that in a book about *phrenology*! Listen again carefully: *whilst they were yet in ignorance of each other's disposition*. Now, how can people find out more about each other? By having their heads read of course. And going into a trance or two as well maybe, just to make it even more exciting! What say you and I set ourselves up to give them advice before they . . .' (Rillie heard the scorn in her friend's voice), 'pledge their troth!' Cordelia began to stride up and down the room, flicking at the books she had been reading. 'You and I of course have never, as it turns out, *been* married—'

'—oh but you were as if married, and—'

'—nevertheless I was not, as we know, actually—'

'—and I have been married, Cordie.'

'*What?*' Cordelia looked at her friend in astonishment.

Rillie gave a small, odd shrug. 'When you were in Wales.'

'You never said!'

'There wasn't much to say. I only saw you twice in all those years, and we never wrote really.'

Cordelia sat down, her eyes wide with incredulity. 'Tell me,' she said.

'Oh well,' said Rillie, and she picked at her skirt as she sat under Aunt Hester's stars and mirrors. After a while she took a deep breath and began. 'He was an actor, Jack, an actor with twinkly eyes – I was always attracted to that sort, Cordie – he was a comedy actor and we worked together several times, we went to York on that circuit, you know, and we went to Hull – that was where we descended from clouds.' Cordelia's face was a picture of puzzlement. 'Cordie, I didn't like to tell you about all the new things in the theatre when you were in Wales, for I thought it might make you sad because it was so exciting, but me and Jack, dressed as angels, we came down from the top of the roof on ropes nightly, like flying! and one night, being close as we descended, Jack whispered to me to marry him. So I did.'

'In Hull?'

'In Hull. On the Saturday before the show.' Rillie paused for

76

a moment and then said quietly, 'I liked being married, Cordie, it was – it was nice to be cosy with someone, go home with someone – with Jack. We used to laugh lots.'

'And then?'

'And then . . .' For several moments again Rillie did not speak. Cordelia had the sense to just wait. 'And then I got pregnant quick and then Jack skipped.'

'Skipped?'

'Afterwards I decided that he had just got carried away and had proposed to me because we was flying and it was exciting. He didn't want to have children cluttering up, he said, our lives. Children didn't belong in the theatre, he said, and he blamed me, that it was my fault. Aren't men funny?' Cordelia stared at Rillie in silence. 'I'm Mrs Jack O'Reilly really, not Rillie Spoons at all. He said the baby wasn't his, that I was a whore. And then Emmanuel—'

'Emmanuel?'

'I know, silly, wasn't it, but my mum liked it and it was my mum who helped me. By that time Emmanuel got the fever. He was only one. He died.' Rillie breathed in and out a number of times, as if to calm herself. 'He died in Ridinghouse-lane actually. My mum wasn't demented then, you remember how she used to be, so kind and good and singing all the time, she helped me lots – oh . . .' She caught at her face, stopped the tears. 'It was awful, Cordie, and later on when Jack was playing at the Haymarket Ma went and waited at the stage door and emptied the chamberpot over him and he knew who she was and he ran away from her.' Rillie gave a half-laugh that seemed to be like a cry, and then she was silent.

'Oh Rillie!' said Cordelia at last. 'I am so sorry.'

Little Rillie Spoons sat there in the basement; only her hands still moving slightly across her skirt, over and over, betrayed any emotion. Her face was now blank. 'The next time I saw you after that was when I found the newspaper. About Ellis. So it wasn't the time to tell.'

77

'But – why haven't you told me this before now?'

'Cordie, by the time you came back to live in London it was all over long ago. And you – don't like talking about weddings and marriage and – and children. You know what you're like. You get angry.'

Cordelia was mortified, stared down at her own hands. So tied up in her own story she had never known Rillie's. She felt a blush of something like shame cross her face. 'I am so sorry, Rillie,' she said again. She got up and poured two very large glasses of port. 'To – to the memory of Emmanuel,' she said.

'Thank you,' said Rillie, but did not, just then, drink anything at all. They sat in silence for a long time and heard the carts rattling by, and the knife man calling, and raucous singing from some customers leaving the Blue Coats public house and rolling down Little Russell Street.

At last Cordelia said quietly: 'Listen, Rillie. I really do have a plan. It's come to me over the last few days and specially after I did mesmerise – or have some effect anyway – on your mum. I am so sick of waiting around for Mr Kenneth or Mr Turnour to come up with some depressing rubbish work that we're supposed to be grateful for, and always counting my money. How many more managers are going to break our contracts and fire us in the middle of somewhere where there's hardly a decent road back to London? We could get murdered too! Is this how we're going to spend the rest of our lives just because we can't do anything else?' She stood and started moving about the room again. 'When we saw the Professor and that mad Irish girl the other day singing "Jim Crow" and everyone shouting and arguing, I was reminded so much of my Aunt Hester that I dreamed about her. She was the one who made money, not my mother, the actress; it was Aunt Hester who supported us even with her face with the scars, and her bad leg. And Rillie, we're *old*! I could lose this place, these rooms, this only security where I grew up! You and your mother could be out on the street, we'll all end up in the work-house in Vinegar Yard—'

'*Don't*, Cordie.'

'Listen, Rillie. Once, when I was quite a young lady, and pleased with myself, my Aunt Hester – I'd never been there even though it's so near – took me back to Seven Dials, showed me where she and my mum had grown up – and it's disgusting, Rillie, it's *disgusting*, rooms full of ten people, rats and cock-roaches, dark alleys and stinking lanes and biting dogs, kids drinking gin, and the streets – you can't call them streets, they're only gutters running with shit – it stank like nothing you can imagine and it's only a few blocks away! It stank much more than it stinks round here or Ridinghouse-lane. Turds coming out the windows on top of you, all that screaming and cursing and shouting, it was like being in hell, and people saying they were our relations and asking us for money. It was different for you, Ridinghouse-lane was always much better than that, and you had your nice dad and he worked at that shop and had some security, but I don't come from anything like that. That's why I fought for Ellis, why I couldn't believe my luck – I was right, wasn't I, not to believe it! – when Ellis said he would marry me just because I could walk and talk like a lady!' She banged the port glass down; it broke, but she took no notice. 'Marry *me*, whose mother and aunt came from the rookeries? Of course I was dreaming, wasn't I? Dreaming when I dined with Lord Castlereagh, dreaming when the Duke of Wellington kissed my hand! Dreaming in Wales for years!'

Rillie saw Cordelia suddenly walk to the water jug and basin. She turned away from Rillie, spat, Rillie thought she might actu-ally be retching into the basin. Quickly Rillie bent and picked up the pieces of the glass, rubbed the port into the floorboards. Never, since her return from Wales, had Cordelia said so much about her past, and never, Rillie thought, had she seemed so angry. Rillie wondered if at last she would talk about her children:

Rillie had treasured their names: Manon who Aunt Hester said had looked like Kitty, her beautiful sister. She heard clearly now the sound of Cordelia retching. And Gwenlliam with Aunt Hester's grey eyes. And odd little Morgan who was fascinated by crabs and seaweed. Never, once, had Cordelia mentioned them since her return.

At last Cordelia poured herself a glass of water from the jug, stalked back, her cheeks were flushed and her hair was tousled and somehow, Rillie thought, even if she had been vomiting she looked absolutely magnificent. 'Well, I've still got my home here, in Little Russell Street, Bloomsbury, a polite address! And I can still walk and talk like a lady! And nobody and nothing is going to take this away from me, and I have made a plan. We've spent a great deal of our lives being cheated by other people, and now you've told me of your Jack as well. What say we have a go!'

'Cheating people?'

'Oh – well, no, not exactly. Helping people let's call it! Listen, Rillie, I've got a bit of money under the floorboards under the stove, not much. Now, think of all those well-off people who were at the hospital, watching the experiments and talking about Mesmerism as if it was the new thing, as if my Aunt Hester wasn't practising it years and years ago! And I've been reading about it in the newspapers. What say it is becoming the latest fashion? I don't know what I did to your mum, but I did feel something strange and we know something happened – oh, I'm so sorry, Rillie, it's not supposed to make people fall over and bang their heads! – but more than that, I've also been reading up on that phrenology business that Aunt Hester also used to know about, and use sometimes. I believe an idiot could make that work, if they were careful. And they say, in the books, that phrenology is a real philosophy, just like studying electricity! So we wouldn't be cheating people, not really.' She picked up one of her pieces of paper. 'I'm going to use the last of my money to pay the rent here in advance for a month and then insert an advertisement in the *Morning Chronicle* and *The Times* and maybe

80

the *Weekly Dispatch* – and anywhere else that seems relevant. Look, look, this is my advertisement.' She handed Rillie a sheet of paper.

LOVE: THE MOST IMPORTANT DECISION.
Trained, mature Lady PHRENO-MESMERIST begs
to announce Knowledgeable Advice given on Marriage Partners.
Do not make a Mistake in this Big Decision.
Discretion Assured. Apply in
writing for Appointment and Terms.

'What's a phreno-mesmerist?'

'Sounds good, doesn't it? I read it in one of the books.'

Rillie immediately started to laugh. 'Are you saying people are to choose their partners by the shape of their heads! You *are* saying that we will trick people!'

'No! Because there'll be some truth in it!'

'Truth?' Rillie stared at Cordelia as if she had taken leave of her senses. 'I couldn't do all this, Cordelia, I know nothing about it! And if you mesmerise people they might fall off chairs and sue us!'

'I won't really do the mesmerism. Though it sounds good, don't you think: *Phreno-Mesmerism*. But really, the main thing mesmerism seems to be useful for is taking away pain, or making people oblivious of pain. People who come to see us won't be in *pain*, will they? They'll just want to talk about love. And I'll read their heads!'

'Well I couldn't! I don't know anything about such things!'

'But you can be my Assistant. No – my Partner – you can be in charge! You can take the money, and calm people before they approach the Sanctuary!' Cordelia was half laughing now, talking very fast. 'We can both use our acting skills! We're mature. We look responsible. Part of my hair is completely white! I thought I might wear coloured scarves and look mysterious. We'll polish up the stars and the mirrors and light the candles like Aunt Hester used to do, and charge – well – six shillings, say—'

'*Six shillings?*'

'And half a guinea for two!' Cordelia was now unstoppable. 'A bit of atmosphere, Aunt Hester said, was really important – she learnt that from the foreign gentleman who taught her – he used to play the flute – oh – I know – you could play the flute, Rillie, in the background, and when we get richer we'll buy a harpsichord or one of those new pianos!' She saw Rillie's unbelieving face, went and sat beside her, actually seized her hand. 'Rillie, I've read and read. Mesmerism is still a bit of a mystery but there *is* a truth in this head thing, this phrenology, even the Greeks said so.'

'The Greeks had heads with numbers on?'

'No, no, not exactly. But they did think that the powers of the imagination and reason and memory all come from different parts of the head! I read it, Rillie! Everyone is always talking about the Greeks, so I'll quote the Greeks! And I'll practise on you first, it isn't a trick, not *really*.'

'We can't get inside people's heads, Cordie! That's what you're saying, that somehow we can understand what goes on inside people's heads and make them choose suitable partners accordingly. Of course we can't do that!'

'But look at what we know! Look at the mistake I made in my choice of partner – and you in yours, Rillie. Haven't we learnt terrible, expensive lessons? And aren't we actresses, aren't we used to looking at people's faces and hearing their voices. Isn't that the skill we've learnt? So, we can *guess*, Rillie! We'll watch their faces and listen to their voices and we will *guess*. It will just be another performance – we're *actresses* – we are used to using *our* faces and *our* voices for certain effects. Are we not then qualified to look carefully at people who do not have our skills and make a pretty good guess at what they're feeling? And then we'll learn up all this stuff about parts of the head (even if we don't really quite believe it) to make our

82

pronouncements sound knowledgeable! I'll learn it all up, just like a part, and I'll dress up and we'll polish the stars!' She jumped up again. 'We could even write to the new Queen! She needs a husband!' Even the mention of royalty could not make Rillie look convinced.

'Is it cheating?'

'Really, I don't give a damn if it's cheating or not!' said Cordelia. 'I want us to get *secure* before we die! I'm so sick of having no money!'

'But it's mesmerism that's popular now, you might have to mesmerise as well and who knows what might happen.'

'Listen, there are plenty of phrenologists advertising their skills. But I am my Aunt Hester's niece, I'll go one better, I'll be a phreno-mesmerist!'

Rillie sat pleating her skirt. Cordelia, silent at last, waited.

'What's mesmerism really for, Cordie?'

Cordelia immediately read from her sheaf of notes. '*Mesmerism strengthens the nervous system, tranquillises the mind and improves the digestion.*'

'The *digestion*?' They started to laugh, and then Cordelia stopped.

'Rillie, I know what my Aunt Hester did mostly. I *saw*. They trusted her absolutely and she made them feel better. That's the only way I can describe it. I think that is what I did for a moment, to your mum. I'll only do the mesmerism bit, or try to do it, if I have to. If it doesn't work I'll tell people they are not suitable subjects, as if it is their fault! Of course I'm not thinking of helping doctors in hospitals or anything really serious like that. But reading heads – I will be amazing! I'll learn it off properly, like I said, just like a part in a play. And you, my partner, can be the money person and the flute person, and the kind person.' She looked at Rillie's face. 'And like I say,' she repeated, 'we'll polish up the stars!'

'Cordie.' Rillie smoothed her skirt again, the strange little movement. 'It's men who start businesses. We're *old women*. We're way past forty. We're too old, surely, to start out on something like this and—'

'Do you feel old?'

'I – I don't know what feeling old is supposed to feel like.'

'*Exactly*. Our legs and arms and brains still work, don't they?'

Suddenly Rillie Spoons took an enormous gulp of port.

'I'll pay the rent at Ridinghouse-lane for a month and then I'll put in eleven pounds, Cordie,' she said. 'That's my savings under my floorboards.'

Seven

Rents were paid. The old, stolen glass stars were polished. Lamps were cleaned. Small and large candles were purchased. Aunt Hester's old flute was part-exchanged just off the Strand where a man gave them ten per cent off an eight-keyed cocoa flute with double keys in German silver. Cordelia insisted they buy second-hand severe-looking painted portraits: one of a gentleman with a white beard, one of a woman in a white cap: 'They will give us gravity,' she said. 'The old man is a grandfather on your maternal line who was a preacher in the church in Ashby de la Zouch. And the severe old woman of course is my great-grandmother from a large land-owning family in Derbyshire.' There was no mention of murder in Seven Dials. How Cordelia should look *exactly* entailed long conversations: should she wear an old lady's cap, for the mature look and even more gravity, or should she be exotic?

'I think I'd rather be exotic,' said Cordelia at last.

Flowing coloured scarves could have been purchased for pennies near Smithfield where stolen scarves were hung on rods; they thought this was too risky ('Imagine if someone came and you were wearing their stolen scarf!'). So scarves were purchased from the second-hand clothes shops in Monmouth Street; they both tried them on, twirling in front of mirrors as oil lamps danced; they draped them round Cordelia's face and shoulders so that she looked mysterious, her face half hidden.

'I think I better get a maid's costume,' said Rillie. 'One exotic personage is enough, we don't want to frighten them away.'

'You're not going to be a *maid*!'

'I'll be a maid *first*. I've played them often enough! I'll just be a maid till I get used to the whole idea and then I'll become something more gay.'

Books were studied, lines were learnt by Cordelia; Rillie practised some of Mr Schubert's nice melodies on the flute, over and over. Cordelia's bed had to be moved into the small back room, beside the stove, where long ago she had slept with her mother. The small basement area at the bottom of the old iron steps was scrubbed and cleaned of leaves and fish heads and apple cores and soggy newspapers – all the things that passing people casually threw down. The basement door opened straight into the main room but they screened off a small reception area with some old screens that they purchased cheaply from a bailiff they knew, they painted them bright blue, and acquired a hat stand. The screens they placed in such a way as to allow Rillie, having met the clients and ushered them in to the Oracle, to enter the back room without being seen, to play her flute. The only thing they could do nothing about was the smell of cooking from the back room, which suddenly became very obvious to them ('We can't be exotic with the smell of pork!'), although keeping the windows open even if they were cold, and lighting many candles, helped.

Always, all through this time, they gave halfpennies to beggars, to keep their own luck.

And then they nearly died of Apprehension.

After all their careful planning and buying and polishing and spending their money and being cold to air the rooms of onion

86

and meat smells, there were no replies, nothing from the newspaper advertisements.

'There are lots of advertisements in newspapers about marriage advice,' said Rillie, morosely perusing the *Morning Chronicle*. 'I hadn't realised.'

'Not like ours,' said Cordelia stoutly. 'They're mostly men offering advice. I am the only lady phreno-mesmerist. We must just wait patiently.'

Every day, each more and more apprehensive but trying to hide it; each more and more nervous, Cordelia would go to the circulating library, Rillie would go to Mrs Fortune's.

'I've got a part as a maid in a private theatre,' Rillie Spoons said valiantly to her colleagues.

In the library Cordelia memorised the numbers on the head, memorised the qualities, used her own head, felt for *combativeness* and smiled grimly. She read that forty years ago some doctors had cut up hundreds of brains and examined the nerves inside. She swallowed hard. She tried not to think too much about mesmerism, about what happened to Mrs Spoons. The calm of her Aunt Hester seemed far away; thoughts about interfering with people's minds made her feel uneasy in a way she didn't understand.

They would meet every day at five p.m. Cordelia's beautiful scarves and Rillie's maid's uniform (in which she looked very well) lay, untouched, in the basement rooms.

And then they got their first letter.

That first late afternoon the hearts of the two actresses beat more loudly than on many first nights they had suffered. Rillie, so neat and tidy in her maid's uniform, in particular wondered if what they were doing was against the law and how her dear old mother would fare if her daughter was thrown into Newgate Prison. She could hardly open the door when they heard the bell outside.

Cordelia, draped in scarves and wearing silver bracelets and hearing her own heart, waited where her Aunt Hester had practised before her. The shutters were closed and candles were lit and mirrors gleamed and shadowed. Cordelia sat beside one mirror in a particular way (they had rehearsed this) so that when people entered the room the candlelight fell not on the woman and the scarves, who seemed no more than a presence, but on the empty chair opposite. It was a very good theatrical effect, even if they said so themselves.

Rillie brought a young couple around the screen. At the sight of their grave, innocent faces Cordelia felt blood rushing to her cheeks. *What am I doing?* She saw a young woman, eyes shining for the man beside her; a goodness seemed to emanate from her although she was obviously extremely nervous. She saw a young man, not exactly handsome, but intelligent eyes, and a gentle manner towards the girl beside him. *I cannot cheat these people.* But then she spoke graciously as she had rehearsed and thought firmly, *I am not cheating them. I am advising them.*

'I am' – they had thought a great deal about this over much laughter and port, and had decided that matrimonial hopefuls would feel more at ease with a married woman to talk to, and that a little foreign blood would not go amiss (and for all they knew he might have been her father) – 'Mrs du Pont. Please sit down' – she motioned them to the old sofa where she had thought she had mesmerised the cat (which now had a new covering) – 'and tell me your names.' Above them Aunt Hester's stars shone.

'Miss Charlotte Neville.'

'Mr Martin Bounty.'

Her heart beat fast. Her performance had begun. 'And you are to be married?'

The girl glanced at the young man, gave a quick nervous smile. 'We hope to be. We hope that you will prove that it is an excellent idea.'

'Phreno-mesmerism does not exactly prove things. But it can perhaps advise if you are suited.'

'Are you – going to make us unconscious?' Miss Neville was extremely apprehensive.

'Not at all. Won't you sit in this chair opposite me, Miss Neville? I shall very gently feel your head first, if you will allow me. The shape of our head shows the shape of our personality, and if it can be shown that your personalities seem to match, it is perhaps more likely that a happy union will be the outcome.' And all the time she watched them carefully. She said the lines she had learnt: 'I can only discover the elements of your character, your intellectual and moral qualities. I cannot promise more than that.' She held the end of one of her scarves. She wished she was in a theatre saying lines that she understood better, playing a character she understood better. She half expected at any moment for them to shout FRAUD! Miss Neville, visibly shaking, made her way to the chair.

'Mrs du Pont,' said the young man earnestly from the sofa, 'Miss Neville has the most wonderful, the most generous moral character of anybody I have ever met. I will do everything in my power' – and he flashed such a loving look at Miss Neville that she smiled through her nervousness – 'to make her happy.' And Cordelia saw: he meant it; his clear brown eyes shone.

'What is your employment, Mr Bounty?'

'I am nothing but a schoolmaster, ma'am.'

'But why do you say "nothing but" – the future of England is in your hands!'

'Oh Mrs du Pont, that is what I tell him,' said Miss Neville, and her anxious face lit up like beautiful lamplight.

Cordelia rose slowly and stood behind Miss Neville. Above them the stars glittered, and very softly, from the room with the oven and the bed, came the sound of a flute. Cordelia put her hands to the girl's head and pressed very gently. She moved her hands to points number 1 and 2. 'Ah,' she said at last, 'you have a most pronounced feeling for AMATIVENESS.'

'Is it something wrong?' asked Miss Neville, immediately alarmed. 'It sounds like something wrong.'

Cordelia was aware of the young man sitting forward, watching carefully.

'No, it is something *right*,' she said softly. 'It is an impulse of affection between the sexes. It is a desire to marry. Nothing could be more right.' She felt the girl relax beneath her hands. 'And here, just above that, is PARENTAL LOVE; again it is well developed. Are you fond of children?'

'Oh yes!' And Miss Neville flashed another loving glance at Mr Bounty. 'Oh yes,' she said again. Mr Bounty was leaning forward, watching Cordelia very carefully, but he also observed Miss Neville tenderly, to make sure she was all right. Cordelia thought to herself: *they will be happy; I believe they will be happy.* Very slowly, without thinking about what she was doing, she ran her hands gently up and down the girl's head, felt her relax more. And then the girl gave a small, childish sigh *and with a terrible jolt Cordelia was in Wales, holding her hands to Morgan's small, beloved head, to still the turmoil inside that seemed to torture him so.* Shaken, she stopped quite still for a moment, then with an enormous effort continued to move her hands very gently over the head, just as she used to so long ago.

'Oh – that's nice,' said Miss Neville, almost in puzzlement. Just as Rillie had said.

For a moment just the sound of the flute and their breathing. Cordelia at last recovered herself.

'It seems to me,' she said, and she spoke very softly, for the girl's eyes were closed, 'that your head shows that you have all the qualities for a loving wife and a loving mother. You have signs of conscientiousness, and you have signs of hope,' and the girl seemed almost to sleep. The flute played and Cordelia smoothed the head in her hands, and Mr Bounty sat in the shadows on the sofa, looking at his girl.

At last Cordelia broke the reverie. 'Now it is the turn of Mr Bounty perhaps.'

Charlotte Neville opened her eyes reluctantly. Then she shook herself slightly and stood. 'Was that mesmerism?' she asked oddly.

'I am a phreno-mesmerist,' said Cordelia. 'It is a combination.'

'It was – very nice,' said Miss Neville shyly, and Cordelia saw that Mr Bounty caught her hand as he moved to change places with her. In the next room Rillie Spoons played on, standing beside the small stove and concentrating on her flute as if her life depended upon it.

As Mr Bounty sat on the chair Cordelia wondered why, when they were so obviously devoted to one another, they had come. 'Are all your parents happy with this match?' she asked as Mr Bounty settled into the chair. 'Were they happy for you to come here today?' The couple exchanged glances and for a moment there was silence except for the flute. Then Mr Bounty spoke.

'My mother, who is still alive, likes Miss Neville very much. Miss Neville's mother believes she has better prospects if she marries the son of a distant cousin.'

'Who is a perfectly pleasant man, whom I do not love in the least.'

'Who is a perfectly pleasant man, whom she does not love in the least,' repeated Mr Bounty wryly. 'But he is richer than I will ever be. However, Miss Neville's mother knows of phrenology and mesmerism and has spoken of it often, so we thought that we might persuade her if you found us – suited.'

'And Miss Neville's father?' Neither of them answered. The flute stopped suddenly and then started with renewed energy, as if Rillie had been catching her breath.

'My father is – a very busy man,' said Miss Neville. 'He is often abroad.'

Cordelia said nothing more, put her hands on Mr Bounty's head. 'Heavens,' she said, almost at once. 'You are I think a most intelligent man, Mr Bounty. I feel here,' her hands were on his forehead, she closed her eyes envisaging Alphonse, 'your fluency of language, your flow of ideas . . .'

'He is attending the new Working Men's Clubs in the evenings,' cried Miss Neville, 'and he didn't tell you that, yet you were able to perceive it – oh Martin, all will be well for us, I know it!'

'I think all will be well for you,' said Cordelia, smiling, 'for I feel the qualities of AMATIVENESS and PARENTAL LOVE,' she moved her hands to the back of his head, 'are strong in you also.'

Mr Bounty pulled back slightly from her hands. 'Plato believed such propensities in a person as you are describing could be told from his face,' he said, looking up at her, 'not his head.'

'Nevertheless,' said Cordelia very quickly, 'they believed that more general matters like reason and memory could be found in the shape of a head.' Her heart was suddenly beating extremely fast: she had not imagined she would be discussing the Greeks in her very first encounter.

She made herself pull his head towards her again, but gently, held her hands on his head. 'I have studied phrenology and its history for – for a long time,' she said. 'Phrenologists believe the shape of the head can also add to our knowledge of another human being. A kind of,' she swallowed, then remembered her lines, 'cerebral physiology.'

'And phreno-mesmerism?' said Mr Bounty.

Cordelia took a deep breath and dropped her hands to her sides, came around to sit on the chair beside him. She saw his very intelligent eyes. She continued with the script and as her heart went faster and faster so did her words. 'Dr Mesmer believed that "animal magnetism", as he called it, could be used to improve the mental power of the person mesmerised. And that it could be used – and I have been at University College Hospital and observed this – to prevent a patient feeling pain. But you, Mr Bounty, appear in need of neither of these things!'

'I believe nevertheless that phreno-mesmerism, which you advertise, is something different.'

'I do not quite understand you.' She felt her head would burst.

There was just the tiniest pause, and then he said, 'Perhaps I am wrong, Mrs du Pont. Forgive me.' And he withdrew from the dangerous discussion with a small, rueful smile. 'It is just that – I have wondered if – all this,' he indicated the room, the stars, the draped mirrors, 'is in the end some sort of trick.'

'How can you say that!' Miss Neville came and stood beside them. 'She has promised us we will be happy! I shall tell Mama.'

'I have not *promised*,' said Cordelia quickly. She called upon all her actress's skills to retain some sort of poise. 'But it seems to me that the signs are good.'

The young man's intelligent eyes looked at Cordelia and then he smiled at Miss Neville. *They will be happy*, Cordelia thought again, and a memory of what that word could mean flew over her heart like a shadow.

Mr Bounty put his hand to his waistcoat pocket. 'Oh no, please,' said Cordelia, embarrassed. 'You must pay my – my Assistant, not me,' and she rang a little bell so that Rillie would know that the first encounter was over. Rillie brought the flute-playing to a graceful close. They heard her footsteps behind the screen. 'I hope Miss Neville's parents will come to the same conclusion I have.'

Her legs were shaking as they left the room.

'I only took seven shillings for the two.' Rillie was so excited that her eyes literally sparkled. 'In case they couldn't afford more. Seven shillings in an hour! We shall rule the world if this continues. How was the flute?'

But Cordelia was unwinding her scarves wildly, scrabbling at them. 'I can't do this, Rillie!' she cried. 'They will catch me out – I don't know enough, I can't do it! Really, Rillie, I can't do it, I must be out of my mind! I don't even know what phreno-mesmerism really is, for God's sake! I'll end up in Newgate for fraud!'

'Course you can do it,' said Rillie, the money still in her hand. 'You were always a good actress. I heard you going on about propensities. Have a port and sit down and don't be foolish. This is going to make us a fortune!'

They were excitedly receiving one envelope from the postman next day when a be-hatted woman alighted from a cabriolet and motioned to the driver to wait. 'Are you Mrs du Pont?' she called, peering down the steps. Cordelia assented, wishing she was wearing scarves. Rillie looked nothing like a maid. The lady came quickly down the iron steps, entered the basement rooms. She observed the stars sharply, which perhaps looked a little odd to a stranger, with the shutters open and no candlelight; what she might have thought, however, was not clear in the half-dark of the basement.

'I believe you saw my daughter yesterday.' Then she moved, and light from the window caught her clearly: her hair was pulled back very severely from her fine-boned face: they could not but notice how sad her expression was.

Cordelia pulled herself together. 'Please sit down, Mrs Neville. Here on the sofa is the most comfortable.' (She observed at once that as soon as Mrs Neville heard her cultured, pleasant voice she seemed to relax slightly.)

'Ah, thank you.'

All three heard horse turds falling and splattering on to the cobblestones above them.

'You think they will be happy?' said the visitor abruptly. 'Your phrenology told you so?'

'Nobody can be certain of these things, but I believe they are well matched, their propensities seemed particularly satisfactory.'

'I myself have seen a phrenologist – Mr Tregunter – you know him?'

Cordelia shook her head. 'It is an art with many practitioners,' she said.

'I did not feel he understood me at all. But then – perhaps I do not understand myself.' Cordelia was surprised at the woman's uncertain manner; she seemed a person of some quality. 'I am not, as you have been told, entirely happy about my daughter's marital plans – and indeed she did not tell me of her visit to you until it was over. I have no wish to make her unhappy but I feel that Mr Bounty – although an earnest young man, and I expect reliable – is not perhaps the right husband for her, although she herself seems to think he is. If you are a parent yourself, Mrs du Pont—'

'I am.'

'—you will understand that young people make mistakes.'

'Mrs Neville, the reason that my Assistant, Mrs Spoons' – she indicated Rillie who stood beside them, still with the letter from the postman in her hands – 'and I feel that we can advise younger people is because of our own personal experience. As well as my training in phrenology and mesmerism of course,' she added quickly. 'We too wish to prevent young people from making mistakes. But I must say to you that meeting Mr Bounty yesterday, and observing his phrenological propensities of course, I would have to say that – wouldn't you agree, Mrs Spoons? – that he is certainly the most intelligent young man that I have yet phrenologically examined.' She cast a quick look at Rillie, who nodded her head.

'Indeed,' said Rillie. 'The most intelligent man you have seen, I am certain.'

'But he has only the money of a schoolmaster!'

'Money is important,' said Cordelia gravely. 'Nobody understands this better than Mrs Spoons and myself.'

Mrs Neville looked unsure as to whether to carry on speaking; suddenly removed her hat, small feathers fluttered. 'You *know* what marriage is.'

'Indeed.'

Mrs Neville concentrated even harder on the feathers. 'Then you know she will need money to protect herself.'

How well I know that, thought Cordelia. 'I agree with you, Mrs Neville. But I also felt that – they were perhaps lucky to have found each other.'

'Oh we all think that, though,' said Mrs Neville. 'At the beginning. Didn't you? Didn't I? What did they talk about?'

'Mrs Neville, they were my private clients. If you came to see me, indeed you have come to see me, you would not like me to repeat your conversation abroad.'

Mrs Neville still stared at her hat. 'Of course,' she said. There was silence in the basement. 'Just answer me one thing,' and she looked at the two women wryly. 'I suppose Charlotte actually paid?'

'Oh no,' said Rillie, 'Mr Bounty paid.'

Mrs Neville considered this. Just as she put on her hat she looked again at Cordelia. 'Do I know you from somewhere?' she said. Cordelia's heart jumped: she understood at once. Mrs Neville was her own age, could easily have seen her on stage years ago. 'I feel as if I have seen you somewhere before.'

It was Rillie who saved the day. They both knew that if the word *actress* passed anybody's lips they were doomed. 'Mrs du Pont has been very well known in her work,' said Rillie. And it was not, after all, a lie.

On her way out Mrs Neville absent-mindedly handed Rillie half a gold sovereign.

Their next client, Miss Lucinda Choodle, had not mentioned her betrothed in her letter.

'I cannot do it,' said Cordelia.

'Yes you can,' said Rillie.

Miss Lucinda Choodle was perhaps eighteen; arrived in Little Russell Street quite alone. She fidgeted when Cordelia held her head, she did not seem interested in AMATIVENESS or PARENTAL LOVE. She could not say why she had come or what she wanted. Rillie's flute wafted in hopefully from the back room.

'Tell me about your – your husband-to-be,' said Cordelia, somewhat bemused. There was a long silence. Cordelia waited. A ridiculous thought came to her: was it the name, *Choodle*? She had heard much worse: she knew an actress who longed to get married because her name was Effie Redbottom. She pulled herself together. 'I would like to help you in your choice if I am able,' she said. 'But I cannot assist you if you cannot tell me your concerns.'

'I think he may be deformed,' said Miss Choodle. 'I do not wish to marry a deformed man.'

'What is his deformity?'

Again Miss Choodle was silent. She looked up at the glass stars that caught the flickering candlelight.

'Is it his face? Does something show on his face that distresses you?'

'No.'

'Is it something you cannot see?'

'Yes.'

'Is it something you think he is hiding from you?'

'Yes.'

'Then you must, I would suppose, ask him about it.'

The girl blushed red. 'I cannot.'

Cordelia felt herself losing patience; reminded herself that patience must now be her strongest virtue. 'Do you – care for this man, Miss Choodle?'

'Yes – but since I have – noticed – the deformity I cannot care the same.' Cordelia actually heard her swallow. 'He has a growth. That is – a – a – protuberance.'

'Oh, I am so sorry. The poor man.'

'But he . . . ' she struggled very hard to find the words, 'he – pushes the protuberance against me. I do not like it.'

A light shone. Cordelia bit her lip.

'Has – perhaps – your betrothed – what is his name?'

97

'Mr Forsyth.'

'Forgive me for this question, but has perhaps Mr Forsyth been – a little forward?'

'I do not know what you mean.'

'Have you allowed Mr Forsyth to kiss you?' She saw the girl's face. 'It is perfectly natural that he should want to do so.'

Miss Choodle spoke sulkily. 'Yes.'

'And is it when Mr Forsyth is kissing you that – that this deformity has – come to your attention?'

The girl nodded, her cheeks red.

I did state that guidance for marriage would be given, thought Cordelia ruefully. Another Schubert song commenced. 'Miss Choodle, has – has anyone, your mother perhaps, spoken to you about – about what happens when a man and a woman marry?'

'What do you mean?'

'Do you wish to have children?'

Miss Choodle looked genuinely surprised. 'Of course.'

Cordelia plunged in. 'Do you know how children come to be born?'

'They come when you get married, I know that.'

Cordelia looked up at the glass stars herself, for guidance: suddenly saw Kitty, her mother, laughing. 'Miss Choodle,' she said firmly, 'children are not born because you get married. Children are born because – because men and women who love each other join together.'

'What do you mean?'

Hell's Spite! 'I mean the protuberance you have noticed must – join to you – enter you—'

'Enter me where? Where?' Miss Choodle looked like a frightened rabbit. 'Where? My mouth?'

'Inside your own body,' said Cordelia briskly.

The girl stood up, shocked beyond belief. 'I do not believe you. I shall report you.'

Cordelia tried once more. 'Perhaps if you could speak to your mother . . .'

98

'My mother is a lady, not a vulgar person.'

Cordelia stood also in her shining new scarves. 'I think you will nevertheless find, Miss Choodle, that what I say is true.'

'Such – disgusting things cannot be true. I do not believe you,' and then she looked at Cordelia and added in a small voice, 'Enter me where?'

Cordelia did her best. Very gently she put her hand on her own body.

The horror on the girl's face was now absolute. 'No!' she screamed. 'I do not believe you!' The flute stopped mid-bar.

Before Cordelia could stop her, Miss Choodle ran out of the room, past the screens (omitting to pay), pulled at the door and ran up the iron steps and out into Little Russell Street.

Eight

At the end of one month, they went over their – rather meagre – accounts. They had had only seven appointments (not counting the non-paying Miss Choodle). Cordelia was convinced that it had all been a terrible (possibly port-fuelled) mistake; worried about Rillie and Mrs Spoons; asked herself over and over how she could have been so foolish; wanted to go back to Mr Kenneth in Bow Street, see if there was any work. Rillie wouldn't hear of it.

'We did well enough for beginners.' And then she added rather mysteriously, 'I've borrowed some money. Enough to keep us going another two months and a few bottles of port. I believe our business is going to expand.'

'*Borrowed?*' Cordelia was deeply shocked. 'Who have you borrowed from?'

'Regina. Our neighbour.'

'*What?*'

'She offered. I told you she had money under her mattress. Her poet money! She insists – she's given us *six* pounds!'

Cordelia actually put her face in her hands as they sat beside the fire in Little Russell Street. She had not been asked about phreno-mesmerism again, or been required to use her skills in Animal Magnetism, nor had the Ancient Greeks been mentioned, but, since that first appointment, had lived in dread that she would be found out. Each time Rillie brought someone round the edge of the painted screen she wondered if this would be the one who would unmask her and shout FRAUD! out through the basement windows. 'There's also the problem of the Nuptials,' Cordelia said wearily. Three more of the clients who had been to see them were slightly hysterical young girls; when Cordelia had managed to sufficiently calm them down for them to talk to her in the dim candlelight, she understood (thanks to the unfortunate visit of Miss Lucinda Choodle) that in each case the hysteria was brought on by the idea of the Wedding Night, about which they knew nothing. 'If we are going to continue we need to compose some – some respectable advice about Wedding Nights for me to offer that will not shock them; we cannot have young ladies running screaming from the place!'

'That's nothing to do with phrenology or mesmerism!'

'But it is to do with Marriage, and it is for Marriage that we advertise our assistance.'

Rillie poured more port, frowning. 'Don't they know *anything*?'

'Their ignorance is extraordinary! They must go around with their eyes closed.'

'Or their ears closed! That's how we learnt round Great Titch-field Street.'

'And me! Of course I couldn't help understanding all that heaving and groaning before I was eight! I only stopped worrying after my mother informed me that those – noises – meant her friends were just having a good time. And . . .' Cordelia stopped for a moment, bit her lip, and then shrugged slightly, 'my mother told me that sometimes gentlemen liked her to give little screams. And that I wasn't to think they were hurting her if I came home early from Bloomsbury Square and had to wait a bit, she was screaming to please them, for the rent money!' And Cordelia gave a sharp little laugh, and it had an odd sound, so Rillie

101

patted her kindly. 'But the people who can afford to come to us now were – brought up very *differently*, obviously.'

'Well, we'll have to go to the St Pancras Circulating Library and copy out something respectable,' said Rillie. 'We can't just make it up.'

'We're not making it up! It just *is*! And after all, I was actually born in a theatre, the most unrespectable place of all!' and then they started to laugh properly, not laughter with odd, sharp sounds, and they poured more port, reminisced about scandals on provincial tours; even Mrs Siddons, they had heard long ago, had got into trouble in Ireland, and their laughter echoed up the iron steps. The fire went down, the port bottle emptied, they fell asleep. When Rillie woke up it was two o'clock in the morning.

'Oh my poor mother!' she said, jumping up, grabbing her cloak.

Cordelia came out into the street with her. 'If we're borrowing money you can't get murdered.'

They found a cabriolet and Cordelia waved Rillie off in the darkness after impressing upon the rather dishevelled driver that she would remember his face.

But they did go to the St Pancras Circulating Library next day, where their mature respectability and their genteel ladies' voices allowed them to spend some time discreetly reading a volume that Rillie had finally come across (having no idea in the world where to look). It was entitled: *The Guide to Health, or Advice to Both Sexes in Nervous and Consumptive Complaints, Scurvy, Leprosy and Scrofula; and on A Certain Disease and Sexual Debility, in which is added an Address to Boys, Young Men, Parents, Tutors, and Guardians of Youth*. Although their suppressed laughter finally collected disapproving looks and they had to leave in order not to compromise themselves, Cordelia was actually shocked.

'Where are the books for girls? No wonder young ladies are hysterical,' she said darkly as they walked back to Bloomsbury.

Terrible, painful, beautiful memories of Ellis and nights and the sound of the sea drifted, uninvited. Rillie had to look away from the desolate face.

They finally composed a speech for Cordelia between them that they would perhaps feel they could say to their own daughters. If they had had daughters to talk to. Cordelia rehearsed in her low and pleasing voice something they had decided to call 'The Gentle Intricacies of the Wedding Night'. Perhaps word spread about gentle intricacies: by the time Rillie did the accounts for the second month, they had made *just* enough money to pay their rents and buy their food. They were moderately pleased, tried not to get too excited. By the end of the third month, they also had three guineas *each* besides, and could start paying Regina some of her money back. But Regina wouldn't take it: absolutely refused.

'What do I need money for except the rent?' she said reasonably, shuffling her cards. 'I'm investing in you!' and she looked quite surprised when both women kissed her leathery old cheek.

Cordelia and Rillie were succeeding. They were making money. They were, quite frankly, exultant. They drank intemperate amounts of port.

All sorts of people started coming down the narrow iron stairs. A businessman brought a flighty girl who kept snuggling in to him in a rather forward manner for a public place, but her eyes were cold and nervous, she kept flicking suspicious looks at the mirrors and the stars as the sound of the flute drifted on the air. She was most reluctant to have her head examined, would not discuss herself with Cordelia in any way: insisted that only her Beloved knew her. Cordelia felt she should warn the businessman but was suddenly and most terribly brought up short: *she might want to entrap him of course but how do I know if she is frightened for her security like my mother with Mr du Pont? What if somebody had advised Mr du Pont not to support my mother? What would have happened to her and Aunt Hester?* She saw that the businessman

103

had some unease, wanted Cordelia to alleviate this. Not for the first time she understood that the shape of the head, what she felt with her hands, confirmed what she saw in their faces. The girl had sat beside Cordelia almost sulkily: Cordelia felt, somewhere above her ears, pronounced bumps where Aunt Hester's books said ACQUISITIVENESS and SECRETIVENESS. *But will he thank me if I say some bumps in their heads are not suited? She has a calculating look. But what will happen to her if I speak against her?* She was entering moral territory she had not prepared for, finally shrugged her shoulders. *What business is it of mine?* She put her hands on either side of their foreheads, stroked their heads imperceptibly gently in the strange, odd way she had, and spoke of AMATIVE-NESS and PARENTAL LOVE and earned another half-guinea.

'If I was to be truthful I would have to see people on their own,' she said musingly to Rillie one night. 'I cannot talk of one partner in front of the other, not always.'

'But they want to have the experience together,' said Rillie.

'I know. But if I was *serious* . . .'

Slowly, though, a trickle of obviously moneyed young ladies who must have heard of Cordelia began, anyway, coming without their beloveds, asking for 'wedding instruction', looking with great interest around rooms so different from their own. So Cordelia, having mentioned AMATIVENESS and PARENTAL LOVE and stroking their heads gently, made her speech about the 'gentle intricacies of the wedding night' (to the music of Schubert). She was in no doubt about why they got away with it all: she and Rillie would laugh over the port bottle in the evenings. 'It only works because we are actresses and have been trained to speak and move like the ladies themselves, and you're playing Schubert instead of singing "Jim Crow"!' And some nights an extremely jolly version of *Weel about and turn about and do jis so, Eb'ry time I weel about I jump Jim Crow* could be heard by anybody passing along Little Russell Street in the darkness.

*   *   *

104

To their surprise the sad-faced Mrs Neville returned one afternoon.

'I want to see if you are better than the practitioner I am used to, Mr Tregunter,' she said severely.

'How is your daughter? And Mr Bounty?'

'They continue to be engaged. They seem to pin much hope on me myself finding you satisfactory.'

Cordelia swallowed. 'I can only suggest.' She moved behind the chair, held Mrs Neville's head, seemed to feel at once a kind of vibrating tension there. She smoothed the hair that was pulled so tightly from her face. Something made her undo a large clasp so that the hair fell; Mrs Neville made no demur but the head seemed at once softer, more relaxed. Cordelia smoothed the tense head gently and knew: *it is Morgan, it is how I used to help Morgan*.

'You have,' said Cordelia after some time, feeling the top part of the head on both sides, 'a great quality of CONSCIENTIOUS-NESS.' Schubert drifted. Cordelia still smoothed the head over and over, calming it.

'What is that?' The voice seemed to come from far away.

'It is – an integrity. A sense of justice. And . . .' Cordelia paused, remembered Miss Neville saying her father was 'often abroad'. 'Perhaps – perhaps you are more often alone than makes you happy. Perhaps you often have to make decisions on your own but you do so because your sense of duty is strong.'

Tears ran, very quietly, down Mrs Neville's face. She did not speak. Cordelia did not speak either. But when after some time she saw that Mrs Neville was recovered she gently caught up the hair again. She came round to sit in front of Mrs Neville at last. 'CONSCIENTIOUSNESS is a very important quality, Mrs Neville,' was all she said.

There was a long silence and then Mrs Neville reached for her hat.

'Thank you,' she said. And after another long silence she added, 'I will agree to my daughter marrying Mr Bounty.'

*   *   *

105

An older couple came to argue about who was to deal with the finances. Cordelia saw that the rather pompous man thought it was his natural right, and that the cheery bustling woman knew (and Cordelia quickly saw that this was very likely so) that she could do it better. Having felt their heads and made many comments on their AMATIVENESS, Cordelia opined that indeed the woman had a larger bump for dealing with money: 'That is,' she said, 'CALCULATION'; but that as the man's DECISIVENESS was so pronounced, might it not be a good idea if she showed her husband what she had done, when she had done it, so that he could be decisive? They went away smiling, paying their half-guinea most cheerfully on the way out. But Cordelia noticed that, on the whole, if couples came together they seemed only anxious to show, in among the polished stars and the mirrors and the glowing candles and the long coloured scarves, that they were happy, and desired to pay money to confirm it.

More and more young ladies came without their partners, and more and more Cordelia found herself talking about wedding nights as she felt their heads. It still said PHRENO-MESMERIST outside the door, but she tried to put ideas of mesmerism behind her: she was a fraud, certainly, but she was helping people in other ways and so it was fair (she told herself) to take their money.

And then one late afternoon an old foreign gentleman came. He did not have an appointment; said he was happy to wait until the other appointments were finished. His clothes were shabby but impeccable; his upright bearing and his thick white hair gave a feeling of great dignity. As Rillie finally ushered him into the main room, his eyes were bright as he looked around, saw the stars. Rillie left.

'Please sit down,' said Cordelia, indicating the sofa from her dark chair. 'I am Mrs du Pont.'

'I see,' said the foreign gentleman. He looked towards her, silent for a moment. 'I am interested in your powers of mesmerism,' he said at last. Cordelia's heart skipped a beat *are inspectors sent round to check up on mesmerists?* She was glad of the shadows. 'You wish to marry?' she asked.

He gave a strange answer. 'I wished to marry long ago,' he said. He spoke impeccable English but with a strong French accent.

'I see.' Her voice was puzzled, unsettled. *He is not like my other customers.* They sat in uneasy silence. Rillie in the next room started to play the flute.

'Ah,' he said. And listening for a moment he seemed to smile.

'How can I – what is it that I can assist you with?' said Cordelia at last.

'Were you, perhaps, once known as Miss Preston?' asked the foreign gentleman.

She did not know if he was some kind of constable or bailiff. Or someone out of the past from the theatre perhaps. Her heart was beating most uncomfortably.

'Yes,' she said in a very quiet voice.

The old gentleman nodded his head. 'I thought that might be so. I used to know your aunt. Hester. In fact – it was she I wished to marry.'

Cordelia was so surprised that she stood up immediately, the scarves drifted down. Slowly she came towards him and sat on the sofa beside him. Her beloved Aunt Hester had never, ever, by the slightest word or hint, spoken of a suitor. It was Kitty, Cordelia's mother, who had all the admirers. She saw that his face was dignified and kind. 'Did you ask Aunt Hester to marry you?' she said at last.

'I did, yes.'

'And . . . ?'

'She said – she said "thank you". ' In a wild flash over which she had no control at all, Cordelia's eyes filled with tears: *I thought she had no one.* 'She said,' he added gently, 'that she could not think to leave her family.'

'My mother and me?'

'Yes. You were only a baby.'

And then suddenly Cordelia understood. 'Were you the foreign gentleman who treated her when her leg was so painful? And then schooled her, taught her mesmerism?'

'Yes.'

'Mr . . . Monsieur – I am so sorry, I do not even know your name.'

'I am Alexander Roland. I came to England from France a long, long time ago and have practised mesmerism for many years in my rooms in Kennington.'

'Yes, of course, I – I remember her speaking of you, of course I know who you are!'

'My first admiration for your aunt arose when I realised that with her damaged leg she walked all the way from here, to see me there. When I saw your advertisement I took the liberty of walking past and I saw the plaque . . . I also note that you introduce yourself as Mrs du Pont. I do remember Mr du Pont.' He was then silent but his silence on Mr du Pont spoke volumes.

'Monsieur – Monsieur Roland,' the words came out in a rush, 'you cannot imagine how fortuitous your visit is. It is *I* who need help from you now – I would be so infinitely grateful for your advice and I will of course pay you; our business is expanding and we hope and believe it will grow more. I think – I do think I may just possibly have the – gift I think it is called, but I do not have it under control, I need help.'

'I wondered.' The flute played.

'Oh – you must allow me to introduce my friend. Rillie!' she called loudly so that Rillie could hear her over the flute. She moved towards the door, calling louder. 'Rillie!' The flute stopped mid-bar, and Rillie appeared almost immediately in her maid's costume, the flat-iron in her hand.

'Good heavens!' said Monsieur Roland, standing at once. 'I

remember that iron! You have it still!' And they saw he endeavoured very hard not to laugh.

'Monsieur Roland, this is my friend and partner, Rillie Spoons. Rillie, this is Monsieur Roland, he is a real mesmerist and he used to know Aunt Hester!'

'Oh!' said Rillie, putting down the iron at once. 'I am so sorry. I thought Cordelia was in difficulty.'

'Miss Kitty Preston,' he said to them both, smiling, 'guarded her sister Hester with her life! That iron was carried under their cloaks very many times, certainly to my rooms the first time they came there!'

'Monsieur Roland,' said Rillie, and she was suddenly breathing very fast, 'if you are a real mesmerist, could you make my mother better? I will pay you for we find our business is likely to expand! My mother is quite deranged, and usually recognises nothing or nobody it seems. But Cordelia did *something*, certainly, and – just for a moment she knew me. I would so – I would,' and they heard the pain in her voice, 'so love her to recognise me again.'

His face was thoughtful. 'Mesmerists are not medical men, Madame Spoons,' he said gently. 'It is one of the misfortunes of the philosophy of Animal Magnetism that some believe that they are. Your mother is properly demented?'

'I think she does not know me, or remember me. It has been the same for some years now.'

'Then, *madame*, it is not possible, I think, to bring her memory back.'

'But she recognised me! She called me Rillie.'

He spoke gently still. 'Because mesmerism can,' he chose his words carefully, 'by an inflow of energy bring a kind of relief, a kind of relaxation, then I think it cannot harm her, and she may indeed in one moment know that you are her daughter. She lives I presume in an eternal present?'

'—and often with no clothes on.'

'Indeed.' He sighed slightly. 'I am sorry.' He seemed to study the floor. 'It is often so, and I do not presume to begin to understand why. But if I can be of assistance, I will be glad.' He made a small bow, smiled at Rillie. And then he turned slowly back to Cordelia. 'It is very unusual, still, for a woman to be a mesmerist. It is often said that it is only men who have the strength. Your Aunt Hester was a very, very unusual woman. The presumption of my visit arose when I by chance saw your advertisement and required to know if you are unusual also. People who pretend to have the skills of a mesmerist do the philosophy infinite harm. Mesmerism is not something to be – trifled with.'

Cordelia quickly lowered her eyes. 'It is as I told you,' she said. 'I think I have the feeling for this, but I do not – understand it. And I do not have it under control.' But after a few moments, when he did not say anything, she shrugged, looked at him boldly. She was Cordelia Preston after all. 'I have learnt all the numbers on the head like phrenologists do. We are earning our living, that is all.'

Rillie at once spoke up. 'Cordelia is in my opinion magnificent. We are not frauds. We were actresses and we are getting old and we couldn't get much work. Cordelia often gives good, sensible advice to people. We used the term *phreno-mesmerist* to get attention, that is true, but really Cordelia is very clever the way she guides people who want to get married just with common sense, even if we do call it by another name. You cannot believe how very ignorant some young ladies are. And Cordelia has certainly studied the phrenology books.'

'Perhaps,' said Monsieur Roland, 'I might have my own head read.' He saw their hesitation. 'I will pay, of course.'

'No! No!' Cordelia was suddenly mortified. 'It is just – I couldn't possibly. You will find me an *amateur*.'

He did not remark that *amateurs* did not charge money. 'Let us try,' he said gently.

'I play the flute,' said Rillie. 'Would you like the flute?'

'Indeed I would like the flute immensely. Unfortunately when

110

I was young I could not afford an assistant and so I used to play the flute myself. For the atmosphere. It seemed somehow to help – for people seemed to expect something like that.'

'So did Aunt Hester, if my mother was away in the theatre,' said Cordelia. 'She would play the flute for a little while before she started.'

'I remember,' said Monsieur Roland, and once more he looked with an unreadable expression at the stars and the candles. 'Occasionally when your mother was away, in the days when Hester was less confident, I myself played the flute in the next room also.'

Cordelia stared in amazement. *Here?* And then a thought flashed into her mind: *he was Aunt Hester's lover. And Aunt Hester never told us.*

'So if Madame Spoons would play . . . but here, not in the other room of course . . .'

'Oh please call me Rillie, *monsieur!*'

'. . . it would bring back many memories for me.'

And so it came about that Miss Cordelia Preston held the old head of Monsieur Alexander Roland, and Miss Amaryllis Spoons played Schubert to her heart's content. By now Cordelia *knew* a head: felt the shape, felt his long, wide forehead, had seen his wise eyes and his kind, hesitant smile, and yet his firmness when he spoke of not trivialising things they might not completely understand. She concentrated closely.

'I feel your propensities, *monsieur*,' she said, 'and they are strong and wise, and there is also,' she felt just above his ears, 'also COMBATIVENESS, which is perhaps belied by your gentleness of manner. But – I feel your friendship,' she moved her hands, 'and your dignity. He has, as you have, Rillie, great benevolence, and here' – she looked over at the marble head, Alphonse, for just a moment, and then felt the front of his head, surprised – 'it would seem you are good with numbers.'

111

And her hands, feeling the frail old skull beneath the soft, thick white hair, smoothed gently, over and over, that way she had, as she had learned with her son Morgan so long ago.

The old man had closed his eyes and they heard a soft sigh, and then there was only the sound of Rillie's flute.

It was Monsieur Roland who broke the atmosphere. He had opened his eyes again and very gently he pulled away from Cordelia's hands and turned round and observed her. 'Will you sit beside me?' Cordelia, her heart beating, wanting his good opinion very much, came and sat on her chair opposite him.

'You have learnt well,' he said. 'I think your observation is very fine and I congratulate you – I am, as it happens, very good with numbers!' He smiled at her. Carts rattled past as usual and from across the road the evening church bells began to ring. 'But if I might say something that may sound odd to you . . . ?' She nodded. Rillie, fascinated, stopped playing. 'Cordelia – if I may call you that – I think your hands are too – personal.'

Cordelia, appalled, nevertheless knew at once, instinctively, what he meant. She remembered the shock the first day, the first customer: feeling the head of Miss Neville and somehow being reminded in a painful flash of memory of something she had tried so valiantly to forget. She knew that sometimes, her hands on people's heads, she allowed herself to think of Morgan and his need to be comforted and calmed. Her face was very red. He saw this and spoke very quietly and kindly.

'Your hands have a touch that is very beautiful, and many people would find such a touch soothing. But that is not mesmerism. Or phrenology. There is perhaps a different energy that you may find, from something like the same source and the same sympathy inside yourself but more' – he was choosing his words very carefully – 'detached. I also believe that phrenology and mesmerism are quite separate from each other. And at their best they are – because of their great power for good or ill – impersonal philosophies. Just as medicine must be.'

112

Cordelia nodded, could not speak. Monsieur Roland made as if to stand. 'No, please!' whispered Cordelia.

Rillie said, 'I'll make some tea,' but the old man demurred.

'This is enough for one day,' he said. 'We talk of infinitely complicated, infinitely difficult, fragile matters.' He picked up his hat. It was Rillie who showed him out; their murmured voices drifted in the dusk.

When she came back, Cordelia was bent over as if she was ill.

'*I miss them so, Rillie.*' She was weeping. 'It is sometimes like a knife turning and stabbing my heart when I least expect it.' Tears fell on to the scarves, on to her gown. 'These, here' – she indicated the room incoherently – 'are the only heads I have held since I left Wales and – and – sometimes – just for a moment – I allow myself to remember those days. He knew! *He knew! It is so shameful for someone else to understand!*'

Rillie held Cordelia in her arms.

When he returned late the next afternoon as arranged with Rillie, Cordelia was pale but recovered. 'Thank you,' she said quietly.

He was grave, and pleasant, said nothing about the previous day. 'This afternoon, Cordelia, would you endeavour to mesmerise me?'

Cordelia and Rillie looked at each other. 'As you know, I have only succeeded once, *monsieur*. It is something that I do not – understand, and I have also wondered if it is perhaps only women who can be mesmerised.'

He remained grave and pleasant. 'If mesmerism is only to succeed with ladies of a nervous disposition who will be open to suggestion at the first hint of the word, then it is a fraud. You advertise yourself partly as a mesmerist, so you must try to understand exactly what it is.' But he spoke gently. 'I am an old man. You see that I walk very slowly. Let us see if you can alleviate even very slightly the pain in my back.'

113

'But – I am a guide for people who are to marry. I – I do not really need the mesmerism.'

'Nevertheless,' he said again. He saw that she was nervous. 'I want you to understand,' he said, kindly but firmly, 'that I, at least, believe that mesmerism is not a trick, not a pretence, not magic! It can be explained by reason and perception. I believe it is a transference of energy. You say you have had success at least once. Let us see if you can repeat it.'

This man loved my beloved Aunt Hester.

'Very well,' said Cordelia meekly. She stood beside Monsieur Roland. She was flushed and anxious.

'May I stay?' asked Rillie, flushed and anxious too.

'Of course,' said the old man, 'and perhaps you would again play, somewhere there in the shadows. Although I know, as I told Hester, that flutes and stars are only *accoutrements*, yet I do think the right atmosphere is important. And your flute-playing is most accomplished.' And they heard Rillie's little squeak of appreciation before she began to play.

Cordelia took a deep, nervous breath. 'You must be stronger than me,' he murmured to her. 'Mesmerism only works if the practitioner is mentally stronger than the patient. And – in my opinion – if the patient is prepared to put himself in the hands of another.'

'Is that why Professor Elliotson uses charity patients for his demonstration? By that I mean patients who are under his command.'

'You have seen Professor Elliotson?'

'Yes.'

'I think it is possible that he may have been partially misled by one or two of his patients, but I admire him immensely, and I do not for a moment think he is a fraud. He is learning what Hester and I knew all those years ago. Mesmerism is completely explainable. It is not – I repeat – magic, but I believe all the same that it is a matter of power – that is why it can be dangerous if it is not treated with honesty and respect. But I

will give myself into your energy. For' – and he smiled at her
– 'my back is very painful.' Still, he saw, she was extremely ill
at ease. 'Many people can mesmerise, Cordelia. More than
anything it is a matter of complete concentration. Breathe
deeply and concentrate on your hands and the long, sweeping
passes, as close to my body as you can manage, without
touching me. Concentrate on the warmth you will feel, when
it works, the warmth of my body as well as your hands – even
though you will never touch me. But I will be open to your
concentration. And then, if I go into a trance, concentrate all
your energy on my back.'

Voices called down Little Russell Street. Rillie was playing
her Schubert very quietly from a corner of the room.
Cordelia, slowly and firmly, breathing in time to the movement of her arms, passed her hands across his head and
body, so close that she could feel, indeed, the warmth, over
and over again.

'Yes,' he said later, smiling at her with his wise old eyes. He saw
that she was exhausted. Stood and took his hat. 'We will speak
again another time. But you are a mesmerist. You took some of
the pain of my back with your absolute concentration and your
particular energy. Your Aunt Hester would be proud.'

When he had gone, Cordelia and Rillie whooped about the
basement rooms as if they were young, port glasses in their
hands, laughing, singing: the world was theirs. Nothing could
stop them now.

'We will have a harpsichord!' they said.

'We will have elegant premises that do not smell of old
cooking!' they said.

'No, we'll have a *piano*, one of the new pianos!'

'I can do it! I can do it! Who cares what "phreno-mesmerism"
is! If we have elegant premises we can treat the nobility and
charge each person a sovereign!'

115

Max Welton's braes are bonny, they sang.

'Who was Max Welton?' they said simultaneously.

Later, the thing that stuck most in her mind was that in some odd way, as he slowly went into a trance, *she felt the pain in his back.*

Nine

As the months passed, and then a year, there were waiting lists.

People spoke of the stars, and the distant music and the woman with the white streak in her hair and the scarves. Cordelia and Rillie's fame spread and grew. People were nervous of Cordelia, often found it easier to talk to Rillie: afterwards they would ask her, so motherly and ordinary compared to the lady with the flowing scarves, if things like that *really* happened on their wedding night? Although the business was still advertised in the newspapers it became clearer and clearer that people were recommending the basement rooms in Little Russell Street to their friends. Sometimes one member of a couple came back again, alone, asked for help or advice. Very nervously Cordelia began mesmerising hysterical young girls, calmed them. Often when they came out of the trance they were tranquil enough to hear, and to begin to understand what a wedding night might entail. Occasionally she asked questions of Monsieur Roland, who continued to visit them; she mesmerised him again, became confident in what she was doing. She held the heads of her clients differently: never again, no matter how she felt, did she stroke their heads as if they were her youngest child.

The young Queen Victoria got married (Cordelia and Rillie presumed she had been in some way advised about the Gentle Intricacies). They learned that Prince Albert, the new consort, was interested in phrenology; after much port-fuelled debate they sent a card to Windsor. They tried to only work in the afternoons, although they were so in demand that the afternoons began to stretch: they told each other that their preference for afternoon working was because of the requirements of Mrs Spoons, and the way light shone into the basement in the mornings. But in truth it was often the port. Monsieur Roland managed to mesmerise Mrs Spoons, who had been carefully dressed for the occasion, and although she became very calm and tranquil she did not say Rillie's name again.

It was as if they had caught a craze just on its ascension, as Cordelia had foretold. The newspapers were full of mesmerism. Magnetic Sleep was on everybody's lips: approving, disapproving; nothing showed its rise clearer than the fact that cartoonists drew cartoons about it, the height of fame as everybody knew. Mr Dickens had written of mesmerism in *Oliver Twist*. It was now opined that Mr Coleridge before he died had written of mesmerism in *The Rime of the Ancient Mariner*:

> *He holds him with his glittering eye—*
> *The Wedding-Guest stood still,*
> *And listens like a three years' child:*
> *The Mariner hath his will.*

The widow of Mr Shelley, the poet, published his poem: 'The Magnetic Lady to her Patient'.

> *Sleep, sleep on! forget thy pain;*
> *My hand is on thy brow,*
> *My spirit on thy brain;*
> *My pity on thy heart, poor friend;*
> *And from my fingers flow*

> *The powers of life, and like a sign,*
> *Seal thee from thine hour of woe;*
> *And brood on thee, but may not blend*
> *With thine.*

And Cordelia understood what Monsieur Roland had told her: it must be an impersonal energy.

> *Sleep, sleep on! I love thee not;*
> *But when I think that he*
> *Who made and makes my lot*
> *As full of flowers as thine of weeds,*
> *Might have been lost like thee;*
> *And that a hand which was not mine*
> *Might then have charmed his agony*
> *As I another's – my heart bleeds*
> *For thine.*

'Professors' of Mesmerism toured the country in the new exciting trains, handed out cards, touted for business. The arguments for and against phrenology and mesmerism were taken to new, acrimonious heights. It was stated that 'mental reform' of the working classes could be achieved through phrenology (to the outrage of many people). It was also stated that mesmerism was nothing but a libidinous art: reports were published of a charlatan in France who had mesmerised a rich businessman's daughter and stolen her honour: NO ONE'S DAUGHTER IS SAFE, thundered the newspapers: MESMERISM IS A SOCIAL POISON. A mesmerist who had run off with someone else's wife had, through his wicked ways (so they read in the newspapers), made her his *marionette*. Professor Elliotson himself was finally denounced as a charlatan because, the Moralists thundered also, 'now the private wards of our public hospitals are visited by wealthy and no doubt libidinous men seeking to witness nothing less (and nothing more) than prostitution'.

119

The Professor left University College, but his fame as a Medical Mesmerist, and his income, grew. As did the income of Cordelia and Rillie.

Finally the Rector of St George's Church, Bloomsbury, called in person early one evening as light still slanted down through the windows, although they had already lit one of the lamps. There was a flurry of introductions and then he sat on the sofa. It took Cordelia and Rillie quite some time to understand the purpose of his visit. He cast little embarrassed glances at Cordelia; it did not help his cause that she was so attractive close to (he had seen her in the street, but never this near); it was harder for him to keep to the point. They gave him a glass of port (wishing very much for one each of their own but fearing it might be improper). He rather quickly imbibed the contents and then, his cheeks rather red, he came to the point.

'Mrs du Pont.' He bowed in her direction rather grandly (or as grandly as is possible from a soft sofa under polished glass stars). 'And – er – Mrs – er – Spoons. I feel it is my duty – I have considered this for some time – to ask you to – *reconsider yourselves.*'

'I beg your pardon?' said Rillie, puzzled.

'In what way would you have us reconsider?' said Cordelia, bowing back in a most ladylike manner.

The Rector leaned back, put his hands together as if in prayer. 'I have of course seen your . . .' He was deeply embarrassed. They exchanged a quick glance: *what* had he seen? 'That is, your plaque.' The two ladies smiled politely. 'It is the mesmeric part of your activities that disturbs me. It smacks – if I may say so, it smacks most dangerously of – anti-religious activity and – being almost opposite my church . . .' His embarrassment hung in the air.

'I do assure your reverence,' said Cordelia finally, 'that we, of course, do not speak of religion – that is not part of our field of knowledge. The mesmeric part of our activities is mainly, I feel, for the alleviation of pain and the restoration of calm.'

'*Exactly!*' He bounced up, began to walk around the room holding his empty glass, Rillie refilling it by following him with the bottle. He could not, it seemed, even when he was peram-bulating, take his eyes off Cordelia. He threw back port. Rillie refilled. 'It is the work of the Lord to alleviate pain. Not man – or woman. The Holy Bible speaks of such miracles but they were *divine* miracles. We cannot have people thinking they were – I have read the books and articles, you see – the passing of natural energy between one person and another. What you say you do, Mrs du Pont, is, if I may be allowed to use the word, close to blasphemy! *You are suggesting Jesus Christ was a Mesmerist!*' The women looked startled, the Rector was breathing very heavily, port spilled on to the floor from the glass in his hand, he noticed this and drank the rest quickly, sat back on the sofa. Port seeped. The room darkened. The three of them sat silently after his outburst: neither Cordelia nor Rillie knew what to say and the Rector was quite spent. Rillie jumped up suddenly and lit two more lamps; Cordelia longed for a glass of port for herself. Carts rattled past: one, they knew from the sound of its rolling barrels, was on its way to the Blue Post public house further down the street.

Finally Cordelia said, 'We of course, sir, I do assure you, intend no blasphemy, nor any irreverence. But – this is how we earn our living.'

He seemed deeply offended by this statement. 'Is there – a brother, or a father, or whoever runs your business, for me to speak to? A man would understand that this cannot continue.'

Cordelia rose grandly. 'We run our own business, your rever-ence. We much appreciate your visit.' She looked beautiful (and intimidating) standing there with her flowing scarves. The Rector found himself climbing the steps from the basement and returning (somewhat inebriated, his housekeeper observed) to his large and beautiful church on the other side of the road.

* * *

121

Monsieur Roland visited them regularly, encouraged them. They were aware from his manner that he still disapproved of the term 'phreno-mesmerist' but saw it brought them customers; he never criticised them. He insisted on the highest standards, even though most of their work was still, in the end, about phreno-logical compatibility and wedding nights.

One Sunday he offered to mesmerise them both, so that they would understand how it felt. Rillie went into a trance at once; she emerged ten minutes or so later, rosy-cheeked and bemused. 'I think it was pleasant,' she said slowly, but she was frowning. 'I can't quite remember,' she said oddly.

Cordelia, despite herself, battled with the will of Monsieur Roland, refused to let go, refused to give him power over her. Even when she began to feel the warmth emanating she held out against him.

He only smiled. 'You are a very strong person, my dear. Nobody will mesmerise you against your will. One day, perhaps, you will trust me.'

She was embarrassed. 'But – I do trust you! I just – I don't want to let go.'

'I know,' he said.'

Most of all Monsieur Roland made them see, despite the shadows and the stars and the mirrors and the flute, two things: that phrenology seemed to be based on knowledge; and that mesmerism was not about ghosts and spirits. Neither activity had anything at all to do with magic.

His modesty was such that it was not for some time that they realised he had himself met Dr Mesmer.

'You *met* him?'

'I did, yes, I was a very young man and he had come to Paris, he had rooms in a hotel there.'

'What did the rooms look like? Did he have stars and mirrors?'

He smiled in the basement. 'I myself had just one or two stars, my own idea rather – just because I liked the idea, some atmosphere. People expected it somehow. But Kitty and Hester took shining stars to – new heights, shall we say?' and he smiled, looking up at the many cut-glass stars hanging and twinkling from the ceiling, 'because Kitty could – ah – obtain things from the theatre. But Dr Mesmer did have mirrors because he believed animal magnetism was reflected by mirrors.'

'Did he have music?' Rillie asked eagerly.

'He had music.'

'What was he like? He was not – not at all a fraud?'

'It is my belief that he was not at all a fraud although mesmerism was most controversial in France, and there were several Commissions of Enquiry. But he did perhaps appear to be a fraud because he used a lot of rather ghostly accoutrements, metal wands and magnets. And he dressed in purple.' The women began to laugh. 'But he spoke about this – skill that has been named so pejoratively after him quite simply. He had done his doctorate on the influence of the moon and the planets on the course of a disease; he believed that he, a healthy man, could by deep concentration call upon a strong flow of energy. This energy could reduce blockages in patients whose nervous systems had become out of harmony with the universe, and bring them back to natural tides and rhythms and so make them well again. That is all he claimed, nothing more. At first he thought the energy came from something in the air around him; later he decided it was flowing from himself. And you know – even these ideas were not exactly new. I have heard from travellers that Chinese scholars have tried for a long time to free blockages in a similar way, using not their own energy, but needles. Even in this country there is some talk of acupuncturation.'

Cordelia and Rillie stared, fascinated. 'Did Dr Mesmer make a lot of money?'

'He became very rich, yes, but I do not think he was interested in money. He wanted recognition for his findings; he believed absolutely in his own theories and would accept no criticism; he wanted it to be accepted that he had discovered a new, salutary physical impulse that could be used for the good of mankind.'

123

'Did you like him?'

The old man laughed. 'I was an impecunious young student – I was terrified of him! I wasn't there to *like* him!'

'But did you?'

He considered. They saw his wise, thoughtful eyes. Finally he said, 'Once, when the patients had gone – he had allowed me to observe him at his work – he asked me if I would like to accompany him on my flute while he played his glass harmonica, and we played an old French peasant folk song that had become popular in my country after the Revolution.' Monsieur Roland gave them a little hum. 'And he kicked up his heels and did a little Austrian folk dance at the same time.'

And with that they had to be content.

Rillie went home later that evening and repeated the story to the uncomprehending but cheerful Mrs Spoons, just for the pleasure of telling of an old man in a purple suit kicking up his heels and playing his glass harmonica.

One late afternoon, dressed demurely and unostentatiously (although by now they could afford very fashionable gowns), Cordelia and Rillie met Monsieur Roland on an appointed corner in Oxford Street. He had planned this outing for some time: said he wanted to take them to three rather different gatherings. 'It will be a long evening,' he had warned them drily. 'And remember I wish to pay for you both.'

First, as dusk fell, he took them to some obviously very expensive rooms in Hanover Square where, on the payment of half a sovereign ('Half a sovereign!' cried Rillie in disbelief), they were given a paper with PRINCE HENRI on it in large letters, and escorted to a seat by a woman dressed in exotic Eastern robes, wearing much jewellery and an Egyptian turban. Flickering candles lit the room: they could see, seated on rows of gilt chairs, many rather well-dressed women and scattered gentlemen, from whom emanated an air of suppressed excitement. White papers saying PRINCE HENRI fluttered and fanned in the room. Suddenly they heard a loud rattle of thunder. Cordelia and Rillie were immediately convulsed into giggles which they sought to restrain, recognising that someone just outside the door was rattling a piece of iron, as happened in the theatre. Lights in a far corner were raised and then lowered again and what sounded like a small orchestra played somewhere.

'*Three violins!*' whispered Rillie.

When a man appeared wearing purple, Monsieur Roland gave his first sigh. The man bowed, clapped his hands, raised an iron bar.

'I am Prince Henri, the Master Mesmerist, and you will see today what you have never seen before,' he intoned. 'We will look into the future, we will look into the void.' He went on in this manner for some time and then beckoned theatrically with his iron bar: a young woman in white (almost certainly the woman who had taken their money at the door) floated to his side, and very soon and with many sighs – as he waved the iron bar in front of her face – she fell into a trance rather fetchingly on a handy divan. There was much business of the iron bar moving backwards and forwards and up and down

After more music and thunder, the lady in white cried, 'I see my dead mother before me! She is – I am almost certain – in Africa!' and her arms raised upwards. 'Mother! Mother!' She then began a sepulchral conversation with this apparition she apparently perceived, mainly about the health of members of her family. Finally, when it got to rheumatics, Monsieur Roland could contain himself no longer. Cordelia and Rillie saw he was literally shaking with anger.

'Fraud!' he shouted. 'You are a fake and a fraudster!' He began moving towards the door. 'Mesmerism is a philosophy for perhaps helping people, not entertaining them as if we were attending some vulgar pantomime!' He exited, followed rather stumblingly by Cordelia and Rillie ('Excuse me,' 'I beg your pardon'), past a row of extremely irate ladies.

Out in the air Monsieur Roland loosened his cravat, breathed very deeply. 'Once people claim they can look into the past or the future, or see the far side of the moon, or talk to dead people, mesmerism is doomed,' he said, still trying to contain his anger. 'Mesmerism is *not* supernatural! It is a physical force. Everything must be provable and it should *never be a performance*! To show its effects, for teaching purposes, yes, of course. To make entertainment for credulous fools, certainly not!' And then, having at last recovered himself, he said to his companions in a rather wry tone: 'You see what I was anxious to rescue you from!'

'But it cost you so much money!' cried Rillie.

'Money well spent, I am sure,' he answered. They had tea in a new emporium in Oxford Street to cheer him up, and to fortify themselves for further rigours.

The second appointment was in Cavendish Square and cost four shillings to enter. Here they saw an audience of very intense ladies and gentlemen; the ladies were plainly dressed and two wore magnifying spectacles; one gentleman ate an apple quickly outside beforehand, as if he too felt fortification necessary. Monsieur Roland gave Cordelia and Rillie a handbill which advertised 'A Display in Phreno-Mesmerism' and Cordelia had the grace to blush.

Again it was rather like attending, they thought, a theatrical performance.

The Phreno-Mesmerist was a serious-looking middle-aged gentleman. He first spoke briefly of the cultural importance of his subject. 'Phreno-mesmerism can find the skills and talents of anybody, anybody from any class, and it can even show a propensity for criminal behaviour. Now: if our behaviour is governed by the shape of our skulls, can we *decrease* or *intensify* our behaviour by exciting parts of the skull? Could we save criminals from their base instincts? Could we influence intelligence, encourage it by stimulating it in this way? Please allow me to demonstrate. I have asked an interested party – someone I have not met before this evening, as I think her husband will verify (a man nodded vigorously in the second row) – to act as my patient. She of course has her husband's permission to do so.'

A rather plain-looking woman stepped up from the second row (encouraged by the man who had nodded vigorously), and walked, pale and nervous, towards the speaker; he sat her down and very quickly put her into a mesmeric trance. But then, instead of continuing to draw his hands across her body, the man stood behind the woman in the chair, carrying out a dialogue with the audience as he did so. 'You will, most of you, be aware of the parts of the skull that phrenologists study. I am going to excite several of these parts by rubbing them.' (There was just the slightest intake of breath nearby, as if *rubbing* was a not altogether respectable word or action.)

'Here for instance is the part of the skull that shows the propensity for MIRTHFULNESS.' He laid his hands upon an area of the woman's skull and began a kind of massage of that part. After several moments the woman began to smile, then smile wider, and then laugh, her head back, her cheeks rosy; she wiped tears from her cheeks and such was the infectiousness of her laughter that members of the audience began to join in, were quickly hushed by others.

'You know perhaps,' continued the practitioner after the woman had recovered and seemed once more trancelike, 'that there is a small part on either side of the forehead that we label as TUNE.' He had not manipulated that part of the head for very long before the woman began to gently sing, something about an old English rosebud. One intense, bespectacled woman, leaning forward amazed, quite forgot herself and began to applaud: she was immediately hushed by other people.

'I shall now,' said the speaker, in a slightly theatrical tone, 'excite that part of the skull we label COMBATIVENESS, sometimes DESTRUCTIVENESS.' It seemed this time as if nothing might happen. And then suddenly the woman rose, seized the chair she had been sitting on, and threw it wildly at the audience.

127

This necessitated a brief interval and during this time Monsieur Roland reminded the others that there was yet another meeting to attend.

Walking in the street Rillie was excited, chattering about what they had seen. Cordelia was very quiet. Monsieur Roland regarded her face. 'Well?' he said.

'I don't know,' she muttered. 'But I don't want to do that.'

'That is phreno-mesmerism,' said Monsieur Roland. Cordelia did not answer.

'Is it a fraud too?' asked Rillie anxiously.

'You must make your own decisions,' said Monsieur Roland.

They finally arrived at some rooms in Soho where a hand-written sign said simply:

LECTURE IN MEDICAL MESMERISM.
ENTRANCE ONE SHILLING.

Here Cordelia and Rillie were the only women present: the large audience seemed to be a mixture of foreigners, mesmerists and – it was clear by their conversation and demeanour – doctors. For the first time Cordelia and Rillie properly understood that Monsieur Roland was held in very high regard. People kept coming up to him, bowing deferentially. However the doctors kept up a low rumble of disapproval even before the lecture started. *Mesmerism*: with what disdain they used that word. *Animal Magnetism*: they laughed as they pronounced it. Three well-dressed speakers sat upon a small stage, impassive.

'I've never been to a doctor,' whispered Rillie to Cordelia, looking disapprovingly at the medical men around her. 'I'd rather ask the advice of an apothecary. I've heard too many stories about doctors: cruel, and don't care if they hurt you.'

The first speaker earnestly put the case that they had heard at University College Hospital: that mesmerism was a tool to relieve patients; that doctors and mesmerists should be working together to alleviate pain; that a patient in a mesmeric trance –

this was proven, not a supposition – could easily endure an amputation, or an incision into the body; the conditions for the doctor to work in were therefore much improved because the patient was tranquil. He spoke in a reasonable, measured way: he could easily have been mistaken for one of the medical men sitting in the audience and he affected not to notice the underlying feeling of disapproval emanating from them. And then, in the manner of Professor Elliotson, the speaker introduced a young woman who had been waiting somewhere outside the room. She was a very different young woman from the Irish girl in her nightdress who could sing 'Jim Crow'; she was a very ordinary-looking young woman of indeterminate class, was dressed simply but well in a green dress, her waist pulled tight as fashion dictated. Her thin face was very pale, almost green also, and it was clear to everybody in the room that she was ill and in pain. The speaker explained that doctors had told the woman she had a damaged internal organ, careful not to claim the diagnosis as his own. He said that his treatment had been 'relieving her symptoms' and he used his words very carefully, he did not claim that he was curing her – but there was an immediate, angry explosion from the audience. The pale young woman sat quietly before them.

Despite themselves the medical men became quiet as the mesmerist began to pass his hands near to, but not upon, the pale young woman's face, and her body, and down to her legs. At once Cordelia caught it: something in the air: electricity, magnetism, whatever anyone wanted to call it. Monsieur Roland sat still and silent beside her; Rillie was leaning forward in the most concentrated attention.

After some minutes the woman seemed to fall into some sort of trance, her eyes wide open; *Fraud* could already be heard hissed from the audience. Someone was not able to contain himself, he was in the front row; he jumped up on to the platform and shouted in the woman's ear. She did not even blink. He pushed at her: her body moved wherever he pushed it. Someone in the audience called *Shame*. The man finally shuffled back to his seat, embarrassed. The mesmerist began passing his hands over and over, over and over, along the diseased part of her body. When he passed his hands very near her waist – the whole audience leaning forward now, alert to any signs of impropriety – her own hands moved in an automatic manner, mirroring his moves, indeed in the manner of a marionette. Not a sound came from the audience watching this odd performance, they seemed mesmerised themselves. When the young lady was at last brought to herself it was as if her improvement could almost be *seen*: she appeared somehow less ill, less troubled, there was some colour at her cheek. Her whole gait as she left the stage was quite different.

'Thank you,' she said to the mesmerist quietly. *Fraud*. The muttered word came again from the audience but with less certainty; there was an odd breathing silence: these were intelligent, educated men, their minds dismissed what they had seen, yet they had seen something: a fraud of course, but it had been cleverly done.

And then the second speaker stood. And as soon as he opened his mouth there was a concerted intake of breath in the crowded hall.

In vain he spoke of the healing powers of mesmerism they had just observed; in vain did he make the old call, rallying doctors to mesmerism's cause. Because as soon as he spoke the whole audience understood at once that he was an artisan, a working-class man; the shock (Rillie and Cordelia understood at once) – no matter that he looked extremely presentable – was the idea of a member of the *working class* speaking to doctors about their own profession.

Monsieur Roland beside them gave a deep sigh. All around them they heard voices, talking more quietly at first, then, as the speaker endeavoured to be heard, louder.

It was simply too much to be borne. It had been bad enough, that grudging interest, the respectable young lady in pale green.

But that a person from the lower classes should have the effrontery to stand before educated middle-class men of medicine and tell them what they should think; that he should in some way presume that he might have power over some of their number, their women in particular: it was intolerable. It all happened so quickly that Cordelia and Rillie only just had time, urged by Monsieur Roland, to move out of the way. The doctors in their respectable suits leapt upon the stage and attacked the mesmerists. The woman in green screamed. One doctor produced (for many evenings afterwards Rillie pondered with delight upon this) a large leg of lamb, which he used to beat one of the mesmerists about the head and shoulders. Real damage might have been done had not someone had the good sense to douse the lights.

Monsieur Roland escorted them home.

'Are the doctors really scared of losing power to mesmerists?' asked Rillie. 'Or are they right to be worried for their patients?'

'Perhaps a little of both,' said Monsieur Roland. 'It's why I wanted you to understand what you are doing. You must respect your skills, Cordelia.'

'Lucky we're trained as actresses,' said Cordelia sourly. 'It's only that we've been trained to speak like ladies that we get customers, it's got more to do with that than any of our other skills.' She stopped walking for a moment and faced them. 'We're absolutely no different from that man who so obviously wasn't a "gentleman". If we're not frauds one way, we're certainly frauds in another,' and she stalked quickly ahead of them, would not speak, even about the appearance of the leg of lamb.

She could not be shaken or persuaded out of her dark mood. Monsieur Roland returned to Kennington. Rillie finally went home to Ridinghouse-lane carrying a small lamp that Monsieur Roland had given her; the local watchman calling the hour bade her good night. She thought of what they had seen, and of Cordelia, with her private pain eating at her heart.

*   *   *

131

Next day as they were changing into their costumes before they started work, long scarves and a maid's uniform, shaken out, put on, as if they were in a theatrical production, Rillie pointed out an article in a newspaper comparing mesmerism to the railways.

. . . Mesmerism is one of the many expressions of a prevailing fever for the novel, the technological, that threatens to destroy the fragile peace, the slow pace and the pastoral world in which life should be lived.

'Hell's Spite!' said Cordelia. 'What pastoral world? What idiot wrote this?'

The name at the bottom of the article was William Wordsworth.

Ten

Rillie began to go on mysterious outings.

Rillie was in charge of their finances and their letters and their paperwork: she knew exactly what they spent, exactly what they earned. They were now, you could almost begin to say, women of substance, but they had not changed their habits accordingly: they still walked everywhere; they still drank port and ate chops cooked with onions on the little stove next to Cordelia's bed; Rillie still went home to Ridinghouse-lane to tuck in her mother and empty the chamberpots. Rillie decided that Cordelia needed to be 'taken out of herself' and made plans accordingly. Rillie was to be seen in other parts of London: in Mayfair; in the area of Oxford Street.

One day she arrived in Little Russell Street earlier than usual, bustled about preparing for the afternoon's appointments, putting on her maid's costume, polishing the stars and mirrors with Cordelia.

'We finish at six this evening,' she said, when the stars were shining to their mutual satisfaction. The shutters were closed against the world outside: the room took on its dreamy quality of candlelight and shadows and the drift of a silk scarf. 'I have an appointment that I wish you to attend.'

'What is it?' Cordelia was settling herself on her chair in the shadows.

'Wait and see,' said Rillie mysteriously.

At six thirty, money safely under the floorboards beneath the stove ('No burglar would think us so stupid as to put it anywhere near a fire!'), the two friends set out. It was spring, cold and bright and the evenings lighter and bells pealing from St George's Church across the road.

'Perhaps we should go to a service,' said Rillie.

'Good heavens, after all that talk of blasphemy, why?'

Rillie smiled. 'Did you not notice, apart from blasphemy, the Rector's interest?'

Cordelia looked genuinely surprised. 'No.'

'Well, he couldn't take his eyes off you!'

'Because he thinks I am an incarnation of evil, Rillie! We never once had a visit from anyone at St George's Church all the time I've lived here, and I was much more noticeable when I was young!'

'You are still very beautiful, Cordie, it is still noticeable. He may be new!'

'Beautiful! Oh Rillie, you need magnifying spectacles!'

'You know very well I already have them.'

'Stronger ones!'

They walked on past the steeple and the big stone pillars. Cordelia glanced at Rillie from the corner of her eye: Rillie's eyes were bright and she walked upright and fast. It did not occur to either of them to call for a hackney coach or take a cabriolet: they crossed Tottenham Court Road, called in at Ridinghouse-lane, and then walked past the Middlesex Hospital and down Newman Street where children with dirty faces called out ruderies and kicked an old ball as night fell. Choruses bellowed out from public houses:

> *Be it ever so humble*
> *There's no place like home.*

'Now, Cordie,' said Rillie as they turned in to Oxford Street. 'Do you realise how much money we have?'

'Enough not to worry about the rent!' And Cordelia gave a little dance as they crossed the road, lifting her skirts away from the mud and the rubbish and the horse dung with one hand and holding on to her hat with the other. 'It was the smartest thing we ever did. We know more about people getting married than doctors or philosophers!'

'Well, we're going to get smarter,' said Rillie.

'What do you mean?'

'I think we should rent premises in Duke Street.'

'*Duke Street?*' Cordelia stopped dancing in the middle of Oxford Street.

'The better end,' said Rillie.

'We can't afford to take rooms in any part of Duke Street!'

Rillie pushed her to the other side of the road before she was run over by an omnibus. 'In ten years' time, if we go on like this, we'll be able to afford to *buy* rooms in Duke Street!'

'I'm not leaving Little Russell Street! That's my home!'

'Of course. And I'm not leaving Ridinghouse-lane. I'm not suggesting anything except that Duke Street is where we have our business premises, and you get your bedroom back, Cordie, and won't have to sleep with the oven! The thing is, I've found some rooms, they are in the basement, but what a basement! It's much larger and with proper steps, not little iron ones like we've got. Two rooms, a lovely big one for you to work in with wonderful modern shutters on the windows. And a small room all for me, for receiving people, and my bureau and my flute!'

'But I can't see quite why. We're so busy as it is.'

'Cordie, listen to me. I think now that we should raise our sights – and so our prices. We can't get any further in a basement that makes our hair smell of onions! We're going to get even richer clients if we work here! We can even put a small brass plate on the railings, I have ascertained that we may. *Lady Phreno-Mesmerist: Guidance for Proposed Matrimony*. We'll be setting up right on the edges of Mayfair – we're very lucky to be able to rent rooms here, for a lot of them are family houses, but Mrs Hortense Parker—'

'Mrs Hortense Parker?'

'Mrs Hortense Parker, the landlady, is a great believer in mesmerism and was most interested to hear of a Lady Phreno-Mesmerist. We will be able to charge double what we charge now, we may even get the nobility, we will be right amongst them! We can hardly fail to prosper! Here – here it is.'

Rillie banged on the highly polished knocker, a servant opened the large door, and they were ushered in to see the large and regal-looking Mrs Hortense Parker, who was, they were intrigued to learn (not knowing such a thing existed), a lady apothecary who walked to Bond Street every day to dispense medicines. Now she gave them mint tea.

Still Cordelia grumbled, but Rillie sailed on with their plans, impervious and reasonable. 'Cordie, we *buy* stars! We *pay* to get the mirrors moved – or buy *more* mirrors! You can buy new gowns in Oxford Street.'

But Cordelia hated Mayfair. It was so much a reminder of the time she had moved there to impress Lord Morgan Ellis. She had lived, briefly the toast of London, for that momentous time before she was (or had understood herself to be) married, not three streets away with her maid and her lovely gowns and her hopes and her dreams. 'I dislike Mayfair. What say I cannot *do* it in Duke Street? Aunt Hester's ghost will not be watching over me. I belong in Bloomsbury!'

Rillie clicked her tongue. 'Cordelia Preston, you are on the brink of becoming a rich woman, and what's more you are going to sleep in your old bedroom in Bloomsbury! What's the matter with you?'

And finally Cordelia shook herself, laughed, even apologised to Rillie. They were moving up in the world and she was complaining! As well as shining stars they bought new gowns, new shoes, new hats, to suit their new surroundings. Rillie at last, to Cordelia's satisfaction, discarded her maid's costume; dressed more like one of the head saleswomen at one of those stores on the Strand. She looked extremely respectable and proficient. Once, on these buying sprees, they passed one of their colleagues from the theatre whom they had known for years, Annie from Mrs Fortune's.

'It's Annie!' said Rillie, her hand up to her face. She simply stood still, did not know whether to move towards Annie or not. Annie did not see them; perhaps would not have recognised them in their finery. The old actress, who had played Ophelia in her time, walked along Oxford Street, her shoes scuffed, her shoulders hunched. They knew it could have been them.

Once they began working from Duke Street they occasionally took cabriolets home in the evenings, or called for hackney coaches and so rode in old second-hand carriages that had once been grand, with ancient coats-of-arms fading on the sides. But Rillie still went home to her mother and Regina and the chamberpots of Ridinghouse-lane and Cordelia still went home to Little Russell Street and the fading stars of glass that her mother had stolen so long ago.

'I don't like not being in Bloomsbury, Rillie, not really,' said Cordelia.

'We must get known among people who live in Mayfair,' said Rillie firmly. 'Then we can practise from anywhere we like!'

Duke Street was like their stage, and then they went home.

Monsieur Roland watched their extraordinary rise in the world with a wry air, declined their kind offer to be part of their business.

'My dears, it is very kind. But I have my clients and my rooms and I am perfectly content.' They tried to give him money but he, very graciously, refused.

Occasionally he mesmerised Mrs Spoons, who seemed a perfect subject; she fell easily into a trance, he gave her busy, smiling, anxious little body some calm; she became still and tranquil and seemed to find it all very restful. Just once she came out of the trance and said, 'Rillie dear, the man is so kind, just as you are,' and Rillie held the moment, like a gift.

Mrs Hortense Parker spoke of them, discreetly, as she dispensed her pharmaceutical products. Ladies, real ladies, began to come to Duke Street with their daughters. Cordelia felt the young, hopeful heads and spoke of AMATIVENESS and PARENTAL LOVE and if the noble mothers were present simply hoped that they were taking responsibility for the intricacies of their daughters' wedding nights. They were able to charge half a sovereign for each person they saw. Some younger ladies came with their betrotheds, and they were able to charge a whole sovereign for two. Some of the young ladies managed to return on their own and ask the questions they had really wanted to know the answers to. However, there was a different feeling in the air, and Cordelia and Rillie felt it, could touch it almost. At first they thought it was because they were in Mayfair and not in Little Russell Street, but it was something else, something more pervading than that. Queen Victoria began to be seen, not in the flamboyant clothes and style of her uncle, whom Cordelia had dined with so long ago, but dressed as a very respectable wife with a very respectable bonnet upon her head. *Family Values* was the new phrase. Cordelia and Rillie gleaned that it was becoming less and less acceptable or respectable for young ladies to appear in public with a man who was not her father or her brother or her husband. Somehow, of course, word about Cordelia got around; young ladies still managed to find their way down the steps in Duke Street without their mothers, but now they came more often with each other, sometimes even leaving a maid in the hall. Despite the new aura of respectability, the young ladies somehow still managed to enquire – once the question had been elucidated by a now very experienced Cordelia – about wedding nights.

'I am so sick of young love!' snapped Cordelia at Rillie one evening.

Rillie suddenly decreed that it was now summer and many of their customers had gone away to the country, and that they should lock up Duke Street for a week and have a holiday themselves.

'A holiday?' said Cordelia (who had never had a 'holiday' in her life), bewildered at this new Rillie with all her new edicts.

'You need a rest from young love and we need a rest from each other, Cordie,' Rillie said, most sensibly.

Rillie somehow managed to organise her mother and the neighbour Regina to Bath, to take the waters. (Rillie Spoons was a sensible woman who had seldom day-dreamed of things beyond her reach, but she *had* dreamed, always, of seeing the elegance of the visitors to that most fashionable of watering-holes.) She had the money to take very good rooms with a water closet, which fascinated the old ladies, but had not banked on Bath being so crowded, and wild and busy. There were rather a large number of incidents, including Regina nearly drowning in a small spa, and Mrs Spoons stealing a silver coffee pot. Rillie regaled Cordelia when they got back, over port in Little Russell Street, with all those stories and more. They laughed till they cried.

'Oh I've missed you, Rillie,' said Cordelia, wiping her eyes. 'The holiday has done you good, you look wonderful, your eyes are shining! I'm sorry I have been bad-tempered. I know how lucky we are.' And Cordelia was hit with a pang: how full Rillie's life still was outside their work, compared to her own with its solitariness and its cheap glass stars.

'We're not lucky,' said Rillie. 'We're hard-working. I missed you too. And we're going to be very rich!' and her eyes sparkled even more and they drank more port than usual and cooked chops and onions with impunity, Cordelia's bed safely in the big front room under the stars. 'And where did you go, Cordie? You haven't said.'

'Oh – I just filled in the time, and went on excursions, and had a rest. You know.' Cordelia did not say that she had been, in one week, travelling through nights as well as days, to Wales and back: to where the tide still went out as far as the eye could see so that the secret rocks and the wrecked hulls appeared; to where the wind blew through the grass and the wild flowers; to where the treacherous sea still crashed against the cliffs of Gwyr. The stone mansion beside the castle ruins was empty and dour, the castle itself fell apart even more ruinously and the old oak tree still grew, gnarled and mysterious, and would not share its secrets. It was Morgan's birthday: she realised he would be *fifteen*. She put the usual advertisement in the Welsh newspaper: *Mother is looking for Treehouse Children. Box——*

Eleven

Cordelia noticed that Rillie's eyes went on sparkling. There was something about her that was different. She covertly observed her friend with curiosity; although Rillie was forty-seven years old, nearly forty-eight and a little stout, she had a new bloom of prettiness about her that shone.

One night Rillie arrived in Bloomsbury late at night, almost like the old days when they were actresses back from somewhere and Cordelia would hear brisk little footsteps clattering down the iron steps and it would be Rillie at midnight, a big stone in the inside pocket of her cloak. Cordelia was sitting by the basement fire drinking port, offered a glass to Rillie who took large gulps.

'Guess!' she said to Cordelia.

'Prince Albert has asked us to Windsor.'

'No, guess again!'

'You have found us other premises.'

'Guess *again*!'

'Tell me,' said Cordelia.

'Now you must keep calm, Cordie, it won't affect anything!'

'*What* won't affect anything!' Cordelia was laughing.

'I'm going to get married again!'

Cordelia was so surprised that she dropped her glass. It did not break, but port seeped into the floorboards where port had seeped many times before. Cordelia did not even notice, poured another glass automatically and handed the bottle to Rillie. 'Are you joking?'

'No,' said Rillie.

With an immense effort Cordelia pulled herself together: she loved Rillie Spoons. Rillie Spoons deserved proper happiness. It was just that the idea of her being married to someone was almost unbelievable: this was Rillie Spoons, whose first marriage Cordelia had only heard of years later; Rillie Spoons, who shared not only her room but her bed with her mother. 'But – you don't *know* anyone to marry, Rillie,' she said.

'Course I do,' said Rillie, her eyes laughing still. 'This is the second marriage proposal I've had since we started our new business!'

Cordelia looked mortified. 'I'm sorry, Rillie – of course you have a whole life of your own I don't even know about. It's just . . .'

'It's just, Cordelia Preston, that you would have had proposals too, I expect, if you didn't live so much inside your heart. Like the Rector!'

'*What?*'

'The Rector is always looking out for you to pass! You've seen him, you know you have.'

'He doesn't wish to marry me! He wishes to convert us and close down our business! He's pompous in his robes, and he's about a hundred!'

'We're about a hundred too, don't forget,' said Rillie. She poured more port. 'He's fifty-two.'

'Who's fifty-two, your betrothed?'

'No, he's forty-two; the Rector is fifty-two, I asked a lady who does the church flowers.'

'Rillie, we're talking about your arrangements, not mine!'

142

'There was a man in Ridinghouse-lane asked me to marry him last year, but my feeling was he wanted looking after like my mum and Regina. I think he thought he'd like to join the group! But I'm talking about Edward.' Rillie's eyes danced. 'Edward is his name, Edward Williams. Rillie Williams – oh Cordie, that's got a nice lilt to it, don't you think? – and he doesn't want me to look after him, he is very happy for me to keep on working – I told him I wouldn't stop anyway so it'll make no difference to us, Cordie dear. Oh I've always wanted to get married again, and be cosy! And he is of course most anxious to meet you.'

'I'll give you and him the phrenology test for compatibility' – Cordelia saw Rillie's outraged face – 'no, I'm only joking. Oh Rillie, it's wonderful! but – how did you meet him? Does he live in Ridinghouse-lane too?'

'No, we met him in Bath the day my mother stole the coffee pot.'

'Well that was a fine introduction to your family!' Cordelia was laughing.

'No, he understood. He had a grandmother, he said, who was deranged, so he took the coffee pot.' Cordelia endeavoured to follow. 'What I mean is, he saw me with the coffee pot and Regina and my mother and our luggage and he asked me if he could help so I asked him to return the coffee pot at least, in as unobtrusive a manner as possible; it was silver you see and I think my mum liked the shine.'

'But that was only a month ago! And you're already getting married?'

'Love moves fast, Cordie! I so hoped he would contact me again when we returned to London and he did!'

'But where will you live? What about your mother? What is his business? And – and you're sure he does not expect you to leave *our* business?'

'On the contrary – I wouldn't anyway, Cordie, you know that. He's very interested in our work, I've told him all about it, how we were actresses – he's not the type to be shocked by that, he is a man of the world, Cordie! – and how we started off in such trepidation, and how successful we've become, and our full appointment books. I brought him past here, showed him our illustrious premises! So we'll work out all the arrangements, Edward and me, but it won't affect *us* – you and me, I mean – I promise! Oh Cordie, isn't it wonderful? At my age! I can't really quite believe it.'

'Has he got twinkling eyes – those eyes you like?'

'*Yes!* He makes me laugh and I make him laugh and we'll live happily ever after! Oh Cordie, I am so happy!'

And Cordelia laughed too, to see the round, joyous face. 'Rillie, it *is* wonderful. I'll make a celebratory dinner on Sunday, we'll ask Monsieur Roland, we'll ask the Rector, we'll ask Annie, we'll have champagne. Have more port!' and soon their singing voices echoed out into Little Russell Street, where perhaps the Rector of St George's, Bloomsbury, was listening.

> *Be it ever so humble*
> *There's no place like home,*

they sang.

They couldn't find Annie, the old actress they had glimpsed in Oxford Street, although Rillie went to Mrs Fortune's rooms to look for her, and Cordelia was only joking about the Rector, but Monsieur Roland was delighted. Cordelia cooked a huge piece of beef in the old stove, stoked the fire, glad again that she now slept in the front room and not beside the oven. She cooked bacon and potatoes and cabbage and carrots, meals like Aunt Hester used to make sometimes on a Sunday. She fried onions: now fried onions could dance to the ceiling should they care to and not float into Cordelia's hair while she was asleep. She bought a bottle of champagne as real ladies and gentlemen did, and lots more port. She pushed her bed to one side, put the table in the middle of the front room, bought flowers. She was so glad not to lose Rillie, so glad Mr Edward Williams was happy that she still work in the business. Somewhere deep inside her she understood she was envious of Rillie's happiness: but she ignored those thoughts *marriage is not for me*. She was genuinely glad that Rillie was happy.

When Monsieur Roland came he was glad too. 'I observe Rillie is most kind in looking after other people,' he said to Cordelia as they waited. 'I am glad she has found someone to care for her.' He had brought yellow roses.

Finally Rillie arrived with Mr Edward Williams. He was a little younger than Rillie but looked at her fondly. He was dressed in a dapper manner, perhaps more in the style of twenty years ago, but it was true he did have twinkling eyes and he twinkled away at Cordelia and Monsieur Roland. They all sat in the front basement room with the shutters wide open to the sunny September afternoon and the glass stars subdued. They had to light lamps, of course, but not so many, and their shadows danced on the walls between sunlight and lamplight as the muffin-man called his wares and the church bells pealed.

Mr Williams, it transpired, worked in a bank. He told them very funny, indiscreet stories about clients; one was a butcher from Smithfield who deposited large sums with bloody hands every week; another turned out to be a confidence trickster who had ladies pay large sums into his account. The manager of his bank even dealt with members of the nobility.

'Which bank is that?' enquired Monsieur Roland, and looked suitably impressed when he heard the name. Monsieur Roland was at his most expansive: told them of being a student in Paris after the Revolution, they felt the energy and the excitement, shivered as it turned to terror. Cordelia recounted her second real role on stage, as a prince in the Bloody Tower. She was four.

'Then what was the first?' asked Mr Williams.

'I believe I was a stolen child,' said Cordelia, reaching for more port.

It was a most pleasant luncheon and with the noble champagne they toasted the happy couple. 'When shall you be married?' enquired Monsieur Roland.

'Soon!' said Rillie, twinkling. Mr Williams, his cheeks red from the port, mentioned tidying up his late wife's affairs.

'Oh, I am so sorry,' murmured Cordelia. 'You are a widower?'

'I am a widower, yes, but not for much longer,' and he smiled at Rillie. 'Although these business matters always take longer than we think. Speaking of which, I hope I may be of service to you, Miss Preston, for Rillie has told me of your – foolish if I may say so – habit of keeping your money under the floorboards. Anyone could find it.'

'Anyone won't,' said Cordelia, smiling, 'I do assure you.'

They went, as did many others that lovely afternoon, for a walk in Bloomsbury Square where the old politician Charles James Fox, who had loved going to the theatre, sat immortalised in bronze watching the theatre of a Sunday afternoon.

'This used to be my – place,' murmured Cordelia to Monsieur Roland. 'This was where I used to come and eat muffins in the night when I was a child.' She knew he knew what she was describing: he had been there, somewhere, in those long-ago days and she had not known. 'And still sometimes I come here to think!' and she smiled a wry smile as he listened. They walked along Bedford Place to Russell Square Gardens where the Duke of Bedford sat heroically forever astride his horse.

'I should like to live in Bedford Place,' said Cordelia to Monsieur Roland as they walked behind. Rillie's happy laughter echoed back and she held Mr Williams' arm. 'Ever since I was a little girl I have coveted these big houses,' and Cordelia pointed out the high graceful windows.

'She must not marry him,' murmured Monsieur Roland conversationally. 'This of course is your field, not mine, but she must not marry him. Ask him again next Sunday. I just need a week.'

The three visitors went off soon afterwards and there was no chance to say more.

All week Rillie sang as she polished stars: Cordelia heard her joyous voice in the next room welcoming or farewelling clients.

'Edward will get us very good returns on our money at his bank, Cordie,' said Rillie as she counted the day's takings. 'Much better than floorboards! He's absolutely shocked at what we've kept hidden! He says rich people don't do that! And he'll help us, of course. He says we need a man to run things properly.'

Cordelia saw Rillie's happy, open face. 'Maybe it would be just as well to wait until you are married before we make these changes,' she said.

'But why?'

'Rillie,' she said. 'Listen, Rillie,' and she began to speak very fast. 'Rillie, I have had a majestic plan and we might need money urgently.'

'What majestic plan?'

'You know how well things are going. We might be able to take grander rooms!'

'Grander than Duke Street?'

'Why not?'

Rillie was disconcerted. 'I thought you weren't interested in that sort of thing, Cordie.'

'Rillie Spoons! You've *made* me interested! Our income is growing every day! Of course we do not need to use your money too, Mr Williams might have something to say about that, but—'

'Don't be silly, Cordie, of course he won't.'

'—but, just for a month. Let's leave our money where it is for just a month.'

'He does pressure me, the dear boy. For my own good. He

147

says he can't help it, that obviously we need a man to take charge of things – *and* he's a banker after all and knows things!'

Cordelia spoke even faster. 'Say it is a surprise, Rillie, just for a month.'

'Grander rooms? All right, Cordie. Oh I am glad we were brave enough to change our lives!' And she laughed happily. 'Where will it end!'

'It will end with us being as rich as the Queen and Prince Albert!' And, unusually, Cordelia hugged her friend. 'If we can't arrange my majestic plan in a month – just leave it to me this time – we'll both put our money in Edward's bank!'

'All right, Cordie.' Rillie was happy. 'I'll tell him.'

Next Sunday in the basement Monsieur Roland, amid the roast pork and the wine glasses and the funny stories they all told, said casually, 'I believe we have a mutual friend, Mr Williams.'

Mr Williams put down his fork most carefully. 'And who would that be, *monsieur*?'

'I believe you know Colonel Arthur?' There was a split second before the answer came.

'Colonel – Arthur?'

'Colonel Randolph Arthur. Prince of Wales regiment.'

'I think there must be some mistake,' said Mr Williams.

'Ah – perhaps,' said Monsieur Roland, and the conversation turned to other things and easy laughter echoed up into the street from the basement.

They walked again in the square but it was colder and they soon came back again.

'I cannot wait for next Sunday,' said Cordelia as Rillie and Mr Williams were leaving. 'I haven't enjoyed myself so much for years. I shall cook more beef,' and Mr Williams bowed low over her hand at the basement door and then followed Rillie up the little iron steps. They heard Rillie's happy voice disappearing down the street.

'It's true!' Cordelia said defiantly to Monsieur Roland as they were left together. 'We have been too much alone since we started our business. We never used to go out walking in the square. He makes Rillie happy and she should do as she likes, it's her money too. We should not intervene.'

'Indeed,' murmured Monsieur Roland, picking up his stick, turning it round and round in his hand, looking down at it carefully. 'But I believe he is quite well known all the same.'

'What do you mean?'

'I have – contacts,' said Monsieur Roland. Cordelia stared at him. With an odd start, she suddenly realised how little they knew of him really: just that he practised mesmerism in Kennington and he had once known her Aunt Hester.

'What do you mean?' she said again, but he saw that he had unsettled her, that she walked around her room, uneasy.

'My dear Cordelia, you are the expert on putative marital relationships.' He waited while she stalked about the basement.

'You know I'm a fraud,' she said quietly at last. 'All I do is guess. I look at their faces. I have learnt the propensities of the head but mostly I guess. It's just – instinct. It makes us money.' She saw his face. 'Monsieur Roland, the mesmerism is something else, something different, I know that. I respect that. But this is nothing to do with mesmerism.'

'Then what does your guesswork tell you about Mr Williams?'

At last she poured herself more port. 'Oh Bloody Spite!' she said. 'All right. I want this not to be true. I want Rillie to have happiness even if I feel envious also. But . . .' She looked at Monsieur Roland, shrugged. 'He talks too much about our money. About how he is going to run the business for us, make us richer and secure, take us over. I did persuade Rillie not to give anything to him just yet. And he tries just a little too hard to entertain us. And' – she looked across at him – 'he knew who Colonel Arthur was.'

'So your instinct and mine were working together, that is all. It was easy to ascertain that he did not work at that bank. Then I went to see Colonel Arthur, having been given his name by a

149

patient of mine.' Cordelia suddenly remembered the great respect shown to Monsieur Roland at the mesmerism meeting. He was powerful in the world he worked in: he would have powerful connections, how could they not have realised it? 'Colonel Arthur has a daughter slightly younger than Rillie who lost a great deal of money in a case of fraud.' He saw Cordelia's suddenly very anxious face. 'No. It was not Mr Williams (not that I suppose he always calls himself Mr Williams), of that I am certain, or I would not have let Rillie go tonight. It was a much younger man. But the word is that there seems to be some sort of group operating loosely together, and they prey in particular – I am sorry, my dear – on unmarried women of a certain age. It is just possible Mr Williams is part of that group. As I say, he certainly does not work for the bank he mentioned.'

Cordelia stood quite still suddenly. 'But – then how could you have been so foolhardy?'

'I do not understand.'

Her heart beat oddly. 'Well, surely you see – now you have alerted him.'

'What can he do?'

'What can he do? Well I suppose he can take Rillie straight back to Ridinghouse-lane and get under her floorboards if he thinks you know anything about him.'

'But I thought you kept the money *here*.'

'Only till the end of each month. Then we pay our expenses and share out the rest. Rillie has hundreds of pounds under the floorboards in Ridinghouse-lane.'

Monsieur Roland looked rather odd. '*Mon Dieu!* Then Cordelia, I suggest we go quickly there. And if I have made a mistake I am very, very sorry.'

They took a cabriolet. It was almost dark. They hurried up all the stairs, could hear Regina reading dramatically to Mrs Spoons from one of the penny pamphlets: '. . . *in a moment*

150

the fatal bolt was drawn, the drop fell, and he was launched into eternity . . .'

'Regina!' Cordelia interrupted at the door.

Regina broke off amicably. 'Hello, dear,' she said to Monsieur Roland. 'Come to do another spell for the old girl? You're good for her, you are.'

'Where's Rillie?' said Cordelia.

'Oh, they didn't come in for long, she went off again with her intended and another fellow.'

'Went off where?'

'They didn't say.'

'Who was the other man?'

'They didn't say.'

Quickly Cordelia went to where she knew Rillie kept her money; the floorboards were up. Mrs Spoons smiled. 'Hello, dear,' she said to Monsieur Roland.

'It's gone!' called Cordelia, and her voice was panicked. 'All the money's gone!'

'No it ain't,' said Regina quickly. 'I've had my eye on him for days, that gentleman friend of hers. I knew they was up to no good.'

'You keep saying *they*.'

'I told you, he had another man with him. I've seen him hanging about. But they don't fool me. I wrapped up all Rillie's money in one of me old papers, I done it days ago, it's all under the bed mattress. They was looking for it tonight though, and got cross with Rillie, they thought she'd cheated them but I just kept quiet. For of course two mad old ducks like us can't be responsible for nothing, that's what they think.'

'Did they take Rillie with them against her will?'

'Against her will? What do you mean? You've seen her, she's very enamoured, ain't she!'

'Regina!'

'Well, he was very angry with her, obvious, and she couldn't understand it, and she was more upset about him being angry

151

than losing her money if you ask me, silly girl. "What is it, Edward? Where are we going?" That's the last I heard, but she went willingly enough.'

'Cordelia,' said Monsieur Roland suddenly. 'I think perhaps we should return to Little Russell Street immediately.' He saw her puzzled face.

'Why? We need to find Rillie!'

'I imagine they will suppose that you are there on your own by now. I imagine they will suppose the money is under *your* floorboards, will they not?'

'What, two weak women alone in a basement?' She was already flying down the stairs.

In Little Russell Street the door was open, they saw it as soon as they ran down the iron steps, and the basement was not empty. Floorboards were up (but not the floorboards under the stove, no one sensible would look underneath the stove). There were two men and one of them, in his effort to prise up a particular floorboard, had gone through the floor on one of his legs and was caught now, one leg hanging into a void, from which a not altogether odorous aroma rose. He saw the two visitors: pulled upwards valiantly, other floorboards split: if it had not been Cordelia's home she might even have laughed, so odd did he appear with splinters of wood all over his lower half and a kind of black mud, and stinking now. Then Cordelia saw something else: *Rillie's nose was bleeding.*

Even all these years later the lessons of the older Misses Prestons had not deserted her. It was her home: she knew where the broom was, knew where to lay her hand at once upon the flat-iron. She launched herself at Mr Williams with the iron and the broom like a whirling madwoman. Monsieur Roland merely tripped the other man (who, splinters and mud attached, was now trying to run out of the door) with his stick. There was a thud on the concrete area outside.

152

'You *pig*!' Cordelia screamed at Mr Williams, and smashed at him with the flat-iron. 'What did you do to Rillie? Look at her face. You *pig*!' Again she smashed the iron into his face. He ducked this time and grabbed the marble head, throwing it: Rillie screamed a warning, Alphonse landed in Monsieur Roland's arms; in the mêlée Mr Williams ran out into the area, grabbed his staggering, filthy friend. They heard the footsteps scrabbling up the iron stairs and disappearing.

'I wouldn't tell them about the floorboards under the stove,' said Rillie Spoons, and her voice was shaking. Smashed floorboards and mud lay about them.

'Hell's Spite!' said Cordelia, bending over, trying to catch her breath. 'Bloody Hell and Damnation! We've got to find a real bank! Regina's got all your money safe, Rillie. I'm too old for this, truly, it's like being back on stage in a number-three tour!'

Twelve

It was almost as if Mr Edward Williams (arrested on some other matter, so they heard from Monsieur Roland, and gone to Millbank Penitentiary) had done them a favour, jolted them at last properly into their new life.

By the time the leaves in Bloomsbury Square were turning yellow and gold and falling into the dirt and the muck and the old newspapers, they had found an extremely respectable banking establishment wherein to deposit their money. And they had moved to a large house just off Bloomsbury Square, in Bedford Place; to one of the beautiful houses Cordelia had dreamed of living in when she was a little girl. When she looked out from the long, elegant windows she could just see the statue of Mr Fox, who had been such a gentleman to her mother and her aunt so long ago.

And this time they moved completely, all of them. Rillie closed up her heart and threw herself into wild activity. There were innumerable bedrooms. There were water closets and inside water taps. They had a garden at the back with grass and trees and flowers and a little stone angel right in the middle. After some discussion concerning the likelihood of Mrs Spoons

154

wandering into a consultation with no clothes on, they moved her and Regina to live on the top floor with Rillie. They knew how much Mrs Spoons loved company; if she heard voices she wanted to join them and, as if some wires had crossed in her mind, you didn't dress up to meet company, you removed your clothes. Regina had only one task: to keep Mrs Spoons occupied at the top of the house in the afternoons when the clients came.

'I'll read to her from my papers in the afternoons,' said Regina, who had taken a great deal of persuading to make the move but had been won over by the water closet. 'She always likes that.'

Cordelia settled into the middle floor; clients came to the ground floor for consultations, next to Rillie's office, and a small sitting room looked out on to the garden. It was even arranged, although Rillie was much against it – 'I can do the housework' – that they would employ servants. In the basement they would have two maids and a kitchen. They drew the line at a footman, settled for a gardener-carpenter instead.

And so, finally, Cordelia said goodbye to the somewhat battered basement rooms in Little Russell Street (where before giving notice they had done their best to replace the floorboards). The landlord (a grandson of the man Hester had done business with) had tried to charge them, of course, but Cordelia would only give him one third of what he asked for and said, very regally, that he should have mended those rotten floorboards long ago. (She and Rillie did wonder if, over the years, spilled port had contributed to the floorboards' fragility.)

Cordelia took several very deep breaths and did not weep as she finally took down at last the old glass stars. But she thought of Kitty and Hester and what the basement had meant to them all, spoke gently to their ghosts as she collected the candleholders and the books and the mirrors and Alphonse, told them she was only going round the corner: she was still living in Bloomsbury where she belonged. *But I must call myself Miss Preston*, she suddenly thought. *I owe it to them*. When she left

155

the basement for the very last time she even waved Alphonse jauntily at the fifty-two-year-old Rector, who happened to be passing, and who managed to look disapproving and blush, both at the same time.

At first they were almost intimidated by their new, large-windowed consulting room. But shutters and curtains kept out all light when they so required, and they had acquired new shining stars and bigger mirrors and the mirrors were draped with coloured shawls. The huge room had an oak floor and beautiful rugs; finally they became recklessly adventurous and bought a chandelier. They purchased fashionable furniture: following the new craze for twirls and knobs Alphonse sat in glory on a large curly-legged table. But Cordelia's clothing remained simple, they were a million miles from the drooping Egyptian-turbanned woman in Hanover Square who had claimed to see her mother in Africa. They discussed a harpsichord or a new pianoforte: somehow they both felt the flute was truer, remembered the ridiculous orchestra of violins and the roll of thunder in other consulting rooms. Cordelia rather shamefacedly spoke of *phreno-mesmerism* with Monsieur Roland, remembered the man they had seen rubbing parts of the lady's head, making her laugh and sing and throw things. *I hated that*, said Cordelia. She insisted on using her real name, against all Rillie's objections about customer continuity and the possibility of someone remembering her as an actress: *I must call myself Miss Preston. I owe it to Hester and Kitty.* Mrs Hortense Parker, the lady pharmacist, helped the transformation by putting a rumour about in Bond Street (most discreetly) that Cordelia's aunt, an earlier Miss Preston, had mesmerised the old King, and that Miss Cordelia Preston, reverting to her aunt's famous name, was already receiving confidential enquiries from the Palace.

Finally they put up a brass plate on the door in Bedford Place that was so discreet as to be almost invisible. It said: *Miss Preston, Mesmerist*. But Cordelia's fame (whether as a phrenologist or a mesmerist or as somebody who gave young ladies guidance) was spreading now whatever she cared to call herself; a brass plate was hardly necessary: clients poured in, new and old.

In vain they offered rooms to Monsieur Roland. Once again he gracefully declined. 'I have my rooms and my patients at Kennington,' he said. 'But of course I shall continue to visit you with pleasure if you are so good as to invite me.' He was especially kind to Rillie, asked her to play the flute for him some evenings as he sat in the garden with the stone angel. 'You are a fine flute-player, Rillie,' he said, and they pretended not to notice the occasional sadness in her eyes.

And quite often Cordelia would visit Monsieur Roland, in his rooms near the Elephant; discussed with him her experiences as she gained, more and more, the confidence to use mesmerism when she felt it might be of real assistance. She still of course spoke to loving couples about AMATIVENESS and PARENTAL LOVE and held their heads gently but in an impersonal manner if that was what was required of her. But that some betrothed ladies were suffering from real fear at what lay before them there was no doubt. Very gently, concentratedly, she mesmerised the most trepidatory of them; when they became calm as they came out of the trance she spoke to them, quite simply, about wedding nights. Then people began occasionally coming to her for the relief of physical pain; nervous about her powers at first, she began to have some success: sometimes, out of nowhere, she briefly felt someone else's pain as her own. She explained all this to Monsieur Roland, who listened, and nodded, understanding.

One Sunday he stood taking his leave at the door of their new house, looking at the new brass plate that said only *Miss Preston, Mesmerist* and smiling. The brass caught the autumn sunshine and seemed to sparkle.

Cordelia held his gloved hand for a moment and then said,

'I will walk part of the way with you, it is such a beautiful after-noon.' She went back for her hat and her gloves, they walked towards the river. All about them people walked also, enjoying the day. They strolled, not speaking much, but in a most companionable silence, down Drury Lane and even here the sun shone between the buildings. Cordelia looked up at the theatre, rebuilt after a fire since her mother's day but on the same spot it had always been; she thought of Kitty and Hester in tableaux when they were thirteen; of her own success.

'Monsieur Roland.'

'My dear?'

'There is something I want to ask you.' Still she stared up at the huge, remembered building; almost for a moment she could smell the greasepaint, and the oil from the lamps, and he heard her sigh: *regret? remembrance?* he could not tell.

She began walking again. 'When I was an actress, just occasionally, the work I did – especially with Mr Kean – just sometimes became,' she hesitated, looking for the right words, 'something different. It – it transcended the ordinary.'

'What do you mean by that?' The autumn sun warmed them as they walked.

'Something – it was something to do with absolute concentration, I think. It was almost – but not quite, I was always in control of it – something outside myself.' He nodded. 'Sometimes I wonder – if this is not too fanciful – if it is not that same kind of – of absolute concentration that takes over when I am mesmerising someone, outside myself almost, yet not.'

'You are beginning to understand your profession, my dear,' was all he said, but he was smiling at her; he saw, suddenly, something stab at her heart. And quite unexpectedly she spoke to him of her lost life in Wales and her children, and, as the Thames came into view, bustling and sparkling and filthy and stinking, silent tears ran down her cheeks.

*   *   *

158

Cordelia and Rillie began at last to understand that Monsieur Roland did much of his work not in his rooms in Cleaver-street, but in hospitals, helping people who were to be cut by surgeons. He did not charge for these services: *I do not need money*, he said. They saw his frayed cuffs.

Finally Monsieur Roland felt confident enough of Cordelia's work to introduce her at meetings as a fellow mesmerist. She felt ludicrously proud: Monsieur Roland, who had introduced Aunt Hester to mesmerism, approved of her too. There was great interest in this oddity: a woman. In public one evening she mesmerised a young woman suffering from some unexplainable illness: she had become paralysed, yet no underlying physical cause could be found. She was carried on to the platform, it was clear she could not walk and her pallor was disturbing to behold. Cordelia spoke of blocked channels, and harmony, in her actress-trained, respectable lady's voice, and began to pass her hands across the woman, backwards and forwards, breathing deeply, concentrating absolutely, feeling warmth, energy. When the demonstration was finished the woman emerged as if something good had happened to her: there was no miracle, she did not pick up her bed and walk, but she was able to partly assist herself when being taken from the platform and had colour in her cheeks: whatever Cordelia had done, it seemed to have been fruitful. Cordelia understood that she was gaining respect. She attended as many meetings and demonstrations as she could. If there were arguments she gave as good as she got but endeavoured, in public, to avoid physical violence and kept an eye out for flying legs of lamb.

Sometimes in the evenings Cordelia and Rillie, having a glass of port in their new sitting room on the ground floor overlooking their new garden and a stone angel to watch over them, pinched themselves (quite literally: they would take hold of a piece of their own arm and pinch, and then throw back their heads and laugh). In a few years they had managed to change their lives entirely and *frissons* of amazement touched them still. They had 'arrived': their practice was spoken of all over London. And their audacious triumph made them laugh over their port, and their laughter was tinged with real glee. An almost unheard-of situation was theirs: they were in charge of their own lives. They had been trained to pretend to be ladies because they were actresses, and they *were* ladies now, respectable ladies. They rented a whole house, with a bell-push for servants, and a water closet. They had earned the right to be gleeful. *By some miracle they had got away with it.*

On the whole the two old ladies seemed quite gleeful also. They still, often, used their chamberpots, could not think to do without them, but Regina spent many happy moments pulling the rope above the water closet and watching the water. The rope led into a tank overhead, which was attached to a pipe and enclosed in a large cupboard. Regina often put her hands into the water closet, pouring water absolutely fascinated her. She would usher in Mrs Spoons to observe while she pulled the rope again. Unfortunately such continuous activity made water pour down and flood the cesspit under the house and Regina had to be persuaded to desist. She began to pine again for the less salubrious area of London that she was so used to. But then she discovered gardening. The idea that you had dirt about your house because you *wanted* it, rather than something to be got rid of, bemused her. She called the garden *clean dirt*. The gardener thought both the old ladies very entertaining company and not at all what he was used to in other gardens. They helped him prune and pull out weeds and sweep up autumn leaves. Mrs Spoons loved the leaves, and threw them everywhere, Regina uncomplainingly swept them up again. Once or twice she muttered darkly about a new murderer, the Bloomsbury Square murderer (but made it clear she did not implicate the gardener).

They had servant trouble. Several maids left, saying the house wasn't quite 'respectable' (they meant the old ladies); Cordelia and Rillie laughed, acquired other maids, chose two sisters, Effie and Flo, who said they felt quite at home; unfortunately they felt at home enough to steal things and had to be replaced also. Finally one maid stayed and prospered and was happy: Nellie, who scrubbed floors and pots indiscriminately and who loved murders and penny papers almost as much as Regina. They decided one maid was quite enough; Rillie could not stop herself bustling about inside, but someone else had to be seen cleaning the front steps.

And Rillie, although she had her own room now, still slept with Mrs Spoons. She spoke little about Mr Edward Williams and the hopes that had been roused in her warm heart; just once, after one too many ports, she stood up to go upstairs with her tousled hair and her red cheeks and tripped on a new rug.

'Edward Williams was a Beast from Hell,' she informed Cordelia very loudly, as she reclaimed herself from the floor.

The only habit they could not throw off in their new, extremely respectable life was that Cordelia and Rillie still walked everywhere: they could not accept the idea of travelling about in a more suitable manner; they enjoyed walking, had walked everywhere all their lives. The two women could often be seen briskly going about their business in the mornings, because there was so much to do; wistfully now in the evenings they usually put the port bottle away after the third drink; they had to be up early, to begin work.

Rillie, as well as helping Nellie the maid because she could not help it, opened all the mail, all the bills, kept a now beady eye on their new, rather large accounts at the impeccable bank they had found. After several months the bank began to look at them with interest and respect. The first time a bank clerk bowed low to Rillie when she came to make an enquiry she looked behind her, to see to whom he was making this obeisance.

Cordelia used the mornings to go to the circulating library. She read the newspapers, kept up with articles about phrenology and mesmerism that were in the newspapers daily. Mesmeric institutes were built all over the country. Phreno-mesmerism in particular, and its role in the education of working men, was discussed vehemently. She found any new books on all these subjects, made a note of meetings they ought to attend. Yet really, in the end, she found she was required to give as much information about the gentle intricacies of wedding nights as about all these other things put together.

Every Thursday Mrs Hortense Parker the apothecary joined them in their new sitting room for port and gossip; some Thursdays she would bring soothing oils in blue and red bottles, the beautiful coloured glass shone in the warm lamplight.

'We are businesswomen now,' said Rillie one day, amazed. 'Not businessmen, but *businesswomen*.'

An infirmary was built, the first to be attached to a mesmeric institute. There were certain doctors who did believe that mesmerism could reduce pain, who wanted their patients to be mesmerised before an operation. Cordelia and Rillie went to observe, saw Monsieur Roland mesmerise a man who had to have his leg amputated; they could not bring themselves to see the operation with Monsieur Roland, who accompanied his patient, but talked afterwards to the man, blood on the sheets, who spoke of his great gratitude to the Frenchman.

'I could not do that,' said Cordelia as they walked home, breathing in the air of life not death as they came into Bloomsbury. 'I could not be sure it would work. I am never going to do anything like that.'

But one morning she was indeed called urgently back to the Infirmary. A woman about her own age was to be operated on to remove her breast: cancer. Somehow she had heard of Cordelia: asked for this woman mesmerist to help her.

Cordelia shook her head in great distress. 'I am – not experienced enough,' she said, but the woman stared up at her with huge, imploring eyes.

162

'I have heard of you,' she said. 'They say I may die. Please be with me.' She had a cultured voice but otherwise in her hospital gown and cap she could have been anybody.

Cordelia's hands sweated, she felt cold, her heart beat unpleasantly: this is not what she had planned. *I cannot, I cannot watch this, I cannot go in there with the doctors.* The doctors waited in their big aprons. Rillie was at home, Monsieur Roland was not there to give her confidence. The pale woman put out a thin, thin hand, towards Cordelia. 'I give myself to your care,' she said. 'Whatever happens.'

Very slowly, and with immense reluctance, Cordelia took off her hat, drew down her gloves.

'What is your name?' she asked the woman.

'My name is Alicia.'

Cordelia stared down at the pale, frightened face and the ghost of Aunt Hester seemed to be there, beside her. *Let yourself rest in my care*, a gentle voice said: Cordelia's, or Hester's, and Alicia heard and the fear lifted from her face as if she had been granted peace. Cordelia stood beside Alicia, slowly passed her own arms downwards, just above the white-gowned body. It took a very short time to put the pale, thin woman into the trance.

'Now then,' said the doctors.

Cordelia stayed at the woman's side as they went into the operating room. The surgeon had a saw and a knife. There were people to hold the woman down. Somehow Cordelia did not scream. Several times as the knife, cutting into the thin body, spurted blood, plenty of it getting on Cordelia's gown, the woman moaned: Cordelia passed her hands over and over, over and over, sweat pouring down her face from the effort and the heat of the room and the smell of so much blood and sometimes the feeling of pain in her own breast. But still Aunt Hester seemed to stand beside her; Cordelia breathed in deeply, passed her hands over and over, her eyes blank before what she could not help seeing; she concentrated on the face, the face of the woman,

163

Alicia, on her pain, tried to pull away pain with the energy from herself, and the movement of her hands.

Finally it was over. They bound the woman's body with bandages, blood seeped through. Now they could give her laudanum, to sleep. Cordelia's heart still pumped blood faster and faster and the ceiling spun about her.

However, none of the Misses Preston ever fainted.

Thirteen

Terrible, harsh winter grasped London that year. The cold nipped at bones; the days hardly became bright before they darkened down again. Bodies were found down alleys, in dark corners: frozen. It would snow, and then the snow would turn to mud and filth and it would rain. And always the metallic smell of the grey bleak fog seeping in under the tightest of doors, through window frames, down chimneys: dark dirt everywhere. But still the people came, to see the Lady Mesmerist, to hear of the intricacies of new lives.

Day after day Cordelia read the newspapers looking for anything about her craft: thus it was that she read that Manon, daughter of Lord Morgan Ellis and Lady Rosamund Ellis, had been presented the previous day to her mother's relation: to Queen Victoria.

She took the first cabriolet she saw back to Bedford Place.

It was the first time that she drank port *before* the afternoon's consultations: Rillie, coming to check something, saw Cordelia emptying a very large glass almost in one gulp and pouring another, was shocked beyond measure: showered Cordelia with pastilles of mint and Indian tea. Cordelia was silent and deathly pale: got through the afternoon's appointments, just, as Rillie's flute played accusingly from along the hallway. The appointments went on longer than usual. Cordelia's head ached and she longed to close her eyes.

'Whatever it is,' said Rillie firmly afterwards, 'you must never, *never* do that again.' Cordelia stared. 'I mean it,' said Rillie. 'I'm going to take half of the money and leave if you ever do that again. You cannot insult our customers in that way. You remember all those actors drinking themselves stupid before they went on stage, how they thought it never showed? You remember them, Cordie, thinking nobody knew? Even today somebody might have noticed. You were *drunk*! It's you who's always saying that we can't get away from ourselves, that our gentility is only a veneer. Our reputation grew so quickly – you think it can't fall down again in the same way?' Cordelia had never seen Rillie so angry: was this kind little Rillie Spoons? '*I'm ashamed of you,*' said Rillie.

Cordelia picked up her reticule and took the small torn piece of newspaper from it. She handed it to Rillie. Rillie stared at the newspaper for some time, expression after expression flitted across her face, but the appearance of Mrs Spoons, staggering under some rather large weights from the kitchen scales, brought the conversation to a close for that moment and by the time the matter of the weights had been dealt with the front door of the big house in Bedford Place had slammed.

Cordelia walked round and round Bloomsbury Square, round and round in the freezing evening, frost hung from the trees; round and round as she had so often when she was a child, her garden of dreams; she looked up for a moment at the listening face of Charles James Fox. There was a bright full moon and small bright stars. *Manon, daughter of Lord Morgan Ellis and Lady Rosamund Ellis, presented to Lady Rosamund Ellis's second cousin:*

Queen Victoria. Not if Her Most Respectable Majesty had known she was meeting only another Miss Preston, after all. Which led to the most painful thought of all, so sharp that it was as if a knife was turning over and over inside her, a real knife, like the surgeons had used. Because she had at last understood (there inside her where the knife was turning) that hidden away in the deep recesses of her heart where our dreams live on, she had still hoped, one day, to *find* her children again, that they would somehow be hers, still. And the newspaper report showed her absolutely that she would of course damage Manon's chances if she ever appeared: an actress-turned-mesmerist, raising questions, muddying the past. She looked up past the statue. She saw the moon. She saw the bright stars – the real stars, not cheap glass ones – winter stars shining so brightly above the square, above the frozen branches. Her children were forbidden to her for ever. For of course they must never know of false glass stars. *She saw the taller fair-haired girl refusing to wave to her mother and the other fair-haired girl bending down to her even smaller, crying brother as the carriage rolled away and the wind blew.* And one more thought came to her, there in the square.

Aunt Hester had told her. *All this was my fault too, for wanting something that was impossible. Ellis could not have married me. Charles James Fox may have married Mrs Armitage who was worse than an actress but the world does not work that way.*

As Rillie dealt with all their letters, it was Rillie who opened the letter next morning that her friend the Post Man had brought to her from Little Russell Street where it had been lying in the dirt at the bottom of the iron steps.

> *If it is you, Mama, about the Treehouse*
> *Children, kindly send word to 7 Grosvenor Square*
> *where I shall be for most of the month of December.*
> Gwenlliam

The letter had been sent from Wales weeks ago. It was already the beginning of December. Rillie did not even think about what was the best thing to do: whether she ought to give the letter to Cordelia, she and Cordelia weren't really speaking anyway; she simply sent an urgent message to 7 Grosvenor Square giving the address in Bedford Place, asking Gwenlliam to call late that afternoon.

Cordelia heard Rillie humming quietly to herself as they were dressing for the afternoon's clients, would have liked to hug her for her general good humour, for her wisdom and her love. But they were still not exactly talking to each other and today Rillie watched the port bottle like a hawk. *Tonight* thought Cordelia *I will apologise to her for my behaviour I have behaved appallingly and I hardly deserve a friend like Rillie.* She thought about how brave Rillie had been about the betrayal of the dastardly Mr Williams, Rillie who had only wanted love. She polished one of the mirrors *I love Rillie* although of course Nellie had already done the polishing.

It was the voice. Absurd as it seemed after so many years, and despite the clipped, yet drawn-out vowels of the nobility, she was certain she recognised the *voice*, and hearing it Cordelia actually made a small sound, a cry, as if she was choking: the room spun and beads of perspiration broke out on her forehead and her top lip and her chest and her legs.

Would Rillie know? But she could hear Rillie in the next-door room, she seemed to be talking normally. Did Rillie think this was just a new client? Was this just a new client? *Am I mistaken?* Any moment then, Rillie would bring the owner of that voice into the big, dark room.

Cordelia's panic was such that for a moment she stared about frenziedly as if to find a place to hide. She heard them moving in the next-door room. As if in a trance herself she sat down on the usual dark chair, quickly blowing out two of the nearest candles so that the darkness was more intense than usual. She pulled the flowing scarves over her head as if she was some sort of gypsy; the drum that was her heart pounded wildly.

The door opened, and a young woman entered. Rillie indicated that the visitor should sit on the sofa, the way she always did, and then the door closed softly behind her. Cordelia saw that the girl – the pale, pale girl – was adapting her eyes to the darkness; then she understood that the girl had seen her.

Cordelia would have to speak.

'How can I help you?' she said, and her voice was like a whisper.

The young woman did not answer at once. Her long fair hair was caught at her neck, she was older, and she was so pale, but it was the same face, the beloved face. Without any sound tears suddenly fell down Cordelia's cheeks in the flickering darkness. She saw a face that she knew, yet did not know: the grey enquiring eyes so like her great-aunt, not beautiful the way Kitty had been beautiful but the same quirky, open face as Hester, and the eyes.

'We were told that you were dead,' said the young woman, and Cordelia heard that the voice trembled.

Very slowly, wondering if she was dreaming, or insane, Cordelia unwound the scarves from her head: they lay there, glittering, across her shoulders. Very slowly she walked towards the sofa and as she walked the words emerged: 'I did not die,' and the girl nodded and the dark flickering room spun round.

None of the Misses Preston ever fainted.

The two women regarded each other. Rillie's flute suddenly began to play.

'I recognised your voice, Gwenlliam,' said Cordelia.

'They said you were dead, Mama,' said Gwenlliam.

Very slowly still, as if she was ill, Cordelia sat beside her daughter. 'I looked for you in Wales so many times but the old house was locked up years ago, and the castle has crumbled even more.'

'Yes.' The flute went on playing, very quietly. Still they sat quite apart, stared at each other. For a moment the silence was so extraordinary that it was as if the room was empty. And then there was a little avalanche of words.

'Gwenlliam, where were you taken? They must have taken you away somewhere almost at once because I returned home straight away and—'

'—and yes, that same day, someone came and just took us away in a carriage. I just had a moment to leave a note in the tree, I did not know where we were going but I thought—'

'—and I looked in the treehouse, it seemed—'

'—and I knew you would. If you were alive I knew you would.' Their voices made small gasping sounds.

'But there was a storm. By the time I got there the stone house was locked up and there was a terrible storm. There was no letter, I climbed into the treehouse. There was no letter at all but I knew you would have left one, if you could—'

'—and I wrote *they are taking us away* but I could not tell you where we were going. They just picked us up and took us away, they took us far north, somewhere near a place called Ruthun I learned afterwards, another old stone house, but nowhere near the sea. I knew you could never find us so far away.' And all the time they sat apart stiffly, staring at each other in disbelief. 'We have lived there for years and years.'

'What – what did you do? How did you live? Who – who looked after you?'

'We had many tutors. Morgan would do nothing but read and paint pictures, even when they sent him to a proper school. But Manon and I learnt – young lady refinements.' *Cordelia saw them all, their birthdays passing with tutors in a stone house and herself back on stage playing witches and faerie queens.*

'And have they' – neither of them specified who 'they' might be – 'have they' – Cordelia was trying to make sense – 'have you all been looked after?'

'In a way.'

'Manon?' She said the name out loud carefully, as if it was precious china.

'Manon has just been presented at Court. She is to be married on Friday.'

Cordelia tried to hide her look of shock. *Manon married?*

She made the next word. 'Morgan?' There was no answer. 'Morgan?' she said again urgently.

'He is – as he always was,' and again Cordelia made a sound, like an odd, choked cry, just as she had when she first heard Gwenlliam's voice. She quickly looked down at her own hands. She saw the little anguished face, the anger, the smoothing of the head, the silence; heard not the flute, but the sound of the sea, children's voices calling to each other across the long, empty shore; bright blue flowers and wild red and yellow flowers bent with the wind. She looked up again and saw the young woman in front of her, and above her the false stars.

She had to ask a thousand questions, or none. Finally she said, 'How did you find me?'

'Just a few months ago Morgan was taken to Cardiff, for his headaches, and—'

'—he still gets headaches?'

'Different. They are different from before. In Cardiff Morgan found the advertisement.'

Cordelia had to repeat the word again. 'Morgan? The headaches are still bad?'

'Yes. But – not the same as before.' She seemed to want to change the subject. 'He likes reading the newspapers.' Words like small shocks: *Morgan's headaches. He likes reading the newspapers.* 'He showed me but I told him he was foolish and he got angry and tore up the paper,' and again Cordelia saw the small, anguished face of the past. 'I do not think that Morgan could manage finding you again,' Gwenlliam said simply. 'It took him too long to recover from – your going. But of course I wondered if it was you and I made up my mind to reply secretly as we were coming to London for Manon to be presented at Court, and then to be married. But – there was no answer. I thought it must all be a mistake.'

'But I did not get a letter.'

'Miss Spoons found it yesterday.' She heard Cordelia's gasp of shock. 'She contacted me at once. Miss Spoons told me when I got here that you did not know I was coming but it was – better this way. It was such luck, Mama, my stepmother requires all my letters from me, but I was just returning from walking in the square, the boy was just there, gave me the letter – I just – turned around and came here – I took a cabriolet by myself, I had never done that before.'

Cordelia tried with all her strength to remain coherent, to speak normally, say something normal. Candles flickered. 'You do not usually – live in London then?' she said.

'No, we do not, we are still in North Wales, but Manon began to come about a year ago.'

'Manon has been living *here*, in London?' *My daughter was here, and I did not know?*

'Yes. And when a husband was found for Manon – it is a Duke—'

'A Duke?'

'—Manon, you must remember how beautiful she is – it was decided we should all come. For the wedding. For myself and Morgan it is the very first time!'

She could hardly say the words: '*Morgan* is here in London too?'

'Yes.'

'In *London*?'

'Yes.' Gwenlliam smiled briefly, oddly. 'You know Morgan and I had always made plans to run off to the new country.'

'What do you mean?'

'We always dreamed of going to America. Where the ships came from. The wrecks.'

'Oh.' And Cordelia too smiled slightly; oddly.

'Of course it was just a dream, but Morgan so wanted to go

172

there! You had always – made it sound so exciting. But London was Manon's dream. Our grandfather – that is the Duke of Llannefydd – has a house in Grosvenor Square.' There was a long silence at last.

'Yes,' said Cordelia finally. 'I know that house.' There were too many unanswered things in the air: neither of them knew how to wade through such dangerous waters. Just the sound for a moment of uneven breathing, the clearing of a throat.

'You look the same, but,' and it was clear that Gwenlliam did not know if she should say the words, did not have the sophistication to cover them up, stared up at the white lock of hair, the words came out in a rush, 'very much older.' In the next room the flute played on. 'America was not new really, it did not really jump up out of the sea.'

'What?'

'Our tutors told us that America was there all the time, it had natives on it.'

'Oh! Oh Gwenlliam, I made it up! I did not know anything at all about America!' And both women, remembering, actually laughed for a second in a surprised manner that a part of their past was touching them on the arm like a ghost, and then their small laughter stopped, and then the silence came again.

The pale girl suddenly leaned forward. 'I walked up and down Little Russell Street as soon as I arrived here. I asked the Rector of that big church if Lady Ellis lived here and he looked quite shocked. It was a very respectable street, he said, but not a street of nobility.'

She does not know. She does not know the circumstances, then, of her birth.

'You remembered Little Russell Street?' said Cordelia faintly.

'And I remembered the stories of your mother, and your aunt.'

And for the third time Cordelia made the same sound, the small choked cry. '*Your* grandmother and *your* Great-Aunt Hester!' she whispered. '*You look so like your Great-Aunt Hester,*' and somehow she at last enfolded the fair-haired girl in her arms

173

and her scarves and they became entangled as they wept. And as they wept the pale girl kept saying, *I do not understand anything*. And at last she stared up through her tears at her mother. 'There are so many questions running around in my head. Why did my father divorce you? Why did he say you were dead? What happened when you came to London?'

Cordelia remembered her vow under the stars in Bloomsbury Square. 'Let us not speak of those things just yet,' she said quickly, and she held her daughter tightly.

And all the time Rillie heroically played the flute in the next-door room, wanting, with all her heart, to make them live happily ever after.

Quite desperate, at last, for normality, they took Indian tea with Rillie in the cosy sitting room, looking out into the garden. The fire was lit and they wore extra shawls against the chill air as a few rays of brief winter sun began to disappear. Suddenly they observed Mrs Spoons walking in the garden, singing quietly to herself, wearing only a petticoat. Rillie hurried out, took the small, fragile old lady inside for more clothes, explaining to her over and over that she would get cold and ill.

'Mrs Spoons is demented,' explained Cordelia. 'She was such a good, kind woman and she is still no trouble to us except that when she hears visitors' voices she takes off her clothes as if she is dressing for dinner. She does not of course remember anything we say but Rillie has lately been trying to persuade her to retain her garments by telling her that she will put the garment-makers in the factories out of work, and how would they live? For Mrs Spoons always had such a kind heart.' Gwenlliam gave a small smile. And Cordelia smiled also with a terrible pain somewhere inside her, because Gwenlliam smiled: Gwenlliam and Aunt Hester, rolled into one.

And then Gwenlliam said, 'Are you really a mesmerist, as it says on the door? Why do you call yourself Miss Preston still?'

Regina appeared with the gardener, carrying an armful of chrysanthemums. 'She got away, damn,' said Regina to Cordelia apologetically. 'I was picking flowers for the rooms.'

'This is . . .' her voice stumbled, 'this is my daughter Gwenlliam, Regina.'

Regina, her wrinkled old face looking through the flowers, said, 'Heavens! A lovely young girl you are indeed. You take care if you go anywhere near Bloomsbury Square. There's a murderer.' And having given her usual warning she set off again behind the gardener. Cordelia thought how odd the household must seem to Gwenlliam.

'Is there a murderer?'

'I don't think so. Regina sees murderers on most street corners. It is her hobby!' There were hundreds of questions in the bewildered girl's eyes. They heard a dog barking.

'But – I must go back,' Gwenlliam said suddenly. 'They will be looking for me, I am not supposed to be alone, and they do not know where I am. The Duke is very strict. And it is almost night.' *It seemed a dark bird with heavy wide wings flew over them, shadowing the angel.*

'I shall accompany you back. At least – to Mayfair.'

In the street Cordelia hailed a cabriolet; the two women sat there in the cold, falling darkness without speaking, without saying the things they wanted; only their hands stayed clasped tightly together. Passing lamps flashed briefly, caught white, exhausted faces. 'Could you come back?' Gwenlliam whispered, as though her words were forbidden words that must not be spoken.

'No, Gwennie.' The old name slipped out. 'You know I could not come back.'

'Could – could I live with you? You are my mother, after all.' Cordelia was stunned: here they were, just approaching the most noble square in London. She had to somehow break this thread. She suddenly rapped on the roof, stopped the cab sharply. As they alighted she felt the reluctance of the girl beside her to put one foot in front of the other, made her keep walking towards the square, towards the big, remembered house; spoke urgently in a low voice as the winter darkness enveloped London. Everything had to be said very quickly.

'I could never, never give you what Ellis has given you. *You must understand what I did not understand when I was your age*: the world is divided not just between rich and poor but between those who are respectable and those who are not – it is the greatest dividing line in the world and I did not understand and I have done you great damage.' Her breath made patterns in the cold night. 'I was an actress, I was the daughter of an actress: it would never, ever be possible for you to have the same place in society as you do now if you lived with me, shared my life.'

'I shared your life till I was seven years old. I was never so happy as then, and I am still respectable now!' But the girl's face was ashen.

'But we were not *safe* and I did not understand that. Safety goes with respectability. It is only because you are respectable and safe that you do not understand the importance of such things. You must stay where you are. But' – for she saw the girl's face – 'I will always be here. I have money and perhaps can help you in other ways that we will not make public. But you must – my God, Gwennie, you must *seize* the life that my mother and my aunt and I have fought for you to have.' And she took the girl's arm firmly and walked her into Grosvenor Square where gas lamps shone at the corner.

And then, having behaved with such courage, it was as if all her strength drained away: she could not help herself. 'You – are *all* here?' Cordelia said again.

Gwenlliam's face was now blank of any expression except exhaustion.

'We are all here.'

She could not help repeating herself. 'Morgan too?'

'Morgan too. Manon is to marry the Duke of Trent. It is very – advantageous, they say, and it will be a very big wedding on

Friday. It is to be in the chapel at Westminster. You see,' she continued, her voice blank now like her face, 'our – stepmother – could not have children. That is why we have been useful after all. Morgan is the heir.'

They must never know. I must never damage their chances. 'This – Duke of Trent? Is he suitable? Is he a good man? And Manon loves him?'

Gwenlliam's pale face turned towards her mother. 'She loves London. She is so happy to be here.' *Is she saying something else? But Manon is happy.*

The huge house on the corner of the square stared down at them forbiddingly. Gwenlliam stopped. 'It is here,' she said shakily. 'This is the house.'

'I know,' said Cordelia more sharply than she meant to. They had made no further plans, again did not know how to proceed; stood, staring at each other, both of them shivering slightly. Cordelia looked up at the forbidden mansion that contained her other children.

'Look,' said Gwenlliam, and she pointed at the bright full moon. 'Your moon,' she said, and in the moonlight she saw that her mother closed her eyes for a moment, as if she could not bear it. And then Gwenlliam said very quickly, 'This is all wrong. I always thought you might be alive. They took us away *first*. And then they told us that they had taken us away because you had died in London when you were with our father – but I knew you could not have got to London by the time they removed us from the castle that very same day.' She took a deep, tremulous breath. 'You – you must not ask me not to. I am going to tell Father tonight that I have seen you and ask him why he told us you were dead.'

Cordelia quickly caught hold of the girl's hand, drew her close, pushed through pain. 'Gwenlliam, listen. Listen.' She spoke urgently, almost a whisper. 'You must listen to me, and be guided by me. *You must not speak of this visit to anyone.* Not ever!' She looked up anxiously at the house, pushed her daughter, now,

177

into the shadows, no one must see. She saw the girl's stubborn face, Aunt Hester's stubborn face. Somehow she had to shock her into understanding. 'Listen to me carefully, Gwenlliam,' Cordelia said harshly. 'I must trust you. You must be – an adult – and understand what I am going to tell you and never breathe a word of it to another soul for the sake of Manon and Morgan. And yourself.' A carriage rattled past. Somewhere a man whistled, there were voices and horses: all the sounds of the city, even in Mayfair. Cordelia looked about her and then spoke very quickly and very quietly. 'You remember I used to tell you about our wedding, the wedding of your father and me that—'

'—that was in the little church, a beautiful, romantic wedding with only Rillie and Aunt Hester and—'

'—and the "cousins", I found out much later, who came with your father, were not part of the family at all. And the vicar, I found out later, was not a vicar and—'

'—do you mean – was it a trick?'

'It was a trick. I went to London that day and when I got there I was told that I was not legally married, that I had never been Lady Ellis and that your father had never been my husband.'

Gwenlliam's horrified, unbelieving face. 'But – *why?*'

'You know something of society now, Gwenlliam, you know why. Your father would never have married me, and I should have known that. I was an actress, not a lady.'

'But we were a *family*. He came to us for years and years.'

'Yes.'

'It was all a lie?'

'We were a family, that part was real. But it was based on a lie. That is why you must never, *never* speak of this visit. If this was known, Gwenlliam, there would be no wedding for Manon. Morgan would not be the heir.' There was silence for a moment, just the girl's breathing as she heard, understood. 'I was never Lady Morgan Ellis,' said Cordelia firmly. 'I am – I always was – Miss Preston.' And in the darkness she nevertheless saw the flash of the girl's amazed eyes.

178

'But I am *sure* the Duke cannot know of this! You do not know what he is like. He would *never* accept us if he knew we were' – she spoke the word very carefully and quietly – 'illegitimate.'

'I am sure he does not know, of course he does not know. Hell's Teeth, Gwenlliam, *you have to understand!* I am sure nobody knows but your father, and the lawyer who met me in London. It was much easier for your father to admit to an indiscreet marriage with the wife unfortunately and conveniently dead. He could not explain the three children in another, acceptable way, and he loved you. I know he loved you, or he would have just left us all. You must remember always that he wanted to keep you because he loved you and – and everything has worked out for the best. If I could come in now and gather you all up into my heart I would. But,' she allowed herself just one endearment, 'my darling Gwennie, you understand now. We cannot go backwards. You have come up in the world. You cannot go backwards to where we were. The consequences would be too terrible.'

Gwenlliam's eyes glittered again in the dark. 'So, in truth, I am Miss Preston also,' and then they heard the huge doors being opened.

'Gwenlliam!' a woman's voice called, and Cordelia knew at once the voice. It was the cultured voice of the real nobility. She immediately turned away.

'Please come to the wedding,' the girl whispered back over her shoulder as she hurried towards the house and up the stone steps.

Cordelia walked quickly away in the darkness.

Fourteen

In the early, freezing, filthy morning Rillie stepped out to the Two Boars Inn and took a hackney coach to Kennington via the Elephant.

When she arrived at Cleaver-street she found to her surprise that Monsieur Roland was entertaining two coloured gentlemen: Rillie stopped just inside the door, blushed in amazement, she had never been so close to a coloured person in her life, even in the theatre. One gentleman wore a turban around his head; the other had marks and swirls carved deep into his face. Rillie was much embarrassed, turned to leave, but Monsieur Roland did not seem in the least surprised to see her; welcomed her with a graceful, polite look, indicated silently with his hand that she should sit by the window, that their business would be over. The man with the strangely marked face was leaning forward now and in a low monotone seemed to be reciting a long poem on one note. Rillie listened for some time, seemed afterwards to have nodded off; when she looked up the coloured gentlemen had just left, their farewells drifted in from the street outside.

Monsieur Roland came back from the door, icy air flowed in

with him so that Rillie shivered. 'I am so glad to see you, Rillie. Have you brought your flute?'

Rillie gave a small laugh. 'We could play together!' she said. 'But I do not have it with me.'

'I have several flutes,' said Monsieur Roland, 'although my own playing is now a little rusty. Come, I have stoked up the fire.'

'Those were – interesting gentlemen,' she said shyly.

'They have the same interests as myself,' he answered. 'The one with the turban can levitate himself from the ground in a state of meditation. Or lie on a bed of nails and be trodden upon. Or walk through fire. He is from India.'

'Oh, I am so sorry I missed part of the conversation, it would have been most interesting to me and to Cordelia. I somehow dropped off to sleep.'

Monsieur Roland smiled gently. 'Perhaps you were put to sleep. The one with the carved face is a very respected man in his own country that has lately been discovered, New Zealand. He is a *tohunga*.'

She was puzzled. 'Do you mean the man with those marks on his face made me go to sleep?' She stopped a moment. 'I – I think I could hear his voice, going on and on. Did' – she was startled at the thought: a stranger, a coloured person – 'did he mesmerise me?'

'It is not necessarily mesmerism. But it all comes from the same type of thinking. We were discussing the different ways we all practise, we are all trying to do the same thing.'

'Not mesmerism?'

'Well – finding different ways to relieve pain.'

'Pain,' said Rillie. 'I need to speak to you about Cordelia.'

When Monsieur Roland had heard the whole story he sat for some time very quietly with his head bent slightly, as if he was perhaps involved in some sort of meditation. Rillie looked about his room: there were the few stars and the mirrors, there was his suit jacket hanging on a hook, there were his overshoes.

181

Nothing was shabby exactly, everything was very tidy. She looked at his face as he sat there: strong and uncompromising, and the thick white hair. He looked like a wise old foreign duke, like paintings she had occasionally seen in art galleries, except that his cuffs were worn. She had to resist an almost overwhelming instinct to pick up one of his flutes and play for him.

At last Monsieur Roland said, 'I feel much sorrow for Cordelia. She will not see them again?'

'She feels strongly that for their sakes she should not. But she is – so terribly distressed, that is why I have come, to ask if you could, somehow, help her. And anyway,' she added stoutly, 'I think she should see her own children, they were stolen from her and it is too much to think she should honourably keep herself hidden at all times.'

'It would be a scandal if the truth were known?'

'Of course it would be a scandal! The children were born out of wedlock and are no more legitimate heirs to the Duke of Llannefydd than all those people littering London who were born to the Queen's uncles when they were young men about town!'

'It is indeed another age,' he said wryly, 'from the time when I was young and the Prince Regent set the tone with his wild evenings in his Oriental palace in Brighton with all those brightly painted rooms.' He saw Rillie's startled face. 'I was invited once,' he said. 'But I realised I was there as – entertainment. I did not go again.'

'I think the Queen and Prince Albert plan to wipe away the memory of those times altogether,' said Rillie. 'They are very staid. And Cordie and I have money now but we are only pretend ladies after all, we are certainly not really staid, we would be found out in an instant. For her children's sake we would never do.'

Monsieur Roland looked at her. 'I do not see you as a pretend lady, Rillie,' he said gravely, but smiling slightly. She was so overcome with such a compliment that she squeaked and then blushed, but Monsieur Roland was on his feet. 'I shall come back

182

to Bloomsbury with you,' he said, and they walked out into the grey, cold morning and he, with his special old-fashioned courteous manner, bowed as he gave Rillie his arm.

Monsieur Roland saw that Cordelia looked so anguished, so haggard, that it was as if she had aged ten years in a night: as if her passionate desire to see her own children was literally warring inside her head with her understanding that to do so would harm them irrevocably. 'Sit down here with me, my dear,' he said, closing the shutters and lighting several candles in his calm, deliberate manner. 'You must help me, if you want me to try to in some way relieve this pain. I cannot do it by myself, not just my energy is needed this time, but your own. If you think that this time you can let yourself be guided by me I want you to look into my eyes.' And nodding to Rillie, who sat in the far corner, he stared at Cordelia for some time, as if willing her to use her own strength and join it to his. 'I will not help you if you fight me,' he said gently, 'but I think I *can* help you.' He saw her face. 'My dear, the reason you cannot allow yourself to be mesmerised is because you think you are losing control. Think, rather, that I am freeing you to have more control over yourself.' She stared. Finally her haggard eyes agreed.

He fixed her with his own eyes for quite some time: she wanted to look away but did not, stared back at this man who she knew was trying to ease her distress. Only then, when her eyes were locked into his, did he slowly begin passing his hands across Cordelia's head and down near to, but not touching, her body; the hands passed up and down, up and down, he breathed in time to the movement of his hands but – and this was different: something else – all the time their eyes were locked together. From her corner Rillie played her flute very quietly. At last Cordelia became still: her face relaxed and her hands unclenched. And then, finally, her eyes closed.

Monsieur Roland sat beside her, not touching her, no longer

183

making the downward passes across her body, and began to talk to her very gently. Rillie only caught little snatches, something about the children and her life, longed to stop playing to hear properly what he was saying. It was extraordinary, she thought as she played, how the lines of pain on Cordelia's face smoothed away. She had known Cordelia mesmerise hysterical young women, make them somehow calm; remembered the young girl in the hospital nightdress, how they stuck nails into her, how she sang *weel about turn about* and danced. She remembered her own mother, just for a moment, saying her name. But this was something different. Cordelia did not move or sing or dance but she seemed to listen quietly to Monsieur Roland, who spoke on and on. Rillie took a breath, chose Cordelia's favourite Schubert song, and played on also, trying to send her own message of love to her friend.

And somehow, when Monsieur Roland had gone, Miss Cordelia Preston's excellent good sense, that she had inherited from the Misses Preston before her, asserted itself.

'Of course we will go to the wedding on Friday,' she said to Rillie. 'Why should we not?'

They went to Bond Street and the Strand; they dressed in clothes they had once only thought to wear on stage. They wore cloaks lined with fur. Cordelia's hat came down at a jaunty angle over her face. Rillie looked rather like an older version of the respectable young Queen, without any accoutrements of state of course, but her bonnet and her gown were not unlike a picture seen in the new sepia-tints that were beginning to be pored over with wonder in some of the new magazines. On the wedding day they mingled with part of a group from an elegant coach, swept into the chapel, found themselves good vantage points in a discreet corner halfway down the aisle. Although Cordelia's heart was beating extraordinarily fast she remained in other ways calm.

But then came the terrible moment.

The bride's family arrived.

A woman walked down the aisle. Cordelia and Rillie understood at once. She was from another world, obviously the mother of the bride: tall, stiff, proud. She was utterly elegant; diamonds shone at her throat; her eyes, as she nodded almost imperceptibly to a few people in the congregation, were cold. This was the real Lady Ellis, second cousin to the Queen. Cordelia quickly lowered her head for a moment: *how could I ever, **ever** have thought I could be part of that world?* – looked up again. Walking beside Lady Ellis was Gwenlliam, the beloved face. She was dressed in pale green with a wonderful pendant of greener emeralds about her neck. Slightly lagging behind, a short, sulky fifteen-year-old boy followed. His hair had been oiled down but jumped upwards, and he kept fingering at his tight collar. Cordelia gave small gasps, as if she could not breathe. Rillie glanced at her anxiously. Organ music sounded. Somehow, as the music swelled, Cordelia caught her breath again, and then was silent *you have to love them enough to put their lives first.* The words that somehow drifted about her brain (the words Monsieur Roland had spoken to her while she was in a trance) lay upon her, and allowed her to bear it. The organ went on with its sonorous music, ladies and gentlemen crowded into the pews, there was a great noise of rather loud voices endeavouring to remember they were in the Lord's house but failing somewhat because of the glamour of the occasion. The boy sitting in the front row stared at the stone floor, still pulling at his collar. And then suddenly there was a rustling, expectant stillness and the organ burst out its anthem.

The bride walked down the aisle, her face covered with a veil, on the arm of her grandfather, the Duke of Llannefydd, who had insisted, and on the arm of her father, Lord Morgan Ellis, who was to give her to her husband. To Rillie it was as if

185

something in Cordelia disintegrated for a moment: the body beside her began to shake. Rillie quickly put an arm around her friend: felt her shaking with passion, but whether it was the passion of love or the passion of anger, Rillie could not tell. Firmly she held Cordelia as the procession moved to the front of the church. Lord Morgan Ellis had the remnants of his once young, handsome face but the features had coarsened and reddened: there was a raddled, undone look about him. And, in the way of gentlemen of a certain size, he obviously wore stays underneath his very fine jacket. At last Rillie felt the caught breath leave Cordelia's body; the shaking stopped; she heard a long sigh beside her: *recognition*? *disappointment*? She dared not look at Cordelia as the organ played on. The old Duke, extremely short of stature, nodded and smiled as he strutted to the front of the church with a somehow malevolent air, or perhaps it was only the way the light from the high windows fell across his red face.

The groom was older but suitably handsome, and when the presiding bishop asked if anyone knew any reason for the marriage not to be ordained, not a voice was heard.

And at last the organ boomed jubilantly, another noble British wedding successfully concluded, and the large marriage party finally walked back up the aisle. Everyone (not only her mother) observed the bride: so beautiful that it made one's heart stop to look at her (beautiful like her grandmother from the rookeries of Seven Dials) as she glanced up triumphantly at her Duke.

And Cordelia saw that Gwenlliam, coming slowly behind, flicked her eyes carefully over the wedding guests, back and forth as she followed her sister up the aisle. Slowly Cordelia lifted one gloved hand.

And Gwenlliam saw Cordelia. Something in her face relaxed: *her mother had come*. Morgan pulled at his collar and stared straight ahead and Cordelia felt the words imprinted on her very soul: *You must love them enough to let them go*.

186

Cordelia and Rillie merged into the milling people outside, turned quickly towards Whitehall. Cordelia's eyes were hooded, but Rillie suddenly caught a glimpse of Monsieur Roland, wearing his best suit, disappearing down towards the Elephant.

Something was lifted from Cordelia.

That night she wept for her children in the privacy of her own room. But now she had seen them: they had become real, not hallucinations from the past. She had held Gwenlliam in her arms just once more and Gwenlliam at least knew the truth. Manon had married a Duke and was safe. Only the face of a fifteen-year-old boy intruded into her dreams, pulling at his collar as his hair stuck upwards unheroically. But one day her son, *my own son*, would be the Duke of Llannefydd: with that she had to be satisfied.

Next day she walked alone along Little Russell Street past the iron basement steps and spoke with the ghosts of her mother and her aunt and heard their pride and their laughter: *the dirty stinking rat-infested alleys of the rookeries, Hester and Kitty running away from a murder to Mr Sim the lamp-man*: these things were now far, far away.

Fifteen

Cordelia went to see Monsieur Roland. Carts and carriages splashed up black melting slush at the crossroads at the Elephant; the bottom of her cloak and her gown were covered in mud as he opened his door in Cleaver-street and ushered her inside. But she did not care about the weather as she sat in his spare, sparse room, where old stars hung from the ceiling.

'I have come to thank you,' she said. 'For what you did for me. Or – to me.'

He smiled his wise smile, produced some old pieces of wood, stoked up the fire till warm flames crackled. 'I think you must also take pride in yourself,' he said. He was silent for a moment and then he said, 'My dear, the ways of the human mind are strange and mysterious. Since the world began, these things – the things that you and I and Hester have begun to understand a little – have been practised. It is nothing new and it is presumptuous of us to think we originated such things. I have talked to men from many cultures: always a society has looked for a way to alleviate pain: physical pain of course – but as you have realised with your clients, there is another kind of pain also. I am sure in a hundred years we will still be trying to find a way.' He looked at her carefully. 'Several of my colleagues have been experimenting with these new sorts of trances. The practice has been called *hypnotism*. It is something like mesmerism as we understand it of course but the – the recipient – is more involved and must use their own energy and their own volition which then somehow works together with the magnetic energy of the exponent. You are a very strong person, Cordelia, it needed your energy as well. Do you understand me?'

'I – I think I do.'

'Because hypnotism involves making suggestions to the patient. As I said to you, I tried *not* to put my will upon yours – but to, by my will, make you aware of your own strength, your own potential, and so help you find your own capacity for dealing with your pain. I was merely suggesting to you how you might do that, helping you to find your own strength. That is all. That is not frightening. Dr Mesmer taught that the magnetic energy of the mesmerist was the only active energy: this new philosophy, this *hypnotism*, includes – and requires – the energy of the patient. I myself feel this is in very early stages of discovery and you know how adamant I am that great care be taken with these fragile things, but obviously the two philosophies are very closely related. And it seemed perhaps a way to help you through what it was necessary for you to do.'

'And – you spoke to me while I was in the trance, didn't you?'

'Yes.'

'About – about being strong enough to let the children go.'

'As I said, I was encouraging you to find your own capacity for dealing with your distress, Cordelia.'

'It was odd. I remembered, and yet did not remember.'

'Part of you remembered perhaps.'

They sat together in silence for some time, just the fire: burning and whispering and crackling. Silence, with Monsieur

Roland, was never an empty thing, but full of thoughts and nuances. Suddenly he sighed heavily. 'I care very much about our work, Cordelia, yet sometimes I fear for it also. I am – I do my best to be – a healer, not a mental manipulator and showman, like the fools we have seen. In the wrong hands the things we have learned, are learning – it is so clear to me that they could be used in a way that is dangerous. We must always – always – be very careful of such fragile power. This "hypnotism" I hope will lead us onwards but there is so much rubbish in the air. I have heard recently from America of preachers – preachers! – who have turned into mesmerists and perform in *circuses*!' It was only in defence of his profession that he ever showed anger. 'To think of pseudo-mesmerists plying their trade at funfairs with acrobats and fat ladies – and now there is another fad: they say people with psychic powers can conjure up spirits who will tap on tables and bring us messages from the dead, *mon Dieu*!'

'People will believe things to comfort themselves, I suppose,' said Cordelia.

'It is credulous,' said Monsieur Roland, but calmly now. And then after a moment he said, 'Is Rillie recovered from the disappointment of her suitor?'

Cordelia looked disconcerted at the change of subject. 'She never mentions him.'

'Not mentioning – as you know, my dear – is not the same as recovering.'

'No, of course not,' said Cordelia, somehow chastened. She had always wanted to ask Monsieur Roland if he still thought of Aunt Hester after all these years, if he dreamed of her the way Cordelia did, but there was always something in his demeanour that prevented her asking personal questions. She again had that feeling that really, they knew nothing about him at all. And yet they loved him and trusted him more than anybody else they knew in the world.

The question came out, rushed, embarrassed. 'When I was

living in Wales, Monsieur Roland, did you still, then – know Aunt Hester?'

'Of course.'

'But – I never met you, when I – when I came back to live with her before she died.'

Monsieur Roland looked down through the flickering, noisy flames for a long, long moment. She thought: *I have gone too far* and her cheeks burned, but not from the fire. And then he said: 'Cordelia, when you came back from Wales your aunt already knew that she was dying. But she knew how much you needed her then. We – said our goodbyes. We knew and understood each other well enough to do that.' Cordelia stared at him, and then looked away. *And I thought she had not known about that kind of love. Like I thought about Rillie. So engrossed in my own life and pain I did not understand other people's.* She sat in silence, and so did he.

'So – when I told you about my life in Wales, my children, you knew of course.'

'I knew. But I felt very glad that you felt able to tell me yourself.'

Another silence.

'I wish you could have seen Gwenlliam,' she said at last. 'She is so like Aunt Hester as I remember her when I was young.'

'Yes,' said Monsieur Roland. After a moment he went on, 'It seemed to me an almost superhuman strength was required of you that day. I took the liberty of attending the wedding myself in case you were in need of assistance' – he saw her startled look – 'but you managed very well without me.' He was smiling. 'I was there, in a dark corner. And I got immense pleasure in seeing remembrances of Hester and Kitty. The bride was very beautiful, as Kitty was. The boy Morgan has something of you about him – I could not put my finger on it – he does not look like you but he is like you.' He noticed, or did not notice, a small tear that ran down her cheek, she brushed it away as if she did not notice either. 'And Gwenlliam – Gwenlliam does, indeed,

191

look as Hester looked. It was interesting – and strange – to see her. I am glad I was there.'

'You are always there, Monsieur Roland,' said Cordelia slowly. And then they were silent again.

She stood at last, took up her cloak. 'I believe,' she said, 'that if – if anything important happens in Gwenlliam's life – in all of their lives – *she felt the old familiar pain, but went with it, like a wave* – I will, now, hear about it. And although it is so painful to me to know there is so much of their lives that I may not share, I have at least seen them all again.'

'Yes,' he said. 'They are real now, Cordelia. They are no longer dreams from the past.'

'That Prince Albert is making a big fuss about Christmas,' said Rillie, pointing to the engraving picture of the fir tree decorated with little candles in the *Chronicle*. It was Sunday afternoon, snowing again outside, almost beautiful falling softly on to the already white garden, yet they knew that not half a mile away the snow turned to filth almost before it reached the ground. They had fires in the rooms upstairs to keep the old ladies warm, and a fire in their sitting room; Cordelia had done all the fires; Rillie and Nellie had made a huge meal of beef and potatoes; Regina had kept them entertained with her newspaper readings.

'But you read this one, Rillie,' Regina had said, handing Rillie a newspaper. 'It's a proper report, not a broadsheet – this is from *The Times* that Monsieur Roland left here the other day, I didn't know proper newspapers could be that int'resting, there's even a war in that place far away called Afghanistan, did you know that? I thought we only fought the French – anyway, anyway, go on,' and old Mrs Spoons, leaning on the table, nodded her head in pleasure at Rillie's voice, as if she might have known this was her daughter. Rillie read with suitable dramatic inter-pretation, because she could not help it, because she had been an actress.

192

'On Tuesday morning last an attempt was made to murder a female named Elizabeth Magnus who acts as a barmaid at the Auction Mart Tavern, in the city, by a young fellow who is employed as potboy in that establishment. It appears that, after discharging a pistol loaded with ball at his victim, which perforated her stays and after passing through her right side, lodged in her clothes, the assassin endeavoured to cut his own throat . . .'

Rillie shook her head at Regina, and then concluded:

'. . . but was arrested before completing his purpose. It is said that slighted love was the cause of this fierce attempt. The female is expected to recover.'

Cordelia had snorted with laughter. Regina then wished to point out the advertisements for Treatises on the Enlarged Stomach, but Rillie – laughing also nevertheless – ushered the old ladies back upstairs for their post-prandial nap. Now Rillie, talking of this new idea of 'Christmas trees', was surrounded by, and immersed in, not only *The Times* and the *Chronicle* but the *Morning Post* and the *News of the World*. She no longer had to read such things in the circulating library, could afford to buy as many as she wished.

'I expect they do things like that to trees where he comes from,' said Cordelia.

'Prince Albert? Yes, well he's a foreigner of course, but shall we do it?'

'What, do a tree like that?' Cordelia stared at the engraving in the newspaper. 'Put candles on, you mean?'

'Why not?'

'We'll set fire to the house!'

'No we won't, Cordie!'

'Where are you going to get a tree from?'

'I can find a tree,' said Rillie firmly. 'It'll be cosy.'

'Do you still mind about Mr Williams, Rillie?' said Cordelia suddenly.

Rillie looked down quickly, pleated her skirt, that way she had. After some moments she said, but not looking up, 'I mind a *bit*. I wanted to have a someone to be mine, even though I'm old. Don't you wish it, Cordie, sometimes?'

Cordelia's face closed up. 'What for?' she said. 'After all.'

'Oh you know, Cordie, cosy, like I said. And also – like a mirror.'

'A *mirror*?'

'Never mind,' said Rillie quickly, and just then they heard the knocker outside. They caught each other's eye: not a crisis of some young lady, on a Sunday? Rillie started to get up. 'Nellie's off seeing her brother.'

'I'll go,' said Cordelia. She automatically picked up the flat-iron as she walked to the door, they kept it handy still.

On the steps outside stood a short fifteen-year-old boy, his slicked-down hair already sticking up from his head. Snow cascaded down as he stood there. For a moment she could not speak, thought she was in a dream, that this was a dream.

'I read Gwennie's journal,' he said in a voice that changed key at least twice in that short sentence. The snow fell on to his hair.

'Come in, Morgan,' said Miss Cordelia Preston, at last, to her son. In the hall, where she replaced the iron, he removed his cloak, nervously shying away from her when she tried to help him, his cheeks red.

Rillie miraculously appeared, bringing normality; the *Chronicle* and *The Times* were under her arm. 'Hello, Morgan,' she said, as if he visited often, 'how nice to see you again, I'm just going upstairs to read the *Chronicle* to my mother,' and she bustled upwards.

'Come in, Morgan,' said Cordelia again, and led him into the warm room and the fire and the scattered newspapers. He did not look about him, kept his head down rather, sat where directed, said nothing.

'Does Gwenlliam know that you have come here?'

'No.'

'Does anybody know?'

'No.'

Silence, only the fire spitting and crackling. Outside the heavy white flakes still fell on to the garden and on to the small statue of the angel.

She had a miraculous inspiration: *he likes reading newspapers.* 'Read the newspapers, Morgan. I am just going to make some tea.' He looked slightly startled.

'Where are the servants?'

'We do have a maid, Nellie, but she has gone to see her brother and I am perfectly capable of making Indian tea. Would you like some?'

'Is there cordial?' Again the voice changed key.

'I think there is cordial. Rillie's mother likes cordial.'

In the kitchen downstairs she began to shake. She breathed in and out deeply but could not stop the feeling that she was in a dream, could not cohere her thoughts, could not think, made the tea, found cordial.

Upstairs Morgan was indeed reading a newspaper, or pretending to read a newspaper, the *News of the World*, something about a murder in Clapham. She placed the cordial beside him. He gulped it down. She tried not to stare at the beloved, remembered face; as she poured tea from the pot she advised herself that if this was a dream she would have woken by now. 'Do you always read your sister's journal?'

'Yes. And her letters. And Manon's letters. They keep things from me.'

'Why do they do that?'

'They think I am peculiar. I shout when I get headaches. Last week I fell over. I am not permitted to fall over in front of the Duke.'

'Headaches?' She tried to keep anxiety out of her voice.

'Not like when I was a boy. These are new. They are different.'

'What do you mean – you fell over?' This was unbearable.

He shrugged. It was like a small pony shaking its shoulders. And then at last he looked at her. 'What I remember most is you took my headaches away. But now you look old.'

She tried to smile. 'You look different too, Morgan.'

'I saw the advertisement for the tree children. I was in Cardiff. I always read the advertisements. Gwennie told me I was being fanciful. If I was not careful to always read her journal I would never have known I was right after all.'

'I see.'

'They told us you were dead.'

'So I have heard.'

'The journal says we are illegitimate.' She did not speak. 'I know what illegitimate means.'

This terrible mess. I have to stop this terrible unfolding.

'Nevertheless, it is something nobody knows about you. Your father has kept it hidden, and I have – never found you until now. I think Gwenlliam should not perhaps have written of that in her journal. It is important that people do not know of it.'

'Why?'

She leant forward but spoke very gently. 'Morgan, you are fifteen years old, I am sure you know very well why. Your papa has done the best for you. One day you will be the Duke of Llannefydd.'

'I do not want to be the Duke of Llannefydd.'

She was astounded. 'Why ever not?'

'I was sent away to school, but I hated it. There is only one thing that I am good at. I want to be a painter.'

'A *painter*?'

'Yes.'

She thought quickly. 'You could still be a painter.'

'The Duke says I may not paint. The Duke says I must do Greek. And Latin.'

'I see.'

196

'Have you seen the paintings of the ships and the sea by Mr Turner?'

'Yes.'

'I can paint like that. I always think of the sea.' She had got used now to the way the childish voice broke sometimes when he spoke, and the sound of a man emerged. He stood abruptly. She stood at once also, somehow alarmed. 'I have brought you a painting.' She followed him as he went into the hall, followed him as he returned with something that he had retrieved from his cloak. On the table he rolled out a painting of the Gwyr coast below the castle ruins. Cordelia gasped, in recognition and pain at what she saw. It was a painting of their past.

She could not speak, turned her head away sharply for a moment. He smoothed the painting with his hand, stared at it, waited. She swallowed several times before she was able to speak.

'When did you paint that?'

'After I had read Gwennie's journal.'

'When did you go back to Gwyr?'

'Never.'

'But – you were only five.'

Silence in the room, only the fire. She stared at the painting.

'What is a mesmerist?' he said.

Slowly she sat down again. 'If you read the newspapers you have probably read about mesmerism.'

'I thought it was for hospitals. So that people can have their legs chopped off.'

'It is used in hospitals, yes.'

'Do you go to hospitals?'

'I do sometimes.'

'Does it work?' The intense little face.

'I *know* it works. But many doctors do not believe in it. Sometimes I go to the London Mesmerism Infirmary. The doctors who work there understand that we can put people into a mesmeric

197

trance, and then it seems that they do not feel pain in the same way.'

'Is it a trick?'

'I do not believe that it is a trick.'

'Did you use mesmerism on my head when I was little?'

She was startled. 'I am not sure,' she said slowly, 'but perhaps some – some energy of mine went into your head and helped you.' She did not want to embarrass him by calling it love. She remembered how at first she had held the heads of the people who came to her in that way, a way of remembering her son. This boy. 'You may not remember that your Great-Aunt Hester was a mesmerist. Perhaps – perhaps I inherited something from her.'

'What was that song?'

'What song?' Yet she knew. He waited. Finally she managed to sing the first words:

> When that I was and a little tiny boy
> With a heigh ho, the wind and the rain . . .

His face stared at her with such passion that she felt as if he hit her. His words rushed out. 'Can I live here and paint?'

The question took her so by surprise that she looked blank, assumed she had misheard. 'What did you say?'

'Can I live here and paint?' This time she was so startled that she stood up again at once, saw dark shadows in her head: *I have to stop this terrible unfolding.* She shook herself. 'Your papa—'

He burst out, a child still. 'The Duke of Llannefydd is like a fat pig!' She tried to hide her shock. 'He is the most horrible person I have ever met, he is a bully and he thinks he is God! God of the pigs!' he said and gave a half-laugh. 'Papa is scared of the Duke, scared as if he was still a *child*! Did you know that? And the Duke cares only for Manon, he spoils her and he insisted on leading the dancing with her at the wedding – he looked

198

stupid, him so short and Manon so tall – and he fell over while he was dancing with her – and he looked more like a pig than ever, with his legs in the air, and now he can't walk, or get up the stairs, and he lives and sleeps in the drawing room at Grosvenor Square with poultices on his legs and drinks whisky and it stinks in there!'

She tried to take in such an unlikely noble picture; for a moment she was silent. And then she said, 'I expect it was his fear of his father that made your papa keep us hidden away on Gwyr.'

'Does he know Gwennie saw you?'

'I – I do not know, Morgan. I do not think so. It was important that she did not tell him.'

'I think he does know. I've been looking at him since I read Gwennie's journal. I see him every day, and I think something has happened, I think perhaps he guesses and he is frightened – maybe he reads Gwennie's journal too. He is frightened and always drinking, imagine if the Duke and Lady Rosamund – we call her the Ice Queen – knew! Then what would happen?' Her heart leapt in fear at what she was hearing, at everything unravelling. 'I think Lady Rosamund would kill him if he knew about you, that you were still alive. She would not be able to bear it, the shame of it! All she ever talks about is 'honour' and 'family'. And the Duke would rise up with his poultices and come round here with a shotgun! If he knew we were illegitimate.'

'*You must not keep saying that word, Morgan!*' She had no idea if he was exaggerating, she felt panic upon panic rising in her heart. 'You are your father's children, he has accepted you as such. You live in his house. You must not talk like that.' A terrible thought struck her. 'Does Manon know?'

'She is too busy with her Duke.'

'There would be no Duke if it – if our story was known.'

'I do not care at all!' And then he did smile properly, for the first time. 'And I do not care if we are illegitimate.' Cordelia did not smile back. She could have hit him.

199

'Morgan. Listen to me! It is all very well for you to be so – nonchalant. But I could not have – if your papa had left all of us – brought you up safely. I had no money of my own. It was for the best in many ways that he took responsibility for you. If we had all been left we would have been in the workhouse long ago!'

'This house does not look like the workhouse. Does Papa give you money?'

She supposed her own son was allowed to ask her such a question, but it felt odd to have to answer to anyone. 'No,' she said at last. 'My work, mine and Rillie's, has made us – prosper. There is no money from your father.'

'Can I live here and paint?' he asked for the third time. 'We could go to America!' and there was a tremor of memory, *their America, the land of carpets and honey and strange fruit*. She answered him violently.

'No, Morgan! It would not be allowed.'

'You could speak to Papa.'

Her heart sank. 'Morgan, I would help you in any way that was possible, but I have not spoken to your father for many years. There is no way in the world that he could possibly acknowledge my existence: you are fifteen, you are old enough in the ways of the world to understand that. And,' she shrugged, 'I do not wish to speak to your father. I do not even wish to see him. Once – long ago – he forbade me to have any contact with you at all.'

'But why ever do you have to do what he says? He lied, he said you were dead. I want you to take away my headaches.'

She froze. *He must not blackmail me like this.* 'I have to keep out of your life for your sake,' she said. 'For all of you.' He stared at her, and his face closed up. She felt his disappointment in her, like a blow.

'I have to go now,' he said and made to leave the room.

Only her son, only Morgan, could have persuaded her. 'I will write him a letter,' she said weakly. 'I will try. And perhaps there will be some way I can help the headaches – perhaps there is something I can do that will – at least relieve them.'

She again followed him out into the hallway, he put his cloak about his shoulders, but childishly, getting caught up. Suddenly she was herself again. She put her hand upon his arm, would not let him shake it off, spoke firmly. 'Morgan, this is not just about your future, it is about Manon and Gwenlliam too. Frankly I do not believe your father will acknowledge any letter from me. But I will write to him about your wish to paint, and about your headaches, if you give me your solemn word that you will not mention any of this. If you do not agree I will not write.' He ducked his head briefly. She saw that she would have to take that for his solemn word. And she saw that he was terrified that, having put her hand on his arm, she might try to kiss him.

'Goodbye, Morgan,' said Cordelia and her son bowed rather awkwardly at the door.

'You can keep the painting,' he said, and then he ran down the steps into the snow.

After he had disappeared into Great Russell Street Cordelia felt something; stared up at the heavy sky.

Again. It seemed as if a dark shadow flew across the house in Bedford Place.

'He was like a rather small Beast of Hell,' she said ruefully to Rillie later, most unwillingly writing a short note to be delivered to Grosvenor Square. 'No good at all can come of this!' But Rillie saw that nevertheless Cordelia's cheeks were flushed and her eyes were bright: she could not help it: she had seen her son. 'Perhaps mesmerism could help his headaches, Rillie?' she said.

'Perhaps it could!' said Rillie roundly. And Rillie saw that Cordelia's eyes kept turning to the painting in incredulity. 'It is – extraordinary – that he can remember that,' said Rillie.

'Yes. It is extraordinary.'

'I wonder how he would like living in a house full of women?' said Rillie.

'Hell's Teeth!' said Cordelia, suddenly envisaging Morgan and Mrs Spoons and Regina all in one room. 'Pour the port!'

Sixteen

They did not expect him once the letter was sent, yet they expected him.

'One would not want to be Lady Ellis,' said Rillie firmly the next evening, by their fire. 'He has aged a lot.' She had finished the day's accounts; she had somehow, true to her word, acquired a small fir tree.

Cordelia actually laughed. 'One would not want to be Lady Ellis,' she agreed smoothly. 'I was so lucky.' She drank her port. Rillie peered up from tying tiny candles to the boughs of the tree, to see if Cordelia meant it. 'Don't let me anywhere near the flat-iron,' said Cordelia sharply. 'When he comes. If he comes.' The curtains were open still, they saw a bright chill moon shining on to their garden, on to the angel who guarded them.

'I am sure he will wear his stays,' said Rillie after a moment, looking up at Cordelia again. 'How that very light blue colour suits you, Cordie, try and wear that gown if he sends a message that he is coming. And you have the advantage, you have seen him and his red face. But he has not seen you, and you have kept your looks and your shape. What a disadvantage that will be for Lord Morgan Ellis!'

'I have to go through with this if he does come, but don't let me anywhere near the flat-iron,' repeated Cordelia. She watched Rillie with the candles. 'Don't you set fire to this house!'

'I'm only going to light them on Christmas Day like it said in the paper.'

Cordelia laughed. 'The tree will be dead by then!'

'No it won't! It's only a few days! I will give it water.'

They heard the knocker.

They heard Nellie running up the stairs from the basement.

When they heard the remembered voice at the door, Cordelia – for all her laughter and anger and disdain – turned white, like a winding sheet. *So soon?*

'No, I cannot do it,' she whispered. 'I will kill him,' and would have slipped out the French doors and into the garden, but Rillie held her.

'It is something – unfinished, Cordie,' she said quickly. 'And – you do look beautiful, in that light gown, I told you.' Cordelia seemed not to hear. Rillie shook her slightly. 'It's for yourself as well as Morgan, Cordie. And for Gwenlliam and for Manon – *you have to do it*. I will be next door. You only need to bang on the wall.'

Rillie left the room. She could be heard speaking to Ellis coldly, giving Cordelia a moment to stand by the long windows, looking out at the dark garden and the bright, bright moon. Cordelia breathed deeply, almost as if she was mesmerising herself. She had the advantage after all, as Rillie said: he had not seen her: the front of her hair was white, as it turned after her visit to the lawyer in the Strand, but she stood there, beautiful still, and graceful, and waited for the man who had changed her life. And who then paid for her life, and her children, with two hundred guineas.

Ellis was accompanied by the perfume of the Macassar oil he used on his thinning hair, and the smell of whisky.

Cordelia turned into the room at last but said nothing; saw that Ellis was startled as he looked at her; he looked away, looked at her again. His face was very red. She saw that, stays or not, he was holding himself very upright.

For almost a minute they stood there beside the uncurtained windows and could not speak: the crumbling stone of the ancient castle and the bright wild flowers that danced in the wind and the deceptive, uncertain sea: they were there suddenly in the silent room in Bloomsbury: memory, loss: the days that were gone.

And Morgan Ellis suddenly, terribly, understood that the days that were gone could never be retrieved; that there was nothing and no money, not even kindness, that could bring back the days when he was young and beautiful and in love. And that sudden knowledge made a small, distressed sound in the throat of a man who had never in his life dared to look back, for fear of what he would see.

Rillie in her little office went through the accounts, arranged to pay bills, every nerve tuned to any sound from the room next door. But it was quiet. At last Rillie relaxed. There was no shouting at all: surely they would come to some amicable arrangement. For the children's sake. Rillie dreamed of Cordelia as some sort of benign fairy godmother to her own children. A young boy in the house might be good for all of them, if that was what they agreed. Cordelia would be happy. And for one brief moment Rillie allowed herself to think of her own little boy, of Emmanuel. He would have been nearly fifteen also.

The clock ticked. The clock chimed. Almost an hour had passed. But – they had a lifetime to settle, after all. Rillie went quickly upstairs to see to her mother and Regina. When she came down again the door to the sitting room was still closed. Something about the stillness at last began to unnerve her. She fidgeted, not wanting to interrupt: perhaps they had become enamoured of each other again and her entrance would be of great embarrassment to them all. At last her prudence got the better of her good manners. She knocked gently on the door. There was no reply. She opened the door and went in.

The unlit fir tree shadowed as the curtains at each end of the French doors billowed inwards. The French doors opened out into the darkness. The room was empty.

TWO

broadside: all the guns on one side of a ship; their simultaneous discharge; a critical attack; a sheet of paper printed usually on one side only containing a proclamation, a ballad, or other popular matter

broadsheet: a sheet of paper printed usually on one side only containing a proclamation, a ballad, or other popular matter

Seventeen

GOOD PEOPLE ALL I PRAY ATTEND!
UNTO THESE LINES THAT HERE ARE PENNED!
THE HORROR OF THIS ATROCIOUS DEED!
ENOUGH TO MAKE YOUR HEART TO BLEED!
BLOOD AND GORE LAY ALL AROUND . . .

The street balladeers sang loudly and with delight: singing loudly in public had been ostensibly against the law for years under the old Vagrancy Act but the sale of songs like this was the stuff of small fortunes. The printers and the balladeers; the writers of the penny pamphlets and the penny broadsheets and the penny broadsides; all these chancers could not, frankly, believe their luck, could not churn out information (real, or imagined) quickly enough, for this was what they dreamed of: this was what sold more than any other occurrence: Murder And The Nobility. Little printing machines all over London worked through the night. Thousands of the penny papers appeared like magic with *NOBLE MURDER* writ large. They circulated all over the country: having speedily consumed their material from the respectable newspapers, they embellished it as far as they dared. And more of Regina's particular favourites, those anonymous little pamphlets entitled *DREADFUL MURDERS,* appeared like magic, price one penny, thus:

THE AUTHENTIC NARRATIVE
OF THE SHOCKING MURDER

Of Morgan, LORD ELLIS, heir to the DUKE OF LLANNEFYDD, One of the most HORRID instances of Crime recorded In the Criminal Calendar of our Country; and including Details of the GRISLY discovery last night of the BODY of the noble lord above.

The body was hardly cold, but that did not deter the balladeers and the penny journalists. The respectable newspapers were also a-quiver but slightly more circumspectly and the lettering much smaller, but the news was the same: SON AND HEIR OF THE DUKE OF LLANNEFYDD FOUND BRUTALLY MURDERED IN BLOOMSBURY SQUARE.

The *Morning Advertiser* thundered immediately:

The terrible Murder of a member of the Nobility in a not unrespectable part of the City must be dealt with swiftly by a Police Force that has been unfortunately inefficient in recent previous cases of this kind. The streets of our City must be made safe. Let us fervently hope that the recent formation of the Detective Division in the Metropolitan Police will this time bring a Swift conclusion to this matter that fills all right-thinking People with Horror.

The lineage of the ancient Llannefydd seat of Wales was everywhere discussed over the breakfast table: in Mayfair of course, but with just as much interest in Whitechapel and Clapham and even the rookeries of St Giles'. Were Lord and Lady Ellis known as the doers of any Good Works? (Lords and ladies had been turning to good works lately as a way of disassociating themselves from their earlier, somewhat rakish,

210

antecedents.) Nobody could quite remember: had there been missionary work somewhere, paid for by them? Information, and misinformation, was being churned out by every printing press in London but some facts were incontrovertible: the deceased was Morgan, Lord Ellis, aged 55, heir to the Duke of Llannefydd; the widow was Lady Rosamund Ellis, daughter of the Duke of Arbotham and related to Her Majesty; one of the daughters had, only weeks before, become the new Duchess of Trent.

THE BLOOD IT LAY UPON THE SQUARE!
BLOOD AND GUTS LAY EVERYWHERE!
A NOBLE LORD, A CRUEL NIGHT!
THE HEAVENS WEPT AT SUCH A SIGHT!

called the patterers all along Oxford Street.

The noble family were spared the agony of appearing in public. A steward from the Duke of Llannefydd's household confirmed the identity of the deceased before the post-mortem was carried out by two surgeons from Guy's Hospital, who had been summoned to a small upstairs room at the police watch-house at Bow Street. The body of the deceased (the newspapers soon informed the populace) had been found by a passing footman after midnight in Bloomsbury Square. There were contusions on the dead man's face so there must have been a fight, but the death was caused by multiple knife thrusts to his body and a great deal of blood lay all about. The said footman had been on business for another duke the previous evening and his every movement could be nobly spoken for, so, no stabber he. There was some confusion as to what kind of murder weapon had been seized: one of the broadsides accounted it a Napoleonic sword, another a shilling knife from St Giles'. A known vagrant had been found asleep – 'inebriatedly unconscious' said *The Times*

– in a far corner of the square behind some bushes and it was said that the aforementioned, although disputed, murder weapon had been found not far from his prone form. He was of course immediately taken into custody: vagrancy was an offence (particularly round Bloomsbury Square, which was considered more salubrious than the streets further eastward). Whether he was being held as a murderer or a drunkard at this stage had not yet been made clear, but the odds for the vagrant did not look very favourable, either way.

The curtains remained drawn at the huge house in Grosvenor Square and the big front door unopened; a phalanx of three constables guarded the entrance from intrusion by the curious. Such impenetrable silence within: such closed doors; such dark rooms, all curtains drawn; such wealth and power and the sudden chiming of clocks. And in the large, dark downstairs drawing room that smelt of poultices, and medicines, and alcohol (which may, or may not, have been medicinal also), the fractious, ill-tempered, short colossus: the Duke of Llannefydd. The small figure of the Duke was apoplectic as he lay there, confined to a large sofa: the shame, the scandal, the loss, and the inconvenience. The funeral could not be arranged, for Lord Morgan Ellis was not yet released to them; the body was still with the surgeons and the police.

Finally, later that cold, shocked day, a police inspector and a constable were reluctantly admitted through the front door in Grosvenor Square; they introduced themselves as Inspector Rivers of the new detective division of the Metropolitan Police, and Constable Forrest, his assistant. The Inspector carried a small, unimportant-looking parcel, something wrapped in newspaper.

I always look for the grief, the Inspector had said casually to his man (a rather eccentric command: the constable had expected, rather, to be sent to look for footprints or torn pieces of clothing rather than grief, but Inspector Rivers was an old hand at detection and much admired among the constables). The two policemen endured the barely concealed disdain of the presiding footmen while they endeavoured to speak to the other servants: there were at least twenty, the interviews were somewhat perfunctory: Lord Morgan Ellis had gone out last night before seven o'clock, that was all they knew; if there were family secrets they were not being spoken of. The policemen then endured the abuse of the Duke himself from his malodorous bed in the drawing room.

'You are indisposed, your Lordship?' enquired Inspector Rivers politely from the doorway of the room and was shouted at louder for his impudent concern; this outburst was followed by the threat of the officers' dual expulsion from the Metropolitan Police Force overseen by the Duke personally if the body of Lord Ellis was kept any longer while one of the finest families in the land danced to the tune of rascally surgeons. And so on. The Inspector and his constable stood stoically in the doorway. When the Duke finally paused for breath and refreshment, waving for whisky, Inspector Rivers entered further into the drawing room and asked if he might speak briefly to members of the family.

'God's Truth! Get out of here!' As he cursed, the Duke indicated impatiently to a footman for his whisky to be larger. He considered himself above the law, and with nothing to say to the common men who had the temerity to stand on the peripheries of his temporary bedroom. Perhaps his appalling rudeness was grief: who could say?

The silence in the room went on. It was very cold; the fire in the huge fireplace spat at the room rather than heating the medicinal air. The Inspector and the Constable observed the paintings on the walls: battles, castles, an elaborate portrait of William IV (as if the new young Queen had never come to the throne). Suddenly they became aware of small movement: a young boy, short, fair-haired, sidling in silently, making for the far corner of the curtained room where he quickly bent over a chessboard where only a small candle-lamp lit his game. This must be the boy Morgan, the new Lord Ellis, direct heir now to the Duke of Llannefydd. The old man had not even noticed his arrival: the police officers did not draw attention to it.

'I do beg your pardon, your Lordship,' said the Inspector finally, 'to be troubling you at this most grievous time, and I do assure you that the body of your son will be returned to you for burial at the first possible moment. In the mean time I am afraid I must, in a matter of such seriousness, ask your permission to speak to your daughter-in-law and her children as well as to yourself.' The Inspector could tell, by the angle of the chess-playing boy's head, that he was listening avidly.

'There is absolutely no reason for you to speak to anybody, and why you should speak even to me and waste my time I cannot imagine! I am ill! Look at me, look at me! I cannot even walk! Why is that fellow standing by the door?'

'As I explained, he is my assistant, sir, Constable Forrest.' From his bed the Duke flashed a look of pure malevolence at the young man, so that Constable Forrest (the Inspector saw) flinched slightly. But stood his ground. Inspector Rivers, imperceptibly, sighed. In his younger days as a new constable the Inspector had held the nobility in great esteem, had looked upon them with awe. He no longer felt able to do that in many circumstances: he had long ago understood that most – not all but most – of the nobility saw people like himself as cut-out cardboard figures, not real people. He did not demean his own profession by thinking the same of the nobility: *Do they not bleed?* he would say to himself, misquoting Mr Shakespeare. This short, fat man in front of him now, lying there with poulticed legs and bandaged knees, drinking whisky and swearing, seemed like something from the stage rather than from real life, but the Inspector had, over the years, seen clearly that the nobility lived so differently that they could not conceive that rules that applied to the general populace also applied to them. Inspector Rivers had also, over the years, developed perhaps his greatest aptitude: an extraordinary patience, which had been honed by his interest in small miracles: the slow development and emergence of butterflies from the chrysalises that hung under dark leaves in his small back garden. This interest had intensified once his daughters had taken up the artistic fashion of many young ladies of the day: the pinning of beautiful butterflies for ever on to a glass-covered board, which they then insisted be hung in the hallway of their house in Marylebone. (The Inspector often regarded the pinned butterflies with silent regret.) The slower and more unobtrusive the emergence of the young winged creatures, therefore, the better it was for them. So the Inspector stood quietly, spoke with the same unobtrusiveness. 'Your Lordship, you surely understand that we must try to ascertain your son's movements last evening.'

'The Commissioners will be hearing from me about your quite unwarranted intrusion. I am the Duke of Llannefydd, not some common suburban . . .' he paused for a suitable word, *'villa-owner!'* Inspector Rivers stood firmly, silent but immovable; finally, swearing loudly again about intrusion in a house of grief, the Duke lunged at the bell pull. One of the urbane, disdainful footmen disappeared to do the ducal bidding. The Duke drummed his fingers, and then snapped them, and from somewhere in this large room with its dark tables and upright sofas and formidable chairs another footman materialised, poured another morning whisky. In the far corner of the room the chess-playing boy was perfectly still, as if his immobility would make him invisible.

Constable Forrest stood stoically by the door, observing everything. He had never been inside a house like this in his life: he was conscious of disappointment: he had assumed something different, something more dashing and magnificent; found himself thinking with sudden longing of his two rented rooms in Vauxhall and his wife and their baby boy and their joy; they had painted one of the rooms and their fire flickered warm on clean brown walls.

When Lady Rosamund Ellis finally entered the room it was as if a further chill entered also: the cold whiteness of the face almost shone above the blackness of the gown. She was so pale, and her face was so haughty and expressionless, that to the two policemen she seemed like some sort of intimidating waxwork. She was followed by her two daughters, and somehow the chess-playing boy slid along the wall again as they entered, tried unobtrusively to make himself one of the group, but his mother flicked her eyes at him quickly, missing nothing. The three young people stood pale with lowered heads. *Is this the grief I should be looking for?* thought Constable Forrest. He knew their ages, had checked them for the Inspector: seventeen, sixteen and fifteen. Lady Rosamund did not take her hawk eye away from her children for a moment; they surely must have felt the look of white ice.

The older girl – this would be the new Duchess of Trent, extremely beautiful even *in extremis* – was in paroxysms of grief that she could barely control: the old Duke glanced at her in some kind of embarrassment but the Constable saw the mother look at her with severity: the nobility were never seen to weep, of course. The middle girl appeared to have been weeping also, her eyes were very swollen, but she stood there now, contained. The chess-playing boy stared at the carpet, but he seemed odd in some way, his head kept moving, he stretched at his neck, as if he was suddenly in some sort of pain. The Constable looked at him doubtfully. The three young people made a very sorry little group, which of course – the Constable understood – was natural in the circumstances. The boy seemed to be in some real distress, he rubbed at the side of his head; Constable Forrest glanced at his mother, but if she acknowledged this distress she said nothing.

The Inspector's questions to the gathered family were brief and to the point, and the required information was quickly elicited: Lord Ellis had had dinner with the family at about six and then he went out. They had not seen him again. They had all been in Grosvenor Square when the news came, except for Lady Manon who was interrupted at a ball by a servant.

'You and your husband came here at once, Lady Manon?'

The beautiful eyes brimmed with tears. 'My – my husband did not come with me. I came alone.' The tears poured down her cheeks, her sister clasped her hand tightly as if willing her to stop. Constable Forrest's kind heart suffered. *Is that the way the nobility do things? Make her come alone?*

'Lady Rosamund,' said the Inspector, 'did you perhaps know where your husband was going after dinner?'

With what seemed an extraordinary effort to make herself speak, she answered him in a sharp, barely polite manner. 'I am not my husband's keeper,' she said.

'It would help us enormously to deal with this most terrible tragedy quickly if anybody could tell us anything at all about what plans your husband might have had.'

It was only then that she actually looked at him for the first time, looked at Inspector Rivers. The detective division of the Metropolitan Police was new, but the delicate art of detection was not, not entirely, and he saw in her eyes something so naked, so strong, that despite himself, despite his experience, he looked away for a moment. *That is venom, not grief*. The room would have been silent had the fire not spat and had the Duke's breathing not been so harsh. The moment went on. There would be nothing more.

'I am so very sorry to have troubled you all,' said Inspector Rivers, 'in a time that must be so difficult for you to bear, but you of course understand that we must try to find out how Lord Morgan Ellis was killed. Just one thing.' For they were all here now and he could show them. He unwrapped the small parcel in his hand, felt the surprise, heard the involuntary gasp in the room. The dagger was the most beautiful object he himself had ever held. The blade was silver and sleek and fine, but it was the handle, the jewelled handle, that caught them, that shone even in the dim light of the curtained room: the jewels on the handle glittered in the lamplight: rubies there, and diamonds. *Not your common or garden ordinary murder weapon*, thought Constable Forrest in amazement, staring from the doorway at

217

the sparkling, shining, beautiful object lying there in Inspector Rivers' hand.

'Where did you get that!' The Duke's voice.

'Do you recognise it, your Lordship?'

'I do not *recognise* it. But that is a piece of most particular and valuable antiquity, obviously. Look at it! Look at it, man! It is priceless. How has such a thing come to be in your possession?' The Duke wanted to see it better, hold it, his hand itched to hold such a beautiful thing; he saw the rubies clearly but could not easily move from the sofa, could not step forward and snatch such a thing, which he would otherwise have done with no compunction. 'How is it in your possession?' he repeated, frustration in his voice.

'This is the murder weapon, your Lordship.'

'Impossible, of course!'

'It was found in the bushes in the square, near where the body lay, covered in your son's blood.' There was an audible sound now in the room, perhaps of sorrow, perhaps of horror. 'I am sorry, these things must be said. It has been accepted by the surgeons and the coroner as the murder weapon.'

Even the beautiful girl had been shocked into attention, the tears froze. But suddenly the maternal presence reared. 'These children are surely not needed further to hear these unspeakable things,' Lady Rosamund said imperiously.

'Do you know this object?' he asked of the young people conversationally.

The girls stared still in horrified astonishment, shook their heads slightly at the dagger shining in the hand of the policeman. It glittered. *It had killed their father*. There was only silence and breathing now, in the room. 'We have lived mostly in Wales,' the middle girl explained at last, as if someone must speak, but her voice shook at what they had seen. 'We do not know such – things.' The boy said nothing, seemed to hold his head now as if he was in terrible pain: it was most unnerving to watch him for, as well as the pain, his eyes shone sharp as he stared at the dagger.

Finally Inspector Rivers bowed slightly to the young people. 'Thank you for your time. I am so sorry about your father.' Lady Rosamund looked at them without speaking. They filed out of the huge, chilly drawing room in silence. The dagger still shone in the Inspector's hand.

He spoke once more. 'The body will be returned as soon as possible but you must know there will have to be an inquest,' he said. 'And I must also inform you, your Lordship, that in these sad but violent circumstances the law will very likely require you to appear at the inquest.'

'Me!' He was outraged.

'You were one of the last people to see Lord Ellis alive.'

The extraordinary voice of Lady Rosamund cut through the air before the Duke could reply.

'I was one of the last people to see my husband alive,' she said. 'I will attend the inquest.'

'I hardly think that you would be expected to—'

'I will attend,' she said. But the Duke of Llannefydd was hardly listening. In the ensuing silence he said an extraordinary thing. 'I want that dagger,' he said. 'I will buy it.' He stared again at the jewelled handle. The Inspector tried to hide his surprise.

'This weapon is not, for the moment, for sale, your Lordship.' And Inspector Rivers turned to go at last, carefully wrapping the dagger again in the newspaper.

'Constable.' Inspector Rivers presumed Lady Rosamund meant himself, stopped, turned back. He saw that she was deliberating between speaking and not speaking, she bit her white lip. 'I will buy it.' The Duke made a sound of outrage; the Inspector tried to hide his astonishment, looked at her very carefully for a moment. She was impervious. 'I seem to remember that long ago, when I first met my husband, he had a dagger like this.'

'How would he have had such a priceless treasure without my knowledge?' the Duke barked. 'He did not have such a piece as this, I would have known. I would have had to pay for it!'

'I have not seen it for many, many years,' she said, shrugging her elegant shoulders very slightly. 'Perhaps he sold it. Or gave it away. Or perhaps I am mistaken. But I will pay what is required. It will be a . . .' For one extraordinary moment Inspector Rivers was sure she was going to say *memento*: if she was, she changed her mind. 'I will buy it,' she repeated. 'I will buy it when it is available.'

Constable Forrest was flabbergasted from his station by the door: *everybody wanting to buy a murder weapon?* It was beautiful, certainly, but their actions seemed to him incomprehensible. He actually shook his head in disbelief and disapproval, but of course nobody was looking at him. He admired the way Inspector Rivers bowed again slightly, implied that the request, at this moment, was not within his grant, prepared to take his leave.

'Lady Rosamund,' the Inspector said, 'your son seemed – ill. Is he quite well? Of course these are terrible circumstances.'

Lady Rosamund was icy once more. 'That is an impertinence on your part. My son is prone to headaches. That is all.' The Duke added nothing: the Inspector finally nodded, went out into the hallway followed by Constable Forrest; the big, heavy front door was quickly closed behind them.

Constable Forrest let out an explosion of breath, as if he had been too nervous to breathe inside. 'Perhaps the nobility show their grief in different ways than us, sir,' he muttered after a moment. 'Except for that beautiful girl, of course. That Duke and Lady Rosamund don't like living in the same house, do they, sir?' And then he could not hide his excitement, looked at the small paper parcel in the Inspector's hand. 'But what a murder weapon! What a *beauty*, sir!'

'Indeed.'

'But funny them wanting to buy it. It's ghoulish, that's what it seems to me, sir.'

'It is invaluable,' said Inspector Rivers mildly. 'I expect they like to own invaluable things. Even murder weapons.' But

Constable Forrest shook his head again: to him, it was inappropriate.

They agreed that Constable Forrest should stay for the moment outside the house with the several other police constables; odd types hung about, showing interest. 'Watch the house,' Inspector Rivers said, and Constable Forrest knew that that command also meant *watch the people*.

Inspector Rivers carried the beautiful dagger away. It looked as though he carried a piece of fish for his supper.

It was a dank, grey, darkening afternoon when he returned to the detective division headquarters at 4 Whitehall-place, off White Hall. The detective division was new. The Metropolitan Police was extremely unpopular with the populace and the detective division in its small separate building was not likely to change this view. The other policemen jeered, chaffed Inspector Rivers and his constables: '*Detect?* What is *detect* that is different to what we do? Just find the bloody buggers!' and they would laugh, not always kindly. Every policeman had heard stories of an oily French police inspector who had obtained glory for his detection: no prancing detectives were required in London thank you very much. 'It's got vainglorious ideas, detection,' said one of the other inspectors sourly, who had hoped for promotion. He repeated the word, he'd heard it somewhere: *vainglorious*. 'Waste of money,' said the other policemen. And it was true that the division was new, and even nervous, and Inspector Rivers only said 'It gives us time to listen,' to the disbelieving mutterings of most of his colleagues. But the Inspector was sure this was a better way, for he had seen much injustice done.

A house had been acquired in Whitehall-place for this very new department; there was a small prison at the back which opened on to a yard called Scotland Yard. The air was grey and wet and cold and the smell of the everlasting fog got into the nostrils with the smell of piss in the yard and the smell of

221

unwashed bodies and the smell of rotten fish: all the smells that lingered always outside, and often inside, any police station. The newspapermen who had hung about the watch-house at Bow Street had arrived here at Whitehall-place now, cold and complaining; wanting something, some news, for in Bow Street the dead body had at last been sewn up, and the surgeons had dispersed. Inspector Rivers smiled noncommittally and said there was no news. They didn't believe him, but finally disappeared into the gloom swearing, slapping their cold hands under their armpits, making for a nearby public house. Dull lamps flickered in Whitehall-place.

London was divided into parishes for local governance: Mr Percival Tunks, the coroner for the parish of St George's, Blooms-bury, who had come to the detective division with his post-mortem report on Lord Morgan Ellis, now put on his hat to go and find himself some repast. As he left the premises he met the Inspector returning the dagger with the rubies and the diamonds in the handle to the safe inside the building; they both admired it one more time, stroked the shining jewels: a strange, exotic murder weapon. Could it have once belonged to Lord Ellis? It was almost – they both felt this and were almost ashamed to feel it – too *valuable* to be a murder weapon. They stared as they placed it in the safe, double-checked the lock. Then they walked together, exchanging information, out on to the wide main thoroughfare of White Hall, where carts and carriages rattled past in the gloom throwing up mud and horse dung. They crossed up to St Martin's Lane, through the cabbages and old chop bones and thin, scavenging dogs. Just as the coroner made to enter a chop house, a boy ran up.

'Mr Tunks, sir! I been following after you, sir, a letter, sir!' A white paper was thrust outwards towards the coroner. Inspector Rivers recognised the boy: he was often to be seen sweeping, for the ladies to cross, the filthy streets round Bow Street with a small dirty broom, sometimes slept on gratings or beside street fires; one of hundreds of them, pale and thin and filthy and no home anywhere. Inspector Rivers gave the boy sixpence while Mr Tunks was staring at the letter.

'Where did this come from?' Mr Tunks frowned at the boy.

'It were given me, sir!' The ragged boy almost burst with importance.

'By whom?' Mr Tunks examined the missive in the light of one of the gas lamps.

'By a person, sir! I couldn't right say who, sir, look at the fog and they dint talk to me, only gave me a shillin' in the gloam, sir, for bringin' it to you after the post-mortem of the 'orrible murder, sir!'

Mr Tunks opened the letter.

All it said was: *Lord Ellis was visiting a Lady Mesmerist in Bloomsbury last night.* The letter was unsigned. *A Lady Mesmerist?* Mr Tunks gave a small grunt of surprise, reached into his pocket, gave the boy tuppence. He might have asked something more but the scrawny boy dissolved into grey shadows.

The phlegmatic Inspector Rivers, studier of chrysalises, had lost his temper only once with his superiors, ever, and it was an anonymous missive that had caused this unusual happening. He had been investigating a murder for the Metropolitan Police some years earlier, long before a detective division had been thought of, and he had received an anonymous note naming a rather odd and lonely working man as the murderer, long before the case had been tried in court. One of the newspapers had been sent the anonymous letter also, and soon the penny broadsides and the balladeers and the patterers had got wind of this, and had named the man accordingly. The real villain had eventually been found but the process had been slow and ponderous (Inspector Rivers knew this); by then the working man had hanged himself above his single bed in his rented room. The Inspector in his frustration had gone to see the Commissioners themselves, had broadly suggested that the penny papers were responsible for the man's death, anger and guilt making him foolhardy. 'You should speak to your masters in the Parliament, or to the King!' he had shouted. 'If the tax was taken off the proper newspapers so that ordinary people could afford them, the broadsides and the balladeers would be out of a job with their irresponsible scandal-mongering!' One of the Commissioners was receptive, the other was not: Inspector Rivers was lucky to hold on to his rank and his job.

So the Inspector, who was of course most interested in the anonymous information (for often such letters were most useful, malicious or not), did wonder if the letter had been sent to the press also. He sighed deeply as he heard the knocker echo into the house in Bedford Place, looked about carefully for any sign of newspapermen. His breath made patterns in the falling early evening air; fog and cold filled his nostrils. His enquiries had found that a Miss Cordelia Preston was the only lady mesmerist in Bloomsbury, possibly in the whole of London. He refused to allow himself to think ill of her until he had made further enquiries, but if the papers got hold of the very word *mesmerism* he would not like to answer for the consequences: he imagined her a little old lady with staring eyes, but, as yet, he wished her no harm.

A maid, her face at once alive with surprise and then, quickly, excitement, escorted him to a small room where a comfortable, pleasant older woman sat at a desk with papers. For a moment he saw her, before she saw him. She looked tired, end-of-the-day tiredness perhaps, and distracted. She looked up and saw the policeman: he saw her eyes widen, *was it apprehension*?

'I am a police detective, ma'am, Inspector Rivers. Are you Miss Cordelia Preston?'

'Thank you, Nellie,' said the pleasant woman. She waited until the maid had left; they immediately heard her voice calling with the utmost urgency, 'Regina! Regina! It's a copper!' and her footsteps running up the stairs. The pleasant woman smiled slightly.

'Nellie is deeply interested in policemen,' she said. 'I am Miss

Spoons, I am Miss Preston's business partner.' She put out her hand in a friendly manner, but he saw wariness in her eyes.

'I wonder if I could speak to Miss Preston?'

'Are you requiring her services?' He was confused slightly, then understood she would mean mesmerism, not anything less salubrious.

'I am investigating the murder in Bloomsbury Square last night of Lord Morgan Ellis. We have reason to believe that he may have met Miss Preston last night before—'

'I am Miss Preston.' He did not see that Miss Spoons blanched at his words, for the voice came immediately from behind him and he turned at once. He stared in surprise: it was not a little old lady with staring eyes at all. Somehow she was *beautiful*. A lock of white hair, a melodious voice, elegant: not at all what he had been expecting. 'I met my maid on the stairs,' she said. She was dressed in hat and gloves to go out, and she was very pale, more than ordinarily pale. She looked quickly at the other woman for a moment, but otherwise she was contained. 'Perhaps you would like to come next door where there is a fire – and perhaps Miss Spoons could join us also.'

'Of course,' said Inspector Rivers. Miss Spoons quickly showed him to a small warm sitting room. For just a moment he was left alone in the room: he had seen that they had been thrown in some way by his arrival, perhaps they were conferring some-where outside, yet the house was silent. In a corner of the room there was a fir tree, someone had placed candles on the branches the way they said Prince Albert did, but they were unlit. He saw comfortable but elegant furniture, he saw mirrors, he saw paint-ings on the walls. One was of a stern patriarchal figure of earlier times, no doubt a relation. One was, oddly, unframed: three childish figures played on desolate, deserted sand, it was eerie and rather beautiful. The fire burned bright, he warmed his hands. Then the ladies entered the room, indicated pleasantly that he should sit, sat themselves also although Miss Preston did not remove her hat and gloves; more friendly anyway than

225

the pale, cold woman in Grosvenor Square. He noted again the white lock at the front of Miss Preston's hair, she was extraordinarily elegant, did not have staring mesmeric eyes of any description. But he saw that the women, pleasant as they were, were uneasy. He tried not to stare at Miss Preston, one did not stare at ladies; she was perhaps a little older than he, looked very pale, yes, but – *beautiful*. He introduced himself properly. And then there was silence: the ladies were waiting for him.

'You will already have heard of the death nearby last night of Lord Morgan Ellis.' It was a statement, not a question.

'We have heard.' It was Miss Spoons who answered. 'It would be hard not to hear, the penny papers have been singing their wares round here since early morning.'

'Indeed.' He looked again at Miss Preston. 'Miss Preston, did you know Lord Morgan Ellis?'

'May I know why you are asking me this question, Inspector?'

It was an anonymous letter but he must use it. 'We have been – given information – that he was known to you.' Miss Cordelia Preston – he saw this – made an immense effort. Expression after expression seemed to flicker across her face; finally she controlled herself again. She looked straight at him, answered in her low, pleasant voice.

'Many years ago, I knew Lord Morgan Ellis well. But it was in – in another life.'

He went straight in. 'We have been advised that he came here last night.' But she had already heard him say that as she came down the stairs; she faltered for only a split second.

'May I ask who advised you of that?' she said pleasantly.

'Did he come here last night?'

She gave a small swallow, her eyes flickered to Miss Spoons, again it was Miss Spoons who answered.

'He did come here last night, yes.'

'Were you expecting him?'

'I had not spoken to Lord Ellis for about ten years,' said Miss Preston.

'But were you expecting him?'

She again hesitated for a split second, flashed another look at the other woman. 'We would be grateful for your discretion in this matter, Inspector. We were not expecting him particularly last evening. But – I had written him a letter. There was some – ancient business we needed to discuss.'

Ancient business. For some time Inspector Rivers was silent. And then he said, 'What time did Lord Ellis come here?'

'Perhaps – nine o'clock. He stayed much less than half an hour. We concluded our business and he left.' The Inspector wanted that to be true. Perhaps they were just old acquaintances, and everything easily explained.

'Was Lord Morgan Ellis a friend of yours?'

She looked at him expressionlessly. 'No,' she said. 'Lord Ellis was not a friend of mine.'

He had seen the house. There were gilt mirrors and warm fires and ancient portraits. He saw their fashionable clothes. *Is mesmerism such a lucrative business?* They had not yet drawn the curtains: outside the long glass doors a well-looked-after garden contained grass and shrubs and a small statue, he could see angelic outlines in the dusk. He had learned long ago in his work not to jump to obvious conclusions, but sometimes obvious conclusions were indeed the answer. The question had to be asked. It would explain, of course, the venom in the eyes of Lady Rosamund Ellis. 'Were you – forgive me asking so soon a question of such a personal nature, Miss Preston, but it does need to be asked eventually in the circumstances – were you . . .' he still tried to find a suitable phrase, they were ladies after all, 'a receiver of pecuniary assistance from Lord Ellis?'

He was very much taken by surprise, because the two women laughed, seemed relieved almost. But if it was not money, what else could it be? They did not laugh nastily, or too gaily, as if they were in some way hiding something: it just seemed to be a small spontaneous sound. 'I do assure you,' said Miss Preston, still smiling at him, 'that my business with Lord Ellis was not of a pecuniary nature. My colleague, Miss Spoons, and myself are businesswomen in a world where – we do realise – there are few businesswomen; we nevertheless earn our own money, and have no need of money belonging to anybody else.' Again he was thrown. *Businesswomen?* That could not be entirely true. There would be a man partner somewhere. There was money, certainly. And then a thought flashed. *The dagger*. The beautiful dagger locked in Whitehall-place. Had it belonged to Lord Ellis long ago, as Lady Rosamund had intimated? Had he, long ago, given it to Miss Preston?

'Can I ask something else – forgive me if these questions seem blunt, but the sooner they are over the better. Did you' – he had to plough on in one way or another – 'did Lord Morgan Ellis – perhaps at some other time in your life – make gifts to you?' He saw their faces. 'I do not just mean money. I rather meant jewels perhaps. Or – jewelled things.' He knew he was sounding clumsy.

'Anything Lord Ellis may have given me was sold long ago, Inspector. I did not need to keep – *mementos*.' That word again. *There is something disparaging in the way she uses the word. There was something disparaging in the way Lady Rosamund Ellis had almost used the word. Was Lord Morgan Ellis a man to be disparaged? Something here. Something*. He cleared his throat.

'There is a small plaque outside – I believe you are a mesmerist?'

'Yes.'

'May I ask who actually runs your business? Who owns it, I mean.'

She at once understood. 'Strange as it may seem to you, Inspector, it is our very own business,' she answered wryly. 'Miss Spoons and myself are the only partners.'

Again he was silent, unsure how to continue; here the fire spat too, as in the other house he had recently visited, but the room, and its inhabitants, were so much warmer. He looked again at the fir tree with the little candles. For some reason he could not ascertain, the boy playing chess suddenly came into his mind. It would be a sad Christmas Day for that strange family. Lady Rosamund had looked so – he saw it again: the look of venom. Again he saw the boy; *is there a reason the boy is in my mind?* Inspector Rivers had learnt to allow his thoughts to range in this odd way: sometimes it was rubbish, sometimes it was useful and his thoughts would give a somersault and he would understand: *something about that boy.* Who knows where his thoughts may have led him at that moment if the door had not slowly opened, and if a completely naked old lady had not entered the room.

Miss Spoons stood at once. 'Oh Ma!' she said, but lovingly, not angry. The naked old lady was followed immediately by another old lady who had rather wild grey hair and was clutching one of the penny broadsides that were the bane of Inspector Rivers' life.

'Sorry, Rillie,' the grey-haired old lady began, and then her eyes took in the uniformed policeman. 'Holy God!' she swore, waving the penny paper at him like a flag as the naked lady smiled kindly at everyone.

A naked old lady and a grey-haired old lady with the broad-sheet flourished: this surreal moment was broken almost at once – Miss Spoons, looking over her shoulder for a brief moment at Miss Preston, quickly and firmly took them both away; they heard the voices outside in the hall for a moment, then footsteps going upwards, then silence.

He saw that Miss Preston did not look particularly embarrassed at the rather extraordinary state of affairs, but she did apologise politely, explaining that the mother of Miss Spoons had lost her reasoning.

'My wife had a mad mother,' said Inspector Rivers, 'I know very well what it can be like,' and Miss Preston smiled. But she did not let down her guard.

He returned to his questioning: his odd train of thought had gone. 'You – did not leave the house after Lord Ellis had gone?'

She did not answer him at once, again expressions flitted across her face and were gone.

'I – I did leave, yes. I felt the want of air. I walked to Drury Lane.'

'You walked alone to Drury Lane?'

'Yes.'

'At nearly ten o'clock at night? You did not call a cabriolet?'

She saw he was shocked and smiled slightly. 'Inspector Rivers, you perhaps do not have experience of this, but ladies who live alone sometimes want to walk by themselves at night. I have done it all my life and I have come to no harm – I have always lived in Bloomsbury and I know the streets well.'

'Do you carry some sort of protection?' He had to say it. 'A knife?'

'My mother and my aunt instructed me long ago in the usefulness of a flat-iron.'

'I beg your pardon?'

'I was taught to always carry a flat-iron in my cloak.'

He remained silent, digesting this odd piece of information. Then he said, 'Did you pass Bloomsbury Square on your way to Drury Lane?'

Miss Preston looked down at her gloved hands. 'I did,' she said, shrugging, 'but it was quiet.' And then she seemed to consider, gave another little shrug, looked up at him again. 'If you are finding it necessary to check my movements, you will find out soon enough where I went. I decided to go to Mrs Fortune's rooms in Cock Pit-lane.' She gave an odd little smile. 'If my story of walking about London streets seems so shocking, you will at least be able to check my destination.'

Inspector Rivers knew very well of Mrs Fortune's rooms in Cock Pit-lane. But he did not quite understand. It was a place frequented by rather rackety actors. 'Why did you go there in particular, Miss Preston?'

She looked at him. 'Surely I do not have to give you a reason, Inspector?'

'I'm rather afraid, Miss Preston, that you do. You may have been the last person to see Lord Ellis alive.' She looked at him with an unreadable expression. 'Why did you go to Mrs Fortune's rooms at ten o'clock at night?' He heard an almost inaudible sigh. Then she looked at him as if she was weighing him up, deciding.

'Miss Spoons and I used to be actresses.'

She saw at once then, his expression. She looked away from him impatiently. Her face, which had been, on the whole, friendly, closed. 'You will most certainly be able to ascertain that that is where I went to.' And as he did not answer she added sharply, 'Neither wielding a knife nor splattered with blood.'

'You did not see Lord Ellis after you left your house?'

'No.'

'You know nothing further about his death?'

'Nothing.'

'Miss Preston, why did Lord Ellis come to see you?' She remained silent. He waited. But she was not going to speak. 'You do not feel able to tell me the reason he came to your house last night?'

'I do not.'

'Miss Preston, Lord and Lady Ellis are well-connected members of the nobility and Lord Ellis has been murdered nearby – this visit is not something you are going to be able to hide, nor your visit to Mrs Fortune's establishment.' She looked at him in alarm. 'It will become public knowledge: you cannot avoid it.' He saw how shocked she suddenly was.

'How will it become public?'

'As I have already said, you seem to be one of the last people to see Lord Ellis alive. In the circumstances you will have to attend as a witness to the coroner's inquest which will be called in the next day or two and you will certainly be questioned there about the reasons for his visit.'

'Questions about *me*?'

'Yes.'

'But – his visit here did not have anything to do with his death. I did not have anything to do with his death. I am not on trial!' *Oh but you will be*, thought the policeman sadly and could not look at her. 'I cannot think our brief meeting had anything to do with his death,' she said in real agitation, 'and I certainly do not consider that I should be questioned about it in public under any circumstances. You will be able to ascertain where I went. I was not murdering anybody!' He listened in silence. 'I read that a man had been arrested,' she said.

'A man was arrested and a very valuable jewelled dagger, the murder weapon, was found near a clump of bushes at the end of the square where the statue of Mr Fox stands. An unlikely murder weapon, we feel, for a poor vagrant.'

She stared at him. 'How did – am I allowed to question you? – how did you know that he had been here?' She swallowed. She was very nervous now. 'It was not a visit he would have spoken of, I am sure.'

She would find out soon enough: she may as well find out now. 'We received an anonymous letter.

'An anonymous letter?' She tried to control herself. 'You take evidence from *anonymous letters!*'

'If they contain evidence. This one contained evidence, did it not? It would no doubt surprise you to know how many of these the police and the coroners and the magistrates receive.'

She stood, threw her next words at him angrily. 'I have been honest with you. You have not been fair or honest with me. I would not have answered a single one of your questions if I had known that all the proof you had of his visit came from *an anonymous letter*! You have deceived me, Inspector.'

'But it was true.'

She tried again to check herself. 'As you now know.'

'Can you think of anyone who knew about the visit who wishes you ill?'

'Nobody knew about the visit! We did not even know about it ourselves until we heard the door-knocker! And we certainly do not wish anybody else to know.'

'Somebody does know.' After a moment or two Miss Preston, with a great effort, calmed herself properly; she even shrugged, but said nothing more and did not sit again. 'You are not – affected in any way by his death,' he said.

She looked at him blankly. 'The pain Lord Ellis caused me happened many years ago. I cannot pretend to further sorrow.'

The fire spat and glowed; outside he saw new snow falling past the French doors on to the tended lawn and the angel; it was night now. Wherever Miss Preston had been going she had now obviously changed her mind, she unpinned her elegant hat slowly but she looked away, was waiting for him to leave. Inspector Rivers was sorry, he stood at last also. He liked her, he liked looking at her; somehow he believed her, more or less, although it was obvious she was holding things back. And there must be a man behind this business venture somewhere.

'As I say, the coroner will hold his inquest almost immediately. You will be required to appear and will receive a notice to do so. I presume you understand that an inquest is not a murder trial but the cause of death must be officially established.' He watched her carefully, her face was still blank. 'You went on, you say, to the rooms of Mrs Fortune, and I will of course make enquiries there. You are – an actress – no longer?'

'I am a mesmerist now, Inspector. As I said.' Almost, she spoke proudly.

She did not seem to understand how the newspapers would seize on the event of Lord Ellis's visit to a mesmerist; he did not know how to warn her. And then they would find out she was an *actress*.

They would make mincemeat of her.

* * *

The Inspector ate a pie from a pieman, sheltering from the snow in a doorway, and then went on to the Bow Street watch-house to report to Mr Tunks the coroner, who was waiting there for him, rosy-cheeked from his chops and ale. Mr Tunks listened, and then hit one hand upon the other in jubilation. 'Good. Oh good, well done, Inspector. Something promising at last! You've saved my bacon, indeed you have, sir! Well, well – he visited a *lady mesmerist*!' He did not observe the look of dismay on the Inspector's face for he went on quickly. 'Now I can call the inquest – good man, Inspector – d'you know, I've already had a note from the Attorney-General – dammit, they always interfere when it is the gentry, well of course, I understand it's different for the nobility – d'you know, there's a connection to the Queen herself! And you better look at this: Lord Ellis was only murdered last night and they want it all settled before Christmas Day – what do they think we are, you and I, magicians?' and Mr Tunks handed the Inspector a newspaper, just off the presses.

> If an Inquest is not held immediately it shall appear once again that the police are without any worthwhile clue that might lead to the discovery and apprehension of the Murderer. We supported the idea of a new detective division: now we expect results. They have a man; they have a murder weapon. What more are they waiting for? It is intolerable that a noble family's grief (at this time in the calendar most especially when we are used to celebrating the birth of the Lord), and their desire for a funeral, must wait on the plodding foot-steps of our police force.

The Inspector kept his face blank but his dismay grew. The murder only yesterday and criticism for the detective division already. And Inspector Rivers knew the quirks of Mr Percival Tunks very well: a volatile mixture of extreme honesty, arrogance and deference. Mr Tunks was a good coroner and a moral man – except where the nobility was concerned: he did actually believe

234

that, for them, different rules applied. And more than anything in this world Mr Tunks hoped one day for some sort of Royal Recognition for his long and undoubtedly loyal service. 'I will visit Mrs Fortune,' said Inspector Rivers stolidly.

Mr Tunks was smiling. 'We've got the dagger, we've got the vagrant but they don't look likely to go together. But now we've got mesmerism and the theatre! That's more like it!'

'But there is certainly no proof of anything at all, sir, regarding this woman. None. Only that the deceased visited her house last evening.'

'But a mesmerist and an actress all rolled into one! She probably acts the mesmerism!' He laughed at his own wit. 'Well, it's certainly enough to be going on with.'

'It's *not* enough!' said Inspector Rivers more angrily than he meant to. 'There is no evidence, sir, nothing at all. But you know perfectly well the papers will crucify that woman.'

'Better than them crucifying us!' said the coroner sensibly, but he patted the Inspector kindly on the back. 'We must call her to the inquest, of course we must, you know that, Inspector. See what they say at that illustrious establishment of Mrs Fortune and let me know later tonight.'

Inspector Rivers sent a message to Constable Forrest, to tell him to come to Drury Lane.

As he left the watch-house, pulling his cloak around him against the cold evening, it was Inspector Rivers' turn to be accosted by a boy; but he knew this boy. There standing patiently in Bow Street, a few yards away from the station doorway, seemingly impervious to the shit and the smells and the snow that here turned immediately to filthy slush as it touched the ground, stood the chess-playing grandson of the Duke of Llannefydd, the boy who had come into his mind so oddly when he was questioning Miss Preston. The boy had his black cloak wrapped about him with some insouciance and he was carrying newspapers.

'Good evening, Lord Ellis.'

'I saw you go in earlier, Inspector.' The voice started high, broke, went low.

'You should have come in, of course. Out of the weather. You are recovered? From your headache, I mean. Your mother told me that you have them sometimes.'

The health enquiries were ignored. 'I wanted to ask you a question. Out here is best.' The Inspector waited. The boy swaggered but was clearly nervous. 'My sister has asked me to sell – a valuable necklace.' Inspector Rivers looked grave. 'It is her own necklace, Inspector, I do assure you! If it was stolen I would hardly ask a policeman for advice! As you know, we have always lived in Wales and I do not know where to go to – make this sale. I thought the most sensible person to ask would be you, for you would know which are regular places and which are not.' Snow fell on the boy and the policeman.

'Surely this is a matter for you to discuss with your family, Lord Ellis – with your mother, or your grandfather.'

'At the moment they cannot give us any attention.'

The Inspector supposed this was true, in the circumstances. It seemed an odd time to be selling jewellery, the day after the death of their father, but the upper classes, he knew, moved in mysterious ways. 'Well, my Lord, I agree it is true you would not be likely to ask my advice if the necklace did not belong to your sister. Bond Street would be the best place. Go to Mr Sheekey, and give him my compliments.'

The boy looked partially relieved. 'Thank you. Although I wish I was selling that dagger!' Inspector Rivers looked at him very carefully indeed. How odd this family was about the dagger.

'What do you mean by that?'

The boy looked surprised. 'Well! Just think of the money you could get for that!' But then his face seemed immediately to close. Again the Inspector waited as the snow fell. 'I have been reading the newspapers. Will there be – a – court case about my father? They do not have court cases about lords, do they?'

The Inspector looked down at the strange boy. 'The law is the same for everybody, Lord Ellis. First there will be a coroner's inquest to try to establish the cause of the death of your father. Any witnesses we find will be called to give evidence then.'

'When?'

'As soon as possible. Even tomorrow. It is the law.'

'Have you got any idea,' the young man's voice faltered on a kind of moving scale of sound, 'where my father was last night? Before – before it happened?'

'Why do you ask?'

'Are you allowed to tell me?'

'Have *you* any idea?'

'No,' the boy answered very quickly. And then he added: 'I just wondered – why he was in Bloomsbury.'

'I see.' It was cold, it stank, both of them were getting wet. 'Well, just between you and me, your Lordship, it does seem that your father was visiting someone in Bloomsbury last night. Did you know that?' He saw the way the boy's eyes stared at him. And Inspector Rivers felt, just slightly, the skin rising on the back of his neck. *The boy knows something.*

'Where will the inquest be held?'

'Upstairs in the Anchor public house.' The Inspector pointed behind them. Light and noise came from the bars and the parlours. Directly next door the upstairs of the police watch-house was in darkness. Suddenly he saw the boy was staring upwards at the watch-house, gave an involuntary shiver, suddenly swallowed.

'Is that where – is that where my father is now? Up there?' The Inspector nodded. 'But there's no lights on.' He suddenly looked about six years old.

Inspector Rivers felt very sorry for him, knew he could not question him further at this bleak moment. 'Your father's body must await the inquest,' he said gently, 'and the watch-house is where it waits. It won't be long but that is how these things are done.'

'I'll have to be going now, Inspector,' said Morgan, and he

237

quickly disappeared down Bow Street, snow falling on his small shoulders. The Inspector watched him, wondering, till the boy turned a corner off Long Acre.

Constable Forrest, message received, caught up with the Inspector just at the corner of Drury Lane. They walked stolidly in their police cloaks, ignoring the weather.

'There's been that much coming and going since you left!' said Constable Forrest. 'I was surprised. The Duke went – he was sort of carried into his carriage, told it to go to his club in St James's. Her ladyship, all black-veiled, "The Strand," she says when her carriage comes round, and then that young boy goes. I passed him on my way here – pile of newspapers as big as your arm!'

'He has just been here, speaking to me.'

'Speaking to you, sir?'

'Yes. He wanted to know where his father was last night and I had the oddest feeling that he knew more.' The Inspector rubbed his neck in frustration: that gesture reminded him of the boy in the huge cold room in Grosvenor Square, rubbing his own.

'The young ladies didn't appear.' Constable Forrest sounded regretful. He thought of the beautiful weeping girl. 'Sad Christmas for that family.'

'Tomorrow, Constable, go and watch this address in Bedford Place. Plain clothes.' There were secrets in that house, he was sure of it. And there would be a man behind that business, some-where. Ladies did not set up businesses.

They walked down into Cock Pit-lane and up the rickety stairs above the pawn shop.

It was almost time for Mrs Fortune's famous theatrical stew to be thrown out. She heated up her cauldron (it actually was a cauldron: she had obtained it years ago from a failed production of *Macbeth*) but the smell was, to put it politely, not, tonight, appetising. She was considering whether she could offer it for one more night at reduced price, 5d, when the police officers arrived. Mrs Fortune was not feeling guilty about any one thing in particular, but she fluttered somewhat all the same: policemen were not welcome in Cock Pit-lane, they brought nothing but bad news, and there had been that murder in Great Titchfield Street of a young actress who had brought the man in here, that had done her establishment no good, though it was nothing to do with her. She prudently offered them some whisky (not risking watering it); they hastily refused an offer of the stew also. As it bubbled, the smell became worse.

'How is it then that I can help you gentlemen?' she said at last.

They brushed the worst of the snow off their clothes, glad of the warming whisky. 'We've come to ask you, if we may, about the visitors you had here last night.'

'Last night?' (Last night she had had a particularly unpleasant argument ending in a physical altercation with one of the younger actresses – *she's a slut, that Primrose*, thought Mrs Fortune viciously – who'd brought in yet another young man: Mrs Fortune knew her place was getting a reputation and she was only trying to make an honest living: *was charges laid by that little cow? I only pushed her.*) 'No, I'm sorry, gentlemen, but I don't remember nothing. Nothing at all, there's all sorts here in the evenings.'

'Do you remember a Miss Cordelia Preston coming here?'

Her face cleared. 'Cordelia? Course, she come last night, didn't she? I remember now, nothing untoward, I hope?'

'No, no, nothing untoward. She is merely a witness in a case we are investigating.'

'Ooooh, a witness! What's she done?'

'She has done nothing, Mrs Fortune, nothing at all.' But their demeanour was very solemn. On one of the tables one of the penny papers had been discarded with its only headline; Mrs Fortune was an extremely quick-witted woman, she glanced at

239

the paper, looked quickly at the officers. 'Last night there was a murder I see, have you come to accuse me of being involved in another murder by any cheery chance? Trying to damage my establishment, are you?' Her eyes flashed with anger and apprehension; she picked the paper up, studied the words. 'Here, look – Lord Morgan Ellis!' And she was actually quiet for a moment and then she said slowly, still reading: 'Ain't that the gentleman Cordelia Preston left the stage for, years ago? Lord Morgan Ellis? Am I right, or aren't I?' *So that is the connection*, thought Inspector Rivers. *She left the stage for him.* Mrs Fortune looked up at them, wondering whether to co-operate or shut up. Her vanity got the better of her. 'Course you know, gentlemen, I've been around a long time – I remember when Cordelia Preston was famous!'

'Was she – famous?'

'Lord yes, pardon my expression, she had her time. There's a few of them still around that's had their time. But then their time goes, drifts away, someone else's turn, someone else's time – oh look, here's Mr Tryfont!' She sounded relieved. 'He was talking to her last night, boring her to death I shouldn't wonder!' She called loudly across the room: 'Mr Tryfont! Mr Tryfont love, here's some policemen looking for you.' Mr Tryfont approached theatrically but at the same time rather warily, looked down suspiciously at the policemen.

'Yes?'

'It's about Cordelia Preston,' said Mrs Fortune. 'You know, I remember now, I said to my girl, "She's looking pale," and where was her cloak? She didn't have no cloak!' The Inspector's eyes hooded for a moment into himself. *No cloak. No flat-iron in her cloak.* 'We wondered, but of course we weren't thinking of murder, not murder!'

'Not murder *again*, Mrs Fortune,' said the Inspector rather unkindly. She looked at him with instant rage.

'That other girl wasn't even a proper actress. She come here, that's all. Nothing to do with me, I run a respectable place!'

'Miss Preston was here then last night, Mrs Fortune?'

'Yes! I told you, yes, stayed here an hour or two, hadn't seen her in a while, her and that Rillie Spoons used to come in, I thought she must be on tour, but someone told me she's gone and been a mesmerist!'

'What about her?' said Mr Tryfont, still waiting.

'She's charged with murder!'

'No, no indeed!' said Inspector Rivers loudly and firmly. 'She is not in any way charged with any murder at all, Mrs Fortune. She is a witness, nothing more.'

'It's the Lord's murder!' said Mrs Fortune to Mr Tryfont helpfully.

'She has been involved in some religious activity?'

Inspector Rivers looked quickly and carefully at the tall actor, who was smirking, rather pleased with his turn of phrase. 'Were you in this establishment last night, sir,' he said more ominously than he might have, 'when Miss Preston was here?'

At his tone of voice the actor began to take things seriously, he could suddenly see the possibilities of drama. He threw back his cloak in his most theatrical manner, leaned with one arm on one of Mrs Fortune's rather battered and stained red velvet sofas. 'Is she dead?' he asked sepulchrally. 'I heard she had become oracular.'

Mrs Fortune assisted his understanding by thrusting the penny paper at him. He read the headlines. Other actors crowded round, understanding suddenly with great interest that *another* murder was being discussed here, right here again at Mrs Fortune's rooms! Was the place safe? Olive the ballet dancer perched prettily on the red sofa arm, shivering slightly. 'But I bought her a glass of port when she come in last night,' Olive said, 'she'd forgotten her money. She talked to me. I told her about me work. She had a lovely blue gown on too, expensive.' Mr Jenks the retired prompter pushed forward, the better to hear. Young, pretty actresses giggled nervously with excitement. The revolting stew continued to bubble, several people moved slightly, to be further from its aroma.

'What's this got to do with Miss Preston?' asked Mr Tryfont.

'She knew him, the Lord, I remembered she knew him!' said Mrs Fortune in very dramatic tones.

'You spoke to Miss Preston last night, young lady?' Olive nodded, tongue-tied now. 'And you, Mr Tryfont?' The Inspector continued with his questioning firmly.

'I did, yes.' Two dwarfs arrived, asking loudly what was happening; they were shushed by the others but their eyes were wide with interest, they pushed to the front like children. Other actors were nodding now, talking about Cordelia, *I talked to her*, but Mr Tryfont's voice was the loudest. 'Some time ago we had been in an unfortunate production together of a play whose name I will not let pass my lips – an old theatrical superstition, gentlemen, forgive me – and last night I was able to recount to her the addition to the cast of an elephant following her departure – not *due* to her departure, you understand.'

'Did she seem in any way distressed?'

'I told you,' said Mrs Fortune, 'she didn't have no cloak and it was that cold last night too!'

'The warmth of your establishment, my dear Mrs Fortune, would have made the chill of the evening disappear.' Mr Tryfont ended the compliment with a flourish, actually sitting down now on the red velvet sofa so that Olive the ballet dancer, perched on the arm, bounced; Mr Tryfont sat back majestically. 'I spoke to her for some time. She was very interested. I did not notice any distress.'

'You wouldn't!' agreed Mrs Fortune rather spitefully, not liking to lose the limelight, having been an actress herself in younger days. 'But I remember you was talking to her for a very long time.'

'There was a lot to tell,' he said languidly.

The smell of the stew had become almost overpowering, several actors were now looking at the cauldron with distaste and the Inspector saw that Constable Forrest was looking rather pale, had his handkerchief unobtrusively to his nose.

242

'Shall I have to appear in a courtroom?' asked Mr Tryfont suddenly, with great interest.

'Not me!' said Olive suddenly. 'I shouldn't be able to talk, I shouldn't, I'm a dancer, that's all.'

'We shall advise you all,' said Inspector Rivers and he hurried Constable Forrest out before he could embarrass them both.

'Good grief!' said the Constable, retching twice and then recovering. 'Sorry, sir. But I wouldn't like to be an actor if that's what they have to eat!' and they both breathed in the slightly more salubrious air of Drury Lane as the carts and the carriages, their lamps swinging, rattled along throwing up mud and cauliflowers and oyster shells and horse shit.

And Inspector Rivers frowned to himself in the darkness: the big house in Bloomsbury and the elegant ladies seemed a lifetime away from Mrs Fortune's establishment.

No cloak.

Eighteen

Very late that same night, the night after the death of her father, Manon, new Duchess of Trent, walked, weeping wildly, round and round one of the grand bedrooms in Grosvenor Square in her nightgown (her beautiful nightgown, for her new, wonderful life). Intense rhythmical moving round and round a room: something caged, something incoherent.

'He just left, Gwennie! As soon as we got the news at the ball last night – he went to Wiltshire! He just went away on his horse – in the night – he said he was going *shooting*! He said cruel things. He said his family never got involved in scandals and – and that the marriage might as well be annulled for all the use I'd been to him!' She wept as she walked and talked. 'I HATE being married. Nobody told me it would be so terrible, Gwennie, so terrible and so ugly – he tried to do such – disgusting things to me, he hurt me and he laughed.' She was becoming hysterical, kept gulping for air. 'Never marry! *Never marry!* It is a trick!'

Gwenlliam was at her wits' end as to how to stop her sister before their stepmother appeared. Manon had changed so much since she came to London, since she became the favourite of her grandfather, the Duke of Llannefydd. She had grown away from

Gwenlliam and Morgan, cared only for London and noblemen it seemed, spoke only of balls and gowns. *I love her dearly*, thought Gwenlliam. Her loyalty to her sister would not let her properly cohere the next thought: *but she is very spoilt*. Gwenlliam's own, complicated grief for her father, her still undigested shock at meeting her mother again: all this was momentarily swallowed up by Manon's abandon and despair; she seemed almost mad with grief and anger and some other thing – some disgust? Or fear? Gwenlliam was out of her depth. Finally she held her sister: half straitjacket, half loving sister; held her, whispered comfort to her, got her over to the bed they had shared before Manon went off so eagerly only weeks before to marry the Duke of Trent. She half lifted her older sister on to the bed, sat smoothing her hair, stroking her arms, her forehead.

'Go to sleep now, dearest Manon, go to sleep. You must sleep.' She stroked her sister's face gently.

'I want to go back, to how things used to be,' wept the girl whose only dream had been to come to London and marry a duke. But the weeping was almost over at last; it seemed the voice echoed into a distant place, exhausted. Gwenlliam stroked the long fair hair and at last her sister's breathing became smoother, her eyes closed. *Never marry*, came the whisper one more time.

After some time Gwenlliam gently disentangled herself, stood, stretched, sat in front of the mirror at the dark dressing table. She could hardly see herself in the candlelit gloom. She brushed her hair. From somewhere a draught shivered the flame, blurring her reflection. She too was so tired she could not even think clearly. Once, long, long ago, she had loved her father so dearly. But that was long ago in another life: he had changed, he was a different man, not the man who walked for miles on the wet sand seeing the shells and the rocks and the seaweed with his children. She had only just understood his perfidy; now he was dead in some terrible way and somehow people like the Duke of Trent called this not tragedy but *scandal*. Slowly she went back

245

to the bed, climbed in, listened again for Manon's even, muffled breathing. She leant over and blew out the candle, lay in the darkness. At once the face of her mother came into her head. *Does she know?* But of course she would know: there was nothing else in the newspapers; the balladeers' voices echoed even in Mayfair. What would she feel? But it was all so long ago. Thoughts drifted. *I want to see her again . . . Is it wrong of me not to tell Morgan? but Morgan cannot keep secrets . . . I should have explained more to Mama about Morgan, the doctor in Wales warned me that these new headaches are ominous, there was nobody to tell but me, 'give him landanum', he said, 'there is nothing else.'* She shied away from the thoughts that raced round and round. She lived in fear of Morgan's health . . . *should I have told her? warned her? . . . I want to see her again . . .* but Manon must be protected, the new Duchess of Trent, Morgan must be protected, the next Duke of Llannefydd: there could be no further scandal, if a murdered father was scandal . . . *it was a most beautiful dagger . . . but it killed my father . . .* At last the younger sister was asleep also.

She woke at once in the night, understood instinctively that the intruder was her young brother, heard his special way of breathing; heard also the rustling sound of paper. When he was young he had got into bed with them, weeping terrible tears for his lost mother, for his childish headaches; these days he scorned his sisters' room, the mess of their clothes and their potions, but she knew him so well: if his new headaches were unendurable he came still in that old remembered way. So, disoriented, still half asleep, she sat up quickly, 'Morgan,' she whispered, 'is it your head? Do you need your medicine?' He stood shivering at the bedside in his nightshirt as she lit the candle, shielding the light away from Manon. Morgan was holding yet another newspaper.

'What is it?' she whispered. 'Have you a headache again?'

'She saw him because of me.' Even his whispered voice broke, changed key.

'What's the matter, Morgan?' She tried to speak firmly in a very quiet tone. He was so odd, you had to be firm.

'He was visiting her the night he died.'

'Visiting *who*?'

'I read your journal. Our mother.' She felt her heart literally leap up inside her. The blood rushed to her face. She stared at him. She thought his eyes seemed mad in the candlelight and she stared at him in disbelief. 'I read your journal. I went to see her.' His teeth were actually chattering, so cold now was the room. Still she stared at him, now in a kind of horror. 'You never tell me anything. It was me that found the Treehouse Children advertisement, not you. And you said I was being wishful and not sensible and then you found her and did not tell me. If I did not read your journal I would never know anything.' He shivered almost convulsively as he stood there beside the bed. She tried to pull herself together, it was true what he said: she had kept it from him, she kept many things from him, but for his own good, he was too – *volatile*. She spoke to him in an urgent whisper.

'Morgan, get in at the bottom, on my side, and keep warm. Do not wake Manon, *you must not wake Manon*, she knows nothing of this.' He pulled the blankets back from the bottom of the bed, got in gratefully. 'Oh, your feet are so cold!' she whispered. 'Do not wake Manon with your feet.'

'We're illegitimate.'

'*Be quiet!*' But the word hung there. Manon turned slightly, gave a small crying sigh.

Then silence in the huge cold bedroom. The house was silent. The square was silent.

'I'm fifteen,' he whispered. 'You could have told me. I went to see the policeman.'

'*What?*'

'I asked him. The policeman. He told me Father was visiting

247

someone in Bloomsbury the night he died. He was visiting our mother.'

Gwenlliam was so dumbfounded that she forgot to whisper. 'Stop it! Stop it!'

He took no notice. 'It was me. I asked her to talk to Father. I asked her if I could go and live with her and be a painter. I did a painting of Gwyr so that she would see I remembered.'

And neither of them noticed a sudden stillness on the far side of the bed.

'You must never talk of this again, never.' Gwenlliam's voice was whispered again but harsh. 'It is over. The past is over. That is what she said.'

'You wrote everything down in your journal. That's the same as telling people! You found her, that she was still alive. That we are illegitimate.' He seemed almost to delight in the word.

'Stop saying that! Stop it! What would happen to Manon if she knew, if the Duke of Trent knew? He would find a way of annulling the marriage, I am certain – and how could you be the next Duke of Llannefydd if anybody knows? Our mother does not want anybody to know. She told me.'

'Manon cries all the time, all she has done since her marriage is weep. It makes her ugly. She was the one who wanted to come to London where everything would be so wonderful! I wanted to go to America! I don't want to be the next Duke of Llannefydd, I want to go and live with our mother and be a painter, you can do what you like.' His urgent words would suddenly be voiced, and then turn to whispers again. 'Listen, Gwennie.' He stopped at last for a moment. 'Listen, Gwennie. I've sold your emeralds.'

'*What?* What are you talking about?'

'The ones Father gave you, for the wedding. I'm sorry, Gwennie, I had to, I will buy them back for you again one day, but now I will need money.' She was dumbfounded. He tried to explain. 'You know they can just take it into their heads to send us back to Wales any time, as though we were parcels! I can't go back to Wales, I must stay here for the inquest.' Still she stared at him as if he was mad. He was enraged that she did not understand. 'What if they say it is *her*? That *she* killed him? She lives by Bloomsbury Square. What say I am needed to explain that she is our mother and she was only seeing him because she was helping me?'

'*In a public court? You would say all this in a public court?*' On her side of the big bed Gwenlliam suddenly saw her life being pulled out from under her, like a rug from beneath her feet, she felt herself falling. She heard their mother's urgent words: *You must understand what I did not: the world is divided not just between rich and poor but between those who are respectable and those who are not.* She saw in her head the faces of the Duke and her stepmother. And why had Morgan sold her most valuable piece of jewellery? Then she heard a name, as clearly as if someone had said it aloud, but it was in her head.

Miss Gwenlliam Preston. She shook her head, as if to shake it away, but it stood there firmly.

Miss Gwenlliam Preston.

On the other side of the big bed there was, but the brother and sister did not notice, so involved were they in their own stories, a silence as loud as a scream.

Afterwards, after the next thing happened, although Gwenlliam wept and shouted in denial, mad with grief and remorse and pain, and Morgan was so pale and so horrified that it seemed he could not stand upright and his head seemed that it might burst; afterwards, after the same policeman came again, asked questions again; after the family of the Duke of Trent refused to acknowledge the family of the Duke of Llannefydd and hurried away to their estates in the northern part of England to escape further scandal and enquiry and gossip – afterwards, then, Gwenlliam and Morgan sat in the huge house in London like wraiths: grief-stricken, consumed with guilt and anguish, their faces as drained of any colour as the face of their dead sister.

249

The Duke of Llannefydd would not speak to, not even to shout at, the policemen on their second visit. Poultices fell off his legs and he drank whisky and stared at nothing, his face completely expressionless, in the dark drawing room. Only Lady Rosamund could answer, still, the further questions that Inspector Rivers had to ask: she did so with icy and controlled speech: her daughter, Manon, Duchess of Trent, had killed herself from grief at the brutal murder of her father. Inspector Rivers looked carefully at the white blank face that did not weep, at the silent, whisky-consuming Duke; then saw the two children, distraught to the point of collapse, who could tell him nothing. *I always look for the grief*, he had said to Constable Forrest. Here was grief.

Gwenlliam had burnt her journal. Morgan had burnt his old newspaper with the advertisement in the personal column (but hid the money in a deep pocket). At the immediate post-mortem there was no doubt at all how the young Duchess of Trent died; the newspapers soon had all the details and more, for an inquest on her death was immediately held by order of the royal household. At first light, while her brother and sister were still asleep, she had been in the mews at Grosvenor Square; she had asked the groom for potassium antimony, saying she had a sick horse in Wales; she died by three o'clock that afternoon in great agony, with burnt internal organs: she lay dressed in her wedding gown, her face twisted in terrible pain, upon her new matrimonial bed in her new Duchess-of-Trent house in Berkeley Square, in London: the dream she had always dreamed. A verdict was found at the inquest in four minutes once the surgeons and the hapless groom had given their evidence: all members of the hastily summoned jury agreed. They saw the sad body in the wedding dress, their faces registered their understanding of how painful the death must have been. Although the young Duchess had been the cause of her own death, ranked in law among the highest of crimes ('evading the prerogative of the Almighty and rushing into His presence uncalled for'); yet nevertheless the jury decided, advised by the royal coroner, that this had happened *in dementia accidentalis*, that is while the poor young lady's mind was temporarily disturbed by grief for the death of her father, and thus she was excluded from the criminal responsibility of her actions.

This verdict allowed her to have permission from the Church to be buried in hallowed ground, with her father.

Mr Percival Tunks, the coroner from the parish of St George's, Bloomsbury, suddenly received a message from Windsor; by order of Her Majesty the inquest of Lord Morgan Ellis must also be opened at once: *now*: so that the body of Lord Ellis could be released for burial: therefore a jury from this parish was, also, quickly summoned. Seventeen good and lawful men from the said parish passed the beer and the crowds and the life at the Anchor on their way into the police watch-house. Before they could view the body, the inquest on the death of Lord Morgan Ellis had to be formally opened; none of the seventeen men liked being in a police station: they stood uneasy in the dark, freezing upstairs hallway with their hats in their hands, answered quickly to their names which the coroner's officer called.

'Humphrey Ditch, baker, North Street.'

'Aye.'

'John Boxall, ironmonger, Bury Street.'

'Aye.'

'Giles King, baker, Gray's Inn Lane.'

'Aye.'

'Joseph Manley, glass-cutter, Gray's Inn Lane.'

'Aye.'

Finally all the names were called and sworn. The jury crowded into the small room indicated to them. The body of Lord Morgan Ellis lay there: oil lamps turned up high had been placed about it so that the injuries were clearly displayed. They saw the marks on the swollen face. They saw all the congealed blood where the weapon had gone in and were glad it was winter, and so cold. Ironmongers and auctioneers shuffled together with the bakers and the policemen as they looked at the body and knew that death, in the end, was no respecter of rank or money. They

251

could hear distantly the life and the cheer from next door, from the Anchor.

'You have all viewed the body?' asked the coroner formally as they crowded together. The jurors nodded.

'You have assessed the injuries?' They nodded and murmured.

'You have seen the murder weapon?' Again they nodded, they had been impressed by the murder weapon shining almost wildly in the gloom, out of place, gorgeous (they had shaken their heads, made low whistles, thought of the value).

Mr Tunks then, as was in his power, did by order of his hand allow, in these special circumstances, the body to be given into the hands of the family of the deceased. He then adjourned the inquest until the day after the next, to allow the double funeral to be held on Christmas Day.

The jury hurried next door for something to drink; Mr Tunks went downstairs, glad also to be away from the body. In the watch-house constables hovered, spoke of other matters, of burglars in Vauxhall; Mr Tunks put on his hat and went out into the freezing streets. He would find a chop house, and ale, and company. He was torn between fury at the majestic metaphorical pushing of his elbow in such a manner, and immense pride that this particular inquest was to be presided over by himself. He had received another message: the Duke of Llannefydd was now bringing his own legal representative to attend the inquest, and when Mr Tunks heard who it was to be his heart had beat a little faster: Sir Francis Willoughby, who, it was well known, advised the Queen. Sir Francis Willoughby would no doubt be instructed by the Duke of Llannefydd to blame the tardiness of the coroner and the police for the death of the young duchess if he could not blame them personally for the murder in Bloomsbury Square. Sir Francis Willoughby would also no doubt believe, as members of the legal profession often did (Mr Tunks had actually trained as a medical man), that a coroner's inquest was a poor thing, an anomaly, because it worked outside the rules and constraints of the legal system,

252

but Mr Tunks pulled back his shoulders as he walked and did not notice the cold. Some inquests were shambolic, that was true – the jury free to question the witnesses, legal representatives putting their oar in, the occasional witness running amok, even evidence destroyed or dropped or stood upon or stolen. The murder weapon, that extraordinary, shining thing, he would keep at all times with his officer. But – Mr Tunks sighed – the upstairs room of a public house was a hard place to keep dignified, there was not the neatness of a proper trial in a proper place. Nevertheless: he would show how a well-run coroner's inquest should proceed to anybody who might be watching, especially to Sir Francis Willoughby, adviser to royalty. He would show that proper caution on the part of a coroner was more important than speed. His mind drifted for a moment to honours, and royal pensions. And then, because he was fond of food, to the goose his wife was preparing for the morrow.

Inspector Rivers, on the other hand, went that evening once more to Bloomsbury.

In Bloomsbury Constable Forrest, lounging unobtrusively in plain clothes on the other side of the road wishing for at least a cup of hot tea as snow fell, was able to report to Inspector Rivers that an old foreign-looking gentleman had arrived at, and not left, the house of the mesmerist.

'What do you mean – foreign?'

Constable Forrest considered. 'He wore his cloak and hat funny,' he said.

Inspector Rivers, not quite understanding why he felt alarmed, stared once more at the unobtrusive brass plaque, banged on the knocker: nobody came. He pulled the bell rope, heard the sound of the bell echo down the hallway of the house. A man had arrived as he had always imagined one would. But were there to be *foreigners* in this case as well as everything else? He was here, he knew, because he wanted to make the inquest of

253

Lord Morgan Ellis easier for that elegant and attractive and mysterious woman, Miss Cordelia Preston, mesmerist and actress. *Long ago she left the stage for Lord Morgan Ellis*. If she would relate to him what had transpired between them on the evening of his murder, matters at the inquest might be able to be directed accordingly. It was not his role to be involved like this but he was uneasy at the way the coroner was being influenced (understood Mr Tunks was being pressured by higher beings for speed and results); realised that Miss Preston, especially when her antecedents were made public, could easily turn from a witness to a suspect, however innocent she might be. And he was here, he knew, because he wanted to see that beautiful woman again.

Miss Spoons herself finally answered the door, seemed bewildered to see Inspector Rivers, looked white-faced and strained. 'I should like to speak to Miss Preston once more if I may,' he said politely.

'Miss Preston is not well,' said Miss Spoons.

'I apologise for the intrusion. But it is of immense importance that I speak to her. With regard to the inquest of Lord Morgan Ellis.'

She finally gave him admittance, but reluctantly; asked him to wait in a large room with a small lamp she gave him. The lamp made uneasy shadows in the room, glass stars shone from above him in an unsettling manner as they caught light from the gas lamps outside. He walked about uncomfortably as if the room held alien forces; picked up a marble head that had numbers all over it, smoothed it with his hand for some unfathomable reason, thought of his dear dead wife and the way her hair fell out before she died. At last Miss Spoons returned and indicated that he should follow her to the cosy sitting room he had entered on his previous visit.

He was not prepared for what he found.

Miss Cordelia Preston seemed almost not to be the same woman. The elegant, attractive, confident person he had met was now pale, distraught, seemed not to notice his presence almost, and her hair was wild. Could this be delayed grief for Lord Ellis? A man, an old man (Inspector Rivers wondered why he felt relieved), obviously the foreign gentleman Constable Forrest had spoken of, stood beside the long windows; the men bowed as they were introduced. The curtains had been drawn, but not entirely; outside he saw again the shape of the angel, poised and hopeful although coated with snow, in the middle of the dark cold garden. The fir tree with its little unlit candle-holders seemed desolate now, Christmas forgotten. The fire crackled: it was the only sound.

When he said gently, 'I am sorry to have come at an obviously unsuitable time, but I need to talk to you about the death,' Miss Preston's eyes filled with tears which then ran unheeded down her cheeks and she did not answer him. It was most distressing and bewildering to see her. He looked at Miss Spoons for some elucidation for this terrible grief: she gave him none. He had to continue. 'Miss Preston, the inquest on Lord Ellis has now been opened and adjourned so that the funeral – funerals – you will likely have heard about the death of Lord Ellis's daughter, Lady Manon – can be held. It will open again the day after Christmas Day and you are to be called and it seems to me that you must prepare yourself for . . .' he paused, 'the intrusion of the Press. I will not be able to protect you from that.' But Miss Preston seemed not to hear.

'She knows she is called,' said Miss Spoons quietly, and she handed him a letter addressed to Miss Cordelia Preston, spinster, of Bedford Place.

Whereas I am credibly informed that you can give evidence on behalf of our sovereign Lady the Queen, touching the death of Lord Morgan Ellis, deceased; therefore by virtue of my office, in Her Majesty's name I charge and command you to appear before me at the Anchor Public House by Bow Street police station at five o'clock in the evening on the 26th day of

December instant, there to give evidence and be examined on
Her Majesty's behalf, before me and my Inquest. Hereof fail
not, as you Will answer at your peril. Given under my seal
this 24th day of December one thousand eight hundred and
forty-two.

Mr Tunks had already sent it. It was signed by him. It was
the form of letter sent to all the witnesses: here in this house it
seemed somehow to contain a tone of menace. The Inspector
handed the letter back to Miss Spoons. He looked again at Miss
Preston. And then suddenly his heart sank. She had worn gloves
last time they had met and he had not seen the contusions on
the back of her hands. He tried not to look at them, there could
be other reasons for such bruises and abrasions, of course there
could, perhaps she had – his mind seized at anything – fallen
in the snow. He spoke with enormous reluctance.

'You have – hurt your hands, Miss Preston?'

She stared down at her hands as if she did not see, but he
saw that Miss Spoons suddenly observed him most anxiously.
He glanced almost surreptitiously at the hands again, and looked
away. He could not believe that he would mind so much.

'Miss Preston.' It was hard to speak authoritatively in the
presence of such sorrow. But whatever was the matter, his matter
was more urgent. 'Miss Preston, I urge you most solemnly, once
again, to inform me of your business with Lord Ellis. It is only
if I have that information that I may be able to assist you by
speaking on your behalf to the coroner. I see that you have some
private sorrow and I am most regretful to be intruding. But I
am not sure if you understand the difficulties you may be placed
in if you do not answer the questions.'

But there was only silence in the room. The foreigner was
looking at Miss Preston; the Inspector could not read the look
on his face.

He made one more attempt. 'Miss Preston, because of the
suicide of that unfortunate young girl – the daughter, you

understand, of Lord and Lady Ellis – one of her Majesty's legal advisers will be present at the inquest to advise the Duke of Llannefydd. They will all be expecting – clamouring for – a very speedy conclusion, and sometimes in those circumstances – mistakes – can be made. I believe you may be in some danger if you cannot adequately advise the court what transpired between yourself and Lord Ellis on the night of the murder. An inquest can be an unruly thing and I adjudge that it is possible you might yourself be called to trial.'

She looked at him with terrible eyes as if she was on trial already, but she would not speak. At last the Frenchman turned to the Inspector. 'I believe Miss Preston understands the difficulties, *monsieur*,' he said. 'But she has difficulties of her own. It is not possible for her to answer you.'

Finally, unwillingly, Inspector Rivers took his leave. He wanted to stay there in the room, understand what terrible thing had happened. But Miss Spoons showed him out, polite but silent.

'Thank you,' was all she said, as she closed the door. He saw again in his mind the bruised, scratched hands.

Of course the coroner would have to be informed.

'Go home,' he said kindly to Constable Forrest who waited outside in the snow, for Constable Forrest had a young family and tomorrow was Christmas Day.

Nineteen

The funeral next day of Lord Morgan Ellis and his daughter Manon attracted more attention, and was an affair more riotous, than the family of the Duke of Llannefydd could have imagined in their wildest nightmares. The bodies would eventually be taken back to Wales, by family tradition, but the funeral was of course held in London, an event of pomp and ceremony and black horses and white lilies, Christmas Day or no. Black carriages, black horses, black feathers, a Welsh gun carriage, members of the British nobility: there had been a great rush at Jay's Mourning Emporium in Oxford Street. (But some stayed away: this was not perhaps a funeral they wished to be associated with. No member of the family of the Duke of Trent: extraordinary cruelty towards the memory of the young girl who had so recently become one of them.) The Queen had sent a distant cousin as commensurate with her consanguinity. But there were huge crowds lining the streets towards St Paul's Cathedral despite the dank dark fog and the drizzle; today was a holiday after all. They pointed and shouted and whispered; some of them ate pies from the pieman, who quickly saw a business opportunity and added a halfpenny to his prices. Such a cacophony of noise in the crowded streets as the hearse and the funeral procession went slowly by: beggars and entertainers mixed with the crowds, and pickpockets; someone was flying a kite, jugglers threw balls into the murky air, people relieved themselves, there were doves for sale in cages, balladeers sang their wares.

NOT ONE BUT TWO, O DESPERATE CRY!
THERE CANNOT BE ONE SINGLE EYE
NOT WET WITH TEARS, FOR THIS SAD STORY,
ONE DEAD IN GLORY OF WEDDING DRESS,
ONE DEAD AND GORY, O WHAT A MESS!

This was not just a funeral. This was – and the words, seething with possibilities, passed from mouth to mouth – *a thrilling event*: murder, suicide and mayhem.

Afterwards the horse-drawn hearse began at once its slow way to Wales, to the family burial place far away. In the closed coach behind, the two remaining children were bundled by Lady Rosamund. They were accompanied by one of the Duke's most trusted serving men, who had orders to see them safely back, away from the present scandal, to North Wales, where they were to await further ducal instructions.

The hearse and the closed coach were seen pulling out of the outer environs of London in the dank grey afternoon.

Twenty

The biggest upstairs room (sometimes referred to as 'the parlour') at the Anchor public house, nearby the Bow Street police station, was large as upstairs rooms went but not large enough for the number of interested parties who felt they had valid reason to be present at the coroner's inquest, the day after Christmas, on the death of Lord Morgan Ellis, heir to the Duke of Llannefydd. The room was often used for important parish meetings as well as inquests and was pleasant enough: pictures of country scenes on the walls; a fire to warm the room (which would soon be stinking hot with the smell of bodies); a large clock on the mantelpiece and a mirror reflecting the crowded room; a shelf for the gentlemen of the jury to place their hats. The curtains were open at the big windows but the morning light outside was grey: lamps had been lit. But there was no disguising the room's whereabouts: downstairs, people crowded and complained and laughed: the morning drinkers; the shady characters trying to have business meetings; Chartists; people trying to board the omnibus for the Elephant or the coach for Bristol, both of which stopped here. The crowds got worse. The coroner's officer called for constables: only those with legitimate reason would be allowed to climb the stairs, followed by the smell of strong ale and the shouts of the populace. When the Duke of Llannefydd himself was half carried, half pushed up the narrow stairs, followed by the widow in black, Lady Rosamund Ellis, there was a flurry of deference and excitement, bowing and nudging: *the nobility*.

The seventeen good and true men, already sworn in when they had been taken to see the body, filed in wearing their best clothes. They placed their hats upon the shelf, and sat importantly, knowing this was a very particular case; the bakers among them had risen even earlier than usual to fulfil their orders before they came here. The man from the *Morning Chronicle* had got in, and *The Times* journalist and the *News of the World* reporter, but the man from the *Globe* still fumed downstairs. Miss Rillie Spoons sat alone, one of the few women present, quiet and unassuming. She observed that one of the jurymen, Joseph Manley, glass-cutter, was known to them; they had purchased glass stars from his premises. Sir Francis Willoughby, adviser to royalty, sat beside the Duke of Llannefydd and Lady Rosamund Ellis watching everything attentively. People unknown to anyone seemed to have somehow obtained admittance, crowded the room; perhaps they were journalists, perhaps they were related to somebody, perhaps they were simply curious. Inspector Rivers sat at the back. Monsieur Roland appeared from somewhere. Constable Forrest, once the coroner's officer nodded, closed the door and stationed himself beside it. But even then, when at last there was some semblance of privacy and calm to allow proceedings to begin, the heavy sweet smell of beer drifted strongly, and pipe tobacco smoke seemed to seep in under the door of the upstairs room.

Mr Tunks entered, observed at once the presence of Sir Francis Willoughby, addressed the room with great severity. He would be in charge: this would not be a shambles. 'In the name of her Majesty as I begin this inquest I wish to advise everybody present, in case they are lacking in this particular knowledge, that a coroner's inquest is not, I repeat not, a court of law. It is an enquiry only and as such it is in no way conclusive and at all times I do abjure all present to remember that the coroner's hearing is a hearing of record only. It is important of course that the proceedings are reported – in that way we may find persons with further evidence who may come forward. But matters which the gentlemen of the jury may be privy to are not necessarily matters which' – he stared very hard at the man from the *Globe* who had now somehow managed to emerge from the mêlée downstairs – 'the general public need have knowledge of. I do hope the gentlemen of the press take my meaning. Innocent people who come forward with evidence must not be directly quoted – this leads to mischief, not justice. *I do not want any spurious reporting from my inquest on matters unrelated to the death of Lord Ellis.*' He peered over his large magnifying spectacles sternly: the journalists looked quite hurt to think the coroner might be rebuking them before the inquest had even begun. Inspector Rivers had to admit: Mr Tunks did his best. But they both knew from experience that the words might as well have been air.

'Call the surgeons.'

At the back of the room Inspector Rivers listened once more to the evidence, having to live with the uncomfortable fact that he had not, entirely, carried out his duty. He had, for the first time in his life, withheld evidence from a coroner. He heard the surgeons remark that the deceased would seem to have been in some sort of altercation, hence the marks on his face. Something, some instinct, had made the Inspector feel that Miss Preston was not a murderess: realising how quickly things might likely stack against her, he had not reported the fact of the marks on her hands to the coroner. *But I could be completely wrong. My instincts are not always correct.* The Inspector moved uneasily in the small hard chair at the back of the room. He observed Miss Rillie Spoons all alone. She sat very upright and still.

The Inspector also saw that the Duke of Llannefydd had been placed upon a special chair at the front and seemed more outraged than ever that he was subject to any kind of common law and was now forced to sit in the upstairs room of a common public house. Beside him, never speaking to him, sat the waxwork-like figure of Lady Rosamund, who had lost a husband and a daughter in a week. The two remaining of her children were nowhere to be seen: Lady Rosamund had not consulted Inspector Rivers when she returned them to Wales. As the surgeons described the state of the dead body and the coroner wrote down their evidence on large sheets of paper – occasionally saying, 'A moment please,' or putting up his hand, Inspector Rivers thought of the odd young person, half-man, half-child, who had waited for him in the snow to find out why his father was in Bloomsbury: Mr Tunks had not agreed that the heir to the Duke of Llannefydd, fifteen years old, should be called as a witness just because Inspector Rivers had had a feeling at the back of his neck. But of course the boy would not have been capable of giving evidence now: Inspector Rivers saw in his mind the siblings huddled together, the boy and his sister, bounded by grief, literally unable to speak when he saw them last, so great was their distress. *I always look for the grief*, he had said to Constable Forrest. And then his mind did one of its somersaults. *But – I saw other grief, that same night. I saw it not just in Mayfair – but in Bloomsbury.*

He saw her face: white, shocked, silent.

Then he saw their young faces: white, shocked, silent.

The white, shocked, silent young couple were in a coach in the rain. Lady Rosamund would have been surprised to know that this coach was heading towards, not driving away from, London.

They had left London for Wales after the funeral, travelled for hours; the coaches had finally stopped at an inn as night fell, not wishing to travel in darkness. All night Gwenlliam and

263

Morgan, wild with exhaustion and pain, whispered and wept together; their pale faces were dimly reflected at a dark upstairs window as they stared out at the wintry, friendless night. They heard a horse whinnying, saw the shadow of the big hearse parked up beside the inn; there their father and their sister lay in their coffins. They stared intently one more time through the darkness at that travelling tomb.

Then, as the hearse and the coach pulled away from the inn the next morning, a commotion occurred. The commotion was caused by the fifteen-year-old Lord Morgan Ellis, who, insisting on sitting outside as the carriage left, had managed, as they turned towards the main road, to throw a sharp stone at one of the coach's horses. The horse reared on the narrow way and the coach teetered and then overturned: they had planned a commotion; what they had actually achieved was a serious accident. Morgan jumped, falling, his head and body hit the cobbles but he picked himself up; Gwenlliam had braced herself against the coach back in preparation and then held on to the brass railing as the coach overturned, she was able to crawl out almost uninjured, was not aware that there was blood on her face. The manservant accompanying them, unwarned, had been badly hurt; people from the inn carried him away. Morgan's leg was bleeding as well as Gwenlliam's face, but they did not notice or care.

In the mêlée the two young people disappeared. They had simply walked away.

They had the enormous sum of thirty guineas about their persons: the money from the sale of Gwenlliam's emeralds.

After the surgeons, Inspector Rivers gave evidence, the footman who found the body gave evidence, each answering questions of the jury when required, occasionally answering to Sir Francis Willoughby. Then the old watchman who went through Bloomsbury Square calling out that all was well; he was certain that all was well on his watch at the hour.

'Which hour?'

'The hour of nine, my Lord.' He then went into a long, rambling account of why he had not called again near Blooms-bury Square, but everyone knew: the watchmen slept in their watch-houses with their gin on cold evenings; the coroner cut him short.

The Duke, called to give evidence, lounged in his special chair, refused to take the oath. 'Why the devil should I take an oath in a public house? I am the Duke of Llannefydd. I take the oath for no one.'

'You will take it for her Majesty,' said Mr Tunks very swiftly, refusing to catch Sir Francis Willoughby's eye. 'It is the law, my Lord, that even peers of the realm must give evidence on oath in this court: the evidence which you are about to give to this inquest on behalf of our Lady Sovereign the Queen touching the death of Lord Morgan Ellis shall be the truth the whole truth and nothing but the truth. So help you God.' The Duke answered all questions rudely, his eyes only shone when he saw again the murder weapon produced. *I do not know it*, he said, but there was avarice in his eyes.

After the Duke, Lady Rosamund imperiously, briefly, reiter-ated the story: Lord Morgan Ellis had had dinner at Grosvenor Square and had left the house thereafter. He had not spoken of his evening plans. The body had been formally identified as that of her husband. She stared at the murder weapon, the beautiful dagger that glowed and shone. Then she shrugged her most elegant shoulders. *I may have seen it in my husband's possession many years ago*, she said. *But I am not certain*. She did not look at the Duke, she did not look at Mr Tunks, she did not look at the jury. She spoke, as it were, to the pictures of country scenes on the walls, or to the windows, where rain fell past. While she was speaking the door at the back suddenly blew, or was pushed, open. Loud raucous voices seemed to enter the court at once, and then leave just as suddenly again as the door was quickly closed by Constable Forrest.

It was already late into the afternoon when the vagrant, Saul O'Reilly, was called as witness, or as a possible suspect. He was a poor specimen indeed. He had been brought from the police station; he shook and trembled and stank and asked for gin. He insisted he was thirty-two years old but looked like an old man and quite incapable of stabbing anybody: he mumbled and stumbled and looked at the jury in incomprehension. 'Well all I know is I was in the Blue Posts there, and I was wuth auld Martin the auld bugger, he knows I was wuth him, you can call him. I meant not to sleep in the square for I been done as a vagrant more times than one but I couldn't keep me head up as I remember it and went for the bushes as a bit o' shelter. I could do wuth a gin, I could, it would help me remember.' No gin appearing, he went on. 'Next thing the constable's knocking at me head. I could do wuth a gin, your Lordship, I could answer better wuth a gin.' His spindly legs seemed to give way.

'Oh couldn't we all, sit him down!' snapped one of the jurymen finally, hungry, tired (they had not had a break, except for pissing, since they began at ten in the morning, it was now nearly five o'clock). 'He couldn't stab a cat!'

The dirty old man suddenly said uncertainly, 'Where's the ladies?' Mr Tunks immediately made a sign to a constable and the unsavoury vagrant was taken away, forestalling any other likely impertinent and unseemly behaviour.

'Call Miss Preston,' called the coroner's officer quickly. He had been instructed by Mr Tunks to get as many witnesses as he could called on this first day, the inquest must be over as soon as possible. More lamps had been lit.

The jurors, some stomachs rumbling loudly, murmured among themselves rebelliously, but stopped for a moment when Miss Cordelia Preston was shown in; a fine-looking woman, they all noticed quickly, not young of course, but – well, fine-looking; then the mouth of Joseph Manley, glass-cutter, fell open in surprise – it was Cordelia, the lady mesmerist, why he knew her well, he liked her, had made her some stars, and here she was, a witness. He muttered this information to his neighbour, one of the bakers: *She's a mesmerist.*

Inspector Rivers saw that Miss Preston was ashen still, but – as if some magic had been somehow wrought, to make her calm – she was now contained in whatever was troubling her so terribly. *There is some mystery that I don't understand: she seems nothing like the people at Mrs Fortune's establishment.* She moved with elegance and grace towards the witness chair; he saw her fine waist, perhaps unusual in a woman of her age; he caught himself, looked away, embarrassed. Somehow he had expected her to be dressed in black: *he had seen the grief.* But she was dressed not in black, but in dark green with a bright, light green scarf about her shoulders that threw her features into fine relief: the high cheekbones, the lock of white hair. The Inspector liked looking at her, was aware of some extra beating at his heart inside his cloak. Saw also, with dismay, the journalists, leaning forward with interest. A woman in the story was what they had been hoping for: that would be news.

When Miss Preston had given her name and sworn to tell the truth in her beautiful voice Mr Tunks began his questioning in a kindly manner, as if he too was pleased to have this attractive woman in his court after a long day. He knew also that Inspector Rivers was worried that the mention of her calling, which was highly unlikely to have anything to do with the case, would go against her and Mr Tunks had it in his mind to protect her in whatever manner he could at this stage in the proceedings. If she refused, however, to answer questions about the night of the murder (Inspector Rivers had also spoken to him of this matter), that would be something else.

'Miss Preston, I believe you knew the deceased, Lord Morgan Ellis.'

'I did.'

'I also believe you saw him on the night of the murder.'

'I did, briefly.' (She spoke firmly as if she had rehearsed, and was sure of, her lines.)

267

Inspector Rivers looked quickly at Lady Rosamund Ellis. She was looking at Miss Preston but her face was quite devoid of expression. And then, oddly, just at that moment, Miss Preston looked across at Lady Rosamund Ellis also and their eyes, for a split second, locked: the Inspector saw it: *Something; they know something*. But he could not say what it was that he saw.

'Lord Ellis came to your house?'

'Yes, sir.'

Sir Francis Willoughby was suddenly on his feet. 'I believe you live very close to Bloomsbury Square, the site of this terrible crime, in a house from which you run your – your mesmerism business.' He made both *mesmerism* and *business* sound immoral: a sound of astonished, excited voices rose in the room.

Sir Francis Willoughby was within his rights, anybody at an inquest was allowed to question a witness. But Mr Tunks was outraged: Sir Francis had deliberately put this witness at a disadvantage before the real questioning had begun. 'Perhaps, my Lord, we could ascertain some relevant facts about the night of the murder first,' he said icily. Sir Francis gave a slight bow and sat again. But the damage had been done, Cordelia Preston had been identified for ever. The jury forgot they were hungry and thirsty. *I told you*, said the glass-cutter Joseph Manley to the baker. The journalists were writing furiously and the face and the bald head of the man from the *Globe* had gone very red with excitement as he tried to spell *mesmerism*.

Mr Tunks continued, seething, forgetting for a moment honours and pensions: this was *his* hearing. He actually contrived to turn his back on the illustrious royal lawyer as he spoke. 'Miss Preston, had you known Lord Ellis for a long time?'

Everybody in the court leaned forward, the room was quite silent. And then she said, 'I knew Lord Morgan Ellis when I was a young woman. But I had not seen him for many years until – until the night of his death.'

'At what hour did Lord Ellis come to your house?'

'Sometime after nine o'clock in the evening.'

'And how long did he stay?'

'For less than half an hour.'

'Had you been expecting him?'

Here she paused. 'I was not expecting him exactly. But I had some business with him that had to be discussed.'

'Ah.' She was co-operating; Mr Tunks wished his next question to be circumspect, and kind, but he had to ask it. 'And what was the business that he had come to discuss?'

Cordelia had remained still and calm as she answered his questions, elegant and contained. Now she moved the green scarf slightly, the lamplight behind her caught the light green colour so that it shone against her darker gown. Inspector Rivers swallowed nervously. *She looks so beautiful. She must answer.*

And Miss Preston did answer, with great firmness. 'The business between myself and Lord Ellis was private, sir.'

'Miss Preston.' The coroner cleared his throat. 'You must know that, in the circumstances, that business has become public, for this is murder and we have to understand what happened. What was the business?' He tried to assist her (his cousin's wife had been much helped by mesmerism). 'Did he come for your professional services?'

'I never discuss my clients.'

'I must ask you again, Miss Preston. What was the business between you and Lord Ellis?'

'I decline to answer.'

There was a kind of underlying murmur in the room now, of unspoken things: a murmur of sex and salaciousness and ghostly practices. Mr Tunks heard it. His questioning was brisk.

'You saw him leave your house?'

'Of course.'

'Did you ever see him again?'

'No.'

'Did you remain in the house?' He knew of course from Inspector Rivers that she had not.

'No. I felt like a walk.'

'In the night?'

'In the night.'

'Where did you walk in the night?'

I walked to Drury Lane.'

'It is dangerous surely for a woman to walk alone in the night in London. You surely did not walk *alone*.' She did not answer, did not go into the usage of flat-irons.

'Where were you going?'

She had to answer. They would know. 'I walked to Mrs Fortune's establishment in Cock Pit-lane.' There was a great flurry of activity and muttering now from where the journalists were sitting: *Did this – could their great good luck be that this woman who called herself a mesmerist used to be an actress?* For of course they knew (all the journalists knew) of Mrs Fortune's establishment. But Mr Tunks declined to give them further satisfaction. The dagger was produced once more. *I do not know it*, she said.

The coroner went back to his earlier question. 'Once more I must ask you, Miss Preston – and this is for your own sake, I do assure you – what your business was on the night of the murder with Lord Morgan Ellis. It seems you were one of the last people to see Lord Ellis alive. For his sake – and, as I say, for your own – it is imperative that you answer.'

Again the Inspector felt his heart, how it beat so strangely under his cloak, but he refused to lean forward in the way of all these people, agog and waiting.

Miss Preston did not satisfy them. The green scarf shone. She stood quite still, pale and calm before the coroner's hearing in the upstairs room. The silence went on and on. Finally she said, 'I believe I am not on trial, but a witness giving evidence pertaining to the death of Lord Ellis. I understand that the only reason you are aware of Lord Ellis's visit to my house is that you were sent an anonymous letter.' She heard the gasp of surprise in court, rode over it. 'I have not tried to hide the fact that he visited me, which I could very well have done. He came to see me, and then he left. I have given my evidence.' The green scarf shone. Miss Preston was adamant. 'I have nothing further to say.'

Sir Francis Willoughby made as if to stand again: the coroner, anticipating him, stood quickly first. 'It is my jurisdiction alone that decides the events here,' he said. He said it to Miss Preston, but to Inspector Rivers it was clear he was also addressing his legal superior. 'Miss Preston, I shall now adjourn my inquest until the morning. This will give you time to think on what I have to say to you. You will be called back to the witness stand tomorrow and you will answer my questions or you will be arrested by my officers for contempt.' He then turned most courteously to the jury. 'I thank you, gentlemen, for your patience over this long day.' He nodded to his officer, who immediately intoned loudly.

'All manner of persons who have anything more to do at this court before the Queen's coroner for this parish may depart home at this time, and give their attendance again on the morrow, Thursday, at ten of the clock in the forenoon precisely. God Save the Queen!'

Miss Preston and Miss Spoons hurried away into the darkness unhindered, not – yet – known to the populace.

At about ten o'clock that evening Inspector Rivers, against all his better judgements, once more banged the knocker and then rang the bell at the house in Bedford Place, heard again the bell echoing through the house. The maid opened the door, seemed minded to close it again but Inspector Rivers was too quick for her, was already inside. Down the hallway a skirt disappeared into a room, a door closed.

And then the foreigner Monsieur Roland appeared, carrying a lamp. 'Come,' he said to the Inspector and they went into the large room with the glass stars. The old man with the white hair motioned to the Inspector to sit, sat opposite him. 'Is it bad?' he enquired.

271

'I think it is bad,' answered Inspector Rivers.

'She cannot speak. She has her very strong reasons.'

'*Monsieur*, you are a man of the world. It is exactly as I predicted. It will be all over the newspapers and the penny broadsides in the morning that a mesmerist is refusing to give evidence in what is already a notorious inquest, a mesmerist who – the newspapers will have ascertained this and writ it large – used to be an actress. You do not understand these things as I do – there will be a murder trial, her life could be ruined by this even if she is the most innocent woman in London! The journalists will be swarming over Mrs Fortune's establishment this evening.'

Monsieur Roland sat very still, thinking. His white hair gleamed in the lamplight. Despite himself the Inspector felt himself relax slightly. As if the Frenchman were wiser than he.

'The Duke of Llannefydd is accompanied by a gentleman of the law. Is Miss Preston allowed to be accompanied by a lawyer?'

'It may make it seem, already, that she is accused.'

'Nevertheless.' Monsieur Roland again sat in silence. Then he said, 'It is not possible for her to speak. Therefore a lawyer could at least deflect the wilder or more irrelevant questions. And represent her interests.'

'Of course. But the coroner would have to agree. It is his decision alone, depending on circumstances.'

'I will come with you,' said Monsieur Roland, and he went into the hallway for his hat.

Twenty-one

The broadsides and the broadsheets were out at first light: the printers had again been up all night, they knew when they were on to gold. One of the papers, the ink only now drying, was illustrated by a most bizarre woodcut last used to illustrate the trial of a lunatic: a clumsy illustration of a fat woman with long flying hair, staring eyes, and a knife.

> **WITH EVIL EYE SHE DREW HIM IN,**
> **INTO HER TERRIBLE HOUSE OF SIN.**
> **HER ACTRESS SKILLS SHE BROUGHT TO PLAY,**
> **AS EVEN IN DEATH'S ARMS HE LAY;**
> **SOME USE AN AXE; THEY SAY A KNIFE;**
> **OR DID MESMERISM TAKE HIS LIFE?!**

Even Regina, Queen of the Broadsides, was deeply offended by this. When Nellie the maid slipped out early in the morning and brought the penny papers back, Regina, having perused them, hid them under her mattress where she kept many things, so that Rillie and Cordelia would not see them. Mrs Spoons, as if she picked up invisible vibrations, suddenly got very angry

273

also, threw her cards everywhere and refused to let Rillie dress her. Monsieur Roland arrived at the house in Bloomsbury carrying *The Times* and looking extremely grave. *The Times* was not so vulgar, ever, as to have very large headlines. But under the heading CORONER'S INQUEST, smaller lettering did proclaim:

Lady Mesmerist, Actress, Last Person To See Lord Morgan Ellis Alive?

Crowds gathered outside the Anchor public house, hoping for a glimpse of the evil lady.

And no sooner were the newspaper headlines in the public domain than various people of all classes appeared at the Anchor, wishing to give evidence at this inquest: Mr Tunks had already summoned the actor, Mr George Tryfont, but now it transpired that other people wished to appear also, people kept asking to speak to the coroner: he had had to decide very quickly who was relevant and who was not. Miss Preston's business partner, Miss Spoons, offered to give evidence. Most flurrying for Mr Tunks was the fact that one of those who wished to speak, who said she had something to say about the matter, was the sister of Sir Francis Willoughby; she refused to be dissuaded, even by her brother (the coroner was privy to raised voices, in the hallway outside the crowded upstairs room). Various doctors, attracted by the publicity and hoping for a devastating death blow to this dangerous cult of mesmerism, were also arguing at the door with Constable Forrest, insisting on their prerogative to attend. All in all, it was quite frankly not the calm that Mr Tunks would have liked.

When the court was finally reconvened, Inspector Rivers saw, with some relief, that Miss Preston was already sitting quietly in the upstairs room, next to a legal gentleman. Miss Spoons was by herself towards the back, and Monsieur Roland effaced himself effortlessly by a window. When Miss Preston was recalled by Mr Tunks to continue her evidence she, another coloured scarf, blue this time, about her shoulders, remained where she was; the lawyer stood, as had been agreed late last night. Monsieur Roland and the coroner had come to a compromise: if the newspapers distorted the evidence given so far, only then was Miss Preston to be allowed counsel, which Monsieur Roland would retain. 'I will decide if there has been distortion,' the coroner had warned them.

The new lawyer brandished several newspapers. 'Sir,' he said to the coroner, 'my client, Miss Preston, is nothing more than a witness in this case, yet the headlines in the newspapers are about her alone. She feels that her privacy has already been breached beyond reasonable boundary' – he waved the newspapers again, including the broadsheet with its lurid woodcut – 'despite the words of warning given by yourself to the press only yesterday. Unless she feels that the questions put to her have some direct bearing on the murder, I have advised my client that she is not required to answer.'

There was a great murmur of rage from the Duke of Llannefydd's party. Inspector Rivers held his breath: would Mr Tunks do his duty or be swayed by the presence of nobility? Mr Tunks rose to the occasion. 'That is not quite correct, sir,' he said to the lawyer firmly. 'Miss Preston is indeed required to answer the questions put to her, as are all witnesses. She cannot be excused. All we are doing at this inquest is to try to arrive at the truth: that is, to find the true answers to questions that may seem irrelevant now, but may turn out to be of great importance. It is not you, nor Miss Preston, but I, and I alone, who will decide if such questions have a relevance. However . . .' He stared malevolently at the gentlemen of the press. The journalists looked suitably humble at his look and at his tone: under no circumstances could they have borne to be excluded from something so sensational. 'You, gentlemen, will say that the penny papers are not your responsibility. I say they get their material from your reports, and I feel that your own headlines were unsuitable. I shall place a heavy fine upon the next newspaper that I feel has overstepped its brief.' Still Inspector Rivers waited. 'For the moment,' continued the coroner, 'I shall, in the circumstances, call other witnesses before Miss Preston, for what they say may have some bearing on Miss Preston's evidence.' Inspector Rivers breathed out at last. 'First I call Miss Amaryllis Spoons.'

Inspector Rivers thought how comforting Miss Spoons looked. She was respectable and pleasant and neat and reliable and it was not lost upon members of the jury and the people in the crowded room that, despite her age, she had, slightly, the air of her Majesty Queen Victoria (or perhaps her Majesty's mother).

Miss Spoons answered pleasantly and clearly: she lived in the same house as Miss Preston; had known her for many years; had known Lord Morgan Ellis slightly many years ago but had never seen him again until the night in question.

'I understand, Miss Spoons,' said Mr Tunks, 'that you are Miss Preston's business partner. Is that correct?'

'That is correct.' There was a slightly uneasy stir at this: women in business was a bit like carriages pulling horses: it was against the instincts of almost everybody in the upstairs room, whatever their antecedents.

'How long did Lord Ellis stay at your house?'

'Less than thirty minutes I should say, your Honour.' Mr Tunks liked it when people called him 'your Honour', although the term was quite incorrect. 'I let him out of the house myself.'

'What was Lord Ellis's frame of mind, would you say?'

She smiled at Mr Tunks. 'It would not occur to me to consider Lord Ellis's frame of mind, your Honour. But he bowed most politely, and I closed the door.'

'And then Miss Preston went out, alone.'

'Yes.'

'Were you worried about her?'

If anyone was to explain to this gathering about flat-irons and big stones in pockets and ladies who knew the streets of London yet were in no way women of the street, Rillie Spoons in her respectable bonnet was the one; she explained. 'We know these particular streets so well, your Honour. We have lived in them all our lives. That part of London is our village.' But yet again, the murmur came. Ladies – real ladies – did not walk alone at night. It was as simple as that.

'You too used to frequent Mrs Fortune's establishment?'

Inspector Rivers looked at the floor. Miss Spoons had to answer: the information could not be hidden now. 'I did, yes. When we worked as actresses, going to Mrs Fortune's rooms was a way of hearing about available work.'

'But Miss Preston is no longer an actress. She no longer needed to hear about available work.'

'Well,' said Rillie, and she smiled sweetly again at Mr Tunks, 'it is fun, sometimes, to hear of the old days.'

Mr Tunks digested this, embarrassed. *Fun?* An odd word, surely. 'Did you see Miss Preston when she came home?'

'I did.'

'Did she seem in distress?'

'Not at all. She and I discussed some of our old acquaintances who were at Mrs Fortune's that night. She gave me news of them.'

'And you never saw Lord Morgan Ellis again?'

'Never.'

She turned to leave the witness place but he had not quite finished. 'Miss Spoons, do you know why Lord Ellis came to see Miss Preston?' There was a moment of absolute silence as Rillie paused in her movement, turned back to face Mr Tunks.

'I have no idea, your Honour. The door to the room they were speaking in was closed.'

Mr Tunks sighed. 'Thank you, Miss Spoons.'

When the name of the next witness was called there was a buzz of excitement, not because it was understood, yet, that this was the sister of Sir Francis Willoughby, but because yet another member of the nobility had suddenly appeared. Inspector Rivers saw that Miss Preston looked startled when she saw her.

The Duchess of Arden, Lady Alicia Taverner, was tall and

277

very thin and most imposing. She took the oath without demur (although she was easily as high in rank, through her own antecedents and her marriage to the Duke of Arden, as the Duke of Llannefydd) and answered the questions in a clear voice.

'Did you know the deceased, your Ladyship?'

'I did.' She did not comment further, looked away from Lady Rosamund and the Duke.

'He was a man of nobility and good works, your Ladyship, as you know.'

'Indeed.' Some unspoken disapproval was perhaps implied by the tone of her voice.

Mr Tunks cleared his throat nervously: *What was this?* 'You have come here because you know something pertaining to his death?'

'I do not – save for one thing.'

'What is that?'

'I assumed, from what I read in the newspapers this morning, that the woman he visited on the night of the murder seems somehow to have been connected to his death simply because of her practice of mesmerism, and for no other reason.'

Mr Tunks was grave. 'It is unfortunate that such a connection has been made, for I have to say again,' (he was looking once more at the journalists), 'that it was not apparent in this court in the evidence we heard that mesmerism comes into this story.'

'I am very glad to hear it. And although my brother,' she bowed calmly at Sir Francis Willoughby (there was a surprised intake of breath in the room), 'does not agree with me, I believe that mesmerism is a power for good, not evil.' (There were murmurs all over the courtroom; angry, louder mutterings from where several medical practitioners were sitting: this was not what they had come to the inquest to hear.) 'I know nothing about the actual death of Lord Ellis, but if the newspaper-reading public must read of the traducing of the reputation of Miss Preston on account of her work as a mesmerist, as part of the activities of this inquest,' (Mr Tunks felt the rebuke), 'then I am here to speak on her behalf.' She ignored the appalled look on her brother's face. Sir Francis Willoughby, deeply embarrassed, pulled at his cravat, tried to look anywhere but at his sister.

'Your Ladyship,' said Mr Tunks, trying to regain ground, 'I am most grateful for your appearance, and I hope that the newspapermen present,' again he glowered at them, 'will take careful note of your words. May I ask you, your Ladyship, if you know Miss Preston personally; or are you speaking generally?'

Very briefly the Duchess looked at Cordelia, looked back at the coroner. 'I do know her, and I know something of her work.'

'Please explain to the court.'

Lady Alicia Taverner, Duchess of Arden, spoke very clearly and concisely. 'Some time ago I had to have a very serious operation. I had contracted cancer. I had to have,' the Duchess paused only very slightly, 'a breast removed.' She took absolutely no notice of the gasp of shock. Did she say *breast*? 'The operation is a most painful one, and the doctors cannot or will not help with the pain, so one must look for help oneself.' The doctors stared angrily but the jurors leaned forward: who among them had not, some time in their life, heard the screams from the hospital wards as surgeons sawed? 'I had been apprised of Miss Preston's skills and summoned her to the hospital. She had not advertised, she had not importuned me or anyone I know: I had simply heard of her.' Lady Alicia, just for a moment, looked down at her gloves, and then straight at the jury. All seventeen of the men were staring at her: some in shock, some in horror, some in admiration. The only sound was the scratching of the quill as Mr Tunks continued to write. 'Miss Preston mesmerised me before the operation, and sat with me during it. I remember moments of great pain and then I remember Miss Preston drawing her hands across my body. I believe I spent most of the operation in some sort of trance. It only occurred to me months later, when I was recovered, that I had not been asked at any time for any payment for her services. Miss Preston is a skilled and professional practitioner and it was not possible for me to

ignore the calumny that has been heaped upon her in the newspapers this morning when I feel so very grateful for her skills.'

She turned, as if she would leave the court: it was a member
of the jury, Mr Joseph Manley, glass-cutter, who called her back.
'Your Ladyship.' She turned again. 'Your Ladyship, excuse me,
but – what does it feel like, this – mesmerism? How does it
work, I mean?'

She remained motionless briefly and then she said: 'It is –
something, something like heat. It felt as if some – power or
energy from another person was assisting me, or bearing pain
for me, I am not sure which.' She looked directly at Cordelia.
'Thank you, Miss Preston,' she said. 'I hope you will consider
this payment of another kind,' and she smiled briefly. And then
Lady Alicia Taverner, Duchess of Arden, was simply gone,
without anyone's permission: the door opened, the sound of
voices and the smell of ale shouted in; the door closed and the
sounds and the smells drifted away. Sir Francis Willoughby did
not look at his clients; wiped perspiration from his forehead: he
was imagining the damage this terrible publicity would do to
his family: she had mentioned *breasts* in a court full of men,
what was the Duke her husband thinking of, to allow it? It did
not occur to him that it was he himself who had identified Miss
Preston's skills to the world, so bringing his own sister into the
courtroom to mention unmentionable parts of the body out loud.

The next witness had received a notice to attend and had been
waiting outside most impatiently. He was wearing a black velvet
cloak and a flamboyant purple cravat, he had been busy shaking
rain from the velvet, it was a terrible day outside. He gave his
oath and named his profession: Mr George Tryfont, Act-or.

Mr Tunks began. 'Mr Tryfont, you saw Miss Preston the night
in question?'

Mr Tryfont began his performance. He spoke as if he were in
a theatre, playing the leading role; his voice carried to every

corner of the crowded room. 'I have known Miss Preston for many years. As you know she is, or at least was, an actress, and we have toured the country in several productions of note in the past, including, several years ago, a performance of a Shakespearean tragedy where I myself played the lead, which name I cannot bring myself to mention for fear of bringing down bad luck upon us, but many of you, familiar no doubt with the adages and superstitions of the theatre, will know to which play I am referring.' Most of the members of the jury looked at him blankly.

'*Macbeth*,' said Mr Joseph Manley, glass-cutter, in a stage whisper. 'He means *Macbeth*, the silly pouncer.'

Mr Tunks tapped with his quill on his desk. 'The night in question, Mr Tryfont, if you please.'

'On the night in question I was having a quiet drink at the establishment off Drury Lane of Mrs Fortune, a well-known meeting place for members of my profession which unfortunately has lately and most certainly undeservedly become somewhat notorious, simply because some unfortunate young lady was last seen alive there and then was next seen dead in the environs of—'

'Thank you, Mr Tryfont, we are only trying to ascertain from you whether Miss Preston was with you that evening.'

'I am leading up to that,' he answered rather haughtily. 'I am setting the scene for you, nothing more.'

'Did Miss Preston come to Mrs Fortune's establishment that evening?'

'She was most certainly there and – Mrs Fortune said you are sure to ask questions of clothes – she wore a delightful light blue gown, and she and I spent some time in conversation regarding the aforementioned production and the employment of an elephant which showed to what depths the management had lowered itself to interest the uncouth kind of audience that we were attracting and the lengths to which they would go – we are speaking of Shakespeare here, your Honour, and—'

'At what time did Miss Preston arrive?'

'I do happen to know the precise answer to that question, it was just after ten in the evening, I had myself just arrived from appearing at the theatre.' He waited. 'That is the Strand Theatre, in case you are interested. I am appearing there.' (He did not say he had seven lines.) 'I am appearing in *Mortals Will Know*.'

'How long did Miss Preston stay at Mrs Fortune's establishment?'

'We spoke for a long time. Perhaps two hours. Yes, I am sure she did not leave before midnight, for I had a lot to tell her. It was after midnight when we left, I remember because I was hungry and had decided to go to another club where the food is more – to my liking. We walked towards Holborn, where I was intending to go, we parted at Great Russell Street.'

'Did Miss Preston seem distressed in any way?'

'About the elephant?'

Rillie Spoons gave a quick, small smile across the room to Miss Preston, who somehow, Inspector Rivers saw, smiled back.

'About anything in particular?' said Mr Tunks. The actor looked nonplussed. 'Did she speak of any difficulties, did she seem upset?'

'Upset? No. Not that I noticed.'

'Was her clothing in disarray? Her pale blue gown?'

'Certainly not. She listened with great interest to my story.' There was a kind of snigger in the room which he caught. He threw his velvet cape across his shoulder. 'I am a leading Actor,' he said, hurt.

'Thank you, Mr Tryfont,' said the coroner.

'Is that all?'

'You have confirmed that Miss Preston was with you around ten o'clock in the evening on the night of the murder and you did not part till after midnight. Thank you. That is all.'

'Wonder where he got his ladies' cravat?' said someone, loud enough for Mr Tryfont to hear. He swept out of the courtroom with a pained look upon his face.

*   *   *

282

When Miss Preston and Miss Spoons saw the next witness enter, their eyes locked for a split second in alarm: Inspector Rivers saw.

'Miss Lucinda Choodle,' called the coroner's officer.

Miss Lucinda Choodle, entering, did not, like the Duchess of Arden, come to the place of witness quietly. She said, 'Excuse *me*,' with hauteur as she had to brush past people in the room, past all the gentlemen; her hat she kept readjusting; she swept her skirts together with her other hand. She looked straight at Cordelia before she turned to the coroner.

'I, Miss Lucinda Choodle, of Paddington,' she identified herself as she took the oath.

'Miss Choodle, what is the reason you have come to this hearing this morning?'

'I have important testimony.'

'Regarding the death of Lord Morgan Ellis?'

'Regarding the suspect, Miss Cordelia Preston, who used to be called Mrs du Pont.'

Mr Tunks showed his outrage. 'Miss Choodle, this is a coroner's inquest, not the Old Bailey. We are taking evidence only to find the facts of the matter of the death of Lord Morgan Ellis. Miss Cordelia Preston is, at the moment, a witness to this case, nothing more.' He fixed the journalists with his stern eye. 'Anybody who states otherwise will be accused by me of libel or slander. It is only for the members of the jury to decide who is a suspect and who is not.'

Miss Choodle was unabashed, went on before she could again be silenced. 'Well I read this morning's newspaper and she seemed like a suspect to me. Miss Preston tells lies. So you should not believe her testimony.' The court rustled. 'Miss Preston has ruined my life.'

'In what manner?' said the coroner expressionlessly.

'Miss Preston used to live in a basement in Little Russell Street. She called herself Mrs du Pont then. She advertised – it was called "matrimonial advice".'

'She was not a mesmerist?'

'She said she was a phreno-mesmerist – well that is what she *said*, that's what the advertisements said. But I made sure she didn't phreno-mesmerise me!'

'Why did you go to see her?'

'I wanted – matrimonial advice. I had heard about her. But she told me disgusting things, lies, that I could not repeat here – or anywhere else.' Inspector Rivers saw that Cordelia and Rillie both sat with bowed heads.

'You are accusing Miss Preston of lying, Miss Choodle. I think you will have to be a little more specific.'

'No. I am not a witness. I am just here to talk about Miss Preston.'

'The hearing is not about Miss Preston, Miss Choodle.'

'The newspapers were all about Miss Preston,' she replied rather pertly.

Mr Tunks looked very severe. 'I repeat: this hearing is about the murder of a peer of this realm, and I can have you arraigned for wasting the court's time.'

'I don't know what "arraigned" is. I have come here because I see it as my public duty. Young girls must be protected from Miss Preston.' Inspector Rivers thought that surely Mr Tunks would stop the witness now. He did not.

'Have you consulted Miss Preston recently?'

'No, I told you, it was when she was living in a basement and calling herself Mrs du Pont. I'm telling you about something that happened more than three years ago – but it ruined my life. I now have to work as a governess. But I was engaged to be married to a wonderful man and I went to see Miss Preston and she told me such – unspeakable things, such lies about my – my dearly betrothed – Mr John Forsyth, if you want to know – and the things she said made me become quite ill.'

Here Sir Francis Willoughby, who had remained silent since the appearance of his sister, suddenly stood up and spoke. 'Miss Choodle,' he said very quickly, before the coroner could object, but most kindly, 'as your name is still Miss Choodle I am presuming that you did not, in the end, marry your betrothed, Mr – ah – Mr Forsyth.'

She found a white handkerchief about her person. 'I did not.' She dabbed her eyes.

'Why was that, Miss Choodle?' Sir Francis Willoughby was a most clever and experienced barrister, had an inkling he was on to something here, could not wait about for the ponderings of Mr Tunks.

'My betrothed – while I was ill – I became ill, you see, Miss Preston made me ill, and while I was ill my betrothed,' she now began to weep in earnest, 'went off and married someone else. I am now – my life is ruined.' She turned to Cordelia. 'You ruined my life!' she cried, and she was suddenly weeping most bitterly. And all around the court they thought of the sad description: *governess*: last resort of a respectable unmarried lady.

The coroner again took charge. 'Miss Choodle, you say that Miss Preston told you lies about your betrothed?'

'Yes.'

'Did she know him?'

'No.'

'So how exactly did she tell lies about him? Did she know *of* him?'

'I do not wish to say any more.'

'Miss Choodle . . .' Mr Tunks cleared his throat, he was always distressed by tears at his inquests. 'Miss Choodle, you cannot come to this hearing and make accusations about a person without backing them up. That is known as slander and could lead to your imprisonment.'

She literally blanched. 'You mean I am doing my public duty and I shall be imprisoned?'

'I mean you must substantiate your claim.'

'I came to do good.'

'What you are actually doing is harm.'

Miss Choodle was so incensed she shouted. 'I am not doing

harm – she did harm! She told me men did things – disgusting things – to women.' She looked quite wildly round the room. 'To their bodies. That Mr Forsyth would do – foul things to my body, that is what Miss Preston does, *that is what Miss Preston tells young innocent girls in dark rooms with candles!'*

If shock, deep embarrassment, and repulsion can make a sound, that was the sound that was heard now in the upstairs room. Mr Tunks actually blushed. This was unforgivable in a public place. Every single man in the room was scandalised. The jurors cleared their throats in outrage, the journalists scribbled with flushed faces. The Duke of Llannefydd's face had gone a purple colour. Sir Francis Willoughby again got out his large kerchief and wiped his forehead: this inquest was becoming most improper and quite out of hand, it was insupportable. As if the door itself was shocked, it flew open: a blast of sound, the smell of ale. Constable Forrest pushed it closed.

And Inspector Rivers, red-faced, caught the eye of Monsieur Roland in shock and dismay. He forced himself to look around the room. Everywhere: closed faces, disapproval, disgust. Angry rain pounded on the roof of the Anchor public house, lashed at the windows. The Inspector knew that Miss Preston's reputation was damaged irrevocably: she could *never* recover from this shameful information, the murder of Lord Ellis was for the moment irrelevant. London society which had given her her living would be closed to her, and she had no man to protect her except, it seemed, an old Frenchman. She could be the greatest mesmerist in the world but she was soiled for ever by what Miss Choodle had said.

She was ruined.

'Thank you, Miss Choodle,' said Mr Tunks in a low voice.

But Miss Cordelia Preston suddenly erupted. She stood shaking uncontrollably with fury as she brushed off the arm of the lawyer beside her; her hat fell from her head but she did not notice. She had understood at once what was lost. From where she was in the room she spoke clearly and angrily to Miss

Choodle. 'Miss Choodle, I very well remember that our whole conversation began because you told me that your betrothed had a deformity.' (She did not see Rillie's appalled face: *Stop it, Cordie! Stop it!*) 'Perhaps you would like to explain to this court what Mr Forsyth's deformity was and how it occurred. Perhaps that could explain your dilemma, and be reported in the newspapers, along with these calumnies against myself!'

Miss Choodle fled, clasping her skirts in anguish, her face red, her tears startled to a standstill on her cheeks: quickly Constable Forrest opened, then closed, the door. The rain drummed on the roof.

'Please come back to the stand, Miss Preston,' said Mr Tunks gravely, and Cordelia now swept back to the witness chair, again shaking off the restraining hand of her lawyer; she addressed the room even before she was invited to, her eyes sparking fire.

'I am a witness at the inquest regarding the murder of Lord Morgan Ellis, whose name has hardly been mentioned this morning. The court instead seems to be intent rather on the murder of my reputation. I will not allow myself to be ruined by a poor, silly, sad girl like Miss Choodle. I never expected to have to discuss my private affairs and my private work in a public place but I did indeed counsel young women, in fact it became a large part of my work, such is the dangerous ignorance of so many respectable girls about the state of matrimony. Nobody will speak to them of these things, not even their own mothers, and the damage done to these young women – and to young men incidentally – is incalculable!'

It was, in its way, magnificent. She spoke of the unspeakable in her beautiful voice, her hair fell in places from its pins but somehow only added to the effect. She looked, Inspector Rivers saw it, wonderful. If Rillie had not been almost paralysed with fear as she saw their careful life crashing down upon them wildly like an avalanche she might have said to herself: *There she is, the old Cordie!*

But the outrage against propriety had been too great. Cordelia was too late in her magnificence. She was now so far from the ideal of womanhood that every man in the room held clearly to his heart that, although they indeed saw her magnificence, she could not retrieve the situation. They thought to themselves, *she is an actress, after all*, and of how they would not like their wives and daughters to hear her words. The sympathy, the attraction, in the upstairs room full of gentlemen with the pictures of gentle country scenes and the lamps and the row of hats, was gone.

Cordelia was breathing hard, trying to control herself. She turned to the coroner. 'This has nothing, nothing whatever to do with the death of Ellis. I beg you to understand what is happening here, and to stop these attacks upon my person.'

'Miss Preston,' said Mr Tunks in judicious, measured tones, 'it seems to me that you have nothing more to lose. What was your business with Lord Morgan Ellis – or Ellis as you rather familiarly called him just now – on the night of his murder?'

Her effort at composure was Herculean. She took a deep breath and stared straight at Lady Rosamund, widow, and mother of a daughter who had committed suicide. Lady Rosamund was like a statue carved in marble as she held Miss Preston's look. For a moment the silence in the court was like a sound. They heard the rain.

'I will not answer,' said Cordelia at last.

The door opened yet again and noise rushed in. Mr Tunks looked up in exasperation, in time to see two bodies shoot into the room as if propelled from a cannon. Obviously caught in the rain, two white-faced, dishevelled young people stood in the doorway dripping water. Inspector Rivers rose in alarm: the two children of Lord Morgan Ellis and Lady Rosamund Ellis stood there; the girl seemed to have bruises on her face. In the boy's hand was a wet copy of *The Times*, folded. The young people at once took in Cordelia giving evidence with wild and angry hair;

288

they also saw the Duke of Llannefydd and Lady Rosamund. For a moment everything was frozen: the crowded room; the jurors' hats on the shelf (one hadn't been able to fit, and was on the mantelpiece with the clock); the flickering lamps caught in the draught from the door. And then the boy closed the door behind them. They saw that he limped, and rubbed the side of his neck over and over.

'Yes?' said Mr Tunks, puzzled, for despite their disarray one could see their clothes, one could see their air: he did not know yet who they were but these were gentry, certainly.

'I wish to give evidence,' said Morgan clearly, his voice breaking as usual.

'Morgan!' Lady Rosamund's sharp voice cut through the air. She moved through the crowded chairs and people, a path somehow opening before her, towards her children. She reached the door. She put her hand on Morgan's shoulder. The white ringed hand shone against his dark, wet cloak.

'My children are disturbed,' she said stiffly back to the coroner, 'which is quite understandable in the circumstances. You will excuse me if I take them from this place.'

But Morgan pulled away, actually grabbed Constable Forrest's arm. 'I will give evidence!' he said loudly again. 'She will try to stop me giving evidence. It is about *me*!' he called across the room. 'I know why my father was visiting her, it was because *I* had visited her!'

After a split second of silence the room exploded into uproar: chairs scraped, paper floated and ink spilt, books fell upon the floor as people conjured up disgraceful thoughts: could the salacity and immorality of this woman go further: she corrupted young boys also? Lamps flickered with incredulity, rain pounded at the window, Inspector Rivers moved to the door, the hat on the mantelpiece got knocked off and then trampled in the general affray. The clock on the mantelpiece pointed to two minutes to one o'clock. At this point the Duke of Llannefydd tried to stand, was taken with a seizure. He pulled at his cravat as he fell heavily

289

forward into the arms of Sir Francis Willoughby who, unable to hold the weight of this peer of the realm, fell also, in a manner most unbecoming to his prestige.

The Thames rose high that particular day because of the heavy rain; water seeped up the alleys towards the Strand, through Hungerford Market: such a stench there of mud and swirling horse dung and human dung and dead chickens and chloride of lime and cabbages and rust and torn floating newspapers with yesterday's stories.

Today's story however went on inexorably in the upstairs room of the Anchor. The Duke of Llannefydd had been quickly attended by the anti-mesmeric doctors present and had been, with difficulty, heaved down the stairs and away to the Middlesex Hospital; Sir Francis Willoughby whispered in anxious tones to Lady Rosamund but Lady Rosamund seemed frozen as her daughter, unexplained blood on her face, refused to attend her mother but sat shivering at the back of the court on a chair that had been quickly found for her, and her son limped to the place indicated by the coroner. It was clear to everyone that the boy had a most terrible headache, his hand kept rubbing the back of his neck and the side of his face, his face was deathly white.

Morgan was wild to speak, pain making him wild; did not look at Cordelia; the coroner, using the omnipotence of his office, signed magisterially, but kindly, for him to wait just one moment. He and Sir Francis Willoughby had finally joined forces, had spoken urgently together (in the moments after Sir Francis was retrieved from underneath the short, fat bulk of the Duke of Llannefydd), in a corner of the room.

Mr Tunks spoke. 'It is the duty of my ancient office to remind everybody here that each death in this world is a personal tragedy for the family concerned. The family of Lord Morgan Ellis has had two tragedies to contend with in as many days, and now the Duke of Llannefydd himself, one of the noble peers of our realm and a servant of our sovereign Queen, has been taken to the hospital. We must find the truth but we must protect the grief of those whose loss is inconsolable, and pray too that the burden will not become heavier. It is the bounden duty of this hearing to avoid – wherever possible – any undue upset to people's personal lives.' He bowed slightly in the direction of Lady Rosamund. 'It has therefore been agreed by Sir Francis Willoughby, her Majesty's adviser, and myself that the gentlemen of the press be asked to leave this hearing.' And Inspector Rivers, despite his feelings of distaste for what he had heard, thought *but Miss Preston's life has already been ruined beyond recall, for her story has been told and the journalists were here, and the world shall know of it.* He minded that this besmirchment even affected him. He had liked her very much, whatever other shocking stories were to now emerge.

The gentlemen of the press were outraged. They were here of right, the truth must be made known.

'Nothing at all is "of right" at a coroner's inquest,' said Mr Tunks pedantically. 'Only I decide what is right at this hearing and I have decided that you shall leave. Nothing shall continue while you are present. When the jury have reached their verdict in this inquest it shall be conveyed to you.'

'I refuse to leave, in the name of press freedom!' shouted the man from the *Globe*.

And all the time, in front of them, sitting now on the chair provided for witnesses should they so desire to use it, the boy's hand rubbed at his neck, at his white, white face, his eyes deep with pain. Nobody who saw could not feel sympathy, he was only a boy. Someone looked round for one of the doctors but they seemed to have gone with the Duke. And then suddenly the boy's body appeared to go into a spasm of agony; it seemed perhaps as if he might have a fit of some kind.

It was Miss Preston, not a doctor, not the pressmen ordered out, who moved. She cast one glance towards the Frenchman, Monsieur Roland. Then quickly, almost silently, she came to

291

the witness chair, and nobody spoke, not even Mr Tunks the coroner.

Afterwards, when it was over, men said they had never seen such a thing, some said they didn't believe what they had seen, but nobody said that it was a trick, or a ploy, or had been planned, for they had all seen the boy's face.

All she had said was 'Morgan,' in her low and pleasing voice. She had touched him only for the briefest of moments, they were sure of that. She had placed her hand upon his head. And they heard a sigh, there in the upstairs room, was it a sigh? a sound, a soft, haunted sound. But whether it was from the boy or the woman they could not tell. Then she had simply drawn her hands down, beside his head, over his head, her hands moved rhythmically over and over. They moved past his head and his neck, very near but not touching, past his shoulders and his back. She had removed her gloves as she came towards him. The contusions were clear on the back of her hands as she worked. The upstairs room was so quiet despite the falling rain and the drinking echo from below that they could hear her regular deep breathing as she passed her hands over and over. Beads of perspiration appeared upon her forehead. After some time it was clear that the boy, no longer rigid, was in some sort of trance. Sometimes his hands moved with her hands, themselves passing near his own neck, over and over, mimicking her movement. And then he was still again. Not asleep, for his eyes were not closed, but very still. Colour came back into his face as he sat there.

At last Cordelia stopped, lines of perspiration ran into her eyes and down her face but she did not heed them. The boy was completely calm now, sat as if he was dreaming in the chair in the upstairs room. Cordelia watched him. Still nobody spoke. Finally she again passed her hands across his face and eyes, not touching, and he stirred slightly and woke, except that he had not been asleep unless people slept with eyes wide open. He moved his neck very slightly and then smiled up at her.

292

'Was that mesmerism?' he said (those nearest heard him say).

'Yes,' said Cordelia. 'That was mesmerism.' And very gently she briefly touched his shoulder.

'That can take away pain, as you told me.'

'Sometimes it can,' she said, and she drew on her gloves and looked at him with an expression they could not read and walked back to where she had been sitting in the room, beside the silent lawyer. *There is something about them that is similar* thought Inspector Rivers, puzzled. And then, all at once, he understood: saw suddenly the unframed painting in the cosy sitting room: the children, *the three children*, playing on the deserted shore.

Morgan turned his head towards the coroner. 'Can I speak now?' he said in a calm voice. The pale face of Lady Rosamund Ellis shone, her eyes seemed to glitter as if they were jewels.

Sir Francis Willoughby was on his feet, spoke urgently. 'Nothing this young man can say,' he said, 'can now be taken as evidence. You have all seen – Miss Preston has used some – some power she has, and it will have affected anything he might say.'

'Then *I* will say it,' came a voice, and Gwenlliam moved from the back of the room and came to stand beside her brother.

'Her power could have reached back that far!' said Sir Francis Willoughby in great anger.

'Then you are bewitched, sir, and the jury and the coroner, for you were all nearer than myself.'

Sir Francis was standing, he expostulated to the coroner, but Mr Tunks, almost despite himself, stared at the girl who spoke and said very slowly, 'Do you swear to tell the truth, the whole truth and nothing but the truth, so help you God?'

'I do,' said Gwenlliam. 'She is our mother.'

Twenty-two

So the shocking truth was public at last, the reason for Lord Morgan Ellis's visit to the house in Bloomsbury was revealed, and the reason for Miss Preston's reticence understood. And Inspector Rivers, who had been looking for grief, had had the answer in front of his eyes and had not, until the last moment, seen.

Once it had been quickly ascertained that the now scandalous Miss Preston had never been actually *married* to Lord Morgan Ellis, Mr Tunks adjourned the inquest early, until the morrow, in the hope that things would become calm while he considered the calling, or re-calling, of certain witnesses. The world was most relieved to understand that Lord Morgan Ellis was of course not a bigamist, and that Lady Rosamund Ellis (distant cousin after all to the Queen) was indeed his widow and not a fallen woman. Miss Cordelia Preston, all those years ago, was nothing more than an actress who had tried to rise above her station. The lord had been sowing his wild oats like many a young man before him: this at least fitted with the inviolate order of life; but he had not been so foolish as to *marry*: a genuine marriage (with an actress of all things) would have raised unpleasant echoes (which the present royal family was doing their utmost to put behind them) of the life of the late, unlamented Prince of Wales, later George IV, and his murky relationship with Mrs Fitzherbert. But it was, nevertheless, a grievous scandal for the house of Llannefydd: the title could have gone to the illegitimate son of an actress! The Duke hovered, alive still but only just, in the Middlesex Hospital, and would no doubt have died immediately had he known what was happening. A second cousin looked at his bloodlines with great interest, for of course the boy would not inherit, not now.

However, whatever witnesses might now be called, about whatever matter, for Miss Cordelia Preston it was no use.

Miss Cordelia Preston's sordid fall was absolute; her reputation was gone for ever. There was something deeply unsavoury about her activities that could never be forgiven, and never be forgotten. It was not just the evidence of illegitimate children. It was the evidence of Miss Lucinda Choodle that brought her down. Miss Choodle was not to be actually quoted verbatim, of course, but what she had accused Miss Preston of was reported coyly, and at length, in all the newspapers all the same. *And she a mother!* An editorial in *The Times* said: *This is the most disgusting exhibition to have been witnessed in a generation.* Cordelia understood that her fall had come, not from the death of Lord Morgan Ellis; not even perhaps from the revelation of the parentage of his children.

She had been undone by the Gentle Intricacies of the Wedding Night.

All the evidence at the inquest was sung about in the streets within the hour, discussed at every Mayfair dinner table that night, written about in the penny papers before it was dark. There had never been anything like it: THE TRIAL OF THE CENTURY as it was called.

SHE LURED HIM INTO HIS ARMS WITH HER EYES,
SHE THOUGHT SHE HAD GAINED THE IMPOSSIBLE PRIZE;
BUT AN ACTRESS SHE WAS, AND AN ACTRESS REMAINED,
FOR THE NAUGHTY YOUNG LORD, HIS GOOD SENSE HAD
  REGAINED.
BUT WHAT MORE SHE HAS DONE – THAT CAN NEVER BE
  NAMED!

sang the balladeers.

But the trial of the century, which was not even a trial but a simple coroner's inquest, was not yet over. For after all the headlines and songs about the nobility and mesmerism and illegitimacy, and the whispered, shocking information about the other activities of Miss Cordelia Preston, it was still not known what had happened to Lord Morgan Ellis on the night of his murder. But of course, *now* . . . the murky picture that had emerged of Miss Cordelia Preston, rumour said, meant that she was obviously capable of anything, even murder: he had scorned her, taken away her children. Interest rose to fever pitch. What more would be revealed on the morrow? Outside the house in Bedford Place, Bloomsbury, crowds gaped and swirled and hoped for glimpses; ginger beer and pies were sold, even more heavy rain did not keep people away and mud and slush flew upwards.

Inside the house in Bedford Place, Bloomsbury, Rillie Spoons administered to Morgan and Gwenlliam (the wild oats of Lord Morgan Ellis): got their feet warm and their clothes dry and their injuries from the coach accident attended to and lots of hot soup. And Cordelia Preston, at last, held her two remaining children to her, Monsieur Roland saw, in pain and joy and grief. He saw confusion and gladness and distress on all their faces so that he almost could not watch (and he thought of Lord Byron's words, which he knew by heart: of the pain, and the power, of love). Monsieur Roland saw how Morgan would not leave Cordelia's side; how he stayed close beside her wherever she moved; how he talked excitedly in his odd, breaking voice about the inquest; about the coach accident; about his painting: that they should all go, and he would study painting, to the new country where the sun shone and people always sang and had honey: to America. But the boy looked ill, flushed, there was something about his eyes: Monsieur Roland made himself look away from any more difficult truths; observed Gwenlliam, who so resembled his beloved Hester. She was watching Cordelia in a kind of bemused, grief-stricken happiness of sorts, cautiously breathing in, it almost seemed, the air of the house of her mother. Rillie Spoons (with some interested assistance from Regina and Mrs Spoons) looked after the comfort of everybody. Regina offered to read to calm them: she had turned, after her difference with the broadsheets, to the Holy Bible and had found some very satisfying pieces (just as good as the penny papers), particularly in the Old Testament: *He took a sword and cut up her body, bones and all into twelve pieces, which he sent around, this way and that*, she intoned with pleasure until she understood it was not really suitable, not just now, and so she turned to the psalms and read of lying beside still waters and Mrs Spoons smiled and smiled at all the excitement, and hummed.

And then Cordelia Preston at last, despite her exhaustion, telling her children that the inquest was not yet over and she must yet deal with this final matter, left hurriedly (her face veiled, pushing her way through the crowds), with Monsieur Roland in a closed carriage in the rain, to meet Inspector Rivers; they met far away from the crowds outside the house and the pieman and the ginger beer pedlar, and the loving, distressed children. They met in the spare, sparse rooms in Kennington near the Elephant and Castle where Cordelia's beloved aunt, Monsieur Roland's beloved, Miss Hester Preston, had first learnt about mesmerism so many years ago.

And at Inspector Rivers' patient insistence (although his manner towards Miss Preston had changed: he could not help it), she at last told them what only Rillie Spoons knew (for had Rillie not waited in the house in Bedford Square in terrible trepidation until Cordelia came home after midnight? Cordelia at last appearing, still wearing only a light blue gown and no comfort against the terrible night): at last Cordelia told them what had happened, the night Lord Morgan Ellis came and the winter moon shone over Bloomsbury Square.

THREE

When Lord Morgan Ellis had seen Cordelia beside the uncurtained windows that night and could not speak, for almost a minute they stood there. The crumbling stone of the ancient castle and the bright wild flowers that danced in the wind and the deceptive, uncertain sea: they were there suddenly in the silent room in Bloomsbury: memory, loss: the days that were gone.

And when that small distressed sound came from him it was like something breaking, and when he did speak he did not know that he was going to say 'my love'; nothing was further from his conscious mind: the words came from his un-conscious heart.

It was as if he had not spoken: perhaps she did not hear. She only stared at the corseted, ageing man in the room. His face, as she had seen at the wedding of Manon, had lost its line: it folded and flushed as he stood there now.

'Morgan wants to paint,' she said.

The voice, the low, pleasing voice that had bewitched him so long ago, confused him even further. With an enormous effort he answered her. 'Morgan will one day be the Duke of Llannefydd,' he said. 'Not a common painter. You cannot think it.'

'Look, Ellis,' said Cordelia.

He turned his head. On the wall of the warm, welcoming room where the fire flickered and there was the scent of pine in the air, there was something uncanny, mysterious. It was an unframed painting of his memory. The tide was out, out as far as the eye could see, so that an old wreck, the rotting wooden hull and the tangled iron pointing upwards, could be seen in the distance. Strange-shaped shells lay in the sand, rocks protruded (the hidden rocks of the high tide that had, when a deliberate light from the wreckers on the shore lured them, caught unwary sailors). Seaweed snaked across the rocks, along the sand. In the background, almost unseen, a small girl bent to an even smaller boy who held up a fish. In the foreground, a girl looked down, studying something, a shell perhaps, and her skirts blew sideways slightly and her fair hair. It was quite clear who it was: it was Manon. Light fell on the horizon and the jagged clouds were tinged with the setting sun: it was a beautiful painting but there was something else there, something unspoken.

'But – he has not been there – not for many years . . .' His voice faded away.

'I know.'

Lord Morgan Ellis stared; bewildered, thrown. 'How did he remember everything so clearly?' And when Cordelia did not answer, he said the words again as if he could not help it: 'my love'.

Miss Cordelia Preston actually laughed. But it was not a mirthful sound. It was a laugh full of incredulity and pain and something else that he heard, scorn perhaps. 'Do not use that word in my presence.'

'Cordie.' She grimaced instinctively at the use of that name. 'Cordie, listen. My father . . .' He could not go on for a moment and then he gathered himself up. 'I will house you somewhere else. I will give you money. You should not be living in Bloomsbury. Bloomsbury was once a place, but it has lost its glory, it is not a place to live any more.'

She was incredulous, astounded, unable to believe what she had heard, but still she spoke low. 'You say to me that I should not be living in Bloomsbury? I come from Bloomsbury. And I have brought myself back from your destruction and built myself a life in Bloomsbury so that I am able to live in this beautiful house and live my life and run a business with Rillie and we support ourselves entirely, we are rich almost and we are respected and we are respectable. And all you can say, after ten years, after your treacherous cruelty and your lies and your deception, is that I should not live in Bloomsbury?'

She felt the loss of constraint beginning in her voice and her manner. She stopped. She forced herself to be calm. She said: 'You must see that Morgan has an extraordinary talent,' and she saw his eyes drawn again and again, despite himself, to the picture of his past. 'If he wants to paint, he may live with me if he desires it and you allow it, and – perhaps my – perhaps mesmerism could help his headaches. That is all I wanted to say to you. Go away, Ellis.' And then very quickly she left the man who had been her life, turned and disappeared through the French windows and into the dark garden. He saw her flicker past the stone angel, saw the shape of her light-coloured dress in the dark. There was a path along the back through a small gate, the gate clanged open as she slipped along the path and down an alley. Then she ran, no cloak, no shawl, her hair falling, to the place she had run automatically to all her life, her garden of dreams, Bloomsbury Square; her boots sounded on the cobbles as she ran across the road.

She did not see the dark-cloaked figure.

The cold, bright full moon, her moon, shone down, lighting her way; she did not notice the cold. She did not stop running until she came to the statue of Charles James Fox: moonlight caught the top of his head; she actually leant against him; and then she bent over at last, she bent almost double in the darkness, trying to catch her breath I am too old to run like this her heart beating against her chest from running, from memory, and most of all from the impassioned, imprisoned anger of the years.

When at last she stood upright she saw the dishevelled figure of Lord Morgan Ellis breathing heavily, unable to run any longer, coming towards her across the road towards the entrance of the square. A coach rattled past, its lamps swinging. 'Wait, Cordie!' he called out across to her in the darkness, wheezing slightly. 'We will – be together again . . .' he was still trying to catch his breath – 'I will arrange it somehow – I will' – he was approaching her now, still puffing – 'find you a

303

place in Mayfair and I will allow – the children – oh, I should not run – to visit you sometimes, it will – be how it used to be,' and he reached her side and reached out to hold her.

Neither of them saw the dark-cloaked figure.

In a moment she was pushing at him: his arms, his body, they were actually physically fighting as he tried to keep her to him and she tried to get away from his grasp. She actually tore at his face, he grabbed her hands away, turning them tightly, hurting them.

'Let me go!' she cried out into the night as the moon shone down.

A sleeping, drunken vagrant stirred, and then, freezing cold, wondered where he was; he bemusedly popped his head out from the bushes. He saw two figures fighting. A dark figure and a light figure.

'Now, Cordie,' said Ellis, and she saw that he had caught his breath now and was actually smiling. 'Remember what I always told you, my dear, dear girl, that I am stronger than you. Let us not have – ebullience – now. I love you. I have always loved you.'

Perhaps it was the word. Perhaps it was the smile. She stopped moving. She was almost stunned with rage. He took it as acquiescence. 'We will live together,' he said. 'In Mayfair. I will set you up in rooms there, I will make you an allowance, and you can leave all this – this ridiculous mesmerism business far behind you. And as I say I will – I will somehow arrange – for the children to sometimes visit you also.' The vagrant listened in a kind of fascinated drunken stupor, his head still sticking out of the bushes.

Ellis had relaxed. His arms were about her, he had her now, as he had always had her.

With all her strength she pushed at his body and his arms, escaped from his grasp and ran, ran towards the side entrance of the square where two gas-lights shone and houses looked down. She was still running, not yet at the gate, when she heard a terrible cry, like a scream, but a man screaming. Instinctively, the sound so horrible, she stopped and turned. And saw quite clearly in the moonlight the arm the dagger the cloak falling back from the face of the woman; the body of Ellis falling downwards; the vagrant stumbling out from the bushes, *inclining towards the bushes still because he was so drunk, but silent with shock.*

And only one word from anybody as the dagger struck over and over.

LIAR! LIAR! LIAR!

Twenty-three

'And you did not run back to help?'

'No,' said Cordelia and she looked down at her still-bruised hands in the large, shabby room in Cleaver-street. 'I did not run back to help.' Inspector Rivers saw that she was shaking with the effort of recounting the story; he believed everything she told him implicitly; he felt sorry for her. But his manner towards her had shifted: Cordelia felt it, understood. He had been affected by all that had been revealed about her, as had every man attending the inquest. He was still kind, but it was a removed kindness.

For a long time the three sat in silence. All three faces were lined with fatigue, pale and drawn. The Inspector thought once more of Cordelia that night, devastated with grief at the suicide of her eldest daughter. And the devastated, grief-stricken children in Grosvenor Square. He was this new thing: a detective: it had all been there for him to find. He pulled at last his cloak about him as if he might leave, but he knew his work was not yet over and it was as if a slight tremor went through his body: *he must make her speak*. He must still pursue the murder: that was his job as an inspector in the new detective division. Of course the

306

answer was here, in this tragedy. There was a fire but it had burned down and Monsieur Roland did not move to stoke it further. They heard the candles spluttering slightly from the draughts that came in under the door and round the window frames. They heard the passing coaches and the carts in the night on the road to the Elephant and Castle.

Monsieur Roland did not look up, but he heard Inspector Rivers' long sigh, as if his weariness with the matter overwhelmed him.

'But why did you go to Mrs Fortune's? Why did you not go home?'

Cordelia did not answer for a long time, stared downwards still at her hands.

'I did go home. I ran out of the square and I ran home as I have done all my life. The square was always my place – my – haven – whatever you wish to call it. I spent a great deal of time there when I was a child, wandering about at night – no, it does not matter,' for she saw questions in his eyes, surprise, 'it was just – my place. I had seen a thousand fights and drunkards and all the things of the night but I had never seen' – she faltered, went on – 'what I saw that night. I ran out of the square and I ran home but – I ran to the wrong place, the place I *used* to live. It was only when I began to go down the little iron steps that I realised what I had done. I was terrified, I felt – insane – I had come to the wrong place, I did not know if Ellis was dead, I could hear that voice screaming in my head still and so – I kept on running – I cannot explain why, I just wanted to get away from that – hideous horrible thing. I am too old to run, Inspector, but I ran, perhaps I was running to Mrs Fortune's, I do not know what I was doing. When I passed Cock Pit-lane I heard them singing, you can often hear singing echoing out late at night, we were always singing. I waited down in the shadows till I could breathe, and I tried to do up my hair – the dancing dwarfs passed me, James and Jollity, but they did not see me. I had no cloak and no money but – anything goes at Mrs Fortune's, we all used to look mad at one time or another, and I went in, and one of my colleagues – Olive, it was Olive the ballet dancer, we always bought a drink if someone had less money than us – Olive bought me a port and told me all about a pantomime she'd done. And then Mr Tryfont talked on and on and on and slowly – I recovered myself.' She stopped at last, exhausted. But still the Inspector had not finished: he had to go on now.

'The woman in the cloak. Did you see who it was?'

She did not even look up from her hands. 'I did not see who it was.'

'Was it your daughter? Was it Manon?'

Cordelia did look up swiftly now in horrified astonishment. '*No!*' She stood up from the chair as if she would hit him and her voice rose and rose in the cold room. 'Of course it was not! I saw the cloak fall back, of course it was not Manon, how dare you say—'

'Was it Lady Rosamund Ellis, Miss Preston?'

Caught, she stood there, understanding. She looked away from him at once. 'It was dark.'

'You have already made clear that it was a woman. Blooms-bury Square is not a big square, Miss Preston. The jury will know that, many of them live nearby. And there was a bright moon, you said so yourself. And you are very sure it was not Manon.'

She looked at him in appeal. 'This is not necessary, Inspector Rivers . . .' She stumbled in her speech. 'The woman – it could, it could have been – any woman—'

'—shouting "LIAR" and killing him?'

'—it could have been another mistress – surely he had other mistresses . . .' And then the words tumbled out: 'It is too much for the children to bear.'

'Who was it, Miss Preston?'

'Please, *please*, for the love of God! Please can we leave it all now? *I will not* say anything more than I have told you! Why should I? Nothing can damage me further! But – the children, they cannot – manage – anything more.' Her eyes flashed at him. 'Human beings can only carry so much pain, Inspector. Their father is dead, their sister is dead, they have lost their inheritance. Are you going to drag their sister's name further in the dirt as well? Or perhaps you want to make them think they have been brought up by – by a murderess! Are they to be called to give evidence in a murder trial against their step-mother after all they have been through? Do *not*, I beg you, put anything else upon them.' For a moment she closed her eyes, seemed to sway there in the room, then opened them again. 'Inspector Rivers, Lord Morgan Ellis told everybody that I was dead.' And finally, unwillingly, hardly above a whisper, she said again, and he could have sworn she was talking also about Lady Rosamund Ellis, 'Human beings can only carry so much pain.'

Silence hung in the cold room.

'Lord Morgan Ellis has done much damage to the people who loved him,' said Monsieur Roland expressionlessly, but perhaps as an appeal to Inspector Rivers also.

The Inspector stood stiffly, his tired, lined face was blank. He spoke officially. 'I will speak to Mr Tunks,' he said. 'I will repeat our conversation of course. You need to understand, Miss Preston, that you yourself are still not clear of being accused of murder.' He could not begin to imagine what the morning news-papers would say about her. 'But – I can arrange that other witnesses are called before you are tomorrow. It will be best – for you – if you do not hear their evidence, if you just tell your story, exactly as you have told me.'

'Not if they speak there of Manon.'

'They will not speak at all of Manon. We know where she was that evening.' He spoke briskly. 'Forgive me, Miss Preston, I am a detective. I had to know what you saw, that is all. I am sorry, truly, for all that has happened to you, and it will be under-stood why you were so reticent to speak. But it must all end tomorrow, and the truth must be told.' He turned finally to

Monsieur Roland. 'And when it is told, whatever else happens, Miss Preston cannot be found guilty of any offence.'

'Other than the ones that have already been put before the public,' Cordelia said without expression.

Inspector Rivers only bowed, and left.

'Come, my dear,' said Monsieur Roland. They were so weary, but it was not, yet, over. He placed the screen around his dying fire. 'We will go back to Bloomsbury now, to be ready for the morning. It will surely be over after tomorrow.'

'It will never be over,' said Cordelia. 'You know that.' She had not moved; remained standing by the cold, dark window.

'But you have your children.'

Light and pain struggled in Cordelia's exhausted face. 'Manon killed herself.'

'This is not your fault,' he said gently.

Aunt Hester; regret; somewhere these things drifted: *this is your fault too, Cordelia.* She looked at Monsieur Roland blankly. 'Manon is dead. I have lost my reputation and any vestige of respect. And probably my ability to earn my own living.' With an effort she stood at last, he saw her exhaustion and her pain. And then despite herself, despite everything, he saw the smile that lit, for just a moment, her lined face. 'But Morgan and Gwenlliam, it seems, have been properly found at last.'

I have my children.

Cordelia lay awake in the darkness, a vision of Manon's face in her mind; felt the cold air all around her in her bedroom; heard the clocks striking: *three*. Saw Gwenlliam's face, Morgan's face . . . The beloved faces . . . somehow the clock struck again: *four*. When it was properly morning she would be back at the coroner's inquest. Surely, then, it would be over.

I have my children.

They thought they had beaten the world, she and Rillie: they thought they had won. They had sat drinking their port and laughing and pinching their own arms: *we got away with it*. But they had not got away with it, after all. They had broken too many rules and nothing could recover them now, nothing. Inspector Rivers had not had to articulate how he felt, what had happened as her life was laid bare in the court. She understood again that, unbelievably, the most damaging revelation of all had not even been that she was the mother of Lord Morgan Ellis's children. It had been the statement from Miss Lucinda Choodle: some line had been crossed then of the unspeakable: the unsayable. Round and round her head all the thoughts ran, over and over, back to the beginning again.

She had her children: two of her children.

But when she thought of Manon, alone in such a painful death, dressing herself alone in her bridal gown, tears fell, unstoppable: *I never spoke to her again after that morning the coach took me along the coast road to London and she would not wave: she had wanted to come to London too*. Round and round her head all the thoughts ran, over and over, back to the beginning again. Suddenly she did have two of her beloved children. But she had lost the means to support them.

She heard the gentle tap on her door, sat up at once. 'Yes?' She stretched out to light the candle, striking the tinder box. It was Gwenlliam.

'I wondered if you were awake,' said the girl shyly.

'Oh come, come in, I am so glad, I could not sleep either, come here, under the covers. Quick, it is so cold.' Gwenlliam snuggled in and they both remembered but did not say *this is how it used to be*.

'I seem not to be able to sleep at all,' said Gwenlliam, 'as if I've forgotten how, I keep seeing Manon,' her voice faltered, she went on valiantly, 'putting on her – oh Mama, her wedding gown.' Gwenlliam was trying so hard not to cry.

'Oh Gwennie, and with everything else we have not even had time to speak of this properly.' She took the girl's cold hand, forced back her own tears.

'I think she heard Morgan and me talking of you.'

Cordelia's heart leapt with pain and fear: *the thing she had feared*. She suddenly sat up very straight in the bed. 'She killed herself because she knew that I was alive?'

'No, no, it was not that. Or not just that, and anyway once Morgan knew, it could not have been kept secret from her. But it was not just that.' Gwenlliam sat up again also, held the quilt about her. 'Something . . .' She stopped and then started again. 'Something happened between her and the Duke of Trent – I did not understand – she said he was – she used the word "disgusting" – that he hurt her, that he laughed at her. She wept and wept and wanted to go back to Wales – but it was because of her that we came here of course, she wanted marriage and London so much and she was always the favourite of our grand-father – that is, of the Duke of Llannefydd. London was always her dream. But then – something happened after the wedding between her and her husband that distressed her in a way I have never seen. I – did not understand.'

Cordelia closed her eyes, so great was the pain, all the pains. She thought, as the tears lay there behind her eyes, of her exas-peration with the ignorance of the young girls, how she and Rillie had gone to the circulating library, trying to suppress their laughter over *The Guide to Health* with its comments on scrofula and leprosy and A Certain Disease of Boys. All the time trying to find a way to talk to young ladies. *And nobody had talked to Manon.* Gwenlliam had not been in court to hear Miss Lucinda Choodle: there would be that to bear yet, also.

And then the door opened again, but not gently.

'Where are you all! Why do you talk without me there? My head hurts so much I cannot bear it, I could not find you.'

Gwenlliam spoke quickly. 'Morgan, where is your medicine?'

'My medicine does not help, I want Mama to take the pain away again!' and as he came towards the bed the candle caught his white, agonised face. 'Mama, this is a different pain, it hurts so *much*.'

The two women quickly got out of the warm bed. Their feet touched the cold floorboards, they flitted in their white night-gowns as they moved about the room, lighting more candles, lighting the fire, motioning Morgan into the bed.

Again they saw the new spasm of pain they had seen in the courtroom; his whole body became rigid. And then unable to help himself he vomited all over the bedclothes.

'Quickly, quickly, get Rillie, get Monsieur Roland, he is sleeping downstairs, the big room with the glass stars.' Gwen-lliam ran.

'Mama, it is different, it is a different pain, I cannot even bear it, something is happening inside my head,' and he vomited again.

Cordelia took a deep breath and stood beside him. The smell of the vomit came upwards: she did not notice. For a moment she held his head as she had used to so long ago, stroked his hair. Then she felt his body convulse again. She moved back slightly and swept her hands over his agonised little face, over and over, she must not weep, she could not help him if she wept. Sweat, not tears, poured down her face as she tried with every inch of her being to force the energy from her own body into his. Behind her, her own shadow huge on the wall moved over and over, shadows of her moving arms swept across the ceiling again and again and again. He fouled himself in the bed and cried out but it was the pain.

'We will never be apart again, Mama?' The voice started deep and ended as the whisper of a child. She smiled at him and her tears fell on him and they saw the sand stretching out for ever, the secret rocks and the sea.

'Never, never,' she said, smiling at him. She knew it was not working but still she tried; she passed her hands over and over; he waited for the release she would bring him as she always had. And so great was his trust in her that when he felt himself floating away he thought that she had saved him.

Her hands went over and over with all her strength and all

313

her love, all the pent-up love of the years over and over. She did not hear the others come, did not hear anything. Until Monsieur Roland gently took her shoulders.

'Mesmerism cannot bring back life, my dear. It is not magic.'

Then Cordelia looked at Monsieur Roland, and understood.

Twenty-four

THE TRAGEDY OF THE HOUSE OF LLANNEFYDD said the newspapers now. The headline was muted, as if trying to soften such further adversity.

The inquest concerning the death of Lord Morgan Ellis was hurriedly postponed for several hours, for yet another post-mortem had to be held, on the death of his son. It was as if a terrible curse had fallen upon this unhappy, misbegotten family; however it was not a curse but an apoplexy the surgeons at the post-mortem said, caused by a haemorrhage of the brain, and the boy could not have lived. They did not understand how he had survived so long.

Inspector Rivers had not been to bed. He had walked home from Cleaver-street, he had walked the streets of Marylebone, thinking of what he now knew, thinking of Miss Preston. *I am wrong to blame her. She has been damaged only by the words of others, and her own courage.* He had sat alone in his cold garden in the night. And then in the early morning they brought him news of the death of the boy.

315

Inspector Rivers walked all the way down to the Strand, stood at the edge of the early morning river. Sea birds dived beside the myriad of small boats; coalmen pulled barges in the gloomy dawn. He imagined the unbearable agony of the woman who haunted his heart. He remembered the words she had used last night: *Human beings can only carry so much pain.*

How could she possibly bear this?

When he was informed of the delay at the inquest he pulled himself together. He believed he knew who had killed Lord Ellis. He went down to the prison cells and talked to Mr Saul O'Reilly, vagrant, who kept asking wistfully for gin. He went again to see Mr George Tryfont, Actor, waking him unseasonably early. He thought again about the dead young boy who had been so interested in Bloomsbury. Then he was long in conversation with Mr Tunks in the Bow Street watch-house while they waited for the inquest to begin again. The coroner kept waiting for word, looking at his big pocket watch.

But Mr Tunks was obdurately and immovably adamant: Mr Tryfont, yes; old Saul O'Reilly, yes. But the coroner knew he would never be forgiven for the damage he had done to the House of Llannefydd by allowing that young girl to speak; and now there was this other death. Unless there was certain, undeniable proof – not a glimpse in the dark by a discarded mistress, an actress and a mesmerist who would not say a name – then the wife of the late Lord Morgan Ellis, *a cousin to the Queen*, could not and should not even be mentioned *under any circumstances*. The suggestion that she should be called as a witness caused him to perspire profusely, he kept getting a handkerchief from his pocket, wiping his forehead: it was absolutely out of the question. He would not permit it. This inquest was moving dangerously close to her Majesty: it could not be tolerated, it was unforgivable: it must conclude.

*   *   *

316

The inquest on the death of Lord Morgan Ellis was at last reopened at midday in the upstairs room at the Anchor; the lamps had been lighted, and the fire, and the top hats lay in rows upon the shelf once more.

There may have been sympathy for the benighted characters in this drama, but the doctors present had a grim, self-satisfied look upon their faces at last: the boy's illness had been a medical matter and the mesmerist could do nothing. (They would not concede that medicine could do nothing either, in such a case.) Sir Francis Willoughby was present but he had no one to advise: the Duke was still hovering in the hospital and Lady Rosamund was not there: *grief no doubt*, they all said, and the jury shook their heads and moved uneasily; they would be glad to be rid of this inquest, there was too much tragedy, they longed to get back for good to their everyday lives and their everyday work and their wives and their children, for it would be hard to be unhappier than this oddly-conjoined family. There was sympathy even for Miss Cordelia Preston, although she was not yet present in the room; they remembered her mesmerising her son only the day before and giving him some relief and they felt sorry it had come to this. And yet they would be glad to be rid of her also from their minds. She did not sit there comfortably. They wanted everything to be finished. They wanted the inquest over.

Monsieur Roland and Rillie Spoons entered together silently. Rillie, drawn, white-faced, sat on the one empty chair, Monsieur Roland stood at the back, near to the doctors. Inspector Rivers watched them as he stood beside one of the big windows.

Mr Tunks had, after his conversation with the Inspector, first recalled, to that man's gratification, Mr George Tryfont, Actor. Mr George Tryfont had already acquired glory for being a witness in such a famous case (had already been offered another role), was most pleased to be called again. He walked very proudly, pretending not to notice people. He appeared bravely in his

317

velvet cloak and his purple cravat once more, as if challenging people to use the word *flamboyant*.

Mr Tunks leaned forward. 'Mr Tryfont, I want you to cast your mind back again, if you will, to the comportment of Miss Preston when she arrived at Mrs Fortune's establishment.'

The actor's voice echoed round the room, bounced back off the walls. 'We talked together for a long time, as I have told you.'

'Yes, Mr Tryfont. She was wearing, you have said, a pale blue gown.'

'Yes.'

'You are certain of that: pale blue? A pale gown?'

'Of course I am certain. I told you.'

'And no cloak.'

'Yes. No cloak. I myself lent her my scarf as we walked to Holborn.'

'If there had been blood upon that gown, or upon Miss Preston, you would have noticed?'

'My dear sir, if *I* had not noticed, Mrs Fortune herself most certainly would have, and all the ladies. They notice such things in minute detail, and have long discussions about the dress of every single woman. But no. I remember she did push up her hair, several times, yes, I remember that now, her hair was – slightly dishevelled – but there was no such thing as blood, certainly. It would have been commented upon.'

'Thank you, Mr Tryfont, for clearing up that matter for us.'

'Is that all?' He was clearly disappointed.

'That is all. Thank you.'

'Should you need me further, your Honour, you could come to the theatre. I am still appearing at the Strand.'

'Thank you, Mr Tryfont.'

'I have a part, small though it is, in *Mortals Will Know*. It has been very well received.' Members of the jury sighed heavily.

'Thank you, Mr Tryfont.'

The next person to be called, rather to everybody's surprise, was the poor old vagrant, Saul O'Reilly. He was brought from the police station where he was still being held, but it had been agreed by Mr Tunks and Inspector Rivers that before he gave evidence he should be given a certain amount of gin. He stood now slightly less dejectedly and his voice was slightly stronger and every now and then he smiled.

'Do you, Saul O'Reilly, swear by almighty God—'

'Oh I do,' said Mr O'Reilly interrupting, smiling, wanting to be of assistance, 'I do that, yes.' Mr Tunks patiently finished the oath.

'Cast your mind back,' he said at last, 'to the night of the murder of Lord Morgan Ellis.'

'Oh I do,' said Mr O'Reilly, 'I do, I was asleep, your Lordship, in the bushes.'

'Did you wake up?'

Mr O'Reilly immediately began to bluster. 'Who says? Who says?'

'Nobody says, Mr O'Reilly. It is just possible that you heard an altercation.' (He noted the man's bewilderment and rephrased.) 'Perhaps you heard an argument of some kind, and if you did your remembrance would be of great assistance to us.'

'I didn't do it. Nobody can say I done it.' His eyes had become careful.

'I think we all accept, Mr O'Reilly, that you didn't do it.'

'On your God's honour?'

'On my God's honour. For one thing there was no blood at all about your person when you were found, and a great deal of blood was spilt. We know that. We only wonder if you witnessed anything.'

'The lady running, you mean?'

The room was suddenly very still.

'The lady running.' Mr Tunks repeated the words expressionlessly.

'A lady ran away. I saw the white dress in the moonlight. She

319

was like a ghost. She ran away from him and then the other lady shouted LIAR! loud like that, LIAR! when she was stabbing him.' There was a great stirring in the room: nobody heard Inspector Rivers' sigh of relief. *She is cleared. He has cleared her*.

'What other lady?'

Mr O'Reilly looked in his slightly befuddled way about him, around the room. Then he looked back at Mr Tunks. 'That dark lady who . . . Is there more gin?'

But Mr Tunks was suddenly extremely brisk. 'There is no more gin. Take him away.' And Mr Saul O'Reilly was taken away, mumbling incoherently.

'Call Miss Cordelia Preston,' said Mr Tunks at once.

Constable Forrest opened the door at the back of the room: Inspector Rivers could hardly bear to look in the door's direction. Cordelia was accompanied by Gwenlliam. They did not hold each other's arms: they walked together but apart, ashen, exhausted and grief-stricken to the point of collapse. Gwenlliam sat on a chair quickly made available by a gentleman, Cordelia walked alone as far as the witness chair, held on to the back of it. She declined to sit; conveyed some sort of unspoken message to the room that she would hold on to this chair but she would not look at it, where her son had been. And Inspector Rivers looked at this woman, the almost unbearable pain and courage.

And, with a shock, understood his heart at last.

Mr Tunks cleared his throat. 'Miss Preston, there is now some comprehension of your earlier reticence. And we are also sympathetic to the unfortunate series of events that have overtaken you.' He turned to the jury. He had something important to say that he, a moral man for all his vanities, felt needed saying. 'It may appear that the actions of the people in this – unfolding story – have directly led to the unfortunate events themselves; and it is perhaps a lesson,' again he cleared his throat loudly, 'a lesson to all, that moral values upheld, and the home as the centre of our moral world, are the lodestones of our society. When these moral prerogatives are broken it can only lead to the kinds of events we have had the misfortune to both hear of and to witness. This is a lesson that might be taken to heart by some people in this court.' He considered bringing in God, he did most sincerely believe in God, but decided to leave it at that. Cordelia stood staring at him: blank, white-faced. 'Miss Preston, you will perhaps now relate to this hearing the events, as you know them, that led up to the death of Lord Morgan Ellis.'

Cordelia held tightly to the back of the chair and related the facts in a voice devoid of emotion: her past, her small annual advertisement in the Welsh newspaper, Gwenlliam finding her ten years later. The only time her voice broke was when she tried to say Morgan's name, telling of his visit, of his desire to be a painter. Somehow she caught herself, somehow she composed herself, related the rest without expression: Ellis's visit on the night of his death, the conversation, his following her to Bloomsbury Square, their physical fight – she actually took off a glove as if in a trance, showed now the bruises on her hand – and her flight across the square. And then hearing the screams, turning back to see him being stabbed. And running to Mrs Fortune's in fear and flight. When she had, almost heroically, finished her narrative she suddenly put both her hands over her face in a gesture of most terrible despair.

The Inspector looked quickly at Monsieur Roland. The old man's concentration was on Cordelia totally, as if somehow willing her (it seemed to Inspector Rivers) to survive this moment.

'Was there anybody else in the square?' asked Mr Tunks quietly. 'Surely there are usually people even at that time of evening, passing by?' Disoriented, confused, she let her hands fall, struggled to answer as she saw once again the dread picture in her head with all the other dread pictures in her head: they saw how agonising it was to her to concentrate. 'There seemed – I think there may have been – somebody by the bushes.' Her ungloved hand fluttered, uncertain, in a way that reminded the Inspector of one of his butterflies. 'Truly, I cannot remember better than that. Somebody. I do not know exactly.'

'Miss Preston, did you hear a voice calling out as you turned back?'

Cordelia stared at Mr Tunks as if she did not understand the question. At the window Inspector Rivers stirred again anxiously. Last night, at Monsieur Roland's rooms, there had still been strength: now she seemed insubstantial, lost. His body was tensed, ready to go towards her: he was sure she would faint. 'In the square,' said Mr Tunks gently. 'Did a voice call out?'

Her hand went up to her throat as if to try and attend to what he was saying, as if she did not see her dead son, there, inside her head. 'Yes,' she said at last. 'I heard somebody calling out.'

'What were the words that were called out?'

'I heard somebody calling "liar", ' she said.

There was such silence in the room that for a moment the ticking of the big clock on the mantelpiece could be heard. Even the journalists had stopped writing. Now everybody understood. Cordelia Preston was the lady in the pale dress who was running away.

Perhaps five seconds passed. Mr Tunks understood that his hopes of preferment (let alone his recent speech to the hearing about the home being the centre of the moral world) would be destroyed if he asked one question more.

Mr Tunks said, 'Thank you, Miss Preston.'

But there was a sound: a kind of hiss from the gentlemen of the jury; the foreman stood at once. 'Miss Preston,' he said loudly, before she had had time to move, 'did you see who it was who stabbed Lord Morgan Ellis?'

Cordelia stared, uncomprehending. Inspector Rivers understood she had no idea where she was or even perhaps who she was. *Human beings can only carry so much pain* she had said. The foreman of the jury repeated his question. 'Did you see who stabbed Lord Morgan Ellis?' Cordelia swayed, turned. And then suddenly saw, in front of her, sitting there in the upstairs room at the Anchor public house, the face of her daughter, Miss Gwenlliam Preston, staring up. The pale skin of the girl's face

322

was pulled back, almost like a mask: she looked about a hundred years old, or seven. Pain flashed like a thunderbolt inside Cordelia's head *the sea and the sand and the secret rocks, the boy and girl with the fish, the beautiful girl with the wind blowing her hair*. And she gave a tiny sigh; Mr Tunks, near to her, holding his breath for her answer, heard it. And then Inspector Rivers, watching her so carefully, saw that it was as if she awoke: she awoke, and realised who she was, as she stared down at the face of her own daughter. Cordelia was the daughter of Kitty and Hester, whose tough spirits had always taught her to keep going whatever happened, and to bear anything.

'No,' she said. 'No, I did not see who it was. I was too far away. There was moonlight, but there were shadows. I looked back and I saw only shadows.'

Mr Tunks breathed out. 'Thank you, Miss Preston,' he said again.

The foreman of the jury would not let the court do this. But he felt the eyes of Sir Francis Willoughby and Mr Tunks boring into him. He was not so foolish as to commit slander in the heightened atmosphere.

'Bloomsbury Square is a small square, Miss Preston. Could it have been someone you knew?'

'I could not see.'

He rephrased his question before Mr Tunks could intervene. 'Are you sure it was not someone you recognised?'

She heard Monsieur Roland's voice: *Lord Morgan Ellis has done great damage to the people who loved him.*

Cordelia Preston saw the line of people: *Herself. Manon. Gwen-lliam. Morgan.* And in that line of people: *Lady Rosamund Ellis.*

'No,' said Cordelia. 'It was not someone I recognised.' *What does it all matter now? What good, if I say the name?*

'Are you certain, Miss Preston?'

'Yes.' *They can never get inside my head.* She looked now unwaveringly at the members of the jury, at Mr Joseph Manley who had made her new glass stars, at all the gentlemen who

323

had already judged her, though not for murder. 'I looked back. But I saw only shadows.'

Inspector Rivers looked down at the floor. *So be it.*

The room remained silent, as if it was not yet over. Finally the foreman of the jury sat back heavily into his chair.

Mr Tunks felt the beating of his heart, caught the eye of Sir Francis Willoughby, cleared his throat yet again. He addressed the hot, stuffy, crowded room that smelt, as usual, of bodies. 'The evidence given to this inquest is completed,' he said. He quickly turned to his coroner's officer. 'You shall well and truly keep the jury upon this enquiry without meat, drink or fire; you shall not suffer any person to speak to them, nor shall you speak to them yourself, unless it be to ask them if they have agreed upon their verdict, until they are agreed. So help you God.'

It was a long time before the jury returned. Nobody, not even the coroner's officer who guarded the door of the small uncomfortable room, heard their deliberations, but he could hear the murmur of voices going on and on. Cold fog lay heavy all that day on the stinking city, and the day was over before the seventeen men returned.

'Have twelve of you decided?'

'Thirteen of us are agreed.'

'What is your verdict?'

Lamps flickered; people held their breath for all their different reasons; below them life went on, they could hear it raucously echoing upwards with the room so silent. The seventeen men, most of them good and true, had done their best (but also they were hungry and cold and longing to get back to their real lives at last, away from all this convoluted unhappiness).

'We find that Lord Morgan Ellis was murdered.' He paused and then added scornfully, 'By a person, or persons, unknown.'

There was something about the way he gave their verdict that implied (to Mr Tunks' discomforture, as the jury had intended) that the matter was, in some way, unsatisfactory.

But the inquest was, finally, over.

The Duke of Llannefydd ceased hovering and returned to Grosvenor Square. The house was empty of all its former occupants. There was some unpleasantness at his club. He ordered the huge empty house be locked up and travelled furiously to Wales, which he hated although he owned a great deal of it.

Twenty-five

The inquest may have been concluded but the crowds outside Cordelia and Rillie's house were huge next day despite the weather; this was the best murder for years and they wanted to see the Wanton Hussies close up one more time, especially the Mesmerist: they drank gin and then wanted to be mesmerised themselves. The funeral of Morgan could not possibly be held at St George's, Bloomsbury that was so near, even if – an unlikely event – their acquaintance, the Rector, had agreed. Cordelia and Gwenlliam wept that he should lie so far away from them.

'He cannot be buried anywhere near here,' said Monsieur Roland. 'The crowds will make it intolerable for you.'

With the help of Inspector Rivers and Constable Forrest the body was taken from a room in the Blue Posts public house in Little Russell Street where the post-mortem had been carried out, to a small church at the Elephant. There the funeral was held on that bitter afternoon; just as they were entering the church, the sun tried to shine, as if to cheer them.

It was a small funeral but it was attended by Mr Joseph Manley the glass-cutter from the jury, who had asked Rillie if he might. Rillie had for a moment clasped his hand in gratitude and told him where to come, and there he stood, his hat in his hand. Inspector Rivers and Constable Forrest stood there also. Mrs Hortense Parker, the lady pharmacist, appeared, held Cordelia tightly for a moment. The only other person in the church was Annie, their old actress friend they had seen so threadbare and so sad in Oxford Street; she rented a small room at the Elephant and happened to see Cordelia and Rillie entering the church in black, had read the newspapers, guessed the rest. She stood at the back holding her thin shawl with her threadbare gloves, not wanting to intrude. The vicar called for God's forgiveness for the sins of the world and for everlasting life for the soul of Master Morgan Preston, one of His children.

'Can you somehow help Gwenlliam at least?' whispered Rillie to Monsieur Roland.

'When she is ready,' he answered quietly.

Finally, in the churchyard, Monsieur Roland and Rillie stood either side of Cordelia and Gwenlliam who wept and wept in the chill afternoon, weeping for all that had happened and all that was lost. They wept until they literally could weep no more and then the coffin was placed in the earth, and then it was over.

Twenty-six

After the funeral Monsieur Roland made them tea in his room in Cleaver-street. He carried exquisite old French cups from person to person, his hands shaking slightly.

And then they went home to the house in Bloomsbury, for what else could they do? it is the dead who are dead and gone; the living have to go home, and Regina and Mrs Spoons were waiting for attention. Outside the house people were ringing the bell, clamouring for attention; turds and cabbages were tossed up into the air and there were gin bottles rolling in the gutters, and dogs barking and pies for sale and birds in cages and they saw a board carried high in the air which said REPENT.

Neighbours had drawn their curtains in horror.

'Do me, miss! Do me, miss!' cried the crowd as Inspector Rivers and Constable Forrest – who had attended them home, alert to what might be happening – somehow got Cordelia and Rillie and Gwenlliam inside and the day drew in and the fog drifted and the crowd murmured angrily, unsatisfied. Someone threw a big stone at one of the front windows; they heard it shatter. Regina shouted down in a rage. Inspector Rivers arrested a young intoxicated person and Constable Forrest escorted him off to the police station; the crowd now threw stones at the policeman, for they hated all of the constabulary.

Night fell. Finally the crowds reluctantly dispersed; when Inspector Rivers saw that the worst was over he came back inside. Alone with Cordelia for a moment in her big workroom with its broken window, he helped her pin a curtain over the hole, promising to bring a piece of wood back later in the evening. Pieces of glass lay everywhere, they reflected flickering candle-light back at the glass stars on the ceiling. The numbered marble head of Alphonse stared impassively. The Inspector picked up the largest piece of broken glass and then straightened up again.

'You did not see fit to tell the whole truth, Miss Preston.' She was on her knees trying to pick up the glass and did not answer. If he sighed she did not hear. There was no point in him saying more: it was not the first time truth had been undisclosed, as he knew; it would not be the first time editorials in *The Times* criticised the detective division. 'Well. It is over now.'

'The inquest, you mean. Not the rest of my life.' But she spoke blankly.

'Why would you protect her?'

'I was not protecting her. I was protecting Gwenlliam.'

He was a policeman, he knew justice had not been done, yet he nodded, understanding. Almost everybody had looked away in the upstairs room yesterday: from the face of the mother, from the face of the girl. People stared at the floor, for it was too much pain to see.

'What will you do now?'

'I have no idea.' Grief and exhaustion made her speak almost rudely. He went on doggedly.

'Miss Preston. I have come, finally, to have a great regard and respect for you.' She was far away from him in her head but she understood that he was somehow trying to make up for his shock and coldness after the revelations of Miss Lucinda Choodle and was grateful. She thought briefly of herself and Rillie, exploding with silent laughter in the circulating library. She

329

thought of the desperation of some of the young women: Miss Lucinda Choodle too. She could not think of Manon. She made herself look up at the Inspector for a moment.

'Thank you,' she said with an effort at politeness. She could not say more about what they spoke of. She changed the subject. 'We have valued your support, and your help with – with' – she had to say the name – 'with Morgan's funeral this afternoon *she saw the agonised face the vomiting* thank you, we could not have managed without you.'

He said, 'I think things are going to be very difficult for you. This inquest has been most cruel. I wonder, would you consider marrying me?'

She was so surprised to hear such words that her ashen face turned red. She got up slowly from the floor, staring at his face, holding jagged glass like a weapon.

'*Marry?*' she said incredulously.

'Yes,' he said firmly. He had not walked the banks of the Thames in the grey dawn for nothing.

'But . . .' she could not think how to answer, 'you are married – I know I have heard you speak of your wife.'

'My wife is dead, Miss Preston. She died four years ago.'

'Oh.' Automatically she said the words. 'I am sorry.' Automatically she went back to the glass. Outside the last pieman still called in a desultory fashion and dogs were still barking in the darkness.

'I am speaking now,' he too bent down for more glass shards, 'at this inappropriate – I know – time because I think you will have a lot of decisions to make rather quickly. I have a small house in Marylebone. You would be welcome – Gwenlliam too, of course. I would be most honoured to assist you both, I think you have been courageous past understanding.' He paused, not for an answer but for his own reflection. 'I have, on the whole, been able to fill my life with work, as you have seen, for this new detective division is time-consuming. And once more' – his voice was wry – 'we have been unsuccessful.' She looked up

330

again briefly. She had not thought of that. 'No doubt we will be pilloried by the press but it will not be the first time. I am not making this offer out of chivalry – although I see what has happened to your reputation and your business – but because I – it seems I cannot get you out of my consciousness. I' – it was he who brought the unmentionable subject back: he spoke doggedly despite the difficulty – 'I was as shocked as everyone else at the – information that was given to the court. But I have since become more – thoughtful than shocked.' She would not help him: he struggled on. 'I imagine that – what you were providing for young women was a service that – that is sorely needed. I have daughters of my own and I would have been more than glad to have somebody of your – strength of character – to speak to them about matters that I cannot.' And all the time he picked up pieces of glass as he spoke.

Cordelia, on the day of the funeral of her son, actually gave a small smile, it touched her face just for a moment. Obviously someone from the detective division could not marry a fallen woman, though it was extraordinarily kind of him to offer. 'Inspector Rivers, I would of course speak to your daughters if you wished. You do not have to marry me to make such advice respectable!'

'I did not mean that.' He hesitated. 'I am afraid my daughters married without the benefit of my wife, or – someone like yourself – to speak to.' And she saw, perhaps, the conflicts and difficulties of a lonely man. But then he smiled also. 'I wish to marry you because I – cannot get you, as I said, out of my consciousness. Perhaps I should say my heart. I would have preferred to ask you at a more suitable moment but I know you will have to be making changes and plans and I wanted to put this into your mind. I will not pester you for a reply but the offer is there and – and I have come to care for you, and about you, which has taken me as much by surprise as it has you. I will return with a board for the window.' And he quickly picked up a remaining piece of glass, smiled again very slightly, and left her. She heard the front door close. She also heard Regina reading aloud from upstairs but could not hear which piece of religiosity it was.

The three women sat in the small sitting room that looked out at the garden and the stone angel; Rillie had lighted the fire and it was warm and she and Gwenlliam were sitting there as Cordelia joined them. She did not mention Inspector Rivers; she did not even think of him. They sat there with their grief and their exhaustion and hardly knew how to converse. Gwenlliam's face was unbearable for them to see: the bones seemed to have risen, the white flesh seemed pulled back over the bones almost – they must not think this – like the face of a dead person. Yet she was trained so well to be a lady that she nevertheless answered politely whenever she was spoken to. As if she did not suffer. As if her face was not a travesty of what a young girl's face should be: as if she did not see her brother inside her head.

'How are you feeling?'

'I am well, thank you.' But it was as if she was not there.

Somehow a bird sang in the darkness, which seemed strange. Rillie, in desperation for words, anything, wondered if birds knew how wonderful a thing flying was: she spoke of flying through the air in Hull, she even spoke of her long-ago marriage proposal in the air and saw that Gwenlliam listened in some surprise to such an unlikely story.

'It did happen,' said Rillie, 'he proposed mid-air.' And she smiled. 'It was extremely romantic! But it was all a long time ago.'

Cordelia saw the small pale vomiting face in the night; she saw the bride so beautiful and that small look of triumph, walking up the aisle; she saw the cloak falling back and heard the man screaming and the woman screaming LIAR, LIAR, LIAR. She could hardly look at her daughter. *What is happening inside Gwenlliam's mind?* She was only sixteen years old. She had lost her father and her sister and her brother, all at once. And her way of life. It would need a miracle to sustain her now and Cordelia did not know if finding her real mother was miracle enough. She did not know how far to intrude; she only held the girl's hand often in her own, so that she might know that Cordelia was here, beside her. In desperation, stopping her eyes from returning again and again to the painting on the wall, she suddenly started speaking of her own mother, of Kitty, Gwenlliam's grandmother. She told of Kitty bringing home under her cloak things that she had stolen from the theatre: shiny jewels, a boot for Mr du Pont's walking sticks. Gwenlliam sat forward, listening intently; when Cordelia described how Kitty and Hester balanced on chairs to pin a piece of stolen sky to the ceiling in the basement room, Gwenlliam made a small sound. It was, of its kind, a laugh.

The evening had to be got through, they could not leave one another lonely with their own thoughts. Rillie suddenly got up for the port bottle. It seemed a lifetime since she and Cordelia had sat here, drinking port and singing. Gwenlliam took a gulp automatically, and then found she liked the warm feeling at the back of her throat, drank some more. The slightest colour came back to her cheeks. Rillie had brought out her flute as well as the port, and played some Schubert. As the mother and the daughter listened to the sweet music there were tears on their faces yet the tears were a kind of relief now also, not the terrible crying beside the coffin. When she had finished playing Rillie asked Gwenlliam if she ever sang.

'Yes,' said Gwenlliam in a small polite voice. 'You used to sing to us, Mama, and I sang those songs.' Her voice faltered only a little, 'I sang to Morgan, to try and help him, for he was so unhappy after you – were gone. And then later our first governess was French.'

'Was she really French? In North Wales?'

'She was from Paris, so she said. Mademoiselle Jacques.'

'What was she doing there, a lady from Paris?'

333

'We never asked her,' said Gwenlliam. 'We spent our time disobeying. But she taught us a song, she said it was about her father although I do not expect that was true, she was inebriated.' If the words surprised them they tried to give no sign, simply willed her to go on. They saw in front of their eyes a sixteen-year-old girl making an enormous effort to be normal. And then, very, very quietly, Gwenlliam, almost heroically, began to sing.

Frère Jacques, Frère Jacques,
Dormez-vous, dormez-vous?
Sonnez les matines, sonnez les matines
Ding dang dong, ding dang dong.

'And Morgan, he used to—' She stopped suddenly.

'Go on,' said Cordelia, touching her arm gently. She took a deep breath, looked at the painting on the wall. 'I think we must talk about him and Manon, Gwennie, not be silent.'

Again Gwenlliam, they saw it, made an extraordinary effort. 'Morgan used to play the bells. The ding dang dong. He hit bottles filled with different amounts of water, to make the tune. He thought of that, I felt it was very clever of him. Our servants had a great many bottles.' Now Cordelia and Rillie did look bemused. 'Oh – this was just at the beginning. We had,' she took a sip of the port, 'two inebriated Welsh servants and an inebriated French governess, because, until Papa brought Lady Rosamund to visit and to say we could be their children, nobody had any idea about looking after us.' *And Cordelia's mind flashed LIAR! LIAR! and the shawl falling backwards.* 'And – and there was no sea, no sea anywhere near, and at first we did not know how to exist, without the sea.' She was silent for some time. Cordelia and Rillie sat not speaking, praying she would be able to go on. 'We were a bit wild, I think, and – and missing you, Mama, and bewildered. Especially poor Morgan.' Again she stopped. 'Mama – I am sorry – I should have told you how ill he perhaps was, how bad these new headaches were. A doctor in Wales had warned me but I . . .' Cordelia made a small sound, Gwenlliam went on again, speaking fast now, as if to fill the night with other words. 'And when Mademoiselle Jacques suddenly arrived unexpectedly the intoxication in the kitchen reached new heights and we ran wild, quite unchecked, I used to think sometimes we were becoming like wild animals almost. But Lady Rosamund changed all that. The Welsh servants were dismissed, and Mademoiselle Jacques. We got tutors and maids and became very respectable.' She drank more port, as if it was allowing her to speak. 'We heard Papa telling Lady Rosamund that you were dead. I think – I think, as I said, that she could not have children, so we were produced. She inspected us as if we were horses, looked at our teeth. He wanted them to come sometimes to Wales but she would not agree, she hated Wales, she said so over and over, she could not stand to be away from London, from society. "We will see," she said to Papa. "Let them mature." As if we were cheese.'

It was more than she had ever said to them about the days that were over. Cordelia and Rillie hardly dared breathe, they did not know whether to break the spell or wait. The silence came down again.

And then Gwenlliam gulped a further large amount of port. 'Do you sing, Rillie?' she asked, like the good polite young lady she was trying to be.

'Haven't you ever heard us sing?' said Rillie lightly. And she immediately, as if she instinctively understood it was now her turn, began to sing also.

> *Max Welton's braes are bonnie*
> *Where early falls the dew,*
> *And, 'twas there that Annie Laurie*
> *Gave me her promise true.*

Rillie still had a fine voice and Gwenlliam stared at her. 'Who is Max Welton?' she asked, and wondered why her mother and Rillie made a noise of, almost, laughing.

'I think Maxwelltown is a place,' said Rillie, 'but at first we used to think it was a man, Max Welton, and that he was the gentleman who owned these braes, whatever a brae is!'

'I know what it is,' said Gwenlliam, 'it is a little slope by the river.'

'Well there you are!' said Rillie. 'Owned by Max Welton,' and she began singing again, and this time Cordelia, shakily at first, joined in.

> *Weel about and turn about and do jis so,*
> *Eb'ry time I weel about I jump Jim Crow*

and they filled their port glasses and they recounted to Gwenlliam their visit to the hospital and the famous professor and all the doctors and the girl in the nightdress singing and dancing and their gradual interest in mesmerism. Gwenlliam emptied her glass very quickly.

And then she said, 'Did Lady Rosamund kill Papa?'

The question hung, beside the painting of Gwyr. Cordelia did not answer at once. *So she has guessed.* And she understood that for Gwenlliam to recover there could be no more secrets. Yet still she could not answer directly: this girl could surely take no more.

'Gwennie, whatever happened, we have to remember – and you know this yourself – you *heard* – that she was told that I was dead. I do not know how she found that I was alive, or how she came to be in Bloomsbury Square.' Gwenlliam stared at Cordelia. Cordelia tried again. 'Her – her shawl fell backwards.' Still Gwenlliam waited. At last Cordelia said the actual words.

'I saw that it was her.'

They heard Gwenlliam's long, long release of breath. 'Why did you not say?'

'Oh God, *I wanted it over*, I wanted to protect you from anything further. We have to forget her. We *must*. She was deceived. She has extorted a dreadful revenge – on you, on him – on all of

336

us.' And for a moment there was silence like a terrible cry in the room and the firelight caught their strained, white faces. 'But – there is something else also. I – I felt sorry for myself for many years, for – what I had lost. But when I understood that she had not known about me and had been so betrayed also and she had not even had the joy of . . .' She almost broke down but she knew she had to finish. 'We had those years of happiness. What did it matter to us, in the end, whether I said it was her at the inquest or not? Manon is dead. Morgan is dead. This is our own private, terrible story. She – it was a kind of insanity, screaming out LIAR and stabbing him. In the end I felt sorry for her also.'

'Why is there water running down the wall?' They saw that Gwenlliam stared upwards with wide eyes. Like a madwoman.

Cordelia's stomach literally jumped in fear. She had said too much. She should not have told her. They should not be drinking port. She and Rillie at once understood that it had been the final shock, that Gwenlliam's mind was lost to them.

'Gwennie,' said Cordelia uncertainly.

'There is water running down the wall,' repeated Gwenlliam, and then Cordelia and Rillie looked up also and saw that it *was* so: water indeed was running at rather a fast pace down one of the walls in the room. They stared in disbelief.

'It's Regina!' said Rillie, light dawning. Water came from the ceiling. 'Oh for goodness' sake! I thought she was bored with the water closet by now!'

The three of them ran up the stairs. Regina had not played with the water closet for months, she was indeed quite bored with it now. But today while the others were at the funeral, feeling the lack at last, Regina had abandoned her Bible and ventured out past the kites and the gin and the people, and on into the streets of St Giles' where she bought one of her beloved penny papers. Luckily there was another murder now: last night a woman had somehow sawn off her husband's head and carried it on an omnibus to Camden Town wrapped in paper, a very satisfying story. But Regina, already angry with the rude crowds outside, was incensed beyond measure to see the penny broad-sheets were using the *very same* witch-like woodcut to illustrate the new story that they had used to malign Cordelia, and she was so deeply offended at this reminder of their misfortunes that she went into one of her towering rages, tore the penny paper into small bits and was trying to wash it down the water closet together with earlier evacuations. There was water every-where, and hundreds of tiny bits of newsprint floated in the hallway.

'Them bastards!' Regina was shouting as she pulled on the rope. Mrs Spoons was sitting on the water closet enjoying every-thing, wet through, paddling her feet in the water like a small child.

'Hell's Teeth!' cried Cordelia. 'Stop it, Regina! Let's have a bit of the Holy Bible, *please!* Go back to the Lord, for God's sake!' Regina stormed off. Mrs Spoons was led away to be dried by Rillie. Cordelia, mortified, immediately made it up with Regina, hugged her and thanked her for tearing up the newspaper: 'You are a good and loyal friend, Regina!' cried Cordelia. 'Forgive me, forgive me, we could not manage without you!' Then she and Rillie and Gwenlliam got on to their knees to clean up; it was at this point that Inspector Rivers finally, with a piece of wood for the broken window under his arm, rang the bell of the house in Bedford Place.

To see the three women who had endured so much, on their knees scrubbing, half laughing even, the scent of port in the air, would have surprised a less instinctive man than Inspector Rivers but he was used to looking for other things: he saw the half-laughter was half-tears; he took off his hat and his cloak and his gloves and attacked with vigour the water coming down the wall.

338

Twenty-seven

It was quite clear that the mesmerism business in Bloomsbury was finished.

There was no more mesmerism, no more phrenology, no more marriage compatibility conversations, certainly no more Gentle Intricacies. At first there were customers, certainly. But not their old customers. Not the young ladies from Mayfair. All that first week people knocked on the door hoping for a consultation so that they could say they had seen the notorious Miss Cordelia Preston. Couples laughed uneasily behind their hands but Cordelia would see nobody, would say nothing of wedding nights. One hopeful client turned out to have connections to the *Illustrated London News*, which shocked them profoundly (it was a most respectable new magazine with pictures). It became clearer and clearer: it would not be done for anyone in society to visit so tarnished an establishment. Their old customers simply melted away. It would have been impossible now even for Lady Alicia Taverner, Duchess of Arden, to come to Cordelia's aid: it was inconceivable. Cordelia was banished from polite society. She no longer existed. And Cordelia's concentration, so vital in her work, had gone *she saw again and again the boy's hair that stood upwards and the eyes shining for America; she saw the bride so beautiful and that small look of triumph walking up the aisle; she saw the cloak falling back and heard the man screaming and the woman screaming LIAR LIAR LIAR.*

At the end of that week Rillie removed, when it was dark, the small sign that they had once been so proud of, and Nellie was instructed not to answer the door. Their life in Bloomsbury was over.

Rillie immediately set about finding cheap rooms. 'We cannot stay here, we cannot afford to stay here,' she said to them all, and her face, usually so cheery, was grim. Their future was too frightening to even contemplate properly. They saw the work-house in Vinegar Yard: the cold, punished faces of the poor, it was a crime to be poor. They saw the beggars to whom they had always given a halfpenny, for luck. They did not know what Gwenlliam thought, for she remained, mostly, silent but observing; did she ever think of Cordelia's fateful words outside the door to the house in Grosvenor Square? *The world is divided not just between rich and poor but between those who are respectable and those who are not – it is the greatest dividing line in the world.* Inspector Rivers was working on another murder (THE CAMDEN TOWN OMNIBUS MURDER); he came to see them when he could; his proposal lay there, unopened; unspoken of even, for he might take Cordelia and Gwenlliam, but there was Rillie and Regina and Mrs Spoons. Cordelia did not mention it to the others.

Monsieur Roland came to see them from Cleaver-street. 'I have visited the boy,' he said kindly, and it *was* kind, for he believed in no hereafter. He looked speculatively at the terrible face of Gwenlliam: Gwenlliam, great-niece of Miss Hester Preston. 'Come back to Kennington with me,' he said to the girl. 'I will bring you back this evening.' The relief of the two other women was so immense that they could not hide it. He would use his healing powers: he would mesmerise her, and help her with her pain.

And then Cordelia and Rillie were, properly, alone for the first time since the inquest.

'Rillie!'

'I know!'

They were in the curtained, shuttered room with the glass stars and the mirrors and Alphonse: the room that was no longer any use. Cordelia looked around her. 'What are we to do?'

'We've got no buggering choice, Cordie. First we have to leave this house as soon as possible.'

'But where will we go?'

'The Elephant,' said Rillie, 'down Kennington Lane.' She was adamant. She ignored Cordelia's shocked face. 'It is one of the cheapest places in London, and Monsieur Roland will be near.'

'We won't get proper work at the Elephant! You think they won't have heard of us? And Gwenlliam cannot live at the Elephant! We will have to go away somewhere where we can work. Do you think they will know of us in Scotland?'

'We know about their graverobbers. Presumably at the moment the gentle intricacies of the wedding night have made us just as notorious there.'

'Rillie, stop it!'

'You're not facing the facts, Cordie. At least in the streets of the Elephant we will disappear.'

'Couldn't we – change our names?'

'Change our names by all means if you think it'll do any good.'

'Oh Hell's Teeth, Rillie! How could we possibly know it would come to this? We thought we were helping those young women – we *were* helping them!'

'We were helping them, Cordie, but it is over now.'

'I thought we were rich! How long can we last? Oh,' (she forgot the smashed floorboards), 'we should never have left the basement! We became too grand. We forgot where we came from.'

Rillie bit her lip. 'Our businesswomen days are over, Cordie.

341

You have to accept that. We would not be able to work in Scotland, that is just a dream. We will have to go back to Mr Kenneth and plead for work.'

'Play old ladies in the provinces? Work with Mr Tryfont?'

'It is like I said. We have no choice. It doesn't matter if actresses are notorious.'

'I thought we were safe for ever!'

'Actresses are never safe,' said Rillie, and her tone – so unlike her – was bitter. 'We should have remembered that.' They sat in silence in the dark workroom where the piece of wood still covered the window and the cheap glass stars hung. 'I have already found two large rooms down there,' Rillie continued at last, 'near the Elephant and Castle coach station, one room for you and Gwenlliam and one for me and Regina and my mum. No stove, but they've got fires, and the cesspool out the back.' She saw Cordelia's unbelieving face. 'If it's any consolation, the rooms are in a street called Peacock-street, which is slightly more poetic than Cleaver-street. Whatever else we plan, we have to leave this house in one week, it eats our money. It will be so difficult for Gwenlliam but there is no help, we haven't earned anything for weeks, our money drains away every day.' Rillie's voice was flat. 'We will never earn money like that again.' And they saw the frayed gloves of Annie, their actress friend, and her hunched shoulders. 'I wish we could be sure that Gwenlliam will be more recovered. But we cannot wait. It is not far from Cleaver-street, we will at least be near Monsieur Roland.'

Cordelia saw Rillie's hunched shoulders. Rillie's shoulders never hunched, it was not in her nature. And Cordelia understood then how far, already, they had fallen. They sat together now, in the room of their dreams, and after so long there it was again: the old chill feeling of insecurity and fear. And it settled at the pit of their stomachs where it had once lived, as if it had never gone away.

When Monsieur Roland brought Gwenlliam back, they saw

that her face was swollen with tears. 'I put some flowers on his grave,' she said. But she was smiling slightly, the ghost of a smile. 'I have also travelled on my first omnibus.'

So they had just one more week in Bloomsbury.

Gwenlliam went each day to Monsieur Roland. Cordelia and Rillie were almost overcome with gratitude, offered him money which he gently refused. But they knew that his way of dealing with pain would help her in some way. The first day they took her all the way to Kennington, despite her protestations that she was a grown woman. The next day they walked with her to catch the omnibus at least, making sure she was safely aboard before hurrying back to the house to begin to pack their belongings. Monsieur Roland brought her safely back. People still hung around the house in Bloomsbury with the odd kite, or pie; sometimes they called out, *Whore!* Cordelia and Rillie closed their ears: stoically they bundled up their life. Rillie allowed herself one newspaper; read to Cordelia an editorial criticising the detective division of the Metropolitan Police. On the fifth day, but most reluctantly, they gave Gwenlliam the flat-iron, instructed her about getting round London alone, waited with their hearts beating unnaturally till she returned: this infinitely precious treasure. They breathed at last when they heard her voice.

That night Gwenlliam asked Rillie if she might – she hesitated as if not sure which word to use – treat her.

'I'm not ill!' said Rillie. 'What do you mean, dear girl?'

'I know you are not ill. But I know that you are – anxious and tired and perhaps I can help just a little bit. Monsieur Roland has been teaching me.' Cordelia and Rillie were astounded. They had naturally assumed that Monsieur Roland had been *treating* her, not teaching her. *What was he thinking of?* They had no business now, he knew that. 'He says,' Gwenlliam added shyly, 'that I – of course we are just beginning, but that I – I may have some skill. But – I think, Mama, I am perhaps too – close to you just

343

now to be able to – influence you.' She half laughed: 'who knows what might happen, our energies and our – strengths – might get all mixed up. But – Rillie?'

They were willing to do anything at all to distract her. Cordelia said, 'I will play the flute,' and fetched Rillie's eight-keyed cocoa flute with double keys in German silver. But when the other two heard her play they laughed so much the whole project was abandoned, for Cordelia was a terrible flute-player: perhaps they over-laughed, trying to be normal; they could not find normality, they drank port instead, and taught Gwenlliam 'Max Welton's Braes' as if to say: *grieving? anxious? us?*

But the next evening when she came back Gwenlliam said again, 'Rillie, may I see if I can?'

So they went with seriousness of purpose into the big room. The glass stars still hung but the mirrors were already stacked up in a pile in a corner. Despite Nellie's loyal star-polishing the room was musty with disuse; Nellie, to whom they had so reluctantly given notice. The board still lay across the broken window. They opened the curtains and the other windows wide for a moment, the cold night air came in; Cordelia caught just a glimpse of her moon. Then they closed everything again and lit the candles. Rillie sat on the visitor's chair. Cordelia sat in a corner, as she had sat so long ago when her Aunt Hester had plied her strange trade in the shabby basement room and had said so gently, *let yourself rest in my care.* She suddenly saw half of her face reflected darkly in several stacked mirrors, looked away quickly. In the distance Regina could be heard intoning that she would lift up her eyes to the hills and find deliverance.

And then Gwenlliam lit an extra candle.

'Look at the flame, Rillie,' said Gwenlliam.

'What for?'

'Because I want you to concentrate so hard that I'll be able to connect my mind to yours. And I *can* do it if you will help me, if you agree.'

Faintly Cordelia's astounded voice came from the corner: she

344

did not mean to interrupt but she could not help herself. 'That is not mesmerism, exactly.'

'Not exactly,' said Gwenlliam serenely.

'I should like to be less anxious,' said Rillie suddenly, 'can you do that? It makes my heart beat too fast and I don't like it.'

'What are you anxious about? In particular, I mean? I know of course we must find some way of supporting ourselves.'

'I see us eking out our savings meanly until they are all gone, becoming mean and frightened and ill. We got away from that – I cannot bear to go back to the *meanness* of it, the way of living. That's why I'm anxious!' And every time she said the word *mean* Rillie's eyes flashed with angry tears.

'Look at the flame, Rillie,' said Gwenlliam, 'look carefully at the flame.' She stood just above Rillie, holding the candle, so that the older woman had to look upwards. She gazed at Gwenlliam, who gazed back unblinking, and then Rillie stared at the flame. And so they remained, in complete silence. To Cordelia's astonishment Rillie's eyes finally closed. Gwenlliam was still: infinitely still. And then, after a moment, she put down the candle and began the mesmeric passes that Cordelia used herself, her hands sweeping confidently over, but not touching, the top half of Rillie's body. Finally (Cordelia hardly daring to breathe), it appeared that Rillie seemed somehow to freeze, Rillie who was always so busy and bustling. Cordelia's heart felt tight in her chest. And then Gwenlliam sat down beside Rillie and began to speak to her. She spoke softly and Cordelia could not hear. But she saw some odd sort of connection between the two women and understood that it was this – philosophy? was it a philosophy? – this practice, that Monsieur Roland had used on her after she had first met Gwenlliam again: it was mesmerism, but it was different. He had called it *hypnotism*. And it was this that had given her the courage to go – in public – to her own daughter's wedding. She was stunned now at how like Aunt Hester at work Gwenlliam suddenly seemed: concentrated, confident: another person.

After some time Gwenlliam stopped talking and just sat there, her eyes, huge in her thin face, never leaving Rillie's closed ones. And then, very gently, she touched Rillie's eyelids and Rillie's eyes popped open, surprised.

'Heavens!' said Rillie, looking at Gwenlliam. 'How am I?'

It was as they sat back in their sitting room later that evening with the flute and the port that Rillie suddenly stopped playing Schubert and said, 'Do you know, my heart is not beating in that horrible way. Thank you, dear girl,' and she smiled: an old, recognisable Rillie smile. And then she said, 'I don't know what you've done to me, Gwenlliam dear, although I know you spoke to me, but I keep having a vision.'

'What do you mean?' Gwenlliam looked startled.

'It's a vision of you, and of you, Cordie dear. The two of you – in some sort of duet.'

'Do you mean *singing*?'

'No.'

'Mesmerising?'

'Not exactly. For some reason I keep seeing you both flying.'

'Do you mean on a rope – like you did?'

Rillie looked puzzled. 'I don't know. I suppose that is the only way to fly! Or perhaps,' she frowned, trying to catch at it, 'other people around you are flying.'

'You are dreaming of Hull, Rillie!' said Cordelia. 'And your proposal in the air!'

'Perhaps,' said Rillie uncertainly, and she half laughed. 'I expect you are right.'

Cordelia knew she owed Inspector Rivers the courtesy of an answer. She did not, of course, think of his proposal in serious-ness: he had been so generous to make the offer but he did not understand: there was Rillie and Regina and Mrs Spoons *I cannot*

346

leave them now, after all we have been through. On the last afternoon she had just put on her cloak and her hat and her gloves when Monsieur Roland arrived back with Gwenlliam; he saw the boxes, the bits of their life piled in the hall: the mirrors and the portraits of pretend ancestors, the quilts, and the pots and pans, and Alphonse.

'Let us walk to the square, you and I,' Monsieur Roland had said to Cordelia. He saw her face, she did not want to go to the square. 'You will have to go back there one day, my dear, to make it real again. So let us make it this day, your last day in Bloomsbury.'

They sat now in their cloaks and their gloves and their hats on an iron bench, not far from the statue of Mr Charles James Fox. The chill, dirty fog was even heavier than usual today, it hung there with its rusty, metallic smell; people were indistinct as they passed by quickly, going about their business. Cordelia heard the muffled rattle of carts and cabriolets. There was shouting and laughter as an omnibus passed, trying to pick up a few more passengers and offering them a cheap ride to Paddington in the gloom. The old oak tree still stood in the corner, its few leaves drifting down: an ordinary day; the square of her child-hood. But Cordelia shivered slightly and not because of the cold, heard the screams in her head *LIAR LIAR LIAR*, felt glad of the benign presence sitting next to her, did not see the anxiety on his face.

'What shall you do, my dear?'

'I have no idea. Inspector Rivers has asked me to marry him, out of pity.'

'I understand that he has become very fond of you.'

Cordelia shrugged. 'I cannot, of course. Rillie and I will try to get some acting work.' She looked around the place she had known all her life, rubbed her gloved hands together over and over. He saw, and suggested they walk. Around the square they became indistinct themselves, heard the sound of their own foot-steps. They walked past the place where stains would be seen on the path if there was no fog: stains of blood. They walked past the bushes that had sheltered the vagrant. He heard her uneven breathing. At last Cordelia spoke. 'Gwennie does have the gift, doesn't she?'

'She has the gift, your gift.' He stopped walking, looked at Cordelia carefully. 'I think you understand now, my dear, that for one person to have power over another's mind, that person must have a strong sense of self, and Gwenlliam, for all that has happened to her, has that sense of self, as you do, Cordelia. A strength. And Gwenlliam has – the other thing. She has some-thing in her soul.' He walked on for a moment, not wanting the words to be anything but simple. 'Gwenlliam has a presence of kindness.'

'A presence of kindness?' But she knew, of course she knew, she had seen it too. Aunt Hester had had the presence of kindness. It was what Monsieur Roland had also. And suddenly she thought: *Gwenlliam was the mother of Manon and Morgan, as best she could.*

'She will always make people feel better,' said Monsieur Roland. 'As Hester did.'

'Yes.' And after some moments Cordelia laughed slightly. 'I have the gift. But I fear I do not have the presence of kindness!'

'You have other things, my dear. You have strength and courage and tenacity.'

She gave him a wry, dry look. 'Thank you.'

He stopped walking again then, leant slightly on the iron railing by the gate, and she saw – like a flash through her head with all the other incoherent flashes – that he was indeed an old man. 'Listen to me, Cordelia. As I understand mesmerism, and what is beginning to be called hypnotism – and, as always, we speak of fragile, precious things – they are forces for good. We still know so little about the human mind and how it works. We are at the beginning. But we must not stop now. You and I

– and I believe in particular Gwenlliam – have a duty to go on learning. In some way or another. No matter what has happened – and I know so much has happened – you cannot – you must not – give up now, because what we do is too important.' Already, so early, it was beginning to get dark, the fog brought the dusk down. The carriages and the cabs began to see to their lights, then the lamplighter came by with his ladder.

'Is hypnotism different – better?'

'I think it can produce an enhanced sensibility in the mind of a person who is being hypnotised, if they are willing to co-operate with the practitioner.'

'An enhanced sensibility' – she struggled to express herself – 'so that they have better – access, if that is the word – to their *own* thoughts and feelings?'

'And to their own strengths. That is what I think.'

Cordelia smiled wanly. 'Well, Rillie's own sensibility was so enhanced by Gwenlliam that she saw Gwennie and me flying through the air, like acrobats perhaps!'

'Whatever happens, you must not let it go,' he said. 'It is our – duty, and our privilege, to make a difference to other people's lives if we have the skill to do so.'

'I will remember what you say,' she said, but her tone was dull.

And they left the railings and began walking again. Cordelia said expressionlessly, 'If it is not out of your way, would you escort me to White Hall on your way home? I should explain things to Inspector Rivers before – before we go to the Elephant.' And Monsieur Roland, who had the presence of kindness, who knew more than anyone how she would miss Bloomsbury, and who worried more than anybody else in the world about what would happen to these dear friends whom he loved, courteously gave Cordelia his arm as the evening fell; she took it gratefully, could feel his long thin bones.

Neither of them saw the cloaked, hooded figure in the gloom.

*   *   *

They came down St Martin's Lane in the fog and the lowering night, and across the road into White Hall. They went to the entrance at the back, through the small yard, Scotland Yard; Cordelia did not want to go into the detective division, a reminder of everything. But it was only a small building after all. She thanked Monsieur Roland, who raised a hand and turned away into the darkness. Luckily Constable Forrest saw her enter, came to her most courteously at once, escorted her to a room where other constables leant over a map with the Inspector.

'Sir?' said Constable Forrest.

When the Inspector saw Cordelia his face lit up; he then immediately cleared his throat and told his men he would return. She saw their eyes flashing with interest: *the wicked mesmerist whore.*

'I hope this is not an inconvenient time? I cannot stay.'

'Not at all. If you cannot stay I will walk back with you, if you do not mind walking through the filth and jollities of Long Acre and Drury Lane.'

'As you know, I am well acquainted with them,' said Cordelia, shrugging, 'for I worked long ago in the Drury Lane Theatre itself, and,' she looked at him defiantly, 'my mother before me. Filth and jollities were part of our life. And you yourself have visited Mrs Fortune's establishment.'

'There is something,' he said, 'about Mrs Fortune's stew.'

Cordelia actually laughed. 'Her stew is well known,' she said. He smiled, offered her his arm, but said nothing more until they had crossed up into St Martin's Lane; the evening traffic swirled about them.

'So, Miss Preston?' he said, but walking still.

'Tomorrow we, all of us, leave Bloomsbury for the Elephant until we decide what to do next. Rillie and I will try to get work as actresses – it is the only work open to us now, whatever Monsieur Roland thinks about the importance of mesmerism.' She said it bluntly, knowing her refusal of him was in her words; she did not wait for any reaction. 'We must go, we cannot afford to stay. And we will somehow find a way of supporting ourselves

350

– oh . . .' She was exasperated with herself, she had not put it well, her words were somehow graceless to a man who had been their friend. 'Inspector—'

'My name is Arthur. I believe I was named after that celtic warrior, some fancy of my father.'

'Arthur then. And please, at least – call me Cordelia.'

'Thank you. Cordelia. I expect you were named from *King Lear*.'

'As I have now told you, my mother was an actress also. And now,' and he saw she grimaced in the darkness, 'Cordelia from *King Lear* is going to live in Peacock-street, past the Elephant.'

'I know Peacock-street.' He looked across at her, saw her face caught by light from a street lamp. 'It will not be – quite the same as Bedford Place.'

'It cannot be helped. Arthur, what I want to say is – I want to say thank you. For your generous proposal of marriage of course. But also,' she spoke slowly now, 'I am very sorry – the inquest – it had not occurred to me that I was making difficulties for you, I could not think of that. But Rillie has told me that in the newspaper there is criticism of your department.'

'Well. Well.' He waved his free hand slightly. 'With the Camden Town Omnibus Murder the murderer was carrying the head and there were a dozen witnesses. So there are no complications there.' They turned into Drury Lane, everything fogbound, that odd muffling of sound that heavy fog sometimes brings. He walked on the outside of the footway, to protect her clothes from the muck and the filth and the fresh horse manure that splashed up from the horses' hooves and the wheels that passed them in the dark; every now and then a carriage light flashed across their faces. 'I live to fight another day,' he said drily. 'Yours, believe me, was not the only inquest where the truth has not, exactly, been told.' He did not say that it was perhaps to her advantage that Mr Tunks the coroner did not want the truth to be told either. 'You have not, I suppose, come to tell me you saw the murderer of Lord Morgan Ellis after all?'

351

'No.' She spoke hurriedly, to get it over. 'I have come to tell you that I cannot, of course, marry you. It is not – it is not that I am not grateful to you, of course I am, we all are. But I could not marry anyone, I think. I have got too used, in the end, to – being independent, I suppose. I have had to be independent, always. And now – too much has happened.' She paused. For just a split second, seeing the terrible pain in her eyes, he put his hand upon hers; she was extremely surprised and hurried on. 'As I said, Rillie and I will try to get work again – we *have* to – as actresses, and somehow support the others. A bit of scandal doesn't hurt actresses. Also you – a detective – could not be married to an actress, and a notorious actress at that' – she ignored his effort to interrupt – 'and I could not leave Rillie and Mrs Spoons. Rillie and I have been through so much and of course she could never leave Mrs Spoons and it was Regina who lent us money when our business first began and we were not certain we would prosper.'

'The old lady who loves murders and reads the Bible?'

'Yes. She had money. We did not ask her how, we think she might have been a patterer or a balladeer, for she certainly loves that very trade still' – and somehow, victims of that very trade, they both laughed slightly then – 'but I wanted to tell you that I appreciate more than I can say what you have offered me at a time when most people will not acknowledge my existence.'

'You have no clients?'

'No clients. Not proper ones. Only sightseers.'

'I am sorry.'

'I wish things were so different – in particular for Gwenlliam. Monsieur Roland has discovered – it is wonderful to know this – that she has it, the – the gift.' He understood, nodded. 'Whatever it is, I believe she is better than all of us.'

'She is a remarkable young woman.'

'Yes,' said Cordelia. 'She is totally remarkable. She is like my aunt.'

They came to Little Russell Street, they walked past the big church and across the road to the old basement, past the one street lamp. She showed him in the shadowy dark. 'This is where my aunt practised mesmerism – for it is an older practice than people realise – and this is where I always lived with my aunt and my mother when I was a child and this is where Rillie and I started our business. This is' – she looked up at him briefly – 'where I ran, the night of the murder.' They stopped outside the house, she looked down at the basement window; in the light from the upper windows he saw her shadowed face, a kind of longing, or memory.

'You – cared very much for this place?' He saw a bleak basement area full of rubbish with little iron stairs leading down, the top of a basement window, a black cat.

'Oh, look who is here!' Cordelia bent down and the cat came to her at once, arched its back. 'Yes,' she said, stroking the cat. 'This is my place. This is my past. But,' and she rose brusquely, brushing at her cloak, 'that is over.'

Then Inspector Arthur Rivers did a strange thing. He took her gloved hand and kissed it. And then, for the shortest moment, he put his other hand to her face, traced her cheek, right down to her neck.

It was so long since any man had gently touched her that Cordelia Preston was shocked at how she suddenly, out of nowhere it seemed, felt. She stared at him, completely thrown. 'I . . .' She could not speak, knew she was blushing but kept staring, yet hoped he could not see such naked feelings in the darkness. She understood how well, somehow, she knew his face now, how much it had shared: Ellis's death, Manon's death, Morgan's death, the inquest. All through those terrors, that kind face had been there, trying somehow to help. And then she dragged her eyes away, tried to pull herself together, looked about her, deeply embarrassed. The Rector of St George's Church, Bloomsbury, was luckily engaged elsewhere. Inspector Rivers remained impassive.

He was a detective. In a way he had his answer.

'I will take you home,' he said, offering his arm again. She took it uncertainly. He felt her hand trembling. 'We shall continue to be friends?'

'Yes,' she said oddly, understanding that he had understood. 'We shall continue to be friends.'

And because he was so immersed in the woman beside him, and because the fog was so heavy, not even the detective – usually so observant, so attuned to the London night – saw the hooded figure in the darkness, watching.

Twenty-eight

That evening they said goodbye to their Bloomsbury house: the high, fine rooms and the French windows and the garden and the stone angel and the water closet; tomorrow morning the handcarts would come, their life would be piled into them for all in Bedford Place to see from behind their shutters, they would go to the two rooms in Peacock-street, near to Monsieur Roland. (Cordelia had been shocked when she saw the two bare rooms in Peacock-street; she had hugged Rillie and they had wept: neither of them had said a word.) And they would be near to Morgan. Manon had at least been buried with her father. Morgan was all alone in the cold earth at the Elephant, a place he had never known.

They sat, as they always had sat, in their cosy sitting room, with their lamps glowing, with the fire burning brightly, the light catching the port bottle and making it shine. Regina and Mrs Spoons were there too, for it was a special evening and they were being cheerful. They had not closed the curtains, wanted to gaze upon their garden one more time, but the heavy fog lying across the night meant they could hardly see the shape of their stone angel, to say goodbye. Mrs Spoons now accepted a small port and smiled with great pleasure at Gwenlliam, who had offered her this delight, and patted the girl's thin arm with her wrinkled old hand. Cordelia knew the effort, still, that her beloved daughter needed to make to stand in this room and smile at Mrs Spoons. Cordelia was making her own effort: she looked at the empty space on the wall: Morgan's painting had been carefully wrapped with Alphonse and the mirrors. She was leaving Bloomsbury: she must not mind; they must just live from day to day with as much courage and as much grace as they could find in themselves. They drank their port and spoke of plans for the early morning, Regina looked out, trying to see her beloved garden in the darkness one more time.

'There's a murderer out in the fog,' said Regina conversationally.

'Oh Regina!' said Rillie, scolding and laughing. She got up to close the curtains but looked into the dense blackness with Regina nevertheless. 'Oh – what is that?' She peered uncertainly outwards.

They all looked out, all five of them, Mrs Spoons copying the others, liking the feel of the glass on her face. Five faces staring out, pressed against the French windows. Nothing at all moved.

And then Rillie said, 'I expect our stone angel was waving us goodbye,' and the five faces peered out into the darkness and waved back, and then Rillie drew the curtains.

Cordelia was only half asleep (she was always only *half* asleep she felt) when she heard the door to her bedroom open. She was at once awake because of the sound, it sounded as if someone was trying not to be heard; she would have called *Gwenlliam? Rillie?* but some instinct warned her to be silent. She remained where she was, absolutely motionless in the darkness; she could hear her own breathing and her heart, the beating of her own heart. *There is a murderer in the garden Regina had said*. She visualised the candle, the tinderbox.

Again the stealthy sound of the door: now it was being closed very softly; Cordelia moved her hand slightly till she felt the matches in her hand. For a while there was nothing; then she heard the sound of someone moving uncertainly about the room; she heard another sound of breathing, not her own; not Gwen-lliam's. She heard a floorboard creak, and then there was silence again.

When Cordelia moved she moved very, very quickly. It was almost one movement to sit up, to strike the tinderbox, to light the candle by the bed. The room flickered as the candle flickered: shadows and shapes and light and dark, and – *of course, how could I not have known, there is a murderer in the garden Regina had said* – Lady Rosamund Ellis, caught, surprised, her form throwing an indistinct shadow on the ceiling. Her hood had fallen back. Cordelia was at once terrified: she had seen this woman's terrible rage.

And then the woman in the dark cloak spoke. 'I have watched this house. I knew your room.' Her high, confident, cultured voice had a rusty quality that frightened Cordelia further. *But she is insane. I must remember she is insane.*

'What do you want?' Cordelia's voice was filled with fear and panic.

They heard each other's breathing. They stared at each other.

'Do not presume to think you can mesmerise me. I am the stronger.' She did not try to whisper.

'What do you want?' Cordelia endeavoured to speak calmly but knew her voice shook and gave away her terror.

'My husband told me you were dead.'

Cordelia gulped in air. 'Your husband treated us both very badly.' The bizarre conversation had somehow begun, as if this was somehow normal. 'You have had your revenge a hundred times, surely.'

'Do you know how I found out where he was going that night?'

'How?' Cordelia's voice was a whisper.

'I read your little letter to him about Morgan.' *Is she laughing, is that laughter?* Shadows, and the flickering of the candle. 'I could not think who you were, why you were writing about Morgan. It did not make sense. It was not *possible*,' (Cordelia heard the fanatical anger, heard the breathing coming faster which made her own breath come faster also, in fear), 'for me to understand that I had lived with a lie for more than ten years. So then, I read Gwenlliam's journal, she thought I did not know she kept a journal, I had not bothered with it for months, it was a most infinitely tedious account.' *Is she laughing, is that laughter?* 'So I understood, then, that Gwenlliam had found you, that you were alive and that,' – the high voice spat the words – '*my husband had betrayed me*. But I, not you, am the one who knew everything about those children. It was I who educated them, I who brought them into society, to the Queen, my cousin – *your illegitimate children*.' (Cordelia tried to get up on to her knees on the bed, felt as if her own panicking breath would make her choke.) 'My husband told me you were dead. I dropped the dagger and could not see it, to take it. Afterwards I thought to make them believe he had given it to you.' *I must remember that she is insane I must not argue with her I must get help.* Cordelia quickly knocked the tinderbox onto the wooden floor. The dull sound echoed *will anybody hear?* but Lady Rosamund talked inexorably on. 'I want Gwenlliam back seeing that she is all I have left of my life for I do not think you are a fit person to be in charge of my daughter so I shall not leave this house,' Lady Rosamund's voice rose higher and higher, 'without taking her with me, she shall be with me not you *because I have been watching you*.' *What does she mean – watching me?* Both women were now breathing in short, jagged gasps, as if broken glass caught at their throats. 'You are not worthy of her; for Gwenlliam is a lady despite her past, you spoke to young women about things that were not your business to mention, and I have seen you with various gentlemen, hanging on to their arms' – her voice was relentless, now the words ran into each other – 'I saw that policeman

358

behave improperly with you in the fog I saw you with a man old enough to be your father I suppose they all are paying customers? I know you asked Ellis for money. *He said to you,'* and Cordelia heard it clearly: betrayal and anger and madness, *'that he would put you in rooms, that the children would see you – a whore! he talked of love!'* And suddenly Lady Rosamund moved with some sort of terrible intent towards the bed; there was a spark of something shining and glittering.

In fear and rage Cordelia literally leapt from the bed: years of pain and anger exploded and caution disappeared, if this woman was mad, so was Cordelia Preston – she literally hurled herself at Lady Rosamund and began screaming out words, hitting the other woman in the face with her fists, fighting to get hold of the shining knife. 'You stupid, stupid, dangerous fool! How dare you speak like that to me. I am not a whore! My life has been ruined by you' – huge shadows danced on the ceiling – *'and yet I saved you, not saying what I saw that night in Bloomsbury Square!'* Cordelia was screaming as if she had never been taught to be a lady, screaming and battering her arms against this woman who had taken everything from her: Kitty and Hester's child, fighting for her life.

The door of the bedroom burst open; Rillie and Gwenlliam flew into the room in their nightdresses, their candles flickered. At once they saw the two women, locked in each other's arms, Gwenlliam screamed and grabbed at Lady Rosamund, pulling her stepmother away from her mother; Rillie came quickly to Cordelia, taking her arms, pulling her away. Almost at once Regina arrived with her chamberpot, she took in the situation at once and pounded the pot on to Lady Rosamund's head; finally Mrs Spoons arrived with her nightdress up around her neck, wishing to share the entertainment.

Before Lady Rosamund fell the beautiful dagger flashed out.

The shadows were suddenly still, and large, and silent, on the ceiling. A knife with a jewelled handle lay there, unnoticed, rubies and diamonds in candlelight. They did not at first

359

understand why not only Lady Rosamund but also Gwenlliam lay on the floorboards of the bedroom in Bloomsbury as the candles flickered. There was a creaking sound. It was Mrs Spoons' knees as she knelt down on to the floor.

'Hello, dear,' she said, as the grey eyes, at last, flickered open.

Twenty-nine

At the Old Bailey, at the trial of Lady Rosamund Ellis for the murder of Lord Morgan Ellis, her husband, and for the attempted murder of Miss Cordelia Preston, her husband's long-ago mistress, not only Cordelia and Rillie but Regina were called as witnesses.

Regina delighted the crowds. She swore, she shouted, she quoted from the Bible. 'THE LORD SEEST ALL THINGS!' she cried, or 'I LIFT UP MINE EYES UNTO THE HILLS!' She knew the language of the penny broadsheets: she gave it to them, very dramatically, like one of her readings to Mrs Spoons. She was, of a kind, a heroine.

'It was a dark, dark night,' she said sepulchrally. 'But before that – you see – I thought I seen her in the gloaming. When night fell I peered into the terrible blackness of the London night and I seen a shape, like a ghost, a very ghost. I was that uneasy when I went to my bed and I lifted up mine eyes to the hills.'

Even Cordelia's status changed – if not entirely. At this trial it became clear (as the inquest jury had guessed) that she had withheld evidence about the murder of Lord Morgan Ellis. Cordelia could not return to being a respectable lady of course:

361

she could never be that, she was an actress and she had spoken to young girls about that other unmentionable subject. But there was now a slight aura of honour about her: she had not, when she might have done, sacrificed the woman – the woman of noble birth – who had succeeded her in the affections of the deceased. If Cordelia could perhaps have gone into a nunnery now, and spent the rest of her life doing good works, she would probably, when she died, have been forgiven.

Mr Percival Tunks the coroner and Inspector Arthur Rivers of the new detective division were extremely lucky to escape with a reprimand. The judge called them both into his private chambers.

'I now understand that the inquest jury were unhappy,' said the judge. (Of course he knew what had happened, of course he saw Mr Tunks' difficulties.) 'Justice must always be done.'

'There was no evidence,' said Mr Tunks meekly. 'I was given no evidence.'

'Nor I,' said Inspector Rivers gravely.

Every day at the Old Bailey Cordelia and Rillie were accompanied by the pale girl, the daughter, stabbed but not killed as Lady Rosamund fell, chamberpotted. The knife meant for Cordelia had found Gwenlliam instead but Gwenlliam's arm, as she tried to restrain her stepmother, was in front of her own heart. The people saw bandages but quickly looked away, away from the face of the girl: the stretched skin, the sunken eyes; it was as if the girl understood that nothing more could happen to her: it had all happened already. *Sixteen years old and a lady and now with nothing*, they said.

Lady Rosamund was brought, silent and disdainful, from Newgate Prison each day; there was a notion to pity her but she would have none of it. She never once looked at the women from the Elephant. She believed she lived by different rules (and had not Mr Tunks, the coroner, thought this also, after all?). It was revealed that there were *two* shining, priceless daggers: a pair. They had been given to Lady Rosamund's grandfather by King George III: her own, private, fortune. Lady Rosamund spoke only once during the whole trial, refusing otherwise to demean herself before common people. She spoke to require the daggers back. 'They are mine,' she said. 'They belong to me.'

Her Majesty Queen Victoria herself was kept informed: they would not hang the accused, of course, for she was deranged. She was not only deranged, and silent, but a woman, and a very noble woman. They lived by different rules, and she had been sorely tried – made mad indeed – by the duplicity of her husband. The penny broadsheets had their day as usual, but people muttered that this was a tragedy, a terrible tragedy: it was much hoped in some circles that Mr Charles Dickens himself might one day do justice to such a story.

On the day the trial finished, sentencing having been postponed so that noble minds could confer, Gwenlliam insisted on going to Newgate Prison. Cordelia and Rillie were appalled beyond belief.

'I must,' said Gwenlliam quietly.

They walked in silence the short distance from the Old Bailey to approach the heavy, iron, guarded prison doors. The girl's arm was still bandaged.

They heard the keys, the rattle of the keys; they heard the echoing footsteps from chill corridors. And then Gwenlliam disappeared with the prison governor. There was a clanging sound of doors closing, others opening. The air was dark and dank and cold and frightening: Cordelia and Rillie waited in terrible apprehension for the return of the extraordinary girl.

At last Gwenlliam came back, her face so drawn, so white; her head held very high; she walked stiffly as if she would break. They did not question her, they waited. They – Rillie, in charge of their money, insisted – took a cabriolet back to the Elephant. They saw her face as gas lamps flashed by.

'She would not speak to me,' said the girl finally. 'I waited, but she did not speak. But I told her that I owed her something: it was her, not Papa, who saw that Manon and I were educated as young ladies, whatever use that may have been to us.' She did not say where such an education had led her sister (they saw the beautiful, distorted girl in the wedding gown). Gwen-lliam's voice was calm but she shivered like someone who was ill. Cordelia took her hand.

'It is over now,' said Gwenlliam in the same flat voice. 'All that life is over now,' and then they arrived home, home to the rooms in Peacock-street. Regina had heroically tried to light the fire but the chimneys were blocked so that not warmth but smoke and soot filled both the big, draughty rooms where the candles flickered uneasily and you could hear the scurryings of tiny things running into dark corners; and where there was no kitchen and no water closet, only the stinking cess pit at the back of the building; and where you must block your ears from cries in the night, for perhaps they were your own.

Thirty

Next day, as the boy climbed up the chimney in his bare feet, pushing the broom upwards and swearing at Rillie (who was swearing back at him), a letter arrived at Peacock-street, via Bloomsbury, brought by a boy from Mrs Fortune; that boy required extra for traversing London. Rillie, who would once have given a shilling, carefully counted out four and a half pence. Soot fell down into the rooms, black dust covered everything: clothes, hair, chairs; finally a dead bird dropped out, a pigeon.

'What a bloody waste,' said Regina, looking at it.

The letter was addressed to Miss Cordelia Preston.

Dear Cordelia,
Come if you will to my premises for I have something arrived there to your advantage in your present trouble.
Yours etc.
Flora Fortune (Mrs) – from her establishment

Great parcels of soot fell, Regina threw the dead pigeon into Peacock-street. Gwenlliam stared: there or not there: they could not tell.

'I cannot,' said Cordelia.

'You must – we will go together.' Rillie was already bustling for their cloaks.

'I do not want to go to Mrs Fortune's establishment.'

'Cordie, you have no choice at all. It must be work. We have to work.'

They washed their faces with cold water obtained from the street, trying to get the worst of the soot off; it was fortuitous that they were wearing mourning clothes for black soot from the chimney lay everywhere. Most reluctantly Cordelia put on her hat and she and Rillie kissed the ashen, lonely girl; they walked the long distance from the Elephant to Drury Lane, arriving as the early afternoon darkness came down. As they trudged they left a little line of black soot from their boots; they tried to plan some future that did not include the workhouse; they turned their eyes from that cruel building as they passed Vinegar Yard and turned into Drury Lane. They climbed the rickety uneven stairs in Cock Pit-lane with little enthusiasm for their destination; it was early, perhaps there would not be so many of their colleagues there at this time: not Mr Tryfont, they did not feel they could face Mr Tryfont. They had done their best with themselves but their clothes, their hair, smelt of smoke and of old food.

Olive the ballet dancer sat spelling out the words from a penny broadside, and Mr Eustace Honour, the clown was strumming at the harp. Their faces lit up as Cordelia and Rillie walked in. 'Hello, hello, my dears!' and Olive gave them both a hug. 'You've had lots of publicity, aren't you lucky, and Mrs Fortune has something for you, she's told us all about it, and I have work for three months! Think of that, dancing at Covent Garden, all found, it is a lucky time – Mrs Fortune! Here they are! Here's Cordelia and Rillie!' Mr Honour trilled the harp in triumph. Mrs Fortune bustled.

'Well goodness me, here you are, you've caused me trouble, girls, but never mind, I have a good heart, and you'll stay now won't you and be good customers!' She seemed not to see they were dressed in black, their pale faces. Or perhaps they all knew very well of Cordelia's terrible times, and had decided mention should not be made, for they had *news*. 'Don't say I ain't good to you, could have knocked me over with a feather duster when the letter came, well I opened it of course, it being so exotic and addressed to my establishment, so it was addressed to me in a way, well well!'

'A port,' said Cordelia and Rillie automatically (but how Rillie hated to part with any of their precious money).

'A port and a letter,' said Mrs Fortune, and when she had taken their money, counting it carefully, she placed in front of them a missive with many markings addressed to Miss Cordelia Preston, c/- Mrs Fortune's Establishment, Cock Pit-lane, off Drury Lane, London. Olive and Mr Honour crowded about and Miss Susan Fortune appeared from nowhere with her large bosom, and James and Jollity, the dancing dwarfs, suddenly materialised, seemingly knowing everything. Surrounded thus by her colleagues and fortified by her port and with Rillie sitting beside her, Cordelia unfolded the (already opened) letter. It was from an address at New York, America.

My Dear Miss Preston,

   Allow me to introduce myself, my name is Silas P. Swift and I am what is known in this interesting country as an Impresario of Artistic Expression and I have what some may call a Circus but what I call an Entertainment Theatre. We are based in New York and we travel the Environs and in particular we travel through Pennsylvania and to Cincinnati where we have large paying audiences. Providence as you may know is the centre it seems of the most interesting practice of Mesmerism and in Cincinnati there is the Phreno-Mesmerism Society. Old and young, in particular in Providence (though I know not the reason), are particularly engaged in this phenomenon. I expect interest to swell should you be amenable to my offer.

367

*Although I have some singers who render the most
respectable songs, and a contortionist, and a dancing bear and
acrobats—*

'—I said flying!' said Rillie. 'I saw people flying—'

*—I have nevertheless realised for some time that the interest
in animal magnetism can be turned to our advantage upon the
stage and that there is room in my popular Entertainment
Theatre for a demonstration of this Skill. We have recently had
the services of a Preacher who has now left us but whose
Appearances have been very popular. He has affected people
greatly, there has been singing and groaning, and he extracted
Teeth. Anything you can do along these lines would be greatly
appreciated, as are instances of Clairvoyance or the seeing of
spirits.*

Cordelia's face was red and pale in turn as she read. She saw
the word again: America.

*Your Fame has travelled before you to these shores. The
unfortunate Circumstances you have been involved in have
been written about at length in the* New York Chronicle *and
the story of the Murder of Lord Morgan Ellis and its Extraordinary Consequences has been eagerly followed (for although
this country is a Republic we still remember our roots). I
understand that as well as being a Mesmerist or Phreno-
Mesmerist, you were once an Actress. What a wonderful
combination for my Entertainment Theatre!*

*I need not tell you, Miss Preston, aware as you must be of
the value of all Publicity, that speed is of the essence while
your name is still on our citizens' lips. You are called here
Miss Preston of Bloomsbury, London, for that is how the
newspapers described you.*

Miss Preston, I believe this is a land where Opportunity

368

comes to those who take hold of it. And you must remember that this is a country where people are very much open to new ideas.

I am willing to offer to you, Miss Preston, an Engagement with my Troupe for at least five months and for a salary to be agreed upon but to be no less than Fifty Dollars per week which I assure you is in every way generous, for you will find that I am a generous man and a fair one, and I am aware of the Allure you would add to my Entertainment. You would demonstrate your skills as – I do assure you – the Centre-Piece of the show – indeed I would place your name above and not below the title of my Show: Miss Preston of Bloomsbury, London.

Your speed of reply is of the essence for as the coming Summer flowers my troupe shall embark upon their new season.

I will meet any steamer or sailing vessel that you send me news of and I will arrange accommodation in New York proper to any requirements which you state.

I look forward to the kindness of your most urgent attention and hope for a most fruitful Partnership.

And I have the honour to remain, ma'am,
Your humble Servant,
Silas P. Swift
Entrepreneur

Cordelia read the letter, Rillie perusing it beside her. Olive and Mr Honour read it over her shoulder (although clearly already apprised of the contents) and Mrs Fortune stood proud that she already knew the contents by heart.

'I wonder, Miss Preston,' said Mr Honour the clown, as soon as he saw that Cordelia had come to the end, 'if you would consider my joining you?' He saw Cordelia's blank look. 'Children do like me,' he said desperately, 'they really do, I could entertain the children while you were doing your magnetism.'

369

'Fifty dollars is twenty pounds,' said Mrs Fortune. 'Murder pays, don't it?' She froze at Cordelia's terrible, immediate stare. 'I mean – involvement,' she said hastily. 'The publicity, I meant!'

'Of course we mean that, dear,' said Mr Honour the clown. 'Won't you think of me?'

'Of course,' concurred Olive. 'We mean we'd all like to be involved in a good murder and writ up in the papers, wouldn't we, James? Wouldn't we, Jollity?' and the dancing dwarfs executed a few tap-dancing steps in excitement.

'America,' said Cordelia faintly, just as Mr Tryfont arrived in a flurry of velvet.

'Miss Preston!' he cried. 'Have you seen your letter! My dear! How did you like my evidence in your show?'

'It was of course excellent,' said Cordelia, her voice still faint.

'We are very grateful, dear Mr Tryfont,' said Rillie. 'I thought you made a particularly fine stand in your cloak and your most fashionable cravat.'

He bowed imperiously. 'At your service any time, dear ladies,' he intoned. 'Perhaps we could join you in America. Perhaps we could even revive the unmentionable play by Mr Shakespeare.' (He seemed to have forgotten the elephant.) The smell of boiling stew began to permeate the large room. It was only five days in the cauldron so it could have been worse, but it was somewhat strong.

'But what if he is a fraudster?' said Mrs Fortune rather sniffily (though of course she recognised expensive, printed notepaper when she saw it).

'A *fraudster*!' bellowed the outraged voice of Mr Tryfont. 'Mr Silas P. Swift a *fraudster*! Mr Silas P. Swift is one of the most well-known entrepreneurs in America! Do you not know that? He knew Edmund Kean! Do you not know that?'

If it wasn't for the smell of the stew, Cordelia, holding the letter in her hand, would have thought that she had, quite simply, lost her mind.

On the way back to Peacock-street she and Rillie kept looking at each other in disbelief. They could not at first even speak. They were totally, utterly incredulous at this astonishing turn of events. Cordelia kept feeling for Mr Silas P. Swift's extraordinary letter in the pocket inside her cloak. They kept stumbling on the uneven surface of the bridge as they crossed the river. And then suddenly, as they passed the coach terminus at the Elephant and Castle, they started to laugh. They laughed until the tears ran down their cheeks. They were extremely lucky not to attract the attention of a constable and be arrested as inebriated street women.

That night, squashed together round the spluttering (but more successful) fire at the Elephant and Mrs Spoons knocking over her chamberpot by mistake, they read the letter over and over and talked of America: America instead of the workhouse in Vinegar Yard. Regina unexpectedly advised of a younger brother in New York, *Alfie-boy* she called him. Gwenlliam, colour in her pale cheeks, kept saying incredulously, *America? The new country?* Rillie sat beside Mrs Spoons, asking her if she would like to go on a boat, on the ocean. Mrs Spoons smiled, the way she always did, for would not she, too, if she could understand, prefer America to the workhouse? *Twenty pounds a week!* they kept saying to each other in disbelief. And never, at any moment, was there any suggestion that they would not all go, all of them, the whole household. They had been through too much: they would have to sink or swim together. There was no question: they *would* go: somehow they must reconcile their high standards, imbued in them by Monsieur Roland, with a circus – for were they not fallen women?

But there in the room the thought hovered, waiting: they would have to tell Monsieur Roland. It was Monsieur Roland, (who never raised his voice) who had shouted that mesmerism was a philosophy for healing people, not for entertaining them.

371

They would go to America. But the price would be the friendship of the man who had helped them most.

'We should tell him now,' said Rillie at last.

So, leaving Regina to intone to Mrs Spoons about triumph over adversity (Mrs Spoons listening in delight as she always did), Cordelia and Rillie and Gwenlliam put on their hats and their gloves and their cloaks and walked slowly, their excited hearts suddenly heavy, to the room in Cleaver-street: Cordelia clutched the letter, Rillie clutched the flat-iron – this was the notorious Elephant and Castle, after all.

They were surprised (Cordelia felt her face flushing and her heart beating oddly) to see that they had obviously interrupted Monsieur Roland and Inspector Rivers deep in conversation. The gentlemen at once saw the faces of the women they had just been, with great anxiety, discussing; they observed their air of nervous excitement. Unable to speak, nodding at Inspector Rivers, Cordelia handed the letter to Monsieur Roland. He took up a candle close to his eyes and began to read. As he read they watched his face: no emotion showed. When he came to the end he stood, handed the letter to Inspector Rivers and walked to the window, looked out at the night; they saw his straight, honourable back, his shadow on the wall beside the window. Cordelia, seeing his stiff, upright body standing there turned away from them, understood how much she owed this man, how she loved him, how he had sustained her. *He will never entertain the idea of a circus. I cannot bear to quarrel with him. But we must go.* Rillie, watching him also, simply thought, *I love Monsieur Roland I will miss him unbearably*, and an unexpected tear rolled down her cheek. She brushed it away in embarrassment.

Inspector Rivers read the letter, still in this odd silence that seemed to have affected them all. He finished it, folded it, and waited, as the ladies did, for Monsieur Roland to speak. Inspector Rivers remembered how he had always looked for a man involved in the business of Cordelia and Rillie, but he knew now he had been wrong. It was Monsieur Roland's blessing they

372

wanted, not his permission. They would go, whatever the old man said.

At last Monsieur Roland turned into the room. They saw his wise old eyes in the candlelight: he saw their anxious, upturned faces.

'You have no choice, of course.'

He heard their sighs of relief, of disbelief; one of Rillie's old squeaks of delight.

'And you will all go of course, all of you.' It was not a question. He knew them. He understood that it would be a journey for them all, he would never for a moment question the wisdom of taking old ladies across an ocean. 'However . . .' He paused. He was infinitely more well read than they, suspected that Inspector Rivers was also. He knew very well how many people had gone to America with dreams, and come back to England with broken hearts and broken lives. He looked at them, saw their sparkling eyes where the candles flickered. 'It may be more difficult than you imagine. America is a – wilder – country.'

'Do you think we cannot deal with difficulties and wildness after what we have endured?' said Cordelia, and now he saw that her eyes flashed in the candlelight.

'I know how strong you are,' he answered her gravely. 'And whatever difficulties you may encounter I understand you must go. And' – he paused for a moment – 'there may be a most positive outcome, after all. This Entertainment Theatre will just be a way for you to get a foothold in America. Circuses come and go. But if you can make a success of it, then despite the notoriety that is sure to be part of your performance, you can then begin to be taken seriously. Both of you, Cordelia. You and Gwenlliam. It is, in a way, a happy chance—'

'Of course it's a happy chance!' cried Cordelia.

'—for I am sure frauds and miracles would abound in a circus, in less honourable hands than your own.'

It was Gwenlliam who moved suddenly, to the window, to the old man who had given her hope.

'You must come with us,' she said.

'No, my dear,' he said, as he had always said to Cordelia and Rillie, but he smiled. 'My work is here.'

'No,' she said.

They all looked at her, astonished.

'You are our teacher. You were Aunt Hester's teacher.' And then she said something extremely odd. 'I have walked with Aunt Hester and held her hand.' Perhaps she was speaking of the long-ago days in Wales, perhaps she was speaking of what she had inherited. The old man said nothing; he nodded imperceptibly. 'You have always made it clear how important the work is. It is only your presence that could help us to be taken seriously in America, and I know you will not like this word but we are your disciples. It is you who knew Mr Mesmer. It is you who will help us to set up a proper practice in America.'

'My dear, I am too old.'

'No,' she repeated. 'The work is too important. Hypnotism will become just as important, as a branch of mesmerism, you have told me that. We will work in the circus and perhaps become even more – notorious – still. I realise that. But we can also use this skill to help and heal people who need us – if you come with us. We cannot work here because we are – unacceptable – but America is a new country, as Mr Silas P. Swift says. It is different there. We are – you say – gifted, and with you to lead us we will work in the hospitals *as well as* entertain people in a circus and people will learn to respect us also. Who cares if we have to mesmerise on trapezes!' Two spots of red colour shone in her cheeks. 'We must seize the time! It is not England, it is *America!*'

Inspector Rivers was leaning forward with great interest, totally caught up by her eloquence, thought again what an extraordinary girl she was. But the other three, Monsieur Roland and Cordelia and Rillie, saw something else.

Gwenlliam was infinitely more starry-eyed than Miss Hester Preston ever was. She was, properly, a lady, which Miss Hester

374

Preston never was. But what they all saw clearly was Hester: no-nonsense Hester, who had limped across London carrying a flat-iron in her pocket, to learn her strange trade.

Thirty-one

Gwenlliam – for the first time since her father's murder, for the first time since her life had seemed to spin and spin around her, faster and faster, out of control – was the first to fall asleep that night when they came back to Peacock-street, where Regina was playing patience and Mrs Spoons was throwing cards in a general manner. The girl lay on the big bed in the back room, the quilt tucked around her, and you could still see it: faint colour in her pale, pale cheeks. In the front room Regina fell asleep where she sat in a chair beside the fire: she snored slightly.

Cordelia and Rillie stayed there, by the fire, on the sofa that had once been used by illustrious clients but was now still coated with soot, and Mrs Spoons sat with them, holding an eight of spades and a Queen of diamonds and humming old songs. They stoked up the fire and piled wood and coal on it in a reckless manner: the fire blazed up brightly, caught their faces, warmed up the smell of old smoke and sausages and the slight smell of chamberpots and shoes. Cordelia and Rillie filled their glasses with port and caught each other's eye and tried to keep the laughter down that bubbled up inside them. The irony of the situation was not lost on them: they had been deprived of their living in England because of their notoriety; they had received this bizarre, amazing offer from America because of their notoriety. 'Here's to the Gentle Intricacies of the Wedding Night,' said Rillie cheerfully.

The candles on the mantelpiece, and the firelight, flickered and caught their faces: a kind of glee. 'Well, if they want Notoriety,' said Cordelia, 'let us for God's sake give them Notoriety! I've been thinking – I'll go to that journalist on the *Globe* in the morning and give him a headline: THE MISSES PRESTON JOIN THE CIRCUS IN AMERICA. And I'll write to Mr Swift and enclose the headline!'

'And I'll go into the shipping office. We shall not of course travel as emigrants and be stowed below – we shall arrive as Eminent Visitors.'

'Can we do that?'

'We *shall* do that,' said Rillie. 'All of us. We must start off as we mean to go on and arrive in style. It seems, as Mr Tryfont says, that Mr Silas P. Swift is a genuine entrepreneur. Now we can spend our money – and to Hell with meanness and worrying! I *saw* people flying, Cordie, I told you I saw people flying, isn't that odd!' and Cordelia nodded: understood that their craft was mysterious still. The fire crackled and danced.

'And for Gwenlliam, I am so glad!' Cordelia said. 'Did you see her face, Rillie? – something new, a new start – away from all this – unhappiness. She has the gift, Rillie, oh Rillie – it will all be all right, in the end,' and Rillie nodded, understanding, saw the sudden tears in Cordelia's eyes, saw her hand go to her face, heard the sob she tried to stifle.

Cordelia waited till she could speak. 'Oh *God*, Rillie! You had a son. You know.'

'I know,' said Rillie. She saw Cordelia try so hard not to break down, try so hard to compose herself. 'He was real, Cordie. You got him back, he was not just a memory from the past. They said he could not have lived long, but you saw him again, he came back to you. You can take him with you, inside you. You and Gwenlliam.'

And Cordelia nodded, wiping away tears with the back of her hand, making a sound somewhere between a sigh and a groan, as she leant her head back for just a moment on the sofa. And then she reached suddenly for the poker and stoked the fire up still further; firelight caught her determined, grieving face.

'Yes,' she said firmly.

'And it *will* be all right, Cordie, now that Monsieur Roland is coming I am not frightened about our future at all,' and Rillie held her old mother's hand tight. 'We're old ladies, Cordie, and terrible things have happened, and yet here we are with a new life! It will be so exciting, Ma,' she said to her mother. 'You will go across the sea in a big boat,' and Rillie drew the boat in the air with her hands. 'It will be such an adventure!' And Mrs Spoons smiled and hummed, as who would not (if they could understand) at the choice of the new country: America. 'And you know really, Cordie,' continued Rillie, 'in a way, we'll be *actresses* again. It'll be quite a relief to be ourselves and not have to be ladies – well, not all the time, but I'll be a buggering lady in the shipping office tomorrow!' and they both laughed, and Gwenlliam stirred and Regina snorted and Cordelia and Rillie put their hands over their mouths to stifle the noise.

Mrs Spoons was humming 'Home, Sweet Home' and the two women joined in, but softly.

> *'Mid pleasures and palaces*
> *Wherever we may roam*
> *Still be it ever so humble,*
> *There's no place like home!*

and they rolled their eyes as they sang, at their home now, at the smoky room in Peacock-street, where cockroaches ran behind walls and the firelight flickered.

'Inspector Rivers asked me to marry him,' said Cordelia.

'I know,' said Rillie.

Cordelia half laughed. 'How do you know? I didn't tell you.'

'I got eyes,' said Rillie smugly. 'He's a nice, lonely, wise man. I like him. What's the odds Monsieur Roland will persuade him to come too?'

Cordelia looked shocked. 'Don't be silly, Rillie. He's a detective. We're notorious.' And she sighed slightly. 'I – I do like him. But . . .' She was silent for a long time. 'I don't know how to love – like that – any more, Rillie. I've forgotten.'

'Rubbish,' said Rillie. 'He'd be a good man to be married to.' And then, looking down at her port glass, pleating her skirt, Rillie said, 'You haven't forgotten how to love at all. All the kinds of love. It's just that you love us too and don't want to leave us. I'm your mirror.'

Cordelia remembered, saw Rillie's face in the firelight. 'What did you mean, Rillie? About mirrors?'

'Everyone has to have a mirror,' said Rillie. 'Someone who knows them better than anyone. I thought that' – she hadn't said the name for so long – 'that Mr Edward Williams would be my mirror. But he was just a Beast of Hell.' Again she pleated her skirt. And then she said, 'If you don't have a mirror you don't see yourself, and that's bad for people.'

Cordelia considered. 'I'm your mirror, Rillie.' Again she stoked the fire. 'Monsieur Roland is the wisest person we know. But he doesn't have a mirror.'

'But I expect your Aunt Hester was his mirror for years and years,' said Rillie sensibly in the soot-covered, bright, glowing room.

'You're a good girl, Rillie,' said Mrs Spoons.

Thirty-two

Dear Mr Silas P. Swift,

Thank you for your letter. As you spoke of the need for Haste I reply at once.

I accept your Offer to perform at your Entertainment as a Mesmerist for a minimum salary of Fifty Dollars per week, under certain conditions. You say you, and America, have Eagerly followed the inquest and further trial upon the Murder of Lord Morgan Ellis. In That case you will understand that I have been reunited with my Daughter. She has inherited the powers of Mesmerism very particularly and is a Most Accomplished Practitioner. We believe that we will attract even more Publicity for you if we work together. I enclose several articles from the London newspapers, including information that may not yet have reached you, informing you of the final outcome of the Trial of Lady Rosamund Ellis, my daughter's stepmother, and of the Particular interest of Her Majesty Queen Victoria in this unfortunate and sad situation, and her desire that one of her own Relations should, rather than languish in Newgate Prison, do good works in North Wales, overseen by her father-in-law, the Duke of Llannefydd.

As the Circumstances of my Daughter's Birth seem to have

become common *Knowledge*, we suggest that we are both billed (above the title of your entertainment) as The Misses Preston of Bloomsbury, London, and my daughter would expect a further Twenty Dollars a week in salary for herself. In addition we would be grateful if you would, as you suggest, find us a large lodgings in New York for ourselves and our Family.

You may be interested to know that (at no further cost to you) we are travelling with one of the most Eminent Mesmerists in the World, himself a student of the great Dr Mesmer. He – Monsieur Alexander Roland – has contacts with some of the more eminent Mesmerists in America (from which contact your Circus can only benefit).

We are also travelling, because of the extraordinary amount of Public Interest in our Every Move, with our own Detective Inspector from the Metropolitan Police of London, Inspector Arthur Rivers, who will be assisting his colleagues in the New York Metropolitan Police Department in several Murder cases.

We shall leave from Liverpool on the paddle steamer BRITANNIA on the 14th inst. You will know that this steamer should take fourteen days to arrive at Boston, and from there we will transfer to the small steamer, LIBERTY, to New York. And in New York we will look forward of course to your meeting us at the quay.

We, like you, look forward to a long and fruitful Partnership, Mr Swift, and I guarantee that the skills of my Daughter, also, will astound you.

I remain, sir,

Yours truly,

Cordelia Preston, of Bloomsbury

*

On the last day, Cordelia and Gwenlliam went to the churchyard where Morgan lay.

They had had a small headstone erected over his grave at the Elephant. It read only:

381

MORGAN
BELOVED BROTHER AND BELOVED SON

Despite the freezing cold there were small signs of spring. There were crocuses at the foot of a bare tree, irregular dashes of yellow and purple. But they felt a painful, terrible regret that this boy, who had so dreamed of America, was staying here. Once more they wept; saw the castle ruins and the sea and the broken hulls of ships that were perhaps from America, pointing upwards, towards the sky. At last, arm in arm, dressed for the last time in the black clothes of mourning, the two women turned away and walked slowly towards the churchyard gate.

They turned back once; two black-gloved hands were raised, just for a moment, in farewell to a life that was gone.

Thirty-three

SOON AS THE HOUSE HE ENTERED
HE STRAIGHTWAY LOCKED THE DOOR,
SOON SEIZED UPON AN IRON BAR,
AND THREW HER TO THE FLOOR;
WITH WHICH HE BEAT HER ON THE HEAD,
AS SHE LAY ON THE GROUND
HER BRAINS MOST AWFUL FOR TO VIEW
WERE SCATTERED ALL AROUND

sang the patterers, and people found their pennies and bought the songs and the broadsheets and the penny confessions and followed the next gruesome story with delight, and the evenings lengthened and the twisted old trees in the middle of London somehow blossomed once again among the carts and the horses and the omnibuses and the smoke and the people and the squalor and the excitement and the exuberance and the life: the London life.

The Times never indulged in large headlines but had had, nevertheless, several insertions concerning the actress and mesmerist Miss Cordelia Preston and her departure, with her daughter Miss Gwenlliam Preston (formerly Lady Gwenlliam Ellis) for America to appear in a circus.

Arriving at the Liverpool docks, Mrs Spoons had squealed and pointed in a most overexcited manner to see a flying pianoforte (it was being transported aboard the *Britannia* with big ropes, bound for the new land); now she smiled and smiled at Cordelia and Rillie and Gwenlliam, who stood beside her holding on to their extremely fashionable hats, and who had paid enormous attention to their attire: they looked like the nobility, but with a flash of bright, brazen gold. The stretch of oily green water grew bigger as the paddles of the *Britannia* churned and steam emerged from a tall funnel. Rillie carried a precious bottle of cayenne pepper in her inside cloak pocket: she had been told on excellent authority that placing it in hot soup counteracted the effects of seasickness. Nearby Monsieur Roland and Inspector Rivers smoked cigars on deck and thought their own private thoughts as England grew smaller. And Regina, who had found an acquaintance of hers on board, was already entertaining the steerage passengers: recounting to them how it was she who had hit Lady Rosamund Ellis on the head with her chamberpot.

'It was full,' Regina said for final effect, and the raucous laughter echoed up from steerage to the first-class deck where ladies, the wild rolling Atlantic and its nightmares still before them, complained about the inconvenient little cabins as they dressed for dinner, and spoke in breathless disapproval of the notorious Miss Cordelia Preston who, it was rumoured, was travelling first-class also.

They had yet to meet Mrs Spoons and Regina.

I am indebted to the writers of the following books:

Mesmerised: Powers of Mind in Victorian Britain by Alison Winter (University of Chicago Press, 1988)

A History of Hypnotism by Alan Gauld (Cambridge University Press, 1992)

Conquest of Mind: Phrenology and Victorian Social Thought by David de Giustino (Croom Helm etc., London, 1975)

Compendium of Phrenology by William H. Crook (Samuel Leigh, London, 1828)

Human Physiology I, with which is incorporated much of the elementary part of *The Institutiones Physiologicae of J. C. Blumenbach* by Dr John Elliotson (Longman & Co., London, 1835–40)

Road to the Stage by Leman Thomas Rede (J. Onwhyn, London, 1836)

Theatre Lighting in the Age of Gas by Terence Rees (Society for Theatre Research, London, 1978)

Death at the Priory: Love, Sex and Murder in Victorian England by James Ruddick (Atlantic, London, 2001)

The Clerkenwell Riot by Gavin Thurston (George Allen & Unwin, 1967)

Curiosities of Street Literature by Charles Hindley (Reeves & Turner, London, 1871)

The First Detectives and the Early Career of Richard Mayne, Commissioner of Police by Belton Cobb (Faber & Faber, London, 1957)

A Practical Treatise on the Office and Duties of Coroners by John Jervis, Rt Hon, Sir, Chief Justice of the Court of Common Pleas (London, 1854)